# Healing House

*Nicole Plumridge*

# THE WOODLOCK CURSE

THIS BOOK IS part of what will be a collection of novels within the Woodlock Curse Series. While each book is a self-contained story, the novels interweave and link together through characters, times and settings.

Each individual novel can be read separately, in sequential order or scattered and at random. Whatever approach you decide to take, all stories will converge and connect, creating a tapestry of tales for you to delve into and explore.

# Also by Nicole

## Erosabel

## Healing House

# Chapter 1

## *Samuel*

Samuel woke with a jolt and sat bolt upright, his forehead coated in a sheen of perspiration. He blinked rapidly. His heart was racing and his breath, caged in his old, decrepit lungs, came out in rasps. Samuel waited for his breath to return to normal, heart rate to slow down. He closed his eyes. The vision crept like tendrils of smoke in his mind's eye. He didn't know whether it had been a dream or a hallucination. It could have been a ghost, or it could be that at the grand old age of ninety-seven, he was losing his mind.

The man had returned. The man Samuel met on his first night at 11 Edgeware Lane, thirteen years ago. The memory of that first encounter was still fresh in his mind, as sharp and crisp as if it had happened yesterday. Samuel's memory, like his old bones and withering body, was no longer as sharp and quick as it once was. But when it came to that house, to that man, the experiences and memories would rise in unbidden waves threatening to submerge and suffocate him. Samuel could remember every detail down to the smells that hung heavy in the air, the weight of the atmosphere as it descended upon him and the fear, the ever-

1

present fear that pulsated through his veins. Those memories were imprinted as if on a delicate tape reel which would replay over and over in his head. It didn't matter if he wanted to reminisce or not. The tape reel had a force of its own, feeding him flashes of those memories, breathing life into them until they felt tangible, real, alive.

His warm bed, the long shadows cast by the furniture, the hard, unfeeling ceiling all crumbled around him. Samuel was transported back to that first night. That fateful night at 11 Edgeware Lane, thirteen years ago. The night he met Willowen. Swollen black clouds blotted out the moon, turning everything below into liquid shadow. Samuel arrived at his new house on Edgeware Lane in the dead of winter. The roads were covered in ice, and hail had battered down on his rusted old car. Samuel remembered arriving at the front door in a flood of relief, his hands shaking from the tight grip they had had on the steering wheel for the past two hours. Samuel's eyesight, like the rest of him, had been slowly deteriorating, and driving in those conditions had been close to suicidal.

The first thing he had noticed was the putrid smell of the house as he opened the front door. The stench hung heavy in every room as if the very walls were gently exhaling the rotten odour. A strong gust of wind slammed the door shut behind him, and Samuel couldn't help feeling like a small animal clamped in the jaws of a predator that slowly caressed his body with its tongue, tasting and digesting him whole.

Samuel tried to ignore the smell and changed into warm clothes as quickly as he could. The wind and hail pummelled the roof with iron fists. Bizarrely, it felt even louder in the house than it did in the car. It was as if the hail was smashing into the house deliberately, the crashes reverberating in invisible waves through the house. Samuel could feel each and every blow in his body.

He curled up on the couch the previous owner had left behind and fell into a disturbed and fitful sleep. Samuel couldn't be sure how much time had passed, but he awoke suddenly. The house was silent and still. The storm that had been raging so violently had passed. But that was not what had woken him up. It took a moment for him to realise what had. He stretched his limbs and strained his ears. He could hear music. Slow, sorrowful music. It was the saddest song he had ever heard, filling him with a melancholy that struck him at his very core.

Slowly, Samuel got up and followed the sound of the music to locate its source. It pulled him like a magnet to the garden. The dark silhouette of a man was visible from the window. He had his back to Samuel, and he was playing what sounded like a flute. He swayed gently as he played, as if he was one with the music. The contours of his body were lit up by a puddle of moonlight. Something about the way he moved sent shivers down Samuel's spine.

Samuel gazed up at the sky. There was no sign of rain clouds, just a blank empty space with a cut-out moon plastered in the centre of the sky. The scene felt strangely surreal. When Samuel had arrived it was almost midnight. He had slept several hours after that but there was still no hint of dawn breaking on the horizon. It was pitch black, with the exception of the spotlight cast down by the moon. It was an endless night and Samuel was trapped.

Gathering his strength and courage, Samuel opened the door and called out to the man, "Hello, there. Excuse me, I'm the new owner of this house."

The man continued to play the flute, oblivious. Inexplicably, Samuel felt his pulse quicken and sweat trickle down his back even though it was mid-winter.

"Excuse me, sir," Samuel tried again. Something felt off about the encounter. It was as if the man couldn't hear him, as if he were wrapped in a completely different world separated from Samuel by more than simply space and air. Samuel reached out his hand to touch him. He was so close he could feel an electric energy radiating off this strange man's body. Before he could touch him, the man stopped playing. The note from the flute was violently cut in half, chopped by the sharp end of a butcher's knife. It left an invisible tinge of blood spreading in the gulf between them. Samuel remained as still as a statue with his hand frozen in mid-air as the man turned around slowly.

Samuel was rooted to the ground, his mouth open in shock. The man's eyes locked with his. They were a swirling lavender grey. Samuel couldn't make out individual pupils, just a mass of rotating smoke, moving like an optical illusion, defying reality. Slack-jawed, he could do nothing but stare.

The man opened his mouth and spoke slowly and carefully, as if he hadn't exercised his vocal cords in a long time. "Willowen," he said, pointing to himself.

Samuel nodded, replying shakily, "Samuel."

Willowen simply nodded, as if he already knew who Samuel was. He resumed playing his flute and turned away. He walked so gently towards the cliff edge it looked as if he was skimming over the tangled tufts of grass that carpeted the garden. Samuel blinked hard and rubbed his eyes with his gnarled knuckles. When he looked up again, Willowen was gone. The music had stopped, leaving a deathly silence looming over the garden. Samuel walked over to the cliff edge where he had just seen Willowen a moment ago. There was nothing. There was no hint he had ever been there.

In a daze, Samuel went back to the house. Had he just imagined that bizarre encounter? Was this what happened when exhausted and in need of a good night's sleep? Nothing like that had ever happened to him before.

Samuel's memory became blurred and hazy as he slipped back into the present, still sitting under his warm duvet in bed. The sensations of a cold, bleak winter night melted into the shadowy corners of his room. He thought he had left all of that behind when he sold the house. But last night, he had seen Willowen again. Although he was no longer living at the house and had nothing more to do with it, Willowen had been standing at the foot of his bed. One moment Samuel was sleeping, the next moment, whether awake or in a dream, he had seen him. The man with the swirling eyes hadn't said anything. He'd simply stared, his eyes orbs of sadness. He'd shaken his head slightly, as if in disappointment. Samuel felt tears trickling down his face.

"I'm sorry," Samuel stammered. "I'm sorry. I tried to help." The tears created rivulets interweaving through the papery wrinkles lining Samuel's face.

Samuel didn't know how long the dream lasted or how long the vision remained there. It could have been a second. It could have been an eternity. Time seemed to crumble and disintegrate into dust during these episodes. Seconds, minutes, hours, the future and the past seem to fall like heavy raindrops around him, creating a confusing blurred image of what was real and what was not. This continued until Samuel woke up and he was alone.

In that moment, Samuel knew he would never be able to leave that house in the past. Although it had been sold and the keys sent to the new owner, the house, its history, its mysteries were woven into the dark fabric of his soul. He would never escape the house. It was his prison. But would the next owner, Sophie Parker, suffer the same fate? She was not connected to the house in any way. She was not part of the dark family history. The question Samuel had been fretting over since the first day he moved into that house came flooding back to him. Should he have the house demolished or let it stand, let it continue to breathe, exhaling its memories and curses? For thirteen years, this question had flitted in his mind, swaying his opinion one way and then the other.

Samuel felt the electric current of change in the air. Willowen was back, and Sophie would be arriving soon at her new house, the house Samuel had sold to her. Samuel knew in his bones that Willowen would be there to greet Sophie, just as he had been there on Samuel's first night. Icy fear flooded his veins, while regret paralysed his heart. He cradled his head in his hands as he began to sob softly. What had he done? Had he just made a mistake that could cost an innocent girl her security, her sanity and ultimately her life?

# Chapter 2

## *Sophie*

*Dear Daniel,*

*My pain is you,*

*As is my love,*

*My words mere echoes,*

*Calling to you in your castles above.*

*Sophie*

The rain was drizzling down the windscreen of Sophie's shiny, red Mini Cooper. Droplets zigzagged down, one after the other in a monotonous routine. She had only just taken her car to the carwash the other day, Sophie thought to herself listlessly. Swollen grey clouds dominated the leaden sky, promising many more hours of thundering rain. Sophie breathed in deeply, inhaling the permanent coffee aroma mingling with the Bath and Body Works vanilla cinnamon car scent she had bought. She somehow took comfort in

England's gloomy weather today. It seemed to be shining a mirror into her soul reflecting back the overflowing well of emotions she was trying her best to repress. The sky's heartache was being released in an endless torrent of tears. For some reason Sophie found this calming.

It was certainly unlike the day of Dan's funeral. The day of her late fiancé's funeral the weather was beautiful, probably the best spring day they had experienced so far that year. The sky had been periwinkle blue with white, fluffy cotton wool clouds floating serenely past a hideous yellow ball of sunshine glaring down at the procession. It was as if the heavens had been mocking her sorrow that day.

Stopping at a red light, Sophie closed her eyes and shook her head, as if that would empty her mind of the memories that kept rushing back to her like the ebb and flow of the tide. She couldn't do this now, not when she still had about an hour's drive ahead of her. Grief was a funny thing. It was as if she was able to store it away in a box in her mind, compact and neat. When she felt the overwhelming need to reminisce, she would usually lock herself in her room, open the shoebox of mementos she kept of her and Dan and cry for minutes, hours, even days at a time. She would lose all sense of time and reality, staring at crumpled cinema tickets and dried up petals from roses Dan had bought her what felt like a lifetime ago. Then she would pull herself together, put the shoebox away and push the memories back to the dark recesses of her mind. She found that system worked well. But sometimes, on days like today, the memories, the feelings, the sadness was like an unstoppable force, bursting through her subconscious, demanding her undivided attention.

Her grief counsellor had told her to focus on her breathing whenever she felt like she was spinning out of control. It seemed like silly, trivial advice and yet Sophie had found that it had calmed her down in several nearly embarrassing situations. She inhaled deeply and exhaled loudly, focusing on nothing except the air entering and exiting her lungs, refreshing her from the inside out. It had been five months since Dan's death and Sophie was trying to make a fresh start. Her counsellor had warned her against the move, saying it was too soon. In her last session, her counsellor had lectured her, saying she needed her support system around her. Making a big life change such as this could act as a trigger. Send her over the edge. It could be dangerous for her. Mentally and physically. She remembered those staccato sentences hitting her like bullets.

Sophie had announced a week ago to her horrified family and friends, and against the advice of her counsellor, that she was packing up her life in London and moving to the cliffs of Dover. She had quit her job as a senior account manager at an advertising firm in central London and put a down payment on her new home. She had flung only her most precious belongings into two battered suitcases and shoved everything else into bin bags which she donated to the extremely grateful charity shops in the area.

She had felt her co-workers collectively exhale in relief when she announced she was quitting. Her boss had given her that patronising look, with her phony drawn-on eyebrows furrowed in fake concern. The memory of her last day drifted into the present moment as Sophie sat waiting at the red light.

"Oh, honey, you need to do what's best for you," her thirty-seven-year-old boss, Linda, had said in response to Sophie's announcement. Tottering in her platform heels, she had walked over to Sophie and put a hand on her shoulder. "You just need some 'me' time. Focus on yourself, you know. I know this great site that sends life-affirming affirmations to your email every single day. I'm subscribed and it's totally changed my outlook on life, made me more Zen, you know," she said, chattering away, her claw-like fluorescent nails digging into Sophie's shoulder. "I think it could really help you, after... well, you know," she said in a hushed voice as if divulging a closely guarded secret. "Anyway, take a look, it's awesome," she said, pulling her phone out of her pocket and shoving it in Sophie's face.

The background of the life-affirming site was white fluffy clouds with birds chirping. Sophie scrolled down and saw a sanctimonious-looking man staring out of the screen. His teeth were whiter than the clouds in the background and his face had that pulled look of plastic surgery. He was leaning into the camera, a pose he obviously thought was confidential and trusting. To Sophie, it just looked creepy. He was Jean Desper and he described himself as a life coach, a mentor and energy healer. It was his mission to help long-time sufferers re-emerge from the depths of their despair and lead their "best" lives. Sophie was not sold. She read one of his affirmations floating in one of the white animated clouds: "Your relationship with YOU is the most important thing for you to focus on right now. YOU deserve your own love. Stop taking yourself for granted. It's time for you to break up with the old you and discover your new BEST self!"

There were more capital "YOUs" than Sophie felt comfortable with. Sophie had never been a fan of these sorts of wishy-washy messages but this one was particularly reviling. She did not believe you could simply inject positivity into your day by reading a silly quote. It wasn't that easy. If it was, everyone would be walking around in a cloud of happiness all the time, much like the clouds floating on the screen in front of her. She glanced up at Linda, who was nodding sagely in agreement with the proclamation Sophie had just read.

"Deep stuff," she said sombrely, her wrists jangling with all the bangles she was wearing as she patted Sophie on the back. "All you need is time to yourself, a good face mask, bottle of vodie and this guy to help get things together again. Then of course there are dating apps to really help you get back in the game!"

"Yeah, thanks for this. I'll check it out properly when I've got the time," Sophie said, silently vowing to never ever revisit the site, even if someone paid her to, much less any dating apps!

"Of course. Give me a ring any time you need to talk," Linda added, in her most sincere sugar-sweet voice she reserved for placating angry clients.

"Sure, thank you," Sophie said again, knowing full well she would never call Linda for anything and that even if she did, Linda would certainly see her name and screen the call.

And that was her last conversation at The Maverick Advertising Agency. After five years in the fancy, glass-panelled building she slid quietly out the back door and didn't look back. She was surprised at her lack of feeling towards the place and her colleagues. Then again, for the past five months, nothing had felt real. She felt she was living someone else's life, making someone else's decisions and was somehow an imposter. She was just waiting for the time the real her would take over so she could give up the responsibility of having to plough through each endless day.

The GPS snapped her out of her reverie. The red light had turned green and she had been driving as if on autopilot, in a trance where the past was the only real thing she could firmly grasp. The GPS was barking orders at her to exit the roundabout. She had to focus and yet her mind and thoughts seemed to be slipping away from her, outside the realm of her control. Each thought was a glittering snowflake being tossed and turned, drifting away from her in the gentle wind. Her memories kept pulling her inward, away from the harsh realities of the outside world, protecting her in an invisible shell. On some days she felt the strength to fight that enticing feeling, but sometimes, most of the time, she let herself be embraced by the sweetness and sorrow of the past. She let it cloud her vision and transport her to a different place, a different world, a reality she could still endure.

As she drove down the winding roads Sophie thought back to all the plans she and Dan had made. They were supposed to be moving into a bigger flat after the wedding, which had been scheduled to take place next summer. A pang of sadness struck her hard, weighing her down, whenever she thought about this. She was still wearing the rose-gold ring with the beautifully cut clear cushion diamond. She had intended to go for the more classic white gold but when she saw the rose gold she fell in love and knew that was the ring for her. The way it sparkled and scintillated in the light made her feel it was calling to her. When she pointed it out to Dan he had wrapped his arms around her waist and whispered, "It's perfect, almost as beautiful as you." She had nudged him in the ribs and laughed, saying that was the cheesiest thing she had ever heard.

Hot tears pricked the corners of her eyes as the memory seemed to melt away. Her and Dan's voices sounded like a distant echo in her mind, radiating from the deepest depths of an ancient well. That was all she had now, just memories of her and Dan, memories that would one day fade and become consumed by the dark greed of time. She and Dan would forever be cemented in the graveyard of the past. When she had broken the tragic news to her family and friends no one seemed to know how to react. She received bouquet upon bouquet of flowers and condolence cards. She had thrown every single flower out, not wanting to have to deal with it when the petals drooped and the flower withered and died. Condolence cards had been shoved into an old Sainsbury's bag and squashed at the very bottom of her suitcase.

Everyone was speechless when it happened. Collective shock coursed through them all, contagious, viral. And then came the pity. A veneer of pity coated their eyes when they looked at her. Their voices were thick with the glutinous substance, sticking to their throats, making Sophie sick with nausea. She knew she wasn't being fair. She knew everyone had the right to grieve in their own way. But she also knew that was one of the reasons why she had to leave. She was being suffocated by their pitying looks, furrowed brows and constant glances at each other when they thought she wasn't looking.

Sophie had found her new home online. She hadn't even visited it, just looked at the pictures and made phone calls and sent emails. Logically, she knew it was not a wise decision but the second she had laid eyes on the picture of the little cottage, she had felt an odd sense of déjà vu. A strange emotion drew her in, enticing her, propelling her forward. It was the first moment of clarity she had had in months. She could almost feel the house whispering her name. The smell of the old wooden floorboards and salty sea air infiltrated her nostrils and left a tangy residue on her tongue. It was like she had been there before, perhaps in a dream. Her instinct told her that this was going to be her home, and she had decided then and there to put down a deposit. It was insanely cheap. Apparently no one had rented it in years. It had just sat on the market, waiting. Biding its time, for her.

The key was mailed to her within a matter of days without any complications. She imagined the house would be a bit of a fixer-upper but she needed a project to work on, not that she knew anything about DIY or house repairs. Her mum's voice rang in her head: "You can't be serious, dear! You simply can't just buy a house without even checking it out first! Look, I know what happened was awful but please, think reasonably. This is a bad investment. I mean, why has it been on the market for so long? There's clearly something wrong with it. You need to think about your future. Just stay here with me and Dad until you can find your feet again." Her mother meant well but that was the last thing Sophie wanted to do. Despite the copious cups of tea and warm, home-cooked meals, Sophie knew that right now she needed to be on her own, to heal alone.

The photos of the quaint little cottage made it look small but sweet. It sat perched on the sea cliff and from certain angles looked as though it might topple right over the edge and crash into the foaming mouth of the sea below. Something about that precarious set-up appealed to Sophie. Sophie's best friend Angie looked very concerned when Sophie showed her the pictures on her iPhone. "Erm, Soph, I'm not sure that's the best set-up for you right now. I mean, what if…" She paused, glancing up worriedly at Sophie. "What if you're in a funk, a bit of a depression, you know. And you're on a cliff…" She stared at Sophie, widening her eyes as if trying to make a point. Angie was never one to sugar-coat anything.

"Don't worry, I'm not going to be throwing myself off any cliffs any time soon," Sophie replied. "I think it will be nice to be by the sea. It'll help clear my head."

"Well, if you're sure," Angie said uneasily. "Do you want me to come with you and help you set up and unpack at least? I'm sure it's going to need some cleaning and maybe some repairs. I mean, the pictures look cute but what if it's a wreck in real life?"

"I'm sure I'll be able to manage it myself," Sophie replied curtly. The thought of forced conversation on the long drive there was too exhausting to contemplate. "But thank you," she added quickly, seeing the hurt look on Angie's face. They had been best friends since GCSE days and the last thing she wanted was to appear unappreciative. Angie had been the rock Sophie had relied on since it happened. Angie had been practical and didn't just stare at Sophie as if she were a ticking time bomb about to explode. "I'll call you when I get there and let you know how it is. I'm a big girl though. You don't need to worry about me," Sophie said, attempting an unconvincing smile.

If Sophie was honest with herself, she was slightly worried. She was twenty-eight and had never lived on her own. When she was at university, at the London School of Economics, she had flat-shared with four other girls. In her senior year, she met Dan at a friend's party. Within a few months they had moved into a tiny but cosy flat together. She remembered when they first got the keys and opened the door to their new home in immense anticipation. This was supposed to be a grown-up moment where they could acknowledge that they were mature, successful adults. Dan had even bought a bottle of champagne and expensive crystal glasses to celebrate. The second the door was ajar, the smell of mould and damp had slapped them in the face. The carpets were dingy and stained while the rims of the windows had layers of grime embedded in them. It was so tiny it felt as if the walls were pressing in on them.

Sophie vividly remembered seeing a large spider scuttle from one edge of the window to the other. Its intricate web had spanned the length of the window frame and was shimmering and undulating in the fading sunlight. Its silver lace decorated all the corners of the rooms. They looked at one another and immediately burst out laughing. This was their home and they were going to make the most of it. They had used their suitcases as chairs and a cardboard box full of cutlery as a table. Sophie had set the table as best she could and Dan had called for an Indian takeaway. It was one of the happiest days of her life. The laughter echoed in her ears before fading back in time, replaced by the patter of steady rain on her windshield. Now she would have to do it all alone.

As she continued her drive, she realised it was getting darker. She had hoped to arrive before 7:00 pm at her new house, but due to her wandering mind she had taken a few wrong turns, and it was now 7:45 pm. According to the GPS she was only twenty minutes away. Vaguely aware of her surroundings, she had noticed the landscape morphing from the busy, cramped London roads to views of fields and open countryside. When she was five minutes away, driving along another narrow, winding road, she attempted to check the GPS to make sure she was going the right way.

"What the…" she muttered to herself, confused. Google Maps was recalculating the route, then suddenly the application shut down. Sighing in frustration, Sophie re-opened the app and waited for it to show her the route. Instead it did the same thing. It was re-routing her in the opposite direction from where she had just driven. It was showing her a route back to London.

"Well, that can't be right now, can it?" Sophie muttered to herself, exasperated. Navigating her way around technology had never been her strong point, and now she found herself growing increasingly frustrated with the GPS's attempts to re-route her back the way she had come. Not only was she frustrated, she was also hungry and starting to feel a little panicked being on these badly lit, unfamiliar roads as the dark curtain of night unfolded around her. The army of trees lining the roads felt like they were closing in around her, looming forwards, cutting off any potential escape routes. She clutched the steering wheel tighter until she reached a fork in the road.

"Now what!" Sophie said, slamming her hand on the steering wheel, panic rising. There were no streetlights nearby at this intersection and she was engulfed in an all-consuming darkness. The night had an eerie feel to it. The knotted trees shook off some of their summer leaves, making soft rustling sounds as they undressed. The only light came from the sliver of silvery moon in the sky casting a pale ghostly glow over the road. She felt a shift in the atmosphere, as if the very air around her had become denser, heavier. More alive.

Sophie started breathing heavily. She broke out in a cold sweat as tears welled up inexplicably in her eyes.

"Stupid damn GPS!" she said through gritted teeth, trying to re-input the address with slightly shaking hands. Instead of re-routing her now, it was simple going berserk, showing her completely random routes, any route but forward.

Just as she was verging on full-blown panic, a man emerged, like an indistinct mirage, from the trees on one side of the fork. He had an ageless face, from what she could see in the shifting darkness, but if she had to guess, she would say he was in his fifties. His silvery hair was combed back into a long, smooth ponytail. He was walking with a gnarled old stick. Despite the aid, however, he seemed to walk with such elegance it almost looked as if he was gliding down the path, his feet and stick barely touching the ground. It was an odd place and time to be out walking, but he seemed familiar with the roads and moved with a confidence that Sophie found reassuring. There was something strange about him too. He looked like a character from a fairy tale that had tumbled right off the pages of a children's storybook. He was wearing a thick jacket and loose, baggy corduroys which were adorned with multiple worn patches. Thick leather boots came up to his knees, and as he walked something jangled in tune with his step. The sound cut through the heavy silence, reverberating through the air. With each step, the sound became amplified, louder, as if the rest of the world was holding its breath. Over his shoulder he carried a strangely lumpy sack. Desperately, Sophie wound down her window and called out to him.

"Excuse me, sorry to bother you, sir, but could you help me find my way?" she called.

The man stopped suddenly. The jangling sound vanished, absorbed into the night. He didn't turn around immediately, and at first Sophie thought with rising dismay that he may ignore her and continue his walk into the growing empty darkness. To her relief, he turned, very slowly, head bent low, and made his way towards her car. Goosebumps pricked her skin. As he got closer, she felt a rush of cold air filter through her open window, too cold for an autumn night. A cloud of icy breath rose from her lips as she exhaled.

As he drew closer, he seemed quite slim and fragile. A strange thought struck Sophie: the man somehow didn't seem solid, as if he lacked substance. He was a blurry outline of a man that could be swept away at a moment's notice by a cough of wind or drizzling rain. When he finally reached her, he peered down at her. Sophie had to catch her breath before she could speak.

A layer of shock dulled her senses. In that moment, time stood still. Nothing seemed to move. The trees had stopped rustling. The leaves had stopped spinning. Even the wind had frozen into silence. His eyes were like none she had ever seen before. They were an extremely pale lavender grey with an ethereal swirling mystical quality to them. They pulled Sophie inward. She felt as if those eyes opened up into a completely different world from her own. She couldn't make out any pupils within the hypnotic mists that gathered in his eyes. She was in danger of sinking into those glimmering pools of lavender and never resurfacing. She could get lost in those dangerous eyes. She could lead an entirely different life. She no longer had to be Sophie Parker, the sad woman who had lost her fiancé. She didn't even have to be human in those eyes. She could be anything.

Suddenly Sophie shook her head, trying to push away the thoughts. She was getting lost in her fantasies again, trapped. She needed to be grounded, to return to the real world. She blinked, looking at those strange eyes, wondering if the man could possibly be blind. She somehow doubted that. The way his eyes were focused on her she felt he could see into her very soul. She averted her gaze to the tree just behind him to break the mesmerising spell.

"How can I help you, Miss?" the old man said in a hoarse voice that sounded as if it hadn't been used in years. It was as if each syllable was a monumental effort for him to produce. His accent was one she hadn't heard before, lilting and melodic.

"I, um… sorry to bother you, but my GPS doesn't seem to be working," she said, holding up her phone as if to prove her point. The old man continued to stare in her direction, not even glancing at the evidence in hand. "So, I just don't know exactly where I'm going. I need to get to 11 Edgeware Lane. I'm supposed to be moving into the house there, you see. It's right on the Dover cliffs. Could you perhaps direct me where to go from here, if you know?" Her voice sounded loud and crass in the blanket of silence that engulfed them. Her presence, her movements, her very breath was obtrusive and out of place.

After a moment, the man croaked, "Number 11, you say." He scrutinised her closely. Sophie felt his eyes pierce her mind and sift through her thoughts, turning them over one by one before letting them fall to the ground like sand sifting through one's fingers. A strange energy crackled around him, making Sophie's skin flare up again in goosebumps. Just as she was about to roll up her window and speed away, he spoke again. "You seem like a nice girl. I wouldn't go there if I were you." He shook his head and heaved a heavy sigh that seemed to express more than mere tiredness but a lifetime's worth of exhaustion and sorrow.

"But I have to go there, I just bought the property, you see," Sophie replied, wondering whether this man was simply mad.

"And you can't return it, I presume?" the man replied wearily.

This was turning into a very strange conversation indeed.

"Uh, no, not really. If you don't know where it is, that's fine. I'll figure out where to go from here," Sophie said, exasperation rising to meet her anxiety.

"I know where it is, my dear. I know these parts like the back of my own hand, like the innards of my soul. I've been here a long, long time," the old man said, locking eyes with her, drawing her in to a secret world. "But I'm just warning you, be careful. That house is not your own and it never will be. Don't claim it. Don't take it. Don't trust it. If I were you I would rather be lost out here in the open than in that godforsaken place."

Sophie was utterly bewildered. The man spoke with such vehemence and passionate vitriol. In confusion, she waited, wondering if he would actually get around to giving her the directions. As if reading her mind, he let out another heavy sigh and said, "I see you are already damned and ready to make your pact with the Devil. So be it. You go left at the fork, drive straight and take the next right. It's a very small road, hardly more than a footpath. Drive down that and it will open up to Edgeware Lane. Number 11 will be the house closest to the edge next to the great big willow tree. From there only Fate can guide you."

Sophie felt a wave of relief. "Oh, thank you so much! You've been so helpful." She peered more closely at the man who seemed to have aged a lifetime in their brief encounter. The lines and wrinkles scarring his face seemed deeper, and his shoulders had slumped as if he was being steadily drained of energy. She must have been imagining it, but even his pallor and colour seemed faded. She had the strange feeling that he might just melt into the background and completely disappear, the substance of his body disintegrating into a thousand pieces, blending into the trees and earth around them.

"If you want, I could give you a lift to where you need to go. It's getting rather chilly and dark for walking. Where is it you're going?" she asked.

The man furrowed his brow as if he was thrown off guard by such a question. "I ask myself that every day," he whispered, staring at the makeshift cane by his side. "Thank you, Miss, I will make my own way," he said more clearly, looking back up at her.

"If you're sure," Sophie said, not wanting to press the matter. "Thank you again." She wound up her window and threw her useless phone into her handbag. She looked up and was about to wave to the old man before setting off when she realised he was gone. She looked in her rear-view mirror and to the side, but he was nowhere to be seen. That couldn't be possible. Had he really just disappeared?

Shaking her head in confusion, she suddenly noticed she could hear the wind, the trees and the leaves again. It was as if cotton wool had been removed from her ears. When she breathed, no icy mist rose in greeting.

There was probably a hidden footpath somewhere amongst the undergrowth on either side of her which he had tumbled into, she thought to herself. But still, that was a very odd encounter. She hoped that not all the villagers in the area were quite so intense. Nonetheless, she followed his directions and sure enough she reached her new house in a matter of minutes.

There were only two other houses on her lane. She drove past them and parked outside Number 11. The weeping willow looked ominous, a looming shadow cut out in the darkness. She turned off the engine and sat for a moment in silence. She could hear the rustling of the trees and bushes around her. It was as if they were whispering among themselves, secret mutterings of bygone times. The crashing of the waves against the cliffs was louder than she had expected. It seemed to be a restless night. There was an electric energy in the air. It was like an undercurrent pulsating through the night, making the hairs on the back of her neck stand on end. Sophie felt as if there were eyes in the bushes, watching her. It was probably just the animals and wildlife, but she couldn't help feeling like an intruder trespassing on the peace and silence that had occupied this area for so long. She wasn't supposed to be here.

Sophie remained sitting for a moment longer, stretching out the minutes for as long as she could. She knew she would have to get out eventually and face whatever the house had in store for her. She noted the overgrown front garden in desperate need of care and saw that one of the upstairs windows had been broken. The windows of the house were staring back at her, defiant, big, black gaping eyes. An irrational jolt of fear crept up her spine, making her shiver. She wished she had arrived before sunset. After dark everything seems more menacing with shadows dancing in the moonlight and even the most innocuous of sounds amplified into something strange and sinister. A little picket fence encompassed her garden, and the wrought-iron gate was open, creaking in the breeze. It was as though imaginary hands were slowly opening and closing it. Sophie felt her heart thudding against her chest. She suddenly wished she was in the safety and warmth of her parents' home, munching on home-made macaroni and cheese, watching *Coronation Street*.

She had to snap out of it. There was no other choice. It was not an option for her to spin around in her little car with a near empty fuel tank and speed back home. This was home now. She would not admit this adventure of hers to be a failure before it began, giving everyone else the satisfaction of being right and her wrong. She felt as if any movement on her part would disturb the natural equilibrium of the place. She realised she had been holding her breath, her muscles tense and rigid. Enough nonsense, she thought to herself. It was time to pull herself together. With what felt like herculean effort, she steeled herself and opened the car door. Salty wind whipped around her. Her mid-length brown hair lashed her face, obscuring her vision. She rolled her hair tie from off her wrist and gathered her hair into a messy bun, planted on the crown of her head. She felt as if the whispering from the trees had grown louder, as if they were suspicious of her arrival. The creaking gate continued to sway open and closed at what seemed like an increased momentum. Sophie was sure she was letting her imagination get the better of her.

She rubbed her eyes, trying to clear the grit and dirt which had just been blown into them. Blinking hard, she turned to face the house. She nearly fell back in shock. It was no longer there. It had vanished without a trace. A ramshackle hut squatted in its place. Splintered beams of wood had been hammered together in a lopsided manner, giving it a gruesome hunchbacked impression. A bird squalled loudly in the distance. The tangle of weeds and grass was gone, replaced with dirt and mud. Nothing had a clear outline to it. Everything was blending together and hazy. The scene was constantly shifting as if unsure of its own existence. Confusion and fear raced through Sophie. She felt like she was in a dream, or perhaps a nightmare.

The sound of children's voices floated through the air around her. She tried to spin around and see where they were coming from but found her muscles were only able to move slowly, as if she were pushing through treacle. The disembodied voices grew louder. At first she couldn't disentangle the voices or words but then she heard a young boy's voice ringing out, loud and clear.

"Is this where we're going to live now, Mummy?" the voice asked.

Sophie willed her head to look downwards, fighting the strong resistance pushing against her. She searched for the boy belonging to the voice but saw nothing. The ground was abundant with knots of weeds and grass. Sophie looked up so fast her neck cracked. There was her house. The hunchbacked squalid hut was gone. Sophie was breathing quickly. She looked all around her. Everything was as it should be, as it was a second ago. She flexed her hands, looking at her slender fingers. What had just happened? From the looks of it, nothing had happened. She was tired and her imagination was wreaking havoc on her senses.

Sophie rubbed her temples and knew it was time for her to be practical and quell her wild imagination. No one was going to set the house up for her. No one was going to help her. With slightly trembling hands, she opened the boot of the car and heaved out her two suitcases. She had only packed the basics and left behind most of the things that had memories attached to them, with the exception of her dusty old shoebox full of mementos. It was interesting to see how many things she could leave behind and how little she actually needed. She had decided she would be more minimalistic when moving into her new place, which was a good thing considering how small it was.

She lugged the suitcases past the creaking gate and shut it firmly behind her. There we go, enough from you, she thought to herself. She walked up the path to the main door, inadvertently casting glances over her shoulder. She felt an overwhelming sense of dread rising in the pit of her stomach, as if a swarm of sleeping wasps had been awoken and were encircling her insides, making her feel sick. There was definitely something amiss about this place. Sophie had been there only a few minutes but she couldn't help feeling unsettled and shaken.

The pathway was so overgrown it could hardly be called a path. It was more a mass of grass and weeds trying to tie knots around her ankles and prick her legs, pulling her away from the house. Sophie fumbled in her purse for her keys. Her hands gripped a large, old-fashioned metal key. It was the type of key people used to have in the old days, she felt. One end was large and circular, its centre cut out in a curving, looped decorative fashion. At the other end was the key portion, looking like part of a jagged jigsaw puzzle. She slotted it into the keyhole and turned. There was a loud click and gently she pushed open the door.

# Chapter 3

## *Samuel*

Samuel was pottering around the kitchen when he was struck by a blinding headache. It came as quick as a flash of lightning, stabbing its dagger into his brain. For a moment all he could see was bright light. It was as if his eyeballs were on fire. He fell to his knees on the hard kitchen floor and pressed his forehead against the cool tiles. Slowly, the excruciating pain ebbed and the burning sensation subsided. Samuel massaged his temples before grabbing the countertop and heaving himself up.

He had been in the process of making himself a cup of tea. The teabag was bobbing in the boiling water while the open milk bottle lay on its side, milk dripping down the counter and on to a puddle on the floor. Samuel took a wet cloth and dabbed the spilt milk. That was the last milk bottle, Samuel thought regretfully. He would have to resort to black tea and sugar now since it was too late to go out to the shops.

He told himself it was just another headache but deep down he knew it wasn't. It never was. He had lived with these headaches for the best part of thirteen years and he knew they portended trouble. Samuel glanced at his watch. It was just past 8:30 pm. He stumbled into the living room and collapsed on the couch. With a shaky hand he placed his tea on the coffee table, not minding when it spilled over the rim of the cup, leaving a stain in the wood. The blinding white light was returning. Samuel rocked his head gently from side to side. He knew what he was going to see when he looked up.

Sitting across from him in a battered armchair was the tall frame of Willowen. He looked faded, almost blurred around the edges. His expression was weary, his body slumped over.

"You knew this would happen," Willowen said slowly.

"No, I didn't think anyone would buy the place," Samuel replied, wincing in pain as the white light became stronger.

"But she did," Willowen said simply, his voice deep and rumbling.

"Yes." Samuel sighed heavily. "She did. Has she arrived?"

Willowen nodded slowly. "I tried to warn her to stay away but she didn't listen."

"I hope you didn't frighten her," Samuel replied.

"I wish I did. Maybe then she would have seen sense and not gone near the place," Willowen said, his voice heavy with sadness. "She's a sensitive type. Samuel, she needs to be careful. You know what awaits her there. You know *who* awaits her there."

Samuel nodded, the bitter wave of regret washing over him once again. He should never have sold that rotten old house. He should have had it demolished years ago.

"What's done is done," Willowen said gravely.

Although Willowen had been able to reply to Samuel's thoughts before Samuel even opened his mouth, he still found it off-putting. Samuel nodded again. The silence stretched between them for some time before Willowen spoke.

"The kids like her."

Samuel gave a sad smile and looked up at Willowen, a man equally bent and broken by life like himself. Willowen never could let them go. He had never been able to accept what had happened to his beloved children all those years ago.

"That's wonderful. I'm glad to hear that," Samuel said gently.

Willowen gazed at Samuel as he slowly seemed to break apart, particle by particle, like glass shattering in slow motion. Each particle sprayed out, glittering shards bouncing in different directions until all had dispersed and nothing remained. He was gone.

Samuel left his cold tea on the coffee table in search of his phone. With fumbling fingers he switched it on and searched for Sophie's number. He had never spoken to her or even seen her during the sale of the house. He knew if he had he would never have been able to go through with it. Everything had been done through an agent. He hadn't even given her his personal number. With guilt spreading like an infernal disease through his conscious, he dialled her number and waited.

# Chapter 4

## *Sophie*

*Dear Daniel,*

*Staring over the sharp edge of a cliff,*

*Wondering whether or not to jump,*

*My hands start to tremble, my legs are stiff*

*And in my throat is a choking lump.*


*Gazing into the sea's luminous eyes,*

*A startling, enticing blue,*

*Luring me closer to my demise,*

*As well as the dream of seeing you.*


*One inch forward and stones give way,*

*Crashing and crumbling to the bottom,*

*Snapped up by the hungry mouth of the savouring sea,*

*Within seconds, completely forgotten.*

*So with this potential new dream of life,*

*Away from the bitterness of unending strife,*

*What's to stop me? Why do I glance back?*

*Why in my sturdy armour of resolve*

*Is doubt determined to crack?*

*Sophie*

It was the smell she noticed first, pungent and acrid. It was a mixture of something burnt and something rotten. Sophie covered her nose with her hand which did little to avail the reeking smell emanating from the very walls of the house. It smelt of disease and decay. Well, she knew what her first mission was: to rid the place of that putrid smell. Her eyes adjusted to the engulfing darkness. She fumbled on the wall for a light switch. A cracked naked bulb hung from the ceiling, offering a small halo of light which did little to brighten up the rest of the narrow corridor. From what she could see the place was filthy. She had to drag her suitcases in sideways to fit through the extremely narrow corridor.

As she pulled them along, plumes of dust trailed her. The walls were bare and in need of repainting. The faded yellow paint that was originally there was peeling, and patches of mould darkened the corners. The corridor opened up to a very small dining area, to the right of which was the tiniest kitchen Sophie had ever seen. There was just enough space for the gas oven, mini fridge, and washing machine which was shoved in the far corner. The entire countertop space was the width of her hand and Sophie did not have particularly big hands. Something told her she would not do much cooking here.

To the left was a living room which would barely fit a small sofa and television. Sophie quickly skipped up the steep, creaking stairs to see what the bedroom and bathroom were like. It was the bedroom window that was broken. A stiff breeze blew the ragged, dusty, wine-coloured curtains, making them move and ripple in unison like a pair of dancers lost in a whirlwind of music. Sophie would have to find something to temporarily board up the gaping hole. The floor directly beneath it was cold and damp from where the rain must have lashed in. The room was an odd shape, almost like an octagon. She puzzled at where the bed would go and how to fit her writing desk in this strangely shaped bedroom. The pungent smell was strong here.

She looked around for a bathroom but to her confusion didn't see one. There must be a bathroom somewhere here, she thought to herself, puzzled. She went back downstairs, careful not to stumble on the steep steps as she went down in semi-darkness. She walked through the tiny kitchen and saw at the end, almost as if it was an afterthought, a tiny closet of a room which had a Spartan toilet, a sink and a shower, but no tub. There was no shower tray, only a drain. Whenever she showered, she would need a mop on standby as the water would surely go everywhere. There seemed to be a dank layer of mould growing on everything in here.

First things first, Sophie decided to get a piece of cardboard, which she luckily had from a cardboard box she had stuffed a few trinkets in. She marched upstairs and carefully covered the hole in the window, plastering it with duct tape. She noticed there was no broken glass on the floor. So the owner must have cleared up the shattered glass but hadn't bothered to fix the window. She rolled her eyes in annoyance. As she let her gaze drift over the room, she noticed a dark, shadowy lump lying in one of the many corners. Sophie moved closer slowly. Then realization struck. Her hand flew to her mouth as she tried to quell the mounting shock and disgust. It was a dead, decaying bird, the cause of the putrid smell.

Sophie fought down the nausea mixed with panic that was bubbling in her stomach. She had never had to deal with such a thing before. How were you to dispose of dead birds? She didn't want to touch it for fear of getting some disease from its decaying corpse. Sophie closed her eyes and took several deep breaths which she instantly regretted after inhaling the rotten smell up close. She had to be practical. She was the only person here and she could not sleep with this rotting carcass in her room. She ran downstairs and pulled out some magazines from her suitcase. The magazines were meant to be her entertainment before she bought a television but now she had a more important use for them. Fortunately, she had brought some cleaning supplies based on Angie's presumption that the place would be a tip. Sophie yanked out the yellow marigold rubber gloves from her suitcase and put them on. Armed with gloves and magazines she went back upstairs. She held her breath as she approached the lump in the corner. Slowly, she moved forward and knelt down. Very carefully, she placed the magazines all around the body and scooped it up gently so as not to drop anything. Despite her care, the crumbling mass shook in her hands, and the tenuous thread connecting the head to the body snapped. Sophie screamed as the head rolled on the floor. Heart thudding in her chest, she scooped up its remains and holding it at arm's length she carried the grotesque bundle outside.

The wind seemed to have picked up and was pushing her with surprising strength. She heard the aggressive waves thrashing the cliff side and tasted bitter salt in her mouth. Now she was outside with the dead bird, she didn't know what to do with it. She couldn't just dump it in her neighbour's bin, the lid of which had blown off and was clanging down the lane until it wedged itself in a bush. That certainly would not be a neighbourly thing to do on her first night.

She had an idea. She walked around the back of the house. There was a small crooked fence surrounding her tiny back garden. Planks of wood were missing at irregular intervals. It reminded Sophie of the wide, leering smile of a gap-toothed old man. Sophie shivered. She hopped over the fence. All she had to do was take a few steps before reaching the cliff edge. She peered over. It sloped gently down. Below she saw the frothy waves, jostling and spraying the cliff. She was instantly mesmerised by the vast, black sea at her feet. The dark depths had a magnetic quality to them, and she felt she was being pulled closer to the edge watching the spellbinding swirling surface. She wondered what lay beneath those raging waves, what strange sea creatures dwelt at such depths. Without thinking she dropped the bundle she was carrying over the edge. The bird's corpse fell like a dead weight whereas the magazines seemed to flutter a moment or two in the breeze before being lapped up by the undulating gloom below. The black sea extended into the horizon forever. In the distance the water appeared smooth and glassy, a glimmering reptilian skin containing a whole new, enticing world beneath its deceptive surface. Sophie took a step closer to the edge and then another. Suddenly several stones crumbled under her feet and tumbled into the darkness below. Before she knew what was happening, the strange dreamlike quality descended softly over her. As she continued to stare downwards she thought she could see shadows moving, balancing precariously on the cliff edge. Thick, heavy raindrops pattered down, but Sophie was oblivious to them.

She saw them land as they dotted the ground beneath her but didn't feel the cool splash.

The wind was whispering to her. She felt it wrap around her, encasing her in a silky embrace, murmuring in her ear. "Shhhh," was all she could hear. She inched forward. More stones gave way, falling into oblivion. With the vanishing stones, the shadows were also gone. Sophie snapped her head up and looked towards the skies. Blank and empty. Not a droplet of rain was being wrung out from above. It was only then that Sophie realised she was shivering with cold. She blinked and shook her head slightly, pulling away from the captivating magnetism of the sea. Hugging herself tightly, she turned quickly and sprinted back inside.

She was shivering badly when she re-entered the house. Sophie dragged her suitcases into the dining room area and opened one up. She pulled out a thick woolly cardigan and wrapped herself in it. Much better, she thought. All she needed now was a nice cup of tea. First, she rummaged in her bag for her phone. She saw a missed call from an unknown number, two missed calls from Angie, five missed calls and three texts from her parents, two texts from stores about promotions and a text from a guy, Martin, who she hated. Martin had liked her before Dan asked her out. He had been one of the guys in her journalism courses at LSE. He had instantly clung to her, messaging her non-stop and calling at all hours of the day. Once she started dating Dan, he had slunk back into the corner and left her alone for a while. After he had heard the news of Dan's funeral, however, he was back in her life like a buzzing fly she just couldn't get rid of. She despised him for thinking that he had some sort of chance just because Dan was gone. She deleted his message without even opening it. She ignored the missed call from the unknown number, not feeling up to dealing with strangers pestering about bank loans or upgrading her phone plan. Guiltily she read over her parents' worried messages. She had promised to call them and Angie the second she arrived in her new, humble dwelling.

She opened her parents' messages first. The first one read: *Hi, how are you getting along, sweetie? Let us know when you arrive. We miss you already! Xxx.* The second one was starting to get more anxious: *Please let us know where you are, Soph! We're getting worried about you. Love you – Mum & Dad xxx.* The third one was downright cross with no kisses at the end: *Sophie – where are you? Please message us like you said you would. We've tried calling a bunch of times. Is everything all right?* Oops, Sophie thought. She sat cross-legged on her unopened suitcase and rang her mum's number. She answered on the first ring – probably up, waiting for the call, Sophie thought guiltily.

"Sophie! At last. I was beginning to get worried! It's 10:15 pm, I thought you said you were arriving around 7:00 pm! Did anything happen? Were you in any accidents along the way? My goodness, this is a relief. So tell me, how was the drive? What's the place like? Remember, you can always come home to me and Dad if it doesn't work out." Her mum said all this without even pausing for breath.

"Hey, Mum, don't worry, everything is fine. The drive went well. I only got a little lost at the very end. And the place…" She paused. She wasn't sure how much of the truth she wanted to divulge. She didn't want her parents to worry about her and the state of the house. She also didn't want her mother to inwardly say "I told you so", after vehemently recommending Sophie see the place before putting down the deposit.

"What's wrong with it?" her mum asked suspiciously. "Is it a dump? Oh, Sophie…"

"Mum, it's fine," Sophie said, quickly making her mind up to sugar-coat the truth a little. Well, perhaps a lot. "Really, Mum, it just needs a little clean, then it will look just like the pictures I showed you. Once I've settled in, unpacked some of my things and made it cosy, I'll take some pics for you and Dad." She said this as confidently as she could, which was difficult considering there was still a thick stench in the air and she was sure she had just seen an exceptionally large beetle of some sort scuttle across the kitchen floor which had deep cracks in the floorboards.

"Ok, just remember the offer always stands. So you're happy there? You think you'll settle in ok? What are you going to be doing for your dinner tonight?" Her mum's barrage of questions started to make Sophie's head spin. She just wanted to be in bed under a blanket, surrounded by silence, cloaked in darkness.

"Well, I've actually got the kettle on now," she lied. "I'm making tea and I'll probably just have some of the tuna you packed for me and some biscuits and then call it a night." Sophie's mum had not only packed cans of tuna, but a couple of cans of baked beans, a pack of whole-wheat sliced bread, a variety of biscuits, several jam jars, Pop Tarts, a box of cereal, several bananas and packets of dried fruits.

"Oh, I am glad the tuna came in handy for you. I was worried about you arriving late and all the shops being shut. But make sure you go food shopping tomorrow! Those cans aren't going to last. I wish you would have let me pack some of my mac and cheese for you in a Tupperware. How are the appliances? Are the fridge and washing machine working? You need to test those, you know. Oh, and have you met any of your neighbours yet?"

Sophie rubbed her temples, exhaustion fogging up her mind and rippling through her body in waves. "No, I haven't met any neighbours yet but I'll give you all the gossip once I do. I'll check out the fridge and washing machine now. I gotta go though, Mum. I honestly just want to eat and sleep right now. I'll call you first thing tomorrow!"

"Of course, you must be tired! Well, I'll talk to you tomorrow then, dear. But please, give me or your dad a ring if you need anything! I mean it, anything at all," her mum said firmly.

Sophie smiled. She knew she could always rely on her parents. They had been with her and supported her through everything. She was an only child, so they had devoted all their energy into her upbringing and happiness. She wanted to thank her mother for everything she had ever done for her and all the sacrifices she had made for her when growing up. Instead she replied simply with, "Sure, thanks, Mum! Goodnight. Kisses to you and Dad."

"Goodnight, sweetheart, love you," her mum replied before hanging up.

Sophie sighed. She didn't have a stick of furniture and certainly no bed to sleep in. The only furnishing that came with the place was the washing machine and fridge which Sophie had not checked yet. It seemed the owner hadn't set foot in the place for months, if not years. Everything seemed to be in a state of dire disrepair.

Fortunately, her dad, a big camping fanatic, had given her one of his sleeping bags which she would use tonight. She sent a quick message to Angie so that she wouldn't be worried.

*Hey, Angie, what do you know, I arrived! Place is all right, bit of a fixer-upper but nthn major. I'll call u tomorrow. I'm sooo tired now and just need to sleep. Miss u, girl xxxxx.*

The last thing she had to do before bed was clean the carpet area where the dead bird had been. She was going to leave the rest of the cleaning for tomorrow. As she was pulling out her carpet cleaner and putting on her yellow gloves, she heard a slow creaking of the floorboards overhead, as if someone was trying to tread with care and avoid being heard. Sophie froze. Each creak grated on her already frazzled nerves. It continued, as if someone was slowly pacing backwards and forwards. Sophie could almost feel the presence of someone right above her. She remained motionless with bated breath. Until, suddenly, it stopped. She stared transfixed at the ceiling and strained her ears, but all sounds of movement had stopped dead. All she could hear was the howling wind outside. Adrenaline coursed through her veins. Nothing but silence and her wildly beating heart pulsated through the air.

She was tired and must be imagining things. Despite her rationalisation, she grabbed a frying pan from her suitcase and tiptoed as quietly as possible up the stairs. Slowly she pushed open the door to the bedroom. Her heart was beating fast and her breath was shallow. The room was small and there was nowhere to hide in the blank emptiness of the space. There was nothing there.

Suddenly Sophie felt the weight of the atmosphere engulf her. The frying pan slid out of her hand and dropped noiselessly to the floor. Everything felt heavy. Any movement required monumental effort. She turned her head slowly, surveying the scene. Instead of the faded lavender wallpaper, rough wood adorned the walls. Sophie could hear whispering. Disembodied childish light voices echoed through time. Sophie strained her ears to hear what was being said but couldn't untangle the hushed tones. A cold rush of air seeped through her bones, bringing with it a heavy sadness. Sophie stood as still as a statue as these strange sensations seeped into her mind and body. Tears welled up in her eyes as she stared at the empty space around her, the strange voices reverberating all around her. She blinked to clear her blurred vision. As the tears slid down her face, Sophie looked around her. With her vision restored, she saw the lavender walls and wine-coloured curtains exactly as they were. There was no sound other than the wind rapping on the walls. The heavy feeling was lifted, and Sophie spun around. She wiped the tears from her face and stared at the damp residue they left on her hands. The deep feelings of sorrow and grief had lifted as quickly as they had come.

Feeling frazzled, Sophie repeated to herself out loud, "I'm the only one living here. There's no one else here. It's just me." Glancing at the cleaning materials she was still holding, she remembered the task at hand. She got on her hands and knees and scrubbed the carpet with soap and water. The smell had certainly dissipated and was now replaced by a fresh, lemony smell. That will have to do, she thought. She would clean the rest of the place tomorrow.

She put the cleaning materials to the side and laid out her sleeping bag. Although she was exhausted, adrenaline coursed through her veins. She jumped at the slightest creak in the house or when the wind howled particularly loudly. She was afraid. She was afraid in this unfamiliar house, in the middle of nowhere. She was afraid to be so far from friends and family. She was afraid of the strange dreamlike sensations that suddenly gripped her with hands of steel, transporting her mind to another place, before disappearing, allowing reality to flow back in. She was afraid she was losing her grip on what was real and what was only in her head. Despite being all by herself she didn't feel alone. Feeling drained and unsettled, she pulled her sleeping bag up to her chin.

"I miss you, Dan," she whispered aloud. "I wish you were here." She felt a warm tear trickle down the side of her face and then another and another. Crying softly into her sleeping bag, exhaustion took over and she finally fell into a disturbed, strange sleep.

Her dreams were vivid and delirious. She dreamt she had built a house out of sand on the edge of the cliff. It had started raining, thick heavy drops, and her house was being washed away, slithering down the cliff edge and into the sea. She tried to run after it and catch it, but the sand kept slipping through her fingers before it disappeared and dissolved entirely. Just then a huge black bird swooped over her, stretching its beak wide. Instead of letting out its usual caw, it spoke. It told her that the house wasn't hers and that she had to leave immediately. If she would just hop on the bird's back, it said, it could take her to a place far away from here, to an underwater palace in the sea. She would be alone but safe there, the bird told her. It blinked and its eyes morphed from deep black to a swirling lavender grey, magnetically drawing her in. Sophie shook her head in the dream saying that she couldn't leave just yet and that she would build herself a new house of sand. A house where she was alone but safe. Sophie stared in horror as the raven let out a blood-curdling scream and shook its head so violently it tumbled right off its body. Despite being headless, it flapped its wings in rage. Its swirling eyes stared blankly at Sophie from the head lying motionless on the floor.

Just then the dream transformed into a completely different scene. She was in a beautiful garden. It was a sunny day and a willow tree stood tall, providing her shade from the strong, unrelenting sun. A little girl dressed in white frills skipped over to her.

"Can you help my mummy?" she asked, in a sweet high girlish voice. She had soft brown curls that framed her delicate face. Her eyes were a stunning emerald green, bright like jewels. A smattering of freckles dotted her nose and cheeks. Her lily-white skin looked luminescent in the afternoon sun. She gazed calmly at Sophie with her jewel eyes.

"Of course, where is she?" Sophie asked the little girl.

The girl looked up at her with large magical eyes. "Over there," she replied, pointing at the willow tree, a small crease forming between her brows.

Sophie looked up and was instantly horrified by the scene unfurling before her. The bending branches of the peaceful willow were ablaze. She could hear high-pitched screams coming from the tree, as if its soul was on fire.

"You must help," the little girl said calmly.

The entire tree was a fiery orange, she could feel the heat roasting and melting her skin. She had to pick up the girl and run but found that her feet wouldn't move. She looked down and saw that roots were growing from the souls of her feet, planting her to the earth beneath her.

"Nooo!" she screamed, as the flames started licking the grass, snaking their way to her. The little girl was standing, already engulfed in the roaring fire. Her eyes gleamed through the scarlet flames. They were the only things Sophie could see. Just as the fiery tendrils were about to wrap themselves around Sophie's legs, she woke up in a cold sweat. The acrid smell of smoke burned her nostrils and polluted her lungs.

She scrambled out of her sleeping bag. Fear gripped her heart. Where was the fire coming from? She looked out the window but didn't see anything. She then sprinted downstairs, nearly tripping on the last step. She tumbled into the kitchen but there was no fire there. The bathroom was clear, as was the living room. She frantically glanced out the window into the front and back gardens. Everything seemed calm and serene after last night's gusty wind. She looked apprehensively at the willow tree, its branches swayed gently. There was nothing out of the ordinary there either. It must have been her dream spilling into reality. She let out a shaky sigh of relief. She started counting her breaths, trying to regain control over her mind and body which was still trembling. What a start to the morning, she thought to herself. At least there's nothing to worry about. It was just a false alarm. She swallowed hard, trying to rid herself of the strange burning sensation in the back of her throat. Everything was fine, she told herself.

She had stowed away a red mini travel kettle in her suitcase which she went to unpack. If there was one thing she could not live without, it was a good cup of tea. She had not really planned what she was going to do once she actually arrived at her new home. Everything had happened so fast. These past few weeks had been a whirlwind, what with finding a house, quitting her job, saying her farewells and then packing up her life and moving here. She realised that once she'd had her tea and given the place a good scrub, she had to come up with some sort of action plan and quickly. She didn't have much by way of savings and the first thing she needed to do was find a job.

The steam billowed from the kettle as the water heated up. Sophie pulled out a battered box of PG Tips from her case and tossed a triangle-shaped teabag into her favourite mug. It was a large, dark blue mug with the constellations outlined in gold decorating the inside as well as outside. She prepared her tea and perched on her overflowing suitcase. It was time to contemplate her situation. It was a cold September morning and Sophie hadn't yet figured out how to work the boiler. She wrapped herself in a large, patterned scarf and clasped both hands around her warm mug of tea. She flicked on her phone and to her surprise saw that it was only 6:45 am. She rarely woke that early without the assistance of her aggressive beeping alarm clock.

The strange dream seeped back into her mind, like the morning mist stealing itself upon the day. The little girl, the setting, the willow tree, it had all felt so bizarrely real. It was so vivid she almost felt like she was reliving a memory rather than pondering on a dream. And the smoke. She had woken up choking on it as it filled her nose leaving her with rasping breaths. She tried to imagine what her counsellor would say. She would probably reprimand her for moving in the first place. Then ask her what she (Sophie) had expected and that of course her subconscious would be overflowing with stress and anxiety and it was all coming forth in the form of bizarre, absurd dreams. Sophie nodded, trying to accept that mundane, rational explanation. Nonetheless, an inexplicable shiver shimmied its way up her spine. She wasn't sure if it was because of the chilliness of the morning or the strangeness of the night before.

"What should I do first, Dan?" she whispered into her steamy cup. It was soothing, sitting there in silence, no one hanging over her, no eyes following her every move. Just as that happy thought drifted into her mind she felt a strange paranoia. Eyes were following her. She was being watched. Someone or something was following her every move. She swivelled around to look outside the kitchen window. Two big black ravens were squatting on the windowsill, staring back at her. Their dark, beady eyes penetrating through the glass. Sophie looked at them crossly.

"Shoo, get out of here," she said, waving her hands at them. She thought that might frighten them away, but they continued to stare stubbornly. With trepidation, she approached the window and rapped on the glass hard with her knuckles. The bigger of the two let out a massive caw in return. Sophie jumped back, startled. Whoever had lived here before must have just accepted them, perhaps even kept them as pets. They clearly thought they owned the place. Sophie rolled her eyes in annoyance at the previous owner. She was clearly stuck with this ominous pair. She turned away, deciding to pick her battle with the ravens later. She had more important things to do now.

She took one last gulp of her lukewarm tea and forced herself to get ready and go into town. She was on a mission to find some furniture and, with a bit of luck, a job. She had decided she would take a break from the high-stress environment of the advertising world. She was hoping she could find a simple job, perhaps in retail, or as a waitress or even a bartender. She just wanted a way to earn a bit of cash and be able to pay her bills. She felt she would be happier living a simpler life for a while, with just the basics. She could hear her counsellor's voice ringing in her ears: "What happened wasn't your fault. You need to learn to stop punishing yourself for it. Inflicting this sort of self-punishment isn't going to do anyone any good, especially not you." Sophie remembered feeling her counsellor's large, icy blue eyes penetrating through her soul. Sophie had wanted to scream at her, tell her how wrong she was. Tell her the truth. Everything was her fault. She had tried to speak but a large lump in her throat prevented her words from becoming audible. She had managed to croak out a few gasps before an avalanche of sobs racked her entire body.

Dismissing these unwelcome memories, Sophie gathered up some toiletries from her suitcase and went to her closet-sized bathroom. She wore her beach slippers to ensure she didn't step on the ring of mould decorating the drain. She made a mental note that on her return she would douse the place in bleach. The water barely drizzled out of the shower head when she turned it on. It was also freezing cold. Sophie sighed, closing her eyes. She had loved the way her and Dan had decorated their bathroom when they moved in together. There were baby blue tiles lining the wall and a big stand-alone tub. Sophie had enjoyed lining up all her beauty and bath products on the shelving space they kept next to the tub. She had loved taking long, luxurious bubble baths using exotic salts and the colourful fizzing bath bombs from Lush. There she could relax and sink into the warm water, letting all her worries from the day melt away and trickle down the drain along with the soapy suds.

Sophie opened her eyes to the bleak reality of the present. She felt the icy droplets sting her skin as water sloshed around the hard, chipped bathroom floor. It was dank and dark in the tiny bathroom. There was a small window near the ceiling to let the steam out, she supposed. Out of curiosity she reached to open it, but it seemed jammed shut. She quickly lathered her hair with shampoo, gave it the best rinse she could with the meagre water supply and put in a leave-in conditioner so she didn't have to prolong her miserable shower. She wrapped a towel around her, shivering as she got out of the bathroom and into the kitchen. The uncanny feeling of being watched trailed her. She spun around and saw the two ravens still perched on her windowsill, staring at her with what seemed to be an intent, scrutinising look. First thing to buy was curtains, Sophie thought to herself, feeling unsettled.

Sophie yanked her make-up bag out of her case and sat on one of the cardboard boxes. Using a tiny compact mirror, Sophie squeezed out what remained from her tinted moisturiser and dabbed that on her face. She felt her skin had a greyish, unhealthy hue to it. It could be because the lighting was so poor in the house, but she also knew she had not been eating well lately, doing any exercise or taking care of herself in general. Today, however, she had to make an effort if she was going to make herself a desirable employee. She rummaged in her bag for her concealer. That was definitely what she needed, considering the dark circles which seemed to permanently frame her eyes. For the past few months she had not cared whether she got enough sleep or how she looked. Life had become one blurry haze she couldn't quite wrap her head around. She swiped on a generous amount of the concealer then patted it down with her favourite Rimmel powder. Next step, she had to make her tired brown eyes appear more awake. Until recently she felt she had been in a groggy coma, somewhere between nightmarish slumber and cloudy consciousness. She blended a little natural MAC eyeshadow into her crease, carefully drew a small wing with her liner and layered a generous amount of her mascara on both her bottom and top lashes. For the finale, she got her favourite, mauve MAC lipstick, pouted and glided that on her lips. She stared at herself in the mirror which had a film of smudges and make-up smears on it. She looked almost like her old self, the self before the accident. The sadness in her eyes lingered. No amount of make-up would ever be able to conceal that. Her delicate features shone in the morning light. Dan had always called her his little pixie. Sophie was slim, had gentle brown eyes which twinkled with flecks of amber gold in certain lights, a small nose and cupid bow lips. Her cheeks had a natural flush to them and her hair, if she took care of it, was silky smooth.

"Only magic and pixie dust could have created a gorgeous creature like you," Dan had said once on one of their valentine's dates. She could hear his deep voice resonating in her head. Sophie immediately felt tears well up in her eyes. She snapped the compact shut and drew in several deep breaths.

"I can't ruin my make-up just after I've spent all this time doing it," she muttered to herself. The last thing she needed was streaky, dirty black tears snaking their way down her face. She needed to look presentable today. Several more breaths and she was ready to continue. She blow-dried her hair with her travel-sized hairdryer and dressed in a somewhat creased cream shirt, straight black trousers, a casual loose-fitting grey blazer and smart black shoes with a hint of heel. She didn't have a full-length mirror yet so she had to trust that everything was in place. She freed a large squashed black leather bag from her suitcase and dumped all her necessities for the day in it. In a file, she armed herself with over a dozen CVs which she was planning to hand out like candy on Halloween. When she was ready she stood up tall. She felt a strange sense of disparity descend upon her. She looked like her old self but felt completely different. It was a collision of the two selves. The before and after.

After months of just mooching around on the sofa, unwashed, hair piled up in a knot on her head, she was actually leaving the house in a relatively decent state. Whatever she was feeling, this must be step forward.

"What do you think, Dan?" she asked out loud to the empty house. "I scrub up ok?" She knew what his answer would be. She heard his laughter like soft music echoing in her ears. "Not bad, not bad at all! You go out and knock 'em dead, honey."

"I'll try," she whispered. The lump had lodged itself in her throat again. She had to clear her mind if she was going to do this. She shook her head, dispelling the memories floating around, as unattainable as the misty clouds draping themselves over the horizon.

Sophie gathered up her things and gave the house a once-over. She was standing in the doorframe leading to the hallway where she could see both the kitchen and living room. Everything around her was quiet and still. It felt too still. Bizarrely she felt as if the house was waiting for her to leave before springing into some sort of action. Sophie couldn't even hear the rhythmic crashing of the waves. The silence and stillness stretched on while Sophie remained rooted to the spot. Any movement would disturb the balance of the house, she thought without knowing why. Or perhaps, it would alert the house to her presence. A sense of foreboding crept up on her. It spread from the soles of her feet, crawling like spiders up her body. The eyes of the house were zeroing in on her. A line of sweat trickled down her back as she stood paralysed.

Suddenly a gust of icy cold air rushed in from between the cracks in the door. Sophie gasped involuntarily at the onslaught of coldness. Forced into momentum, she grabbed a thick scarf and wrapped it around her. Shivering slightly, Sophie stumbled to the door.

She stepped outside where she immediately felt warmer. It was as if the house itself had suddenly dropped below freezing. The shrill caw of the ever-watchful raven caught her attention. It had spread its large inky black wings and cut through the air purposefully to the willow tree. Once it had settled on a branch, it turned to face Sophie. Sophie frowned at the unusual behaviour of the bird. Deciding to ignore it, she listened to the waves crashing against the cliff and was surprised at how loud the sound was when moments ago it had been mute. The air was sharp with the bitter taste of salt.

Sophie got into her car. It was a chilly day and she turned the heating up. She turned on her GPS, searching for the location of the town centre. Again, however, her GPS was acting haywire. This time it was pointing directly at the cliffs. It wants me to drive over the edge of the cliffs, Sophie thought to herself. She had heard about people getting themselves into rather sticky situations all because they had taken every direction the GPS issued as fact and hadn't used an ounce of common sense. Well, I'll just try again after driving a little out of this area, she thought to herself. Perhaps there was some sort of interference where she was, she didn't really know how these things worked.

She started up her car and noticed immediately how low on fuel she was. First stop, petrol station, she thought to herself. She drove away down the narrow road she had come from yesterday, savouring the views around her now that everything was bathed in the cold sunshine glow. Sophie turned on the radio and listened to the eight o'clock news for a few minutes before flicking through the music channels. She left it on a station playing oldies from the eighties. Sophie had always felt she had been born in the wrong decade, misplaced in time. She had always loved reading classical novels such as Jane Austen's and the Brontë sisters' books. She would have been happy to have lived in what seemed to be a simpler time rather than the fast-paced lifestyle modern life required. Her nostalgia made it easy for her to break free from the clutches of reality, through daydreams or those precious moments before sleep. For as long as she could remember, she had one foot in reality and the other in the clouds. She was a dreamer, and at times, her fantasies felt more real than reality itself.

She checked her GPS which seemed to be behaving itself this time. There was a little village only five minutes away by car called St. Margaret's at Cliffe. She decided to drive there to fill up then park somewhere and take a walk around. It was a clear, crisp day. The sky was an electric blue with a few wispy clouds hanging overhead, looking as if they had been painted on in a single brushstroke by a lazy artist. There was no wind and everything felt still and serene. The golden sunshine melted into the road in front of her, creating fluid, dappled patterns through the leafy trees. It was as if the road was shifting as the patterned shadows rippled along.

Sophie reached the petrol station and filled up. It felt odd to be doing such a normal, mundane task in such a new, unfamiliar environment. She could see inside the newsagents. There was a man behind the till talking in a friendly, open manner to someone who appeared to be a regular customer. It seemed bizarre to her that people were continuing to live their regular lives when her entire world had been shattered. She was starting a brand-new journey while people around here were going to their usual cafés, their regular jobs, visiting the same shops. That sense of routine, even if it was another person's, gave her a sense of calm, a feeling that all was not wrong with the world. Despite the never-ending litany of tragedies that could unfold, time continued its ever forward march and everyone continued to step in time with it.

Lost in thought, words began to dance around in her head and join together, forming ropes of rhyme. Sophie had not only loved reading the classics growing up, but she had always been a prolific writer. She had loved writing short stories of children going to fantastical worlds and embarking on mind-boggling adventures, fairy tales of wrathful gods and witches and beautiful maidens. Since Dan's death, she had poured her heart and soul into lines of poetry, weaving words and phrases together until she had a beautiful tapestry overflowing with sadness. She kept a brown leather notebook in her bag at all times and was constantly jotting down her poems and the random words and ideas that flitted around her mind like restless birds trapped in a cage. She would then type them up and save them in a folder labelled "To Dan" on her desktop. This strange little ritual gave her a sense of peace and soothed her aching soul, even if it was just for a few minutes.

As she got in the car she spent a few minutes scribbling down the latest rhymes that were darting around in her head before taking off. She smiled and brushed a tear that had found its way out of the corner of her eye. She sighed, checked her appearance in the mirror and drove off.

Sophie had always wanted to be a writer. Her friends and family had always thought that would be the career she would choose. She had studied journalism although she really wanted to study English Literature. She wanted to lose herself in the arcane mysteries of Latin and study ancient texts and myths. Her heart lay amidst books that when opened heaved a sigh of glittering dust. That avenue, according to her guidance counsellor, Mr. Jameson, was not a safe, secure one. Those were soft subjects which would not generate a steady income in the future. *A writer's journey is one of the loneliest journeys in the world*, she remembered him saying in a stern, unwavering tone.

Somewhat intimidated by Mr. Jameson's words, she had decided on a different route and studied journalism. She had enjoyed the degree but her heart was never truly in it. She had always found it difficult to stay within what she considered to be the brutally short word count that most journalistic content required. She had always loved exploring ideas, creating life from words, experimenting with sentence structure, which for her took countless pages. As a result of her lack of passion for journalism, she accepted the first job she found in London at the Maverick Advertising Agency as a Junior Account Executive. She had enjoyed it at first. It was her first real job, first real salary. However, the glamour of the advertising world faded quickly and left Sophie with the sense that she had missed her real calling in life, the calling she felt deep within her soul to create something beautiful, timeless and true.

She found a parking spot and wedged her little car in between two hulking SUVs. Holding her stomach in, she managed to squeeze out of the car without getting any dirt or marks on her clothes. Heaving a sigh of relief, she marched on. She had decided she was going to take it easy. She wasn't going to stress about getting a job immediately. She would just pop into some shops in between meandering and exploring and see if they had vacancies. No pressure, she told herself. She tugged her blazer around herself more tightly, trying to prevent the chill from sneaking under her clothes.

The village was quaint and peaceful. It was a Saturday morning and a heavy drowsiness seemed to cling to the air around her. She decided she would get a bite to eat before her CV distribution mission. Just as this thought drifted into her mind, she realised that she was actually ravenous having barely eaten anything since yesterday's lunch. As if to confirm that fact, her stomach growled angrily. She strolled into the first café she came across. It was called The Mean Bean Coffee Shop. That was something that had first struck Sophie as she drove through the area. There was a total lack of chain restaurants, cafés and shops. The area seemed to support local establishments, and as a result Sophie found herself captivated and enthralled by the names of the places. They stirred the imagination and made her mind wander into fairylands and faraway places. The imaginative thread in her mind spun stories centring around the enigmatic and fanciful names.

She had walked past the Lantern Inn, and on the other side of the road spied a shop selling all sorts of knick-knacks called Peacocks' Lair. Her imagination took her off on an escapade where she envisioned several men, old and young, in a small rickety rowboat, silently flowing down a canal in the dead of night. The only light to guide them was the faint glow of a single lantern. They had to travel under the guise of darkness for fear of getting caught. In her mind's eye, the men stumbled upon the Peacocks' Lair where a sultan sat on a throne comprising jewels and precious stones. Vicious but beautiful peacocks strutted around the sultan in their hundreds. Their bright green and royal purple feathers were studded with diamonds and scintillating crystals. Sophie made a mental note to check what knick-knacks a shop like Peacocks' Lair had to offer, sure that there would be nothing as elaborate as what she had envisioned.

The bell tinkled as she entered The Mean Bean Coffee Shop. Immediately she felt as if she was being embraced in a warm, comforting hug. She was enveloped by the bitter coffee aroma mingling with sweet baking smells. She inhaled deeply, feeling the tension from the cold outside slide off her body and evaporate into the delicious air.

She went up to the counter and ordered a large cappuccino, cheese and tomato toastie, with a blueberry muffin for after. The young man behind the counter, with the name tag Ben, was smiley and friendly.

"New in town?" he asked, as he prepared her cappuccino.

"Yes, actually, how'd you know?" Sophie asked.

"It's a small town," Ben said, smiling. "You have family or friends here?"

"Nope, just me. I moved here recently for a fresh start, you could say."

"Well, you've chosen a great place! Nowhere better to have a fresh start than a place by the sea! It washes everything away, gives you a clean, blank slate to work with," he said, passing her a tray with her breakfast on it.

"That's exactly what I want, a blank slate," Sophie said, smiling, mentally turning the page of her life's story to a pure snow-white page. Beautiful and blank. She thanked him and took the tray to a window seat. She chose a particularly battered but comfortable-looking brown leather couch which she sank into. She took a long sip of the hot coffee and stared out the window, lost in her thoughts. She checked her wristwatch which had been a gift from Dan. It was 8:45 am. She wondered if it really was possible to start again, with a clean slate. She didn't think so. All those previous pages had so much life etched in them. In her mind's eye, the dainty book containing her life's story suddenly morphed into a slab of heavy grey stone. Instead of feathering her story lightly amidst its pages, she was clutching a rough object akin to an ice pick. She started carving through the stone. With each letter, she cut through her skin and blood dripped from the stone. Soon there was so much blood pouring from her hands that the entire stone had turned a slippery, ghoulish red. Like scarlet teardrops they trickled down her arms, landing at her feet. Only then did she look up and see what she had carved: Sophie Parker. 1991–2019. It was her tombstone set in her tiny garden by the sea. Shaking her head violently, Sophie reeled in her imagination. One of the customers was giving her a strange look. Sophie coughed, busying herself with her food.

She felt she was slipping into a deep dark place. Somewhere she could lose her way in the shadows of her soul. It was easy to get lost in a maze but not so easy to get back out. Before she let her thoughts cascade down that dark alley of her mind to a place which was unknown and tinged with fear, she finished her food and went up to the counter.

Ben was cleaning and stacking mugs in a regular, rhythmic way which Sophie found soothing.

"Hey, I'm not sure if you have any vacancies going at the moment, but I would like to pass you my CV in case anything comes up," Sophie said.

"Yeah, for sure! We don't have anything at the moment as we just hired a barista last week. But you know how things are. Someone joins, someone leaves. I'll hang on to this and keep you in mind," he replied.

"Thanks. That would be great!" Sophie said, feeling uplifted. "Bye then."

"See you round," Ben replied, waving the cloth he was using to wipe down the counters.

That was one CV down, plenty more to go. She decided to see if they needed a shop assistant at the Peacocks' Lair. She would like to work in a place with such a name. She crossed the road and felt the little village was stretching its sleepy arms and letting out a great yawn. More people were on the roads and waiting at bus stops. She saw a shop assistant in the window of the Peacocks' Lair setting up a little display of china dolls staring lifelessly ahead, their glassy eyes catching the light.

Sophie entered and smiled at the lady. As she was the only person in the shop, Sophie walked up to her and asked about vacancies.

"I'm afraid we have nothing going right now, lovey, but if anything comes up I can give you a ring," the lady said, kindly. She had silver streaks in her hair and slight creases around her eyes, giving her a happy, relaxed look. Sophie thanked her and decided she would stay a bit to take a look around the shop. The people in this village so far seemed very nice and friendly, she thought, making a mental note to pass this vital piece of information along to her mother.

Sophie walked slowly around the shop, eyeing the vintage-style clothing, picking up little glass boxes that always seemed to come in handy and rifling through some of the books the shop had squeezed into an old wooden bookshelf. She caressed their spines lovingly and let her eyes glide across all the different titles. Each book held the promise of transporting her to a different reality, a magical world not bound by the confines of their world. Reading was her balm. Reading and writing were the best ways she could escape the prison of her mind, which had kept her shackled to her sorrow.

She typically enjoyed fantasy, psychological thrillers and historical fiction, yet her hand gravitated to a somewhat more serious title, *An All-Encompassing History of the Cliffs* by Samuel J. Woodlock. The title interested Sophie. It was not a particularly large book, she thought, to be considered all-encompassing. She flipped through the pages, enjoying the papery smell that wafted like a sweet perfume to her. There were glossy pictures in the middle of the book. Sophie liked it when books did that, freezing reality at a certain moment in time. She would read the book and then flip through those sleek, black-and-white photographs of people, places, and scenes faded by time, lost in the memories of the cliffs and sea air.

She was about to head to the till when one of the china dolls on the display caught her eye. Her face was bathed in the golden glow of the morning sun and the jewels on her dress scintillated, casting a spray of diamond pinpricks on the opposite wall. Sophie touched the fabric of the doll's dress. It was a rich scarlet with a smooth velvet texture. Threads of gold were stitched into the hem of the dress and there was matching delicate gold lace on the bodice. She had soft, wavy, brown curls that fell gently around her shoulders. The glassy eyes that stared blankly at Sophie were brown with golden flecks glittering in the light. Sophie felt mesmerised by the beauty, attention to detail and care someone had put into creating this doll. Sophie had not played with dolls in years but somehow felt drawn to this one.

"That's a lovely choice," a voice said from behind her. Sophie turned to see the woman who had been arranging the display standing behind her.

"Yes, she really is beautiful," Sophie said, admiringly.

"We just received the donation today. There was nothing on the box to indicate where it came from. But her and the rest of them were in it," the woman said, gesturing to the other dolls on display.

"Well, I think I'm going to go for this one," Sophie said, handing the doll and the book to the woman.

"Sure. That will be £10.50, love," the woman said, wrapping the doll carefully in pink tissue paper before placing her in a box.

Sophie paid, thanked the woman and headed back into the street. She wondered at her decision to buy a china doll when she barely had money to buy groceries, but she somehow felt the purchase was worth it.

She walked around several more cafés, restaurants, pubs and shops distributing her CV. She stopped by Shelley's Tea Room for some lunch and, of course, Shelley's famous tea. It was a quaint little restaurant full of mismatching furniture, clashing prints and bizarre paintings that made customers tilt their heads sideways. She ordered a steak sandwich, fries and red bush tea. So far she liked the village. It was peaceful and friendly, the buildings old and quintessential.

She passed a vintage furniture shop called Hearth & Homes. She had decided she would order the bulk of her furniture online but would get a few essentials if she saw anything particularly enticing. She loved the woody smell of the furniture as she entered the shop. It felt like a time capsule, peeling away several decades. She decided to get several pieces so that they would include free delivery to her home. She chose a large wardrobe with a built-in, full-size mirror. She also picked out a bedside table, chair and her favourite piece, a writing desk. She fell in love with the writing desk the moment she saw it. It was somewhat narrow width-wise but had shelving space going upwards, which made it very tall. It folded out and could be locked with the use of a heavy, metal key. She unlocked it and opened the space out where she would write. It was the perfect size to fit her laptop. Behind the writing space were six little compartments where she could store her stationery. Above that there were two glass-panelled shelves where she could store larger items. She appreciated how it utilised space vertically so that it could fit easily into her tiny oddly shaped bedroom. She told the salesman what she had chosen while also handing him the last CV she had.

"Sure, we can deliver for free," he said. "Where is it you live?"

"That would be 11 Edgeware Lane, right on the cliffs," Sophie replied, checking the receipt with a nervous fluttering in her stomach. She glanced up as the man didn't seem to have heard her. He was staring at her, mouth slightly ajar, brows furrowed.

"So you just moved in or something?" he asked quickly, diverting his attention to the delivery forms.

"Yes, I quite like it so far. And I love this little village!" Sophie said.

"Right… and the house? How are you finding the house?" he asked, in a strangely deliberate manner. Sophie was not quite sure what he was trying to imply.

"It's fine, if a bit run-down. I called a window repair company earlier because the upstairs window is broken. It needs a good clean, but I think I'll be happy there," she said, smiling.

"The upstairs window, huh. I knew the guy who sold the place to you. He was a bit of a recluse. He said it was a strange house. Never could quite figure what he meant by that," the man said, thoughtfully.

"Really? I only spoke to his agent on the phone. Did he say anything to you about why he was selling up or where he was going? The agent wasn't particularly chatty," Sophie probed, her curiosity peaked.

The man blinked and stared at her, as if he had forgotten she was there. He cleared his throat. "Um, no, I don't know where he went. Last I saw him was in this shop actually. He said his time on the cliffs was over. He didn't really elaborate, man of few words, that's for sure. He was really old and eccentric, you know. Quite the character."

Sophie was on the verge of telling the man about the strange encounter she had had on the road on the way to Edgeware Lane. She wanted to ask him what he thought the old man had meant by saying the house was not her own. The salesman, however, seemed to be in a rush, handing her the paperwork for the delivery and not quite meeting her gaze. She decided to drop it and perhaps pass by another time to ask about the previous eccentric owner of the house. Something about their exchange made her feel as if she were on a cliffhanger, on the edge of an unfinished tale.

"Thanks, and I'll keep you posted if we have any vacancies. Bye," the man said, snapping her out of her reverie.

"That would be great. See you around," she replied, although his back was already turned as he walked away into the storeroom rubbing his temple.

Sophie felt unsettled after that conversation but couldn't quite figure out why. It was as if something had been said, or rather implied, that had thrown her off balance. She felt like the salesman had purposefully left out some vital information, like a missing puzzle piece that she needed to make sense of the conversation. The elusive feeling stayed with her, gathering overhead like a cloud of uncertainty.

She continued her day fulfilling her chores. She passed by a quaint, old-fashioned-looking tea room called Tea and Biscuits. What an adorable name, Sophie thought. The décor was warm and comforting. It looked as if it had been transported back in time. The sign was written in large old-fashioned lettering along the front of the shop. There was another sign swinging in the light breeze of a vintage-looking picture of a cup of tea and a biscuit. Sophie took a brief peek inside the café through the window. She was surprised to see several women dressed in what appeared to be old-fashioned, dated clothes. Sophie wondered whether there was a themed gathering that day. The women were all wearing long dresses with high necks and long sleeves. Three out of the four women there had large hats daintily perched on their heads. The women were chattering away, sipping tea from small white teacups. Sophie stared for several more moments, allowing a sense of ease and calm to descend upon her. Something about that scene brought a sense of timeless tranquillity with it. Sophie made a mental note to revisit the café at some point. She had to finish up her errands for the day before allowing herself time to sit back and relax.

She went food shopping, called a company to get the Wi-Fi up and running, ordered the rest of the basic furniture she needed online from her phone, all the while hoping against hope that she would get a call from one of the dozen places she had handed her CV out to.

It was a strange feeling going home to a new place. It didn't seem quite fitting to be calling it home just yet. It didn't belong to her. It didn't have any of her memories woven into the fabric of the air encased within it. It was unfamiliar to her touch and her tread was not yet a part of the rhythm of the beating heart of the house.

Once home, she decided to get to grips with the cleaning. As she was scrubbing the countertops in the kitchen, trying to get them spotless, she felt a sudden wave of that increasingly familiar heavy drowsiness descend upon her. Sophie felt surprised at the sudden heaviness she felt in her limbs. When she arrived home she had had a quick coffee to pep her up and keep her going for the rest of the day. Instead she felt she could barely keep her eyes open. She rested her arms on the soapy countertops, taking a moment's break from the arduous task of cleaning. She then looked at her arms. Something was wrong. She had been wearing rubber gloves while cleaning but when she looked at her hands, the gloves had vanished. Sophie shook her head in confusion, moving as if in slow motion. Her mind felt like it had turned to thick sludge, trapping her thoughts and sinking them into a well of murky oblivion. Nothing made sense. She looked at her hands again. No longer were they the pale, long-fingered hands she had known all her life. Instead the palms were rough and the skin the colour of coffee. In her delirious confusion, something caught her eye. Sophie glanced up, her head inching upwards slowly, slowly. She caught sight of two children, one boy, one girl, of the exact same height. Their clothes were ragged and old. They were running to the cliff edge. The crooked picket fence that encased the back garden was gone. They were getting closer to the edge. They were too close. The children were tipping their heads over the edge, as if to get a better look at what lay at the bottom. And then, they slipped.

"NO!" Sophie shrieked, finding her voice as well as her regular momentum. She moved fast, sprinting outside. She jumped over the picket fence which remained planted in its regular position. Heart pounding in her chest, Sophie looked over the edge of the cliff expecting to see two mangled bodies dashed on the rocks below. There was nothing. Sophie blinked and rubbed her eyes. The sea was calm and almost unmoving, the rocks undisturbed. Sophie looked from side to side. There were no children, no bodies. Sophie wondered why she hadn't heard a scream, or even the slightest sound, come to think of it. She held her hands up to her face. The rubber gloves, apart from dirt marks from the fence, were exactly as they were. Sophie collapsed onto all fours, staring hard at the sea and rocks over the edge. She was sure she had seen two children. She was certain she had seen them tumble over. But clearly, she was wrong.

The old man's pale lavender grey eyes returned. They swam in front of her, spinning and churning softly like mist rising above a lake. The house was not her own. But then, whose was it?

# Chapter 5

## *Samuel*

Samuel had tried to call Sophie but without any luck. He resorted to writing her a letter. It would be a brief note, simply opening up a communication channel between them. It felt surreal writing a letter and addressing it to that house that had continued to haunt him in his dreams and visit him like a waking nightmare during daylight hours for the past several years.

Shaking off the feelings of bitterness and remorse, he tried to compose a well-written, friendly letter to the house's new owner.

*Dear Ms. Parker,*

*Please accept my sincerest apologies for not introducing myself sooner. This is Samuel, the previous owner of 11 Edgeware Lane. I am writing to you in the hope that you are doing well and have found everything regarding the house to meet your standards and expectations. Please reach out if there is anything amiss or if I can help you in any way to settle into your new home.*

*I lived there a total of eight years and the house remained on the market another five years after that before you purchased it. Therefore, I expect there to possibly be some repair work or general maintenance that may need to be done. Again, please let me know and I can cover any of the necessary expenses.*

*It is a beautiful, old, strange house and I hope you are able to make it your home.*

*Yours truly,*

*Samuel*

Samuel re-read the letter. He could sense the guilt oozing from the ink, dripping down the page and trickling like tears of accusing blood onto his quivering old hands. He had always found the house oddly beautiful, even when it terrified him. The way the sea sprayed it, each droplet reflecting the light, made it look like a dream cottage from a fairy tale. The willow tree with its slow undulating vines reminded Samuel of silent monks in peaceful meditation. When the house wasn't crackling with unknown life, filled with haunting shadows, it could actually be the most calming haven on earth. Time flowed differently within its walls, as if the past, present and future were all merged together, fused in unison. Samuel believed it was moments like these that captivated him, drew him deeper into the house, making it impossible to contemplate moving or selling the place.

As these thoughts flitted in his mind, Samuel stared absent-mindedly at the letter still in his hands. The edges of the paper suddenly appeared faint and blurred. He stared harder but found it was becoming increasingly difficult to focus. Before he knew it, the letter had dissolved into nothingness. Samuel looked around the room. The walls were melting away before his very eyes. The still weather outside was replaced with a lashing wind and hard pellets of rain. Samuel could taste the sea on his tongue. He knew where he was. With one more blink, the comfort of his home had vanished entirely. Instead he was standing next to Willowen on the edge of the all-too-familiar cliff. Willowen was younger, his face less lined with age and sorrow. He didn't respond to Samuel's presence. It was a dark night with a vicious storm brewing on the horizon.

"Quick, get down," Willowen was saying in hushed tones. A stunning woman with coffee-coloured skin and wild black hair was running from the hut. She was carrying a small girl who could have been about four or five years old on her hip. The blustering wind tossed her thick locks of hair, making them twist and turn wildly like ferocious, hungry snakes. A look of sheer panic swept over her face.

"Are they all here?" she whispered frantically to Willowen, tears mingling with the thick droplets of rain.

"The twins and Danior are here," Willowen said, gesturing next to him. Samuel peered over the cliff edge. Balancing on a knife-edge were three children. There was a boy and a girl, twins who were locked in a tight embrace, balancing precariously on the narrow ledge. Squashed next to them was a small, slim boy, his back flat against the cliff, eyes tightly shut as if he could imagine this nightmare away.

The woman exhaled a sigh of relief. "I'll go down first, then you give me Edwina," she commanded. She passed the little girl into Willowen's arms. The girl was sucking her thumb and started to cry.

"There, there," Willowen said, gently. "We'll be ok, Eddie, hush now."

The woman carefully lifted herself down from the edge of the cliff and onto the ledge. Several rocks crumbled underfoot, and she stumbled. The twins gasped in unison.

The woman dug her nails into the rocks and turned ever so slowly.

"Pass me Edwina," she called up to Willowen.

"Are you sure? You're on steady footing?" he replied. The sound of horse hooves was rapidly approaching.

"Yes, yes, give her to me!" yelled the woman, her voice drowned out by the crashing waves.

Deftly, Willowen passed the crying child down to the woman and slipped off the edge of the cliff and onto the ledge with the rest of his family. He raised a finger to his mouth to silence them.

The horse hooves slowed to a halt. Samuel turned to see who was approaching. Two men wearing a uniform consisting of black trousers and a long buttoned-up black coat with heavy boots and hats came marching forward. They both held heavy truncheons. Samuel noticed that one of the truncheons had spikes on the end.

They gazed right through Samuel and walked straight to the hut.

"Get out!" the more rotund one yelled as he smashed the wooden walls with his truncheon.

"Filthy rats, we'll find you," the slimmer one said, kicking the ramshackle door down.

Samuel heard more clattering and smashing of objects as the two men searched the hut. Just then the horses started whinnying as if panicked. They stomped their hooves furiously, rocking the wagon that was attached to them. Despite the downpour, Samuel did not feel any of the raindrops as he walked slowly over to the wagon. Peering in,

Samuel almost recoiled in horror. The wagon was a human cage, crammed with about ten people. Men, women and children had been packed in tight, their grubby hands clutching the bars, their hair and clothes drenched. Apart from a woman rocking a small child on her lap while singing a hushed lullaby, they were all silent. They gazed furtively at one another. Fear, like a dark shadow, loomed over them all.

None of them seemed to see Samuel, except one. An old woman squashed in the corner was humming to herself, her eyes rolling back as if in a trance. Suddenly she snapped out of the trance-like state and stared directly at Samuel, her head slightly tilted. Their eyes locked. Abject fear and sadness pooled in the pit of Samuel's stomach. He knew their future. He knew what awaited them. Just then the two men came stomping back.

"Gypsy filth," the slim one said, spitting at the cage.

"No one's there. But we'll get them. They'll return to this dump, like flies to shit," the larger one said.

"Then we'll have caught the lot of you," the slimmer one jeered, slamming his truncheon on the metal bars. Those nearest the front flinched, letting go of the bars before their fingers got crushed.

"I'd like to see you try your black magic spells once the noose is around your neck!" the rotund one said. "Won't be able to hurt anyone else then, will you! Serves you right, bunch of disgusting witches!"

The gypsies were being persecuted, and Samuel knew those in power would succeed in their barbarous purge. They were rounding up all of the gypsies in the town. They had probably succeeded in getting most of them, but this family, the family balancing on the slippery rocks of the cliff edge, had evaded detection for now.

The two policemen gave the cage a final rattle, laughing as they did so. They heaved themselves up on to the horses and rode away, dragging the cage with them, until they were all swallowed up by the gloom.

Samuel rushed over to the cliff to see if Willowen and the others were all right. To his shock he didn't see anyone there. All of a sudden he couldn't hear the storm, the crashing waves or the whistling in the trees. It was as if the sound had been turned off. The scenery around him started to fade and crumble. The thick muddy earth under his hands became soft and fluffy. Samuel looked up. Instead of the looming dark sky he was now staring at the familiar faded blue wallpaper of his walls. He found himself on all fours, in a crumpled heap by his writing desk. He felt bruised and broken. Had he fallen and hit his head? Slowly checking each limb, flexing his arms and testing the muscles in his legs, he was relieved to find he had not sustained any injuries.

The room was warm and comforting. The air outside was silent and still, no hint of a storm. Had he just had an incredibly intense dream? Or had he just experienced a memory? A memory of a time that did not belong to him? A memory that was not his own?

# Chapter 6

## *Sophie*

*Dear Daniel,*

*In the cracks and crevices that bloom like a blackened flower,*

*The voices whisper and mumble,*

*The shadows stretch long, tall towers,*

*Within the floorboards there's a reverberating rumble.*

*It is difficult to see through blurred eyes,*

*But I feel you are there.*

*You hover somewhere just out of sight nearby,*

*Existing in a world separated by more than air.*

*Your gaze burns the back of my skull,*

*Your light and shadows dapple the floor,*

*Your icy breath makes my blood run cold,*

*I live suspended in perplexity and fear forevermore.*

*And yet, you and I are connected,*

*Woven together through ribbons of time,*

*Tied by death, tragedy and souls heavily weighted,*

*Spectres haunt this house and heart of mine.*

*Sophie*

It was the dreams that disturbed Sophie the most.

They shook her to the very core. She had unpacked, the new furniture had arrived, the fridge was stocked with Sophie's favourite, easy to make food and yet she was feeling unsettled. She had been living in her new home for a week and every night she had been having the same dream. It had changed somewhat from the dream she had had on her first at 11 Edgeware Lane. She dreamt that she was looking for Dan. She was desperately searching the house for there was something very important she had to tell him. As she was searching the bedroom, she saw the little girl from her previous dream hiding in the corner, next to the dusty wine-coloured curtains. The girl looked up at her with big watery emerald eyes. Tears slid down her cheeks as she pointed silently to the open window. Sophie turned and saw to her horror the branches and leaves of the weeping willow tree were a mass of furious oranges and bright, dancing reds. She could smell the acrid smoke, coiling and slithering like snakes through the open window. Waves of heat rippled over her skin while her lungs filled with the fumes making her feel dizzy and light-headed. The last thing she heard was the little girl whispering something inaudible as the crackling of the flames consumed them both.

Sophie would wake up from this dream sweating profusely, wild-eyed. What scared her most was how real it felt. It didn't have the typical hazy, blurred-around-the-edges effect dreams have when trying to recall them the next day. There was no straining of her mental faculties to dredge up details of the dream. The frightening part was that it didn't feel like a dream at all; it felt like she was reliving a memory, someone else's memory. She knew that sounded ridiculous, and her first instinct was to ask Dan's opinion.

It was 6:12 am and Sophie was bolt upright. "Well, what's going on, Dan?" she demanded, staring at the ceiling above her for answers. "Just tell me what this weird dream means!" she exclaimed in frustration, thumping her fists on the bed. The silence was deafening. Sometimes she was so sure she could hear what Dan would have said in a certain situation that she actually had to turn around and make sure he wasn't in the room. The silence that surrounded her now was suffocating. As the seconds stretched into minutes, the silence was about to reach its crescendo. Sophie jumped out of her new bed, slipped on her fuzzy robe and slippers and went outside. She needed the fresh salty air to clear the cobwebs of the dream that were clinging to her mind.

It was a calm morning. Sophie hopped over the low fence and clambered onto the cliff edge. She had found a spot she liked. There was a large, smooth rock wedged deep into the earth. Sophie liked to sit there and watch the bewitching waves swell and crash against the rocks before gradually retreating. Today, however, the waters were still. The sea's luminous surface was a sparkling carpet of dancing light with pockets of darkness. Sophie watched how it shimmered and shone, stretching endlessly out into the horizon. Since moving here, whenever she felt low or anxious, she would come out to this point and instantly feel soothed by the eternal sight of the sea. Her problems and worries seemed to dissolve in the expansive, timeless view.

Instinctively, she turned to glance back at the house. She frowned as she saw a flickering light in one of the windows. She blinked several times, but the pinprick of light continued to dance. Sophie felt a wave of uncertainty ripple through her body. She stood up and walked slowly through the damp grass of her back garden into the house. It looked ominous with all the lights off except that one strange orb of light in the window. She felt the house looked slightly lopsided from this angle, as if it were trying to dive into the sea. The dark windows gaped unseeingly back at her. She reached the back door, its red paint chipped and peeling.

As soon as she stepped into her house, she had the uncanny sense that she was not alone. "Hello," she whispered into the dim room. Her voice seemed to hang in the air. Her first irrational instinct was that there was a fire. Despite not being able to smell any smoke, the air felt heavy, as if the molecules that made it up had suddenly become denser. She felt as if gravity was stronger and was weighing her down. If only you would sleep better, you wouldn't feel so strange, she berated herself mentally.

She entered through the kitchen and went to the dining area where the light was. She tiptoed in with trepidation. A nameless fear was pulsating through her body. She wasn't sure why but there was something about that strange, dancing light that held a tight grip on her heart. She had the sensation that she was walking in a trance, bound by some sort of spell. To her surprise, when she entered the dining room, she saw that the candle in the centre of the table was alight. It was a tall candle in a gothic, brass candleholder. She hadn't remembered lighting it since her arrival here yet there it was flickering in front of her very eyes. The yellow flame teasing her with its sprightly dance. Sophie glanced around the room. She was quite alone. She stood transfixed for what could have been seconds, minutes or even hours. Time had lost all meaning. The clock's regular flow was distorted, disrupted. It was no longer straightforward and continuous like an arrow shooting its target. Instead it was jilting, fragmented, rising and falling like waves on the beach. Shards of time lay scattered around her and she, Sophie, had to pick up the pieces and put them together again to form a coherent story.

The longer she stared at the flame, the more energy it seemed to gather, flickering faster, rising higher. An ethereal calm replaced the choking fear she had been feeling only moments ago. Just as the flame was leaping to new heights, an icy gust of wind burst through the house, swinging the door open wildly with a bang. Sophie jumped. Goosebumps flared up her arms and legs, and her teeth started chattering. An unearthly chill seemed to be coming from the house itself. All was still outside. Not a single tree was windswept nor a leaf ruffled.

With the candle blown out, Sophie shook herself out of her trance. She had to investigate. Make sure no one else was there. She ran quickly through the house to make sure no one was lurking in the shadows with a lighter or a match, sneakily lighting candles in strangers' homes. Of course, there was no one and Sophie came full circle back to the mysterious candle, standing innocently in the centre of the table. She wondered if there could be a scientific explanation, some sort of spontaneous combustion type theory.

Sophie knew she would not be able to go back to sleep now so she headed to the kitchen to make herself a warm, comforting mug of tea. With her hands clasped firmly around the solid cup, everything felt better. She curled up on the couch, sipping her tea. She glanced out the window several times as she still had the eerie sensation that someone or something was there, just out of sight.

You're being paranoid, she thought to herself. Yes, she had never lived alone before. Sure, this was a huge life-changing decision she had made, and she might be feeling slightly anxious over it. But still. This was her home and she was perfectly safe here.

Failing to convince herself, she tried to shake off the unwelcome feeling by switching on the TV. Just over an hour had gone by since she'd awoken and she was wondering if she could find anything good on at 7:30 in the morning. She took out her brown leather-bound journal, which was always close at hand, as the voices of some morning show or other rattled on in the background. She decided to write about what happened and wrote several lines of poetry about a mysterious flickering light, dancing and spinning in a whirlpool of all-consuming darkness. She drew a quick sketch of a candle with arms, legs and a face doing a dance with another candle. It made her laugh and as she closed her journal, she felt at ease again.

She must have slipped into a deep sleep without realising. The TV voices in the background and the warm tea must have lulled her into a comforting deep slumber for she was awoken by an aggressive ringtone. She woke up startled. She had been having a strange dream where she was walking around the house but this time without fear, without the desperate need to find her late fiancé Dan. Everything felt different. Everything looked different. Nonetheless, she knew she was in the same house perched on a distant cliff at the edge of the world.

She had been walking with a calm purpose from room to room, feeling the texture of the rough wooden walls, the creaking floorboards underfoot. There were no burning smells, only scents of the old wood, the dust clinging to the curtains and a faint crushed flowery scent mingled in the air. There were unfamiliar voices echoing in her dream. She was sure the disembodied voices were the TV voices, creeping their way into her subconscious. But still, the voices had strange accents and it was hard for her to discern what was being said. There was also a distant, rhythmic tapping that continued in the background of her dream.

"Hello?" Sophie said, somewhat groggily.

"Hello, is this Sophie Parker?" a man on the other end asked.

"Yes, this is she."

"I'm just calling from The Acorn Café. You gave me your CV a few days ago. Well, you're in luck as we're hiring," the man said enthusiastically. "Could you come in today, if you're still interested? I can show you how things work, give you a rundown of the place and then we can decide if you're up for it."

Sophie rubbed the sleep from her eyes and smiled. "Yes, I would love that. I can be there in about half an hour."

"Sounds great. See you in half an hour, Sophie. Oh, this is Luke, by the way, manager at The Acorn Café."

"Great talking to you, Luke. Thanks!" she said, before hanging up. She was thrilled. She had been busy this past week with setting up the house. However, she had a nagging fear that once the majority of the set-up was done, she would slip into a dangerous lull with nothing to do and no one to see. If she wasn't kept busy, she knew her mind would meander down dimly lit distant alleyways of the past opening up to a city of lights twinkling and blinking at her, enticing her to stay within the warm glow of the past. Without anyone to pull her free from this world, this shimmering illusion, she knew she would disappear entirely.

These fears could now be dispelled as she had found a new anchor to help steady her lost ship. She quickly turned off the TV and dashed upstairs. She slapped on some make-up and threw on a pair of black, straight leg trousers and a crisp white shirt. It was nearly October and the weather had cooled substantially. Sophie looked out the window. It was a still day, the chill hung unmoving in the air. The sky was icy blue, bathing the ground below in a spreading bruise of cool purples and greys. She shrugged on her old but warm parker jacket and headed out.

Just as she opened the front door, she heard the distinct sound of a meowing cat. She turned, expecting to see a cat in the doorway, perhaps slinking between her legs trying to escape the cold weather outside. To her surprise, there was nothing there, no cat in sight. The sound had been very clear in the silent morning air. She quickly glanced back inside and then in the surrounding undergrowth that fringed her house. She shook her head. She was already late and had to get a move on it. If it was a cat, it would be sure to show up later.

She remembered The Acorn Café. It was a brightly decorated coffee shop. It had mismatching fabrics and brightly coloured cushions with frayed edges and little mirrors embedded within the stitching. The cushions were perched precariously on the spindly chairs. The couches had tasselled edges and there were paintings of beautiful women wrapped in silk scarves with glittering jewellery. It was strange décor choice in Sophie's opinion for a café which she thought should be cosy and calm. The Acorn Café had a strange electric energy about it.

She entered the café. There was a big sign in slanted cursive writing above the bar that boasted: "The Acorn Café – proudly serving the richest coffee in town for 170 years!"

A tall, slim man approached her. "Hello, I'm Luke. You must be Sophie."

"Yes," she said, returning his firm handshake.

"Perfect! Well, thank you for coming in. Would you like a coffee before we get started?"

Sophie, feeling it would be rude to say no, politely acquiesced. "I'll have a cappuccino, please."

"Great choice. Hey, Chris, one cappuccino for the lady," Luke said, waving at one of the young men behind the bar.

"You got it," Chris replied.

"So that's Chris over there, making your coffee. And there's Kalina clearing up the plates. The one at the till is Jeremy."

"Ok," Sophie said, trying to make a mental note and remember all the names.

"Thanks, Chris," Luke said, grabbing Sophie's cappuccino and handing it to her. "Let's go downstairs so I can tell you a bit about the place."

"Sure. How much is this?" Sophie said, raising her cup enquiringly.

"On the house. All baristas get a free cup of coffee a day and discounts on the food. And if the food is about to expire, you can take it home for free." Luke whispered the last sentence as if it was some sort of conspiracy. Sophie nodded along.

They went down a narrow staircase to the basement area and sat at a small table in the centre of the cluttered room.

"So let me tell you a bit about us. As I'm sure you have noticed, there aren't many chain stores around these parts. We like to keep things local and support small enterprises."

Sophie nodded appreciatively. "I like that. The world could do with more originality and less cookie-cutter stores."

"My thoughts exactly!" exclaimed Luke. "Well, there's a little story behind this café. It's certainly not your average café. I'm sure you saw our sign behind the bar. We've been around for a long time."

Luke proceeded to adopt a deep, sombre tone as he got into storytelling mode. "Well, this place was opened sometime in the 1800s essentially as a soup kitchen. It served basics to the poor. I think at some point during the mid-19th century a band of gypsies came to this town. It was a cold winter at the time and some of them were looking for work and shelter. One of them took up work in the soup kitchen. She brought with her all sorts of interesting and weird recipes. They said she made the best coffee along the coast. Her name was apparently Acorn. Whether or not that was her real name, this place has been named after her in appreciation for feeding the poor and homeless all those years ago."

Sophie nodded, enraptured. She wanted to know more about the mysterious travellers, the old town, about Acorn and what happened to them all. Before she got the chance to ask for more details, Luke continued.

"Anyway, I'm sure you're not interested in all that history. How's the coffee, by the way?"

Sophie had been so focused on his story that she had forgotten all about her coffee. She quickly took a sip. It was delicious and creamy. The rich coffee flavour was balanced out perfectly by the foamy sweetness.

"It's great!" she said enthusiastically, taking another long gulp.

"Ok, so do you have any questions? Have you worked as a barista before?"

"I worked as a waitress for a bit during university," Sophie replied.

"Well, it's pretty much the same then. I'll show you how to make some of the drinks. You'll just have to practise and memorise that. You know how to work a till?"

"Yup," Sophie replied, feeling adequately qualified for the job.

"Great. Let me show you how it all works upstairs. If you're free today, you can observe and see how things are done. Then we can discuss your shifts. We'll start you off part-time for the first month and if you like the job and want to continue, we'll take you on full-time. How does that sound?"

"Sounds perfect!"

Sophie followed Luke back up the stairs, feeling a lightness in her step. Not only did she have a job, but she had one in an exotic little café with a fascinating history. She wondered if the artist of the paintings on the walls knew of the tale Luke had told her. The beautiful twirling women had striking, proud features framed by waves of dark hair rippling in the current of movement. They certainly radiated a sense of mystery, of other-worldliness.

She was introduced to the team she would be working alongside. Kalina was thirty-four and from Poland. She gave Sophie a small smile but then quickly busied herself with stacking the dishwasher haphazardly. Jeremy was quiet with brown hair, hiding behind a pair of thick glasses. He was a university student trying to earn some extra pocket money, which was probably going to go on the purchase of textbooks, if Sophie were to make an educated guess. Chris was energetic and had wavy hair, the colour of the pebbles and sand that lay scattered on the beach. He explained he was taking a gap year and saving up so he could travel for a solid six months.

Sophie enjoyed the happy, fun atmosphere and watched carefully what everyone was doing. She had waitressed before and knew once she got into the swing of things it would all be familiar and easy. Sophie tried to give general answers to their questions, not wanting to divulge too many details about her life or why she had decided to move to the small cottage on the cliff.

Sophie drove back home several hours later. She had not noticed the time until Luke said she'd done a good job observing and could go home if she wanted. She could start work the day after tomorrow at 7:00 am. She thought it might be a good idea to buy a bike so that she could cycle to and from work every morning. It was so close there was really no need to be driving.

Although her little cottage was only minutes away, as she drove she felt a change in the weather. It had been cold but still by the café. Closer to the cliffs, she could hear the wind whistling, sweeping up the discarded leaves and spinning them in whirlpools. The waves seemed restless and the sky had become overcast, clouds hanging low and ominously in the sky.

As she arrived, she frowned. She had remembered closing the gate and yet there it was creaking open, that invisible hand playing tricks on her again. The wind must have unhooked the latch as usual. She would have to get it mended. She did not like the way the gate moved eerily backwards and forwards creating that scraping sound that made Sophie's hair stand on end. She decided she would also oil the hinges when she had the time.

She cast her gaze up at the house as she approached the front door. It looked gloomier than usual. Across the house and garden, angular shadows created a patchwork quilt of various shades of darkness. Sophie paused before unlocking the front door. It was a strange feeling and she couldn't explain it, but she didn't feel welcome. The house radiated hostility. The wind rushed around her, its whistling growing louder. She had the odd notion that it was speaking to her, warning her. She felt its strength pushing her away from the house. Something was telling her that she did not belong.

She shoved the key in the lock with determined force and it clicked open. She shook her head, telling herself she was being silly. Maybe she had just had an overwhelming day, she thought. She had not met or interacted with anybody new since Dan died. That was what was probably causing all this anxiety to bubble up inside of her. All she needed was a nice cup of tea. Without taking off her jacket, she headed to the kitchen. She would need to get the heaters fixed. Even with them switched on she was freezing. Rubbing her hands together, she reached out to for the kettle. Before picking it up, something caught her eye. She gasped. Her hands flew to her mouth. An army of ants were marching as fast as they could across her kitchen floor and counter. There were so many they looked like an eerie rippling shadow across the floor. They moved with a collective speed she had never witnessed in ants before. They were running. Running from something.

Sophie stepped back, shocked. She didn't know what to do. She would have to call an exterminator. There were so many ants, but where were they coming from? Could the cracks and crevices of this old house really house so many of these little beasts?

Suddenly, the ants were irrelevant. Almost as if they didn't exist. Their gruesome shadow receded in her mind's eye into nothingness. She felt the temperature drop, the atmosphere shift. Not even her warm, thick parker jacket could prevent her arms flaring up in goosebumps. She wasn't alone. She could feel it. She could sense it. Her breathing became shallow and rang loud in her ears. The house was unnervingly silent, mocking her. Even the wind outside had stopped wailing. The silence was heavy. Too heavy.

She closed her eyes, not wanting to turn around, as if by closing them she could block out what she knew was there. Dread and fear gripped her in equal measure. They paralysed her physically and mentally, leaving no room for rational thought. Slowly, forcefully, hands trembling, she turned. From the kitchen doorway, she could see straight into the living room. Her heart stopped beating at the sight. The day before, she had lined up several candles on the windowsill and put one on the radiator next to it. She used to love candles. They made her feel warm and cosy.

Now, they made her blood run icy cold through her veins turning her into a statue, frozen in time. All of them were alight, their wicks burning furiously in the darkness. Dancing, taunting her. Just as she was staring in horror at the candles' menacing glow, the television started flickering, switching itself on and off. Sophie was rooted to the spot.

Her legs like heavy bricks of lead weighed her down. Her whole body was shaking uncontrollably. The air around her was thick and she felt as if she was suffocating. Her lungs desperately tried to draw breath, but the sludgy air wouldn't enter.

Fire. She could smell fire. Her head started to swim. All she could see were floating candles meshing into one monstrous orb of wrathful light. A rush of heat permeated the room and beads of sweat trickled down her back. The intense cold was gone. All she could feel was the onslaught of heat and a deep sense of foreboding. It was the rush of fire and it was going to consume her. That was it. She was going to die. Fear was somehow around and inside her. It was palpable, saturating the condensed air. She could taste its metallic tang on her lips and tongue. Panic flooded her body, adrenaline pulsating through it. She felt a dark presence, somewhere just out of sight, creeping around her, revelling in her fear.

Her heart was beating so fast she felt it might rip through her chest. With all her strength, she forced her leaden legs to move. The ants. She saw them. She was one of them. They were running and suddenly she was too. She ran in the same direction as the ants. She dashed out the back door, towards the cliff edge.

The cold wind whipped her face. Sophie was gasping for breath. Her lungs felt heavy with smoke, polluted. She ran to her favourite rock and placed both her hands on its cool surface, breathing deeply. Sweat and tears intermingled and traced the contours of her face, before splashing onto the rock. She didn't know what had happened. Sophie fell to her knees. Her stomach heaved, making her retch. She closed her eyes. The all-consuming fear was starting to dissipate, dissolving into the salty air and sea below. She was becoming herself again. The sun was dipping into the horizon. Its golden rays spilled onto the skin of the water below it. The sound of the rushing waves was soothing. Sophie thought she could hear a muffled voice coming from the sea. Her heart beating fast, she glanced to her left where the sound seemed to be coming from. An old woman was waving at her from slightly further down the cliff edge.

"Hello there, neighbour, come on over here," she heard the woman say. The old woman was real. Solid. She was there. Sophie wiped her face with her trembling hands, trying to regain her composure. She was meeting her neighbour for the first time and looked a wreck. Sophie waved back to signal she had heard and was coming over. Sophie took several deep breaths before patting down her hair and shakily standing up tall. She donned a weak smile and, without looking at the house, walked over to the old woman.

# Chapter 7

## *Sophie*

*Dear Daniel,*

*I feel like I'm falling,*

*Like a shooting star,*

*Cutting through the soft velvet sky,*

*Saying goodbye to the cluster*

*Of pinpricks that bring light to the night*

*Glowing a golden glow,*

*I leave a fiery trail,*

*A violent blood-red gash,*

*A wound bleeding through the darkness,*

*As I venture along towards the end.*

# Healing House

*Almost there,*

*I see my doom,*

*Amidst the heavy gloom,*

*The deep frothy sea to me looms,*

*As the foamy waves from its depths bloom,*

*Like a flower's petals opening wide,*

*The tide rises high*

*And snatches me from the eternal sky.*


*Drowned in the darkness,*

*Struggling against the sea's herculean strength,*

*I feel myself crushed by its might,*

*As slowly, slowly, the sea extinguishes my faint, failing light.*

*Sophie*


The old woman had a wide friendly smile. "Come on in, honey. You don't look too well. Have you had any tea?"

Sophie glanced at her watch. It was only 6:35 pm. She had thought it was much later somehow. Time seemed to have become twisted and warped in that house. She dared not even look at it. Its looming shadow lurked in the corner of her eye. Its grotesque presence haunting the corners of her mind.

"No, I haven't," she replied hoarsely.

"Well, I was just about to put the kettle on and make some sandwiches. This is the perfect time for us to get to know each other a little bit. I don't get many visitors these days," she said, wrapping an arm around Sophie and leading her towards the door.

Sophie felt warm and safe in the old woman's arms. She could have cried tears of relief that she didn't have to return immediately to the house of shadows next door. The house that was not her own. That house.

"My name is Isabelle," the old woman said as she ushered Sophie into the living room.

It was a small and cluttered room, but it was so cosy that Sophie immediately felt her muscles loosen up and relax. She was ensconced in a fluffy, overstuffed sofa, leaning into cushions bearing decorations of dogs wearing an assortment of uniforms. There were two large bookcases, crammed with books. Sophie removed her shoes and let her feet sink into the luxuriously soft carpet decorated with pink hued blossoms, pale green foliage and delicate lilac butterflies. The relief must have shown on her face.

"You poor thing. I'm so sorry I didn't come over sooner to introduce myself and have you over. Being brand new to a town is never easy. You know, it's just my back, makes doing things impossible these days. I was in bed all week last week. I had to have the nurses come to help me get to the bathroom." She let out a jovial laugh. "Still, I should have sent a casserole over," she said, tutting at her own neighbourly shortcomings. "What did you say your name was again?"

"It's Sophie. Please, don't worry about it! I completely understand. It's all actually been quite a smooth process and the people in the town are so friendly," Sophie replied, feeling strength seep back into her bones and a warm, healthy flush spread on her cheeks. It was warm and toasty here, unlike her draughty house next door with its inexplicable temperature drops. The house that was not her own.

"Oh, I'm so glad," Isabelle said as she bustled into the kitchen, clattering around with pots and teacups.

"Let me help you," Sophie called out, struggling to free herself from the mass of cushions encasing her.

"No, please, you stay put," Isabelle replied firmly. "You're my guest and I will not have you up and about. You look like you've had quite a day as it is."

Sophie pulled out her compact mirror from the bag still draped over her shoulder. She was shocked at the face staring back at her. Her eyes were dark and wild. Smudges of mascara rimmed her eyes along with dark shadows from one too many sleepless nights. Her mid-length hair was tousled and matted in places. She quickly pulled an old, damp tissue from her bag and rubbed at the mascara stains. She concluded Isabelle must be quite short-sighted or just very polite.

"How do you take your tea, love?" Isabelle called out.

"Milk and one sugar, please," Sophie replied, slipping the mirror and tissue back into her bag. She tried to comb out some of the tangles with her fingers before her host returned.

"Here you go," Isabelle said, handing over a large steaming cup of tea. The mug was delicate china and had little red paw prints dotting the edges.

"Thank you so much!" Sophie said gratefully, taking a deep gulp of her tea.

"Ah, you're most welcome," Isabelle said, setting herself down carefully into a worn armchair opposite Sophie. "Nothing like a good cup of tea to put the world to rights, eh!"

"Couldn't agree more." Sophie smiled.

"So tell me a bit about yourself then. Where do you come from and what drove you to these parts?" Isabelle asked.

There was something about the woman that made Sophie feel at home. She felt as if she was talking to her grandma, who had died several years ago. She felt she could tell her anything. She felt safe.

"Well, I wanted a fresh start. I was looking for a small cottage, something within my budget and this came up in my searches. I can't really tell you why I decided on this place. It was a strange feeling, as if the place was calling out to me. It was almost as if the house chose me rather than the other way around," Sophie said whimsically, before realising how odd that sounded.

Isabelle, however, was nodding. "Destiny called you here. Well, I certainly am pleased about that. The neighbour before you was lovely but a bit of a hermit. I barely got two complete sentences out of him during the entire eight years he lived here. I mean, I'm not much of a talker myself but he was pretty much a mute."

Sophie smiled inwardly. She could already tell that Isabelle certainly was a talker and had probably scared the poor, quiet man away. "You've lived here all your life?" Sophie enquired.

"Yes, born and raised here. I have two sons. They're grown-up. One is married and living in London and the other is working in Spain. I always secretly wanted a girl, you know," Isabelle said, leaning in and winking at Sophie. "They're just so precious, aren't they? Don't get me wrong, I love my boys with all my heart, but a girl really is a gift. What about you then? Are you married? Children?" Isabelle asked.

It was as if all the emotions and sadness Sophie had been carrying around with her and trying to suppress welled up to the surface at those innocently asked questions. Before she knew it, big heavy tears were sliding down her cheeks. Her chest heaved with uncontrollable sobs.

"Oh, there there, my dear," Isabelle said, suddenly next to her on the sofa. She put her arms around her. "I could tell there was a sadness in you. It's ok." She rocked her back and forth like she would a child.

Sophie clung onto the woman she had just met, soaking her lilac-smelling dress with a torrent of tears. "I'm sorry," she spluttered.

"That's ok, no need to explain and certainly no need to apologise."

Several minutes passed before Sophie could catch her shaky breath and blow her nose. "I'm really sorry," she said thickly. "Life has just been hard for me right now. I moved here because…" She paused and inhaled sharply. "Because my fiancé died. I needed a change. I couldn't live in a place haunted by the memories we had made together." Sophie dabbed her red, swollen eyes, noticing streaks of black smudges appearing once again on the tissue. Today clearly should have been a waterproof mascara day, she thought blandly to herself.

"Oh, you poor dear," Isabelle said, her voice low and heavy with concern.

Sophie glanced up but to her relief did not see pity in Isabelle's eyes. She couldn't stand the pity or the uncomfortable silences that usually followed this announcement. Instead, all Sophie saw was kindness and a sense that this woman had faced her own heartache at some point in her life.

"That's a terrible thing to go through," Isabelle stated. "Of course you needed a fresh start. I hope you find it here."

Sophie felt her breathing relaxing again, her heartbeat slowing to a normal rate. "I hope so too. I just don't know how to move on. It's a constant pain. I can't rid myself of it and I don't even want to!" Sophie exclaimed, surprised at herself for confiding in this woman she barely knew. Once she had started though, the words tumbled out of her mouth in a desperate rush to be heard. "I feel if I'm not sad or unhappy then I'm forgetting Dan, and I never want to forget him. If it hadn't been for me and the stupid wedding planning he might still be alive. I had been pressuring him to meet with the caterers and double-check the venue. He was tired and had been rushing to one of these meetings when the accident happened. A lorry was speeding and ran a red light. They crashed and…" Sophie struggled to say the words, "Dan died on the spot." Silent tears were caressing her cheeks again. They were no longer the uncontrollable sobs rocking her entire body. They cascaded gently down until she swept them away with her sodden tissue. "It's all my fault," Sophie whispered.

"Sophie, dear, you can't tell yourself that. It's simply not true. Do you know what I believe?" Isabelle asked. Before Sophie could answer, she continued, "I believe people have little numbers hovering just over their heads, invisible to the naked eye. These numbers are their birth dates and death dates, and no matter what happens in their lives these numbers will never change. No matter what you could have done differently, the accident would still have happened and he still would have died. Destiny is cruel and capricious. We cannot entirely rule our own fates, let alone those of other people. You need to forgive yourself, Sophie. It doesn't matter where you go or how far you travel. You will constantly bear this cross if you don't forgive yourself first."

Sophie stared at her hands. She knew deep down that what Isabelle said rang true. She nodded, a lump in her throat prevented her from speaking.

"Now, what about those sandwiches!" Isabelle said, clapping her old, veiny hands together. Sophie smiled at the sudden gesture. "How do you like cheese and cucumber sandwiches? It's not much but I've also got some chocolate Hobnobs we can have with our next cup of tea."

"That sounds wonderful," Sophie replied. A sense of peace came over her, like a soft, feathery blanket. It was a feeling so tranquil it made her eyes feel heavy with sleep. She just needed to close them for a minute and she would be fine. She nestled into the embrace of the warm comforting sofa, resting her head on a cushion depicting a dog wearing a frilly shirt, bowler hat and monocular. She breathed in the scent of fresh laundry and fabric spray. She would open her eyes in a moment, she told herself. Before she knew it, her head had slumped. She was breathing deeply, lost in slumber. It was her first proper night's sleep since the accident.

Sophie slept until midday the next day. She woke to the sound of music drifting lazily from the kitchen. She noticed a thick, fuzzy blanket had been draped over her while she slept. She also saw freshly baked cookies piled high on a tray on the table in the centre of the room. She stretched and got up to find her unwitting host. She felt fresh and lively. She realised she had had an uninterrupted night's sleep for the first time in months. She had not even had any of those bizarre recurring nightmares she kept having since moving there. She felt as if she hadn't dreamt at all last night, she had just fallen into a still, dreamless slumber.

"Oh, you're up!" Isabelle exclaimed. "You slept like the dead last night. You didn't even move a muscle, not a twitch. I hope I didn't wake you up with this racket. I just can't cook without listening to something. It's that damned tinnitus playing up in these old ears of mine again. I'm making us that casserole for lunch I promised you!"

"Oh, you don't have to do that, Isabelle. Please, don't trouble yourself!" Sophie said. "And I'm so sorry for just falling asleep on the couch last night. I can't believe I did that!"

Isabelle laughed. "No worries at all, dear! We're neighbours now, that's pretty much the same as family in these parts. Anyway, you looked like you needed a good rest. I'm glad you were able to sleep. I've put the kettle on, and the cucumber sandwiches are in the fridge if you want something to nibble before the casserole is ready."

Sophie made them both some tea. Isabelle put the casserole in the oven and they resumed their seats from yesterday, before the interlude of night.

"Can you tell me more about the previous owner of the place? I'm curious to know more about the house," Sophie said, feeling a strange uneasiness drape around her like an invisible curtain. She didn't want to talk about the house. But she knew she had to.

Isabelle stared thoughtfully into her teacup before answering. "Well, he was old, made me look as if I was in the prime of my youth," she added, letting out a hollow laugh. "He kept himself to himself. His name is Samuel, although I always called him Sammy and he never seemed to mind. He seemed to prefer his own company but there was something very lonely about him. I have a sixth sense when it comes to understanding people. You know, he would stand exactly where I saw you standing the other day, by that rock on the cliff edge. Sometimes I would catch him standing, staring at the sea for hours. I felt as if he was searching for something while he was here. I don't know if he ever found it. I believe he wrote a book. I have it here somewhere and have been meaning to get around to reading it, but my eyes aren't what they used to be.

"You know, I believe there was a deep well of sadness within him." Isabelle looked up at Sophie and stared at her directly in the eyes. "I understand what it's like to feel crushing sadness. A sadness so strong it makes it hard to breath. You feel like you will suffocate or go mad. I don't talk about this often, but I did have a baby girl. She was my firstborn, before my two sons came along. She died just as she entered this world. I still remember holding her in my arms, the warm bundle that she was. She let out a small sigh and that was it. Her first and last breath. She died with a small smile on those red rosy lips of hers. I was devastated at the time, of course. But now I understand, she was never meant for this world. Some people just aren't. She was fated to be an angel, my little cherub in heaven. Her name was Cassandra.

"Although me and Sammy didn't really talk or have dinners together, we connected on a deeper level, a level beyond words. I believe sorrow pulls people together, and Sammy and I were drawn together as if by invisible strings. You must think I'm losing my marbles rambling on like this," Isabelle said, as she glanced up at Sophie, snapping out of her reverie.

"Not at all," Sophie replied. "I think it's completely true what you're saying. That's why I had to leave my friends and family in London. I just couldn't connect with them any more, I guess. I'm so sorry to hear about your daughter. I can't imagine what you must have gone through," Sophie said, reaching out to hold Isabelle's fragile, papery hand.

"Thank you, dear," Isabelle replied, patting it. They sat together in silence as time lazily stretched out its hands. Seconds and minutes ticked by until Isabelle said suddenly, "Now, let me go check on that casserole of ours."

They ate in the kitchen. Isabelle insisted on packing the substantial leftovers for Sophie in a Tupperware.

"I know you young people these days. You just don't know how to feed yourselves! I keep having a go at my sons, Jim and Gabriel, living off microwave meals. Gabriel's wife should know better though, but of course she works full-time. It baffles me that no one is there to take care of the home and children nowadays. That's the most meaningful job out there, isn't it? But what do I know? I'm just an old woman living in bygone times," Isabelle said, smiling.

"I couldn't agree more," Sophie said, hugging Isabelle. She felt as if she had known her for years rather than the few hours she had actually spent with her. Perhaps that was what Isabelle meant by connecting on a deeper level, transcending the constraints of words and time.

"Do you have any friends around here yet?" Isabelle asked. "Anyone from work? I think you should reach out and maybe have someone stay over with you in that house.

I never quite understood but Sammy said the house had a way of getting under his skin. I sometimes felt he was almost frightened of it. I'm sure it's nothing, but shadows loom large in the darkness when you're alone."

Sophie hadn't thought about the strangeness of the day before. It somehow felt like it had been a dream in retrospect or a figment of her wild imagination. Perhaps she had been hallucinating the blurred candles and marching ants due to her lack of sleep. It all sounded very fantastical in the warmth and safety of Isabelle's home.

She nodded. "I was thinking of calling up my best friend in London, Angie. She's a freelance graphic designer so she can bring her work here for a few days." Sophie had not been thinking that at all but now she said it out loud, it sounded like a good idea.

"Well, that's lovely. I'd like to meet this Angie when she gets here," Isabelle replied.

"Of course." On her way out she asked, "Did you ever visit the house? Samuel's house?"

Isabelle paused, an indecipherable expression flitting across her face. Finally she replied, "Yes, twice." Her brow was slightly furrowed. "The first time I was dropping off some mail. For some reason his letters had ended up on my doorstep. I knocked on the door and didn't get an answer. You must understand this is a friendly village, so I opened the door and was planning to leave them on the entrance table, but something caught my eye." Isabelle paused, the crease between her brow deepening. "I could have sworn I saw a shadow, moving inside the kitchen area. I thought to myself, if it was Sammy, he would have opened the door for me. I was worried it was an intruder. I'm honestly not really sure what happened after that. I walked to the kitchen and suddenly had a dizzy spell. I nearly fell over, but Sammy had returned from his shopping and caught me by the arm. There was no one else there, just me and Sammy. It was probably my eyes playing tricks on me," Isabelle said, sounding unconvinced. "Sammy didn't say much but I could tell he was furious. He told me he was having repair work done and it wasn't safe for me or any other visitors to enter. He made me promise never to enter again without his permission. I didn't see any repair work though…" Isabelle finished, her voice trailing off, the memory slipping back into the dark recesses of the past.

"I see," Sophie said, trying to sound casual. "And the second time?"

"The second time I was checking up on the place after Sammy moved out. You know, he left a lot of his things behind, just upped and left. So I gathered up some of the stuff and took it to one of our local charity shops. No shadows the second time round thankfully! Strange place," Isabelle said, under her breath more to herself than Sophie. "But I'm sure you've made it comfortable and cosy. Perhaps all it really needed was a woman's touch."

Sophie nodded and smiled back. The smile didn't quite reach her eyes as a ripple of anxiety spread through her body. She waved farewell to Isabelle and turned to face her house. She studied it side-on. There was nothing intimidating or daunting about it, she told herself. The cold afternoon sunshine bathed it in a shimmering, ethereal light. It looked rather peaceful. Pensive.

"This is why I shouldn't live alone, Dan. You always said I let my imagination get the better of me," Sophie whispered to the wind. She could almost feel Dan's warm presence as he walked with her back to the house. She felt safe.

As she jammed her key into the lock, she took a deep breath. There was nothing to be afraid of, she told herself. As the door creaked open, Sophie was met by a calm stillness. Breathing deeply, Sophie tiptoed into the living room where the candles appeared to have been burning wildly at their own free will. They were perched innocently on the windowsill. Sophie gathered them up and placed them carefully in a cardboard box by the mantelpiece. She didn't need all those candles out anyway. She sealed the box with tape and ventured into the kitchen. She checked under the sink and in the corners of the cupboards but there was not an ant in sight. She exhaled loudly, feeling her tense body unwind.

"You see," she could imagine Dan saying. "There's nothing there, you scaredy-cat. You really should be a proper writer what with all those stories and fantasy worlds you've got going on up there." Dan had teased her about her fanciful imagination, but he had always encouraged her to write. He said her talent was wasted at The Maverick Advertising Agency and she just needed to be brave and follow her dream and actually write something.

Sophie had not been brave though. She liked the security of having a regular income and a steady schedule. There was always an uncertainty, a certain risk with writing. Dan would be proud of me, making this move, she thought to herself. She had dived, head first, into a murky pool of ambiguity and doubt. Although it was unclear what she was doing or where she was going or whether she had hit rock bottom, she knew she had made the right decision. Nothing that used to be true and solid in her life was so any more.

The past few months, Sophie felt she had been trying to capture something ephemeral, something that was no longer there, whether that was Dan himself or her love for him which had nowhere to go, no one to cling on to. She now knew she had been fighting a losing battle, like trying to catch light in the palm of her hands. It was an omnipresent force and yet she couldn't touch it, couldn't feel it. This was to be her new existence, where uncertainty was the only certainty. She thought back to the first dream she'd had since moving into 11 Edgeware Lane. It was not just a house of sand that had crumbled and then been swept away by the ever-ravenous sea. She had built a life of sand, a life which had dissolved at a moment's notice. Whether it was fair or not, the only thing she could do was to build another one and hope this one would stand the test of time.

As these thoughts cascaded through her mind, tumbling one after another like a waterfall, she sensed the familiar feeling that she was being watched. She spun around and sure enough the ravens were there. This time there were three of them. Their mean beady black eyes and sharp angular beaks pointed in her direction. One of the birds had something clasped in its beak. It could have been a tissue or a piece of paper. Sophie couldn't be sure since the moment she turned the raven with the unknown object in its beak spread its dark plumes and flew away.

# Chapter 8

## *Samuel*

To his disappointment, Samuel had not received any correspondence from Sophie. He couldn't blame her. It was rather late to reach out now. Guilt weighed heavily on his conscience. He sometimes woke up terrified at night after having one of his recurring nightmares. Heavy crates were being loaded on to his chest by a man without a face. A dark undulating shadow hung where the face should have been. The man mechanically loaded one crate after the other on top of Samuel. Samuel was powerless to stop him. He could neither speak nor move as the burden steadily increased, crushing his body, splintering his bones and tearing through his lungs. He would wake up barely able to breathe.

He was also experiencing more frequent headaches. They were not average headaches, and no amount of painkillers would get rid of them. They blinded him. He felt as if a pure white light was exploding from the insides of his eyes. Snakes of fire slithered around his temples, tightening their coils until the pain was unbearable. Samuel was soon able to predict their occurrence. He would start losing focus, and his thinking became confused. Bizarre images of people and places would dance before him in his mind's eye. They would take on a reality of their own. The sensations this imagery evoked was so powerful that Samuel would not be able to tell what was real and what was a hallucination. It was all a confused mesh of colour, movement, light and shadows.

He had already had a couple of nasty falls due to these headaches, which made him start to doubt his ability to live on his own any more. He had always been an independent man, not needing or relying on anyone for his entire life. Some might view his existence lonely and empty. But he had known from a young age that this would be his cross to bear in life. He was destined to walk his road alone. Now, however, he was being presented with new difficulties which were not so easy to solve. The idea of moving into some sort of assisted living facility for the elderly sent shivers down his spine.

Although Samuel never socialised or came into contact with many people, apart from when he went shopping for groceries, he always managed to keep himself busy. He considered himself to be a small self-sufficient island and had always cultivated and maintained many solitary hobbies. These days Samuel spent much of his time writing when his eyes allowed it. They would tire easily but when he was fresh in the morning he would write notes in his journal, observations and philosophical essays. He had had moderate success and acclaim as a writer in his younger years. He had focused mainly on writing dense historical books, factual and to the point. He liked to target small, unknown groups of people, communities or societies rich in their own unknown customs, obscure beliefs and arcane rituals. He had not quite made enough money simply writing books, especially since they appealed to such a niche market. To subsidise his writing income, he also gave lectures and presentations in universities for history students. It was a modest living, but it was enough for him.

When he wasn't writing, he was pottering around in his small, neat garden. Since the sun was making an appearance, Samuel took his tea and gardening tools and headed outside. He felt calm and at peace with nature. Even as a small boy, getting his hands stuck in mud or climbing to the top of a tree had always provided endless fun and escapism. He sat heavily in his favourite, rickety, old fold-out chair. It had bright yellow stripes that had faded somewhat over the years. The fabric was stained with grass and mud and fraying at the edges. Despite its dilapidated state, Samuel loved that chair. He had bought it in a car boot sale coming up to twenty years ago. He looked upon the chair as an old friend. With the sun beaming down on his face, Samuel relaxed. His eyelids slowly started drooping as a heaviness he could not fight overcame him.

Lilting music drifted softly through the air. It blended in with the background music of nature, the crisp leaves rustling, the birds twittering high in their branches. It was beautiful and familiar. It was rich and sad. The music was so sad it crushed Samuel's heart, bringing tears to his eyes. It was a flute. Samuel continued to listen with his eyes closed. With the melancholy music playing in the background, Samuel fell into a dark dream.

He was sitting cross-legged on the damp muddy earth. He was part of a large circle of people. It was dark and the night air was still and heavy, saturated with plumes of swirling smoke. They were sitting around a blazing fire where a woman was chanting. Samuel looked at the faces around him, lit by the reddish glow of the fire. Most of them had dark skin which looked as if it had not been washed in a long time. Men wore tattered, baggy clothes adorned with multiple mismatching patches sewn on. The women, however, wore brightly coloured dresses, swathed in purple and red scarves. Some of them had glittering jewels interwoven in their hair. Scintillating against their thick black locks their hair looked like a carpet of stars. Kohl lined their eyes giving them a harsh beauty. Some of them wore heavy gold bangles which clattered gently as they swayed in tune with the woman chanting. Although their outfits had a veneer or extravagance and glamour, on closer inspection, Samuel could see where the edges were frayed and wearing thin.

Samuel looked at the woman chanting. He recognised her. He knew who she was. And next to her was her husband, Willowen. He was playing the flute, surveying the scene.

One of the women in the circle then shrieked hysterically, "Tell us, Erosabel, what do you see?"

She was quickly hushed by an older woman sitting next to her. "You can't rush these things, Lottie. Let me talk to her."

The woman faced Erosabel as the fire continued to spark and fly higher between them. "Tell us, who have you met, Erosabel, on your voyage to the dead? Have you come across the first person riddled with the disease? Was it black magic from one of us? Are the townspeople right in their persecution and hanging of us gypsies? Or was it brought on by someone or something else? Tell us what you see, Erosabel."

Erosabel continued to chant. Swaying side to side violently, she opened her eyes. They rolled back in her head as she started shaking. Her entire body was twisting in convulsions. Willowen stopped playing and knelt down next to her, gently placing a hand on her shoulder.

She immediately stopped. Her head slumped forward. She spoke, her voice harsh and deep. It was not the same voice Samuel had heard that night on the cliff edge. It was a man's voice.

"I was a sailor. My name was James," she said, as her head snapped up. Her eyes were still rolling towards the back of her head, revealing only shining white orbs.

"James," the older woman said. "Tell us your story."

Erosabel continued in the strange, harsh voice. "I had been at sea for many years. Travelling to escape the noose and earn my riches. I travelled to faraway lands. One of the ports we docked in was riddled with the pox. No one could escape it. We left quickly seeing only decay and disease and no riches were to be got. But it was too late. One by one our crew fell ill. We tossed countless bodies overboard. We even threw live bodies overboard once we saw their bodies were infested with the pox. I still hear their screams and pitiful pleas ringing in my ears right before they drowned. I will never be free of their voices. When we arrived in Dover we only had a quarter of the men we had set out with. And we all had the pox. We knew it and we still went back to our families, ate at their tables and slept with our wives. We all died soon after, taking so many lives with us to the grave." Erosabel hung her head heavily, letting her chin rest on her chest.

"I knew it," cried the young hysterical woman called Lottie. "It's not us! It was never us!" She rocked backwards and forwards on the spot, her wild eyes searching the faces of those in the group. "We need to tell them, tell the police! They'll listen to her," she said, pointing at Erosabel. Her panic was contagious. All those in the circle shifted uneasily. At this point everyone knew someone who had been taken away by the police. Rumours of torture and unlawful hangings had spread through the gypsy encampment like wildfire. They were being accused of using witchcraft, necromancy and black magic to spread the disease that was wreaking havoc on the townspeople. Neighbours in the town who had once been intrigued by their music, fortune-telling abilities and adventures were now pointing the finger directly at them, accusing them of death and destruction.

"Quiet, girl," the older woman snapped, sensing the rising panic within the group. "James, have you met any gypsies in the realm of the dead? The persecuted ones? What has become of them? Were they tortured?"

Just then Erosabel started to shake violently. Her head tipped back as she began to froth at the mouth. "I see them." Erosabel choked as spit trickled down her chin.

"That's enough," Willowen said, fear glinting in his eyes. "Erosabel," he said, shaking her shoulders.

"I see them," Erosabel shrieked. Her eyes rolled violently, tears streaking down her face, intermingling with the white foam bubbling from her mouth. "No, no, come here!" she spluttered. She raised a quivering hand. She was so close to the fire her hand rose straight into the flames, but she did not react. The flames licked her hands greedily, scorching them with their fury.

"Erosabel, wake up!" yelled Willowen, snatching her hand from the glutinous flames.

"Logan and Joni! I can't leave without Logan and Joni!" Erosabel choked out. She clutched her throat, gasping for air. She was suffocating.

Confusion and panic spread across Willowen's face. "The twins are in their beds asleep. Erosabel, wake up, this is madness!"

Erosabel's eyes snapped open. "In their beds asleep," she echoed absently. Her breathing returned to normal as the frothing foam trickled down her face. Her eyes were a piercing blue, unlike any Samuel had seen before. She closed them gently and lay limp in Willowen's arms, her head tilting back.

"That was too much for one night," Willowen said, the fury evident in his voice.

"We had to know," the older woman said calmly. "She needs rest and she will recover."

Willowen shot her an icy look before carrying his wife in his arms and taking her away from the ring of fire.

Samuel turned to see where Willowen was taking her. To his surprise he didn't see them at all. Instead his old shed was transplanted there, in the middle of the enigmatic, mystical scene. It stood out against the background like a sore thumb. He turned to see the faces of the rest of the gypsies but instead was met with the naked trees and tangle of barbed bushes of his garden. Samuel blinked several times. He was sitting in his fold-out chair, and the sky above was littered with flickering stars, like the jewels embedded in the gypsies' hair. His cold half-finished tea waited by his foot. Samuel only then realised how cold he was. He had fallen asleep and must have been out there for hours. His muscles were stiff and rigid to the point where he could barely move. He limped forward as one of his legs was completely numb. He would draw himself a warm bath to loosen up his frozen muscles. Before shutting the door, he turned around. He couldn't tell if his eyes were playing tricks on him, but he was sure he saw the outline of a man carrying a flute melt into the scenery of the garden. He blinked and it was gone. Only the ghostly shadows of the trees and their bare, angular branches looming down on him remained.

# Chapter 9

## *Sophie*

*Dear Daniel,*

*He exists only between the lines of my poetry,*

*My pen leaks inky pools of his blood,*

*His body is the page I write upon,*

*A body on which my words caressingly flood.*


*His heart beats in time with each and every scrawl I make,*

*The lines on the page stretching out forever guide me to his soul,*

*Our minds are intertwined with ropes of rhyme,*

*Connected through the curves of the words, making a sentence whole.*


*Yet as I reach the last line,*

*As I write the finished score,*

*Your image blurs with the tears swirling in sad eyes of mine,*

*With the bullet of a full stop, you exist no more.*

*Sophie*

"I'll have one large double macchiato with skimmed milk, one medium cold brew, one small flat white with soy milk, and two medium vanilla lattes, one with regular milk, cream and half a pump of caramel but no caramel on top and the other with soy milk and no cream or caramel but add a pump of hazelnut syrup instead. Ok?"

Sophie listened to the long order, feeling increasingly daunted. It was her third shift and she had been getting the hang of it, but today she had been thrown in the deep end of the pool. Jeremy had called out sick and there was no one to cover him. Although Sophie had been briefly trained on how to make the hot drinks she still got confused. The only other person there was Kalina, and she was decidedly looking away and cleaning the already squeaky-clean tables. They were so clean in fact that you could pretty much see the reflection of your face in them. Sophie felt a stab of frustration and glared at the back of her head. It was 8:00 am and rush hour time. All the groggy working professionals needed their caffeine fix to get pepped up for the long day's work ahead of them.

"Excuse me, did you get that?" the girl demanded, glancing up from her smartphone. She was very thin, had a short, stylish haircut and was wearing a garish teal pant suit. A pair of large, Chanel sunglasses sat on top of her head although there was no sign of the sun making an appearance at any point during the day.

"Yes, yes, got it!" Sophie said, trying to smile through gritted teeth. "Uh, Kalina, could use a hand over here," Sophie called over. Sophie spotted the teal-suited girl rolling her eyes.

"Just need to tidy up this table," Kalina said, without looking up. The table in question had one tray and one mug on it. Sophie made an effort not to join the teal-suited girl in rolling her eyes as well. Sophie spun around, ready to tackle the coffee machine. She eyed the growing queue in trepidation. She didn't want to be on the receiving end of the wrath of a stream of un-caffeinated human beings this early in the morning. She turned to the machine. She could do this. She'd seen the others work the machine before. She began to twist the knobs, press buttons, stir, spray cream and caramel, pour into takeaway cups and there, done! Just as she was putting the cups into the cup holders, she turned around and accidentally bumped into Kalina who had magically teleported to the till where she was printing out the receipt for the girl. As if in slow motion, the cup containing the large double macchiato with skimmed milk wobbled and tipped over.

"Oh no! I'm so sorry!" Sophie exclaimed. The coffee splattered Kalina's smart, leather shoes and sprayed all over the floor.

Kalina sighed and said simply, "You take the orders and I'll clean this mess up."

Sophie nodded meekly as Kalina went to get the mop.

"Seriously! You had to spill *my* drink. Now I have no choice but to wait for you to make me a new one. But don't worry, it's not like I have an important job or am in a rush or anything. You just take your time!" the girl spat viciously, her pale blue eyes cold with undisguised fury.

Sophie was taken aback by the vitriolic tone and cutting sarcasm. This girl really hates me, Sophie thought, befuddled. Quickly, eyes downcast, Sophie made a new macchiato and mumbled an apology as the girl flounced away with her coffees in tow.

"Tough crowd, huh," said a disembodied voice from somewhere in the queue.

Sophie glanced up from beneath her heavily mascaraed lashes to see who was throwing her some crumbs of kindness. A tall man with dark hair and eyes wearing jeans and a smart blazer was looking at her with half a smile playing on his lips.

"Don't worry, my order is easy. One large cappuccino and cheese croissant to go, please," he said politely.

Sophie smiled and let out an exaggerated sigh of relief. "That's good to hear," she said. "Just give me a sec." Cappuccinos are easy to make, Sophie thought to herself as she tapped the milk jug on the counter confidently. She felt the man's eyes lingering on her. She hoped he wasn't scrutinising how she made the coffee. She already had one customer watch her barista skills and tell her that she was doing it all wrong and to just let a more experienced staff member take over. Nervously she poured the coffee into a to-go cup and handed him his warmed-up cheese croissant.

"Here you go," she said, smiling.

"Thanks," he replied. After waiting expectantly for several seconds, he added, "How much is it?"

"Oh, right, that will be £5.25," Sophie said, feeling suddenly flustered.

"I've only got a twenty. Could you break this up for me?" he asked, fishing out a twenty-pound note from his wallet.

"Sure."

"Hey, are you new around here? It's just I haven't seen you before," he asked, watching her count out his change.

"Yes, actually, I just started working here a few days ago."

"Welcome to the town. I guess I'll see you around. I'm a regular here," he said, flashing her a brief, slanted smile.

"Right, see you around," Sophie replied, swiping a stray lock of hair from her face and securing it tightly behind her ears.

"Bye then," he said, lingering a moment longer before raising his hand in farewell.

Before Sophie had a chance to reply, the next customer had barraged her way in demanding a large Americano with a string of babyccinos. Sophie glanced down and saw a set of identical twins in a buggy and then another set of twins standing next to the woman who was presumably their mother, tugging on her skirt.

"Mummyyyyy! We want to goooo," one of them was whining.

"Yeah, noooow, Mummy!" the other chimed in.

"Well, you need to wait until I get my coffee," the mother snapped back.

"But we want our chinooosssss," the two older twins said in unison.

"Did you not hear me? I already ordered them!" their mother said, exasperated. "Sorry about this lot, always demanding," she said to Sophie.

"No problem at all," Sophie said. "Your babyccinos will be ready in no time," she said to the older twin boys. One of the younger ones in the buggy started crying which immediately set off the other one.

"Great, just what I need," the mother exclaimed. "You see, this is why I never leave the house!"

Sophie wasn't sure if she was talking to the older boys, to herself, to Sophie, or perhaps she had totally lost it and was talking to the plastic toy phone she had just thrown back into her bag. Sophie decided to give a sympathetic smile and nod understandingly.

"What have we got here!" Sophie exclaimed. "Babyccinos all round!" Sophie handed out the mini cups of sugar and foam to the boys and the large Americano to the mother.

"Thank you," the mother replied, attempting to pay with a plastic toy card before realising it wasn't going to work. "Oh, sorry about that," she said, stifling a laugh. "My brain is so scattered with this lot. I need to have four sets of eyes, six sets of hands and ten sets of feet to keep up with them all!"

Slightly taken aback by the terrifying monstrosity this image conjured up, Sophie smiled weakly. "No worries at all! You've got lovely kiddos. All boys, right?"

"Yep, four boys under the age of four! God help me," she said, before patting the crying twins on the head.

"Here you go, hunnies. Some sugar to cheer you up." She glanced up at Sophie. "I'm sure parenting manuals wouldn't recommend babyccinos for two-year-olds, but when you're a mum, those manuals are the first thing to either go in the trash or get eaten. I've resorted to bribery, blackmail, threats, extortion, you name it," she said, winking at Sophie.

"Hey, no judgement at all over here," Sophie said, laughing. She liked how genuine and easy-going this woman was.

"I'm Georgey, short for Georgina but please never ever call me that. You'll be seeing a lot of me here. There are a lot of mum and baby coffee dates around some of these cafés. Just thought I'd introduce myself. Oh, and the older set of twins are Leo and Nate. The younger ones are Aiden and Patrick," she said, gesturing to the two in the buggy, both of whom had already spilled their babyccinos down their tops and were giggling hysterically. "You'll never be able to tell each set apart. I still get them muddled all the time," she said, ignoring the messy tops and sticky hands waving below her.

Sophie laughed. "Well, they're all gorgeous! And it's nice to meet all of you." She waved at the two little conspirators in the buggy, making them giggle even louder.

Kalina was serving the next customer. She stared at her watch pointedly.

"Oops, well, I'd better get on with my job," Sophie said in an undertone to Georgey.

Georgey smiled. "Well, I can't be standing around chatting all day, not with this lot. See you." Georgey heaved the double buggy to the door calling over her shoulder for the other two who were busy having a sword fight with the wooden mixing sticks.

"Leo just stabbed me, Mummy!" Nate yelled. "That's not fair."

"Well, you're playing sword fight. Isn't that the whole point of the game? Someone stabs someone else," Georgey was saying as her voice drifted out of the coffee shop.

Sophie smiled to herself. Had she just sort of made a new friend, she mused to herself.

"Be careful of that one," Kalina said, gesturing to the closing door. "She talks and talks and talks if you let her. And those kids, don't get me started!"

"I thought she was quite nice actually," Sophie replied, not caring much for Kalina's comments on her potential new friends.

"Nice? She never shuts up. Maybe she's nice if you're deaf," Kalina said huffily before attending to the next customer.

Sophie decided to ignore Kalina's opinions and busied herself with making coffees while Kalina worked the till.

It had been a long shift and when the clock struck 3:00 pm Sophie was ready to get out of there.

"See you, guys," she said, waving to Chris and Jess who had come in for the afternoon shift. Jess was sweet. She had just graduated from university with a bachelor's degree in psychology. She was applying for jobs in clinics in London and was working at the Acorn in the meantime. She had a doll-like face and a massive crush on Chris. They both waved after her.

"Hey, Chris, could you help me move those supply boxes over there? I was trying to do it on my own, but I need someone who's big and strong to help me," Sophie heard Jess say meekly to Chris.

"Sure thing," Chris replied.

The bell on the door tinkled as Sophie slipped through it, smiling to herself. She wondered if Chris could tell Jess was flirting with him with all the subtlety of a ton of bricks. She wouldn't be surprised if he was utterly oblivious. Men could be so dense sometimes.

Sophie untied her bike from the bicycle rack. She had been thrilled to find a bike her size at one of the charity shops on the high street. Sophie had wanted to get a bike since moving to her new home but didn't want to pay for one at full price. She had a job, but she still had to count her pennies and spend carefully. The bike was a faded red colour and had a rusty wire basket clipped on the back. She found the basket feature particularly useful. She hadn't yet been to the beach since moving but today she had put her swimsuit on in the ladies bathroom, underneath her clothes, and packed the rest of her stuff in the little basket.

As she hopped on the battered saddle of her bike, she felt a wave of excitement ripple through her body. She felt as if she was going on some sort of marvellous adventure. It was just her, her bike and the unexplored beach. She had Google mapped the route before setting off, but she figured she would just ask around if she got lost. It was a friendly town and everyone was only too willing to help. She had packed some food from the café which was about to expire, as Luke had mentioned on her first day. A packet of Bakewell tarts, lemon cake, a breakfast roll and a takeaway cup of coffee were stashed in her wire basket. She steadied herself on the bike and started her journey. It should only take her ten minutes or so to get to the seaside as long as she didn't get lost along the way.

She cycled past the now familiar shops on the high street. She felt the wind caress her face, smoothing the worry lines and stress away. She suddenly did not feel tired at all. Her body felt light, exhilarated. As she cycled on, the landscape around her slowly morphed and changed. The road became narrower once she cycled on to Sea Street. High walls of trees sheltered her on both sides. She looked up at the sky for a moment, inhaling deeply. It was 3:05 pm. The sunlight wasn't the same greyish, weak sunlight it had been in the morning. It had become stronger and yet still maintained a softness as it filtered lazily through the wiry branches of the trees. Soon the sun would set and the architecture of the landscape around her would change yet again, Sophie thought to herself. Everything changes, every hour, every minute, every second, she mused. The light embracing her was just another reminder of the constant imperceptible changes that occur throughout life.

As she cycled, the trees on one side cleared and opened up to reveal an expansive field. The hills undulated far off into the horizon. She wondered what secrets lay behind each swell of earth. She almost felt like veering off track to investigate the mysteries of the open field but decided to press on. The beach was calling her, and she wanted to reach it before sunset. Glancing over her shoulder, she let her eyes soak in the view of the patchwork quilt of fields before continuing on her journey.

As she entered Bay Hill Road, she passed several quaint houses lined up peacefully. She couldn't help but glance into several of the windows of the houses she cycled past. The warm, yellow tinged light inside looked inviting and cosy. Nonetheless, she relished the sharp, crisp air of the outside world. It felt refreshing on her skin and in her lungs.

An old stone church stood on her right, next to the village's graveyard. Tombstones marked the final resting place of the town's inhabitants. It felt strange to think about it, but she decided she would like to be buried there when her time came. She was still new in town but somehow she felt a deep connection inside her with the place. She had felt it when she first saw 11 Edgeware Lane on the internet and she felt it now as she passed the cold tombstones, surrounded by an aura of silence and other-worldly magic. This was home.

Pressing on, she passed a lively pub on her left. A crowd had gathered outside and were laughing loudly, clinking their drinks together, one toast after another. Their peals of laughter melted into the background as she continued her journey forward. She saw a sign pointing her in the direction of St. Margaret's Beach Bay. There was also a sign for The Hope Inn. She paused at the signpost as she balanced on her bike. She wondered what The Hope Inn offered its guests, a new life, perhaps? A fresh start with hope on the not so distant horizon? Over the past few months, all hope of happiness and a future had withered within her, a drooping flower close to death. These past few weeks, however, something had changed inside her. The sadness still washed over her in waves. But there was something else now, a small spark within her that was spluttering to life again. It was a glimmer of hope telling her that she could still live and feel alive. There was more out there for her to discover. There was something beyond the wall of sadness and grief and only she, Sophie, could figure out what it was that was calling her.

Sophie reached the parking lot. It was only 3:20 pm. She had made it before sunset. She tied her bike to a bicycle rack and decided to go on foot from there. It was mainly deserted as she had expected on a cold day in mid-October. There was a huddle of people bundled in hats and scarves buying food from the Riverside Snacks hut but apart from them it was just her and the beach. An airplane left a white gash in the sky above, cutting the heavens open. Sophie stared at it as she sat down on the rocky pebbles of the shore. The sharp wind whipped her face, tossing her loose hair around in every direction. Sophie unpacked the little picnic she had brought with her and settled down to eat. She sipped her coffee which was now cold.

The rushing waves, screeching seagulls, smooth pebbles and salty air engulfed her senses. Although it was cold and the sun was setting, Sophie kicked off her shoes and traced the outline of the waves lapping the shore. The gritty sand and pebbles stuck to the soles of her feet. She walked until there was no one in sight. It was just her and the sea. She had reached the end of the world. She ventured closer to the water's edge, its magnetic energy reeling her in.

A wave rolled up to meet her and crashed onto the shore. Foam sprayed into the air and freckled her face. The residue of the wave gently lapped her numb feet. Sophie gasped. The water was freezing. She didn't know what it was but there was something about the open expanse of water that soothed her. Perhaps it was the timelessness of it, the fact that so many souls before her had taken comfort at this exact same sight. Alternatively, perhaps it was the ruthlessness. The cold sea waters were harsh and cruel. Nature was fickle and tempestuous. It was not fair, but nor did it pretend to be. It reminded her that sometimes bad things just happened. There may be no rhyme or reason to them, just the cruel hand of fate wielding the pen of doom, etching the stories of their lives. The waves continued to roll up in a rhythmic regularity. Sophie was wearing her swimsuit underneath her layers but didn't feel brave enough to face the freezing waters.

She watched the fiery sun dip into the sea, its red haze spilling like blood onto the undulating surface. Red tinged clouds stretched out over the horizon. The white chalky cliffs stood tall and proud silhouetted in the background. Their edges were sharp and angular, like cut-outs pasted onto the background. Sophie felt as if she was in a dream world, a dark fairy tale. She had somehow stepped into a parallel reality where everything continued to look and sound the same, but it all felt different. She felt different.

As if in a trance, Sophie stood up and took off her thick parker jacket. She peeled off the layers of clothes underneath until she stood in her swimsuit. She didn't even feel the cold. The breeze, the icy waters didn't touch her. She felt as though a film of protection coated her skin, impermeable to the biting chill engulfing her.

Before her rational brain could kick in and tell her that what she was doing was madness, she ran, head first into one of the thunderous waves. The water crashed around her, flooding all her senses. She couldn't think of anything except the shock of cold which inundated her body. She surrendered herself to it. Her limbs felt stiff. It felt as if thousands of pinpricks of ice were stabbing every inch of her skin. The salt stung her eyes and clung to her lips. The sand was rough under her feet. It shifted underneath, making her lose her balance several times. She moved slowly forward, allowing the ebb and flow of the water to drag her in deeper. She stared up at the sky.

The sun was now a mere sliver of orange, about to be consumed by the ever-hungry sea. The world was spinning around her, faster and faster. She had lost any sense of orientation or feeling in her body. As she continued to gaze upwards she thought she could see pinpricks of light peppering the inky black sky, a carpet of stars. Suddenly another wave crashed on top of her, sending her underwater. The world was muffled beneath the waves. Sophie felt confused. She was in complete darkness. She couldn't tell which way was up or which was down. Suddenly the water pulled away and Sophie desperately gulped in the air. Another wave rolled menacingly towards her. Without the sun, the water had morphed into a thick black shadow, threatening to devour her.

Sophie felt afraid. She was lost in a sea of darkness. She swivelled around in the water, desperately trying to find the direction of the shore. Before she could turn, another wave crashed into her, making her lose her footing. She was submerged again under the sea's shifting surface. Her arms flailed wildly, trying to swim to the top, wherever that was. She gasped for breath. Her lungs were burning, desperate for air. Another wave was already on top of her. Sophie inhaled lungfuls of seawater and started to choke. The waves were circling her, capturing her in a deathly embrace, making her feel light-headed and dizzy. She was stuck in this hellish vortex. Her stiff limbs felt ready to give up, to succumb to the battering of the waves. The incessant battering of the waves.

Suddenly she heard a voice. At first it sounded like it was coming from the sky or the sea or the very air itself. The voice was resonating from everywhere and nowhere at the same time. Sophie thought she was imagining it. Then it became clearer and she could make out what was being said.

"Hello, there! Hey, you, do you need help? I'm coming in," a man's voice bellowed.

Sophie spun around, the fog in her head clearing slightly. Was it a mirage, a sea-induced hallucination? There was a man standing on the shore, throwing off his shoes, getting ready to dive in. She could see the shore. Sophie tried to call out, but her voice was lost in the sound of the waves and the wind whipping the air into a frenzy. She heaved her frozen body closer to the shore which wasn't as far away as she had imagined.

The man had rolled up his jeans and waded in. The water was almost up to his waist when he reached her.

"Jesus Christ, is this really the best time for a swim!" The gentle moonlight catching the water's surface reflected his face back at her. His face was familiar but she couldn't place it. Her head was swirling. All she could think about was how cold she was.

"Here, let's get you to shore. You're shivering." He put his arms around her as they stumbled to shore. Luckily, Sophie had thought to bring a towel which the man wrapped snuggly around her shoulders. He took another long, scrutinising look at her face, half bathed in shadows and silvery moonlight.

"Do I know you?" he said. "Hang on, you're the girl who served me coffee today at the Acorn. Oh my God, what are you doing here? And at this time? And in this weather?" he exclaimed, staring at her incredulously, as the reality of the situation sunk in.

Through chattering teeth, Sophie replied, "I felt like going on an adventure." She then let out a shaky noise, somewhere between a laugh and a sob.

"Well, I think you've definitely had quite the adventure. That water is freezing. Let's get you warmed up," he said, rubbing her with the towel.

Sophie was too cold to resist. Her muscles felt as if they'd frozen over and couldn't move. Once she was pretty much dry, he covered her with the parker jacket and tried to pat his jeans dry.

"How about you get in my car and I'll turn the heating up. You're frozen. If we get you in there now, you'll warm up and dry properly and then you can put your clothes on. Otherwise you'll just get your clothes all wet and catch your death!"

"I probably shouldn't be getting in a stranger's cars at night wearing only a jacket. What kind of girl do you take me for?" she said, bizarrely giving another shaky laugh.

"Well, I really don't know what kind of girl I take you for, going for a swim in the sea, alone, in October, at night!" he said emphasising each part of his statement with mounting incredulity. "Come on, you'll freeze. I swear it's safe and if you want to get out once you've dried up, be my guest."

He offered his hand to help her stand up. Sophie accepted it and stiffly got up. She felt as if her muscles might snap. He helped gather up her things and they walked to his car which was parked nearby.

The man quickly started the engine and blasted the heat. "There you go. You'll be better in no time. We just need to defrost you a little."

Sophie had to admit she felt blood circulating in her body and her muscles loosening up at once. "Thanks," she said, sighing and resting her head back. She suddenly felt exhausted.

"No problem. I just didn't want to see you drowning out there. Is this sort of thing normal back wherever home is for you?" he asked curiously.

Sophie let out a snort of laughter. "What, in London? No, this thing certainly is not that normal there."

"Ah, so you're a city girl. Ok," he replied. "So what brought you to Dover then, Sophie?"

Sophie's head snapped up. "How do you know my name?" Her senses roused into full alert mode. She was in the car with a total stranger, wearing only a swimsuit under her jacket. Of course he was a freak. How could she have trusted him? She sat bolt upright, ready to jump out of the car in a second.

"Hey, hey, calm down! Didn't mean to freak you out. Your name is right there, on your name tag," he said, pointing hurriedly at the purple collared top she had to wear at the Acorn.

"Ah, right, of course it is. Sorry," Sophie said, slumping slightly in the chair. Now that she had come to her senses she realised how utterly and completely bizarre her behaviour must appear to this man. To say that she wished the chair could just swallow her up would be an understatement. To make matters worse, she remembered he said he was a regular at the Acorn. So she would be reminded on a daily basis of her foolish, crazy behaviour.

"Well, yes, I'm Sophie and I moved here from London a few weeks ago for a fresh start and to get away from the city. You know, too many cars, not enough parking, pollution's a real problem there. It's overcrowded as well," she said distractedly, rattling on. She had never given the air quality or population of London a second thought. Clearly the cold saltwater and seeped into her brain and made her delirious. "Anyway, who are you? What's your name? And how come you're here? Are you stalking me?" she asked, shooting the questions at him like bullets.

The man chuckled. "Well, it's nice to meet you, Sophie from London. I'm Matthew and no, I'm not stalking you. I'm a university lecturer at Canterbury College but I live round here. I come here most days after work. Nothing clears my head like a good long walk on the beach."

"I can top that any day with a dive in the ocean," Sophie said drily. "Now if that doesn't wipe your head clean like a blank slate nothing will."

Matthew looked at her, an expression somewhere between amusement and perplexity shifting across his face. Sophie smiled weakly. This was not like her. She was not the joke cracking type and certainly not the absurd, appalling, word-vomit joke cracking type.

Sophie cleared her throat. "Um, I think I'm dry enough to change into my clothes now."

"Great!" Matthew said, smiling.

There was an uncomfortable pause while Sophie waited.

"Oh, right, I'll just wait outside if you want to change in here," Matthew said, looking away.

"Thanks," Sophie replied.

He stood outside the car, his back to her. Sophie watched him as she quickly changed into the barista clothes she had been wearing that morning. It had been a peculiar day to say the least, she thought. Time felt as if it had been stretched out and elongated like saltwater taffy. Her morning shift felt like light years away from her now, sitting in Matthew's car getting changed. She slipped her parker back on and then rapped on the window. Matthew turned around. Only then did she get a good look at his features which were lit up under the moonlight glow. He was decidedly handsome with a strong jaw, short dark hair and soft dark eyes. He had olive-toned skin and a wide smile. Sophie shook her head slightly. There was no point becoming infatuated by a handsome stranger when he must clearly think I'm bonkers, Sophie thought to herself.

Matthew opened the door. "There, feeling better now?"

"Yes, much better. Thank you so much, you've been so helpful."

"No problem at all. I like to rescue the odd damsel in distress every so often," he said in a mock smug tone.

"Odd certainly is the operative word," Sophie replied.

"Hey, I didn't mean it like that," Matthew said, nudging her playfully. "There's no denying it though, I haven't met many girls quite like you around here."

Sophie raised her eyebrows and nodded slowly. She wasn't quite sure if that was a compliment or whether he was simply alluding to how crazy she was.

"So can I do the chivalrous thing and drive you home, Sophie?" Matthew asked.

"Are you sure? I mean, I don't want you to go out of your way for me. Also I've got my bike tied to the rack there. I could just cycle home." Sophie's limbs were so stiff she knew she would not be able to sit on her bike let alone cycle all the way home.

"Which one is it? The boot of my car fits both mine and my daughter's bikes, so it will definitely fit yours," he replied.

Sophie gestured to the red bike. As Matthew got out to deal with the bike and the boot, Sophie felt a sinking feeling in the pit of her stomach. She didn't even know this man and yet she couldn't help but feel disappointed to hear he had a family and was probably happily married. The story she had begun weaving in her mind's eye quickly unravelled to reveal a useless pile of string.

He would go home today and tell his wife about this half drowned, mad girl he had fished out of the ocean. Perhaps they would have a good laugh about it while making a toast to their own well-balanced, perfect lives, clinking expensive glasses of sparkling wine, or hey, why not pop open a bottle of champagne for their mid-week, casual drink. He would go to bed proud of himself for doing a good deed, while she would go to bed feeling utterly mortified.

"There we go, done!" Matthew said, as he climbed back into the front seat. "So where do you live? I'll drop you there."

"Number 11 Edgeware Lane," Sophie replied. "If it's out of your way don't worry about it."

"No, that's about a fifteen-minute drive from my place. It's not out of my way at all," he said, smiling at her. "I've heard funny things about that place and its previous owner. Everyone around here has. They said he was crazy. Did you meet him when you bought the place?"

Sophie's brow furrowed. Almost everyone she had given that address to had some sort of cryptic comment to make. "No. I actually bought the place online. I only spoke to his agent once or twice over the phone. Everything else was done over email. I kind of wish I had met him now though. Everyone seems to have something to say about him," Sophie said thoughtfully.

"Wow, that's pretty brave of you. Buying a property just like that. You really wanted to get out of London then? The pollution and overcrowding were that bad, were they?"

Sophie glanced up at him but saw he was smiling.

"Well, to be honest, it wasn't London's poor air quality or the dense population that made me want to leave. It was more than that. It was personal circumstances. I don't know if I want to talk about it now though," she said, her voice lowering to almost a whisper.

"Oh, of course," Matthew said quickly, a look of concern flashing across his face. "I hope I didn't say anything to upset or offend you. I joke around a lot, but don't take anything I say too seriously."

"No, no. It's not that. You've been great. Really, thank you for everything today."

They sat in silence for the rest of the way back. Matthew cast sideways glances at her when he thought she wasn't looking. As he drove up to her house he said, "Look, if you need anything, anything at all, just give me a call." He took out a pocket notebook and scrawled his number on it. "You moved out here alone?" he asked, trying to sound casual.

"Yep, I did," Sophie replied. "Thanks for this. I'll message if I need anything."

"Or if you want to get a coffee sometime, maybe," he said, clearing his throat.

Sophie smiled. "Sure. And I guess I'll see you at the Acorn, Mr Large Cappuccino and Cheese Croissant. You see, I remember my regulars."

Matthew laughed. "Yes, I'll see you at the Acorn. Have a good night."

"Thanks again," Sophie said as she got out of the car with her soggy swimsuit and towel. She walked past the creaking gate swaying in the wind and up to her front door. She felt his eyes watching her. As she slipped inside the house, she heard his car drive away. A wave of uncertain, confused feelings rushed over her. She was too exhausted now to try and figure them out. What she needed was a best friend to confide in. Before she went to bed, she sent off a hurried text to Angie.

*Hey, Ang, how're you? I miss you. Listen, if you're thinking of taking a graphic designer's retreat any time soon, my place is open for visitors. Pls come visit soon if u can! We need to catch up, I have so much to tell u xxxxx*

Just as she hit the Send button, Sophie collapsed onto her bed, fully clothed, minus the shoes and parker jacket. She fell immediately into a deep, dreamless slumber.

# Chapter 10

## *Matthew*

Matthew parked his car absent-mindedly, his thoughts somewhere else entirely. What a strange experience that was and what a strange girl. He had been drawn to her the moment he saw her fumbling with coffees and change in the Acorn. But now he was even more intrigued.

He checked his phone and groaned inwardly before getting out of the car. There was a missed call from a foreign number. He was sure it was Clare getting in touch. Whatever it was about, it could wait until the morning. Clare had a knack at reaching out during the worst possible times. Matthew checked the area code of the number and saw it was from France. No surprise there, he thought to himself. She had always wanted to go to Paris and live a romantic life, swanning from one café to the next. He guessed she was living the life she had always wanted. She had certainly never been satisfied with her life in Canterbury with him and their daughter. It had been too drab and colourless for her. He had spent years running after her, trying to provide her with the extravagant lifestyle she so desired but in the end, he had inevitably failed. He was just a professor of philosophy who enjoyed spending time with his daughter and walks on the beach. That clearly had not been enough for Clare.

Matthew sighed, pocketing his phone as he walked into his house. It was fruitless trying to analyse where things went wrong with him and Clare. The only real regret that weighed heavily on him was that Heather was caught in the cross hairs of their messy relationship. Clare had wanted to whisk her away on an endless stream of adventures. In the end, Heather had said she wanted to stay in school and be with her father. It should have been a moment of triumph for Matthew, but instead he just felt dejected and hopeless. She had only recently stopped asking when Mummy was coming back. He still caught flashes of sadness and disappointment in her eyes when the other mothers came to the school to pick up their children or brought cookies in for the bake sale. It broke his heart knowing there was something missing in little Heather's life that he could neither fix nor fill.

Matthew entered the living room. The babysitter, Lauren, was watching a movie on his widescreen TV and greeted him with a wide smile.

"She's fast asleep in her room," Lauren said softly, not wanting to disturb the peace that had settled over the house like fairy dust. Lauren eyed Matthew and his damp jeans. "What happened to you?" she asked, eyebrows raised.

"Just a mishap at the beach," Matthew replied briefly. "Nothing to worry about."

"Right," Lauren said, refraining from prying further.

"Sorry you had to stay later than usual," Matthew said, paying her extra for her time.

"No worries, I don't mind at all," Lauren replied, as she headed to the door. Her gaze continued to flick between the damp, sea-smelling jeans and Matthew's face.

Matthew avoided her gaze as he walked her out. "Bye, then," he said, raising his hand to wave goodbye.

"See you," she said, before heading in the direction of the nearest bus stop.

Lauren was in her final year of A levels and was great with his daughter, Heather. Heather was always excited when Lauren was coming to babysit. Matthew tiptoed to his daughter's room and peeked through the gap in the door. She was sleeping like an angel, her soft brown curls framing her face. She was snuggled up with three of her favourite cuddly toys, a faint smile playing across her lips.

Matthew gently closed the door and headed for the kitchen. He took out a bottle of red wine and quickly prepared a microwave dinner. He poured himself a large glass and switched on the TV. He flicked through the channels without much interest. He switched from the news to a reality show about couples being stranded on an island and being tempted to cheat on one another. Finally he settled on a documentary about the Amazon rainforest which he listed to half-heartedly. The images of the rainforest kept slipping in and out of focus as his thoughts strayed from the poisonous dart frogs in the rainforest to more appealing thoughts of Sophie and the bizarre experience on the beach. Who was she and what was she trying to get away from? There was something about her that seemed wounded. Her soft brown eyes expressed a deep-seated pain. Matthew wanted to understand it, to understand her. He hoped she would call him. He wished he had asked for her number but that might have come across as too forward.

Either way, he knew she worked at The Acorn Café so he would be bound to run into her sooner or later. He couldn't help but wonder what would have happened to her if he had not been taking an evening stroll by the beach. He hadn't been planning on going for a walk there that evening. He had wanted to head home early so that he and Heather could have dinner together. That plan had fallen to pieces after a late work meeting with the rest of the faculty. It had been a meeting about revamping and improving their online portals and making them more accessible to the students. It had been one of those meetings where all the professors had groaned inwardly and slumped at the end of the hour, wondering how they could possibly cram this time-consuming project into their already full schedules.

Matthew had called Lauren and stayed late at the university trying to get a head start on the work which would be piled up and waiting for him the next day. Since he had already missed dinner with Heather, he figured he would take a walk by the beach. The sea air always helped him to relax and unwind after a long, tough day. He had been struck by how rough the sea was that evening, crashing down on the seashore with what felt like deliberate vengeance.

Matthew had been staring blankly at the swell of the incoming waves when he had spotted her. At first he thought he was imagining things but as he strained his eyes, he could make out a pair of flailing limbs that were quickly submerged by one tumultuous wave after another.

The poor girl had been half drowned and shivering all over. What had she been trying to do out there? She hadn't made much sense when he asked. Matthew was left baffled by her behaviour, with more questions than answers.

Just then he remembered the faded red bike in the boot of his car. He smiled, feeling a tenuous connection with her. He had already polished off two glasses of wine and was considering a third. As he would not be driving tonight, he decided he would drop the bike off first thing tomorrow morning on his way to work. He took out his notepad and scrawled a short message which he planned to put in the wire basket. He re-read the message and then crumpled it in a ball; too forward. He drafted another, only for it to meet the same end. Before he knew it, he was surrounded with a small pile of scrunched up wads of paper. He was being ridiculous, he thought. He just needed to write a short, snappy note that would hopefully catch her attention and persuade her to call him, rather than overanalysing it all. He felt he was back in school, writing a note to his crush in class. He took a long sip of wine, wrote a brief note, folded it in half and made a firm decision not to read it again until the next morning.

With a slightly giddy feeling he hadn't felt in a long time, he put his wine glass in the sink, changed into his pyjamas and climbed into bed. He lay there staring at the ceiling for some time before succumbing to sleep. His dreams were a swirling mash of freezing waves and notes he had written lying sodden on the beaches shore, being lapped up and spat back out again by the constant flowing waves. Sophie's silhouette was in the distance, far and unattainable as moonlight. One minute she was there, the next, gone.

# Chapter 11

## *Sophie*

*To Angie,*

*True friendship is like a rose that never dies,*

*It remains rooted in the earth's warm body of rocks and soil,*

*It endures through stormy hurricanes and the wind's painful cries,*

*When dawn breaks, the rose remains true and loyal.*


*As time dissolves the years, it will continue to grow,*

*From a mere rosebud to a blooming flower,*

*Seeds of happiness and joy it will sow,*

*Seeds of hidden depth, strength and power.*


*True friendship is like a rose that never dies,*

*To you its sweet fragrance does not lie,*

*The secret of the bond and beauty of the rose,*

*That is one only the best of friends can ever know.*

*Sophie*

Sophie woke to her alarm at 7:00 am and to a friendly text from Angie. She read the message through sleepy eyes.

*Soph! Omg, that is exactly what I need! Let's plan it. If you're not busy next weekend I can drive down on Friday and stay a couple of days? How does that sound? Eeeek, so excited! Miss u more, hun xxx*

It was Thursday today. That meant she would only have to wait a week. She quickly dashed off a response to Angie.

*Next Friday sounds perfect! Can't wait! PS bring wine ;)*

Smiling to herself, she stumbled out of bed. She noticed the sheets were gritty from sand and her barista clothes were all wrinkled.

"Damn it!" she whispered to herself. She had an 8:00 am–12:00 pm shift today. She quickly sifted through her closet in search of her spare purple top with the Acorn logo that Luke had given her. She checked the laundry basket. Sure enough, crumpled under heaps of clothes, was the spare Acorn top.

"Ugh, of course," she muttered furiously. She grabbed the pile of clothes smothering the spare shirt and threw them on the floor. She gave the shirt a shake but instantly knew she couldn't wear it. It felt and smelled damp. She threw the useless shirt on the floor. It was already 7:15 am and Sophie knew she would be late if she kept dithering. Abandoning the dirty pile of laundry carpeting the remainder of empty space on the floor, Sophie flew downstairs to have a quick shower. She smelt of sweat, salt and the sea.

She did her best to clean herself under the cold weak drizzle of her shower. To save time, she grabbed her toothbrush and toothpaste from the sink, which was a mere step away from the shower, and brushed her teeth aggressively while washing out the soapy shampoo suds from her hair. As she was rinsing her hair, she suddenly felt a rush of heat from the shower. She had never had more than a lukewarm shower at best in this house. The heat was unusual. She welcomed the sudden warmth, allowing it to sink into her muscles and relax her. She closed her eyes and continued to massage her hair. A strange heaviness began to spread through her body, starting at the top of her head and spilling downwards through her veins. Her hands suddenly felt too heavy and she let them rest at her sides. She opened her eyes slowly and looked down.

Her coffee-coloured hands had balls of slime and seaweed oozing between the fingers. Shock coursed through Sophie as she continued to stare dumbfounded. Those weren't her hands. Where had the slime come from? Sophie was about to scream but the muscles in her jaw were frozen. She couldn't move. She started shivering uncontrollably as the green slimy seaweed started shifting, changing colour. Soon it was no longer seaweed at all. Sophie's heart was racing furiously. The water was hot, too hot. It scalded her skin, burning her to her very core. The steam whipped around her, blurring her vision. Fingers of blood slid down her arms from where the lumps of seaweed had been. Within seconds, the shower tray was a pool of thick, scarlet blood. Sophie tried to fight against the heavy, sluggish feeling overcoming her. She lifted her head. A scream remained lodged in the back of her throat. She caught her reflection in the pane of the glass shower. Someone else's eyes stared back at her. No longer could she see her warm, brown, doe-like eyes. They had been replaced with deep blue eyes glittering malevolently back at her.

With all the strength she could muster, she raised her fists and slammed them against the glass, making it quiver, threatening to shatter. Sophie stared at the glass. Her haunted eyes, filled with fear, stared back at her. She looked down. There was nothing there, no blood, no seaweed. Her hands were her own again. There was no hint of mist or steam. The water had turned icy cold.

With tears in her eyes, she turned off the shower and grabbed a towel. Her hands were shaking so badly she struggled to wrap it around her body. There's nothing there, there's nothing there, she repeated to herself. Be reasonable, Sophie, you can see with your own eyes, there's nothing except an empty, grotty little shower.

She ran upstairs, trying to get as far away from the creepy bathroom as she could. She then saw what time it was. She felt as if she had been in the shower for an eternity, stuck in limbo between a nightmare and reality. When she looked at her watch, however, she saw she had only been in the shower for no more than five minutes.

Sophie tried to focus her mind on what she still had to do to make herself presentable for the day. She had to get dressed and get ready for work. In an attempt to refocus her scattered brain, she strode over to the wardrobe and fumbled about with her clothes. She pulled on a clean pair of black pants and a pink-collared jersey top, the closest match she could find to the purple Acorn one. After a five-minute blow-dry, she quickly slapped on some mascara and a berry tone lipstick. She couldn't manage more make-up than that with her quivering hands. She checked her watch, her heart still pounding. It was 7:46 am. She dashed downstairs, realising with a sense of dread that her bike was still in Matthew's car. She could always take her car but then there would be the issue of trying to find somewhere to park and she would be even later.

As she left the house and locked up, to her surprise she saw the faded, somewhat dingy red bike perched right outside her door. There was a note fluttering gently in the wire basket.

*Thought you might need this ;)* it read, in Matthew's slanted handwriting.

A warm glow kindled inside her as she read the short, simple note. She stared at it for a moment, enjoying the warm sensation spreading throughout her body and the smile dancing on her lips. It was just what she needed to help her recalibrate, settling her mind and body. Her watch glinted in the sunlight, reminding her she was already late. Hopping on her bike, she cycled as fast as she could to The Acorn Café. Putting all thoughts of the strange bathroom incident aside, she instead let her mind drift to more pleasant thoughts of Matthew with his dark eyes and slanted smile.

Despite her best efforts, she arrived at 8:14 am, a whole fourteen minutes late. As it was just her luck, she saw Luke behind the bar, chatting to a customer. He caught her eye as she slunk in.

"Morning, sunshine. Late start?" he said in a friendly tone.

At least he wasn't mad with her, Sophie thought. "Don't be mad," Sophie said, shrugging off her coat. "Do you have a spare Acorn top I can wear today," she said, glancing down and scrunching up her face at the offending pink shirt she was wearing.

"Hmm, not sure if I have one your size, Parker. You know what, I'll let you off today. Not sure if you noticed the décor around here, but everything is a bit mixy matchy. You blend in pretty well," he said, smiling at her.

"Thank you! I'll wash the other tops tonight and make sure they're good to go for my next shift," Sophie promised.

"No worries. That's a nice colour," Luke said, gesturing at her top. "That colour suits you."

Sophie glanced up and smiled, feeling slightly unsure how to respond. Fortunately a particularly harried customer arrived.

"I'll deal with this," she said quietly to Luke who smiled and stepped back from the bar.

"I'll be downstairs if you need me," he replied, descending the stairs to the basement.

Sophie took orders and served coffee, all the while keeping an eye out for a tall, handsome university professor to walk through the door.

"Waiting for someone?" Jess asked innocently, noticing Sophie's head snap up every time somebody came through the door.

"Oh, nope, not really. Just a little distracted today, I guess," Sophie replied.

"I see," Jess said, unconvinced. "Didn't sleep well last night? You know, I've got this new concealer if you want to try it?" she added, eyeing the dark circles around Sophie's eyes.

Sophie smiled. "No, I stayed up pretty late yesterday but I'm all right, thanks." At that moment the door opened, and her eyes instinctively flitted towards it.

"If you let me know who you're waiting for, I could help keep lookout. I have your back, you have mine," she said, winking. Sophie sensed Jess loved a good gossip.

"Right," Sophie said, letting out a strained laugh.

"Just a thought," Jess said, shrugging her shoulders.

At 12:20 pm, Sophie figured she'd made up her late time well enough, slipped off her apron and was out the door. She couldn't help but feel disappointed. It felt tangible, as if weights of disappointment and fatigue were tied to her legs and arms. She tried to shake it off by telling herself she was being ridiculous. He was married, settled and happy, what could he possibly want with a train wreck like her? And what about Dan? How could she do this to him? It had only been seven months since he had passed away. Before that, they had been together for nearly six years. How could she even think of wiping out six years of happiness, comfort and security for a brief encounter with a stranger? She felt furious with herself and her straying, unfaithful feelings. The imaginary weights strapped to her limbs seemed to multiply in heaviness.

She felt she was being dragged downwards into the earth as she slowly shuffled along the high street. Gravity seemed to be working extra hard today. It was as if she had aged several decades in a matter of seconds. Her shoulders drooped and her eyes felt weary. She watched her feet moving mechanically, one foot placed in front of the other, the motion out of her control. A chilling ache spread through her bones, gnawing away at her insides. All she wanted was to curl up on the hard floor beneath her and shrivel away like a dying autumn leaf disintegrating into the wind, any trace of its memory whisked swiftly into nature's cavernous well of oblivion.

"Hey there, is that you, Sophie?" a loud, friendly voice called. It sounded like a distant echo to Sophie's ears, as if she and the voice were separated by a transparent film, existing in two different universes. Nonetheless, it hauled Sophie out of her reverie. She looked up to see Georgey's friendly, smiling face peering into hers.

"You don't look well, love," Georgey said, concerned. "Are you ok?"

"Yeah, I'm all right. Just didn't sleep too well last night."

Georgey raised a sceptical eyebrow. "Come join me and Tilly here for a spot of lunch," she said, gesturing at a red-haired woman with long red nails. "You look like you need a decent meal. Maybe a drink or two. Or hell, maybe the whole bottle!"

Tilly nodded, clearly in agreement with the final statement.

"Oh, I don't want to disturb you two or get in the way of anything," Sophie quickly responded, not sure if she could face lunch and talking with other human beings.

"Don't be a silly sausage, you're coming to lunch with us," Tilly exclaimed loudly.

Something told Sophie it was going to be a loud lunch, but she smiled and nodded in acquiescence.

"We were just debating where to go," Georgey said, filling her in on missed conversation. "How about The Smugglers' Cove? They do the best fish and chips round here!"

"Yeah, the Cove sounds good to me," Tilly replied.

"Well, I'm always a fan of fish and chips," Sophie said, joining in.

"Perfect. To the Cove. We like you already, Sophie. Someone who's not picky about their food is a keeper in my books." Georgey laughed. "Can't be dealing with vegetarians and vegans and pescatarians and I-only-eat-free-range-cardboard-arians." Georgey rolled her eyes as Tilly chortled.

"Booze and food. That's all you need for a good life," Tilly stated with a philosophical bow of her head.

"Where are your two sets of double trouble today?" Sophie asked, remembering the four sandy-haired boys from the café.

"Oh, it's Daddy's day today. He works four days a week. So one day a week he drops the four-year-olds off at school and takes the toddlers out so that Mummy can have some time to feel like a normal human being again," she said, laughing.

"Ugh, wish I had such a considerate hubby," Tilly said, rolling her eyes. "Both my girls are at school now, but I've got about an hour and a bit before I have to do the school run."

"Well, let's get a move on then. I'm starving," Georgey said, breaking into a brisk stride.

"Hey, doll, not so fast. You may not be a fan of heels but I'm wearing my Tory Burch boots today," Tilly said, clicking after them.

Georgey rolled her eyes affectionately. "You have to excuse Miss Fashionista there, always bringing up the rear."

"Well, not everyone is blessed with your fabulous height, now, are they, George. Although, this one's actually pretty tall and slim actually," Tilly said, gesturing at Sophie. "You lucky ducks!"

Sophie smiled. "Well, I don't think I'm half as glamorous as you are!" Sophie glanced at Tilly's luscious red hair tied up in a sleek ponytail, long lash extensions and swinging hoops dangling from her ears. She looked like she had stepped out of the glossy pages of a magazine.

"Oh, she's a flatterer! Thank you, dear," Tilly said, beaming from ear to ear. "Can we keep her?" she asked, bouncing her perfectly plucked, arched eyebrows at Georgey.

"Don't give this one too many compliments, they go straight to her head," Georgey said in a loud whisper to Sophie, earning her an elbow in the ribs from Tilly.

They entered the restaurant and chose a comfortable table by the window. It was a bright, cold day. The sun was streaming in, illuminating the white tablecloth and bouncing off a glass vase of freshly picked flowers.

"I think we're ready to order," Georgey said, waving the menu at one of the waiters.

None of them had even opened the menus yet.

"Three of your best fish and chips, please," she said, nodding at Tilly who was picking at a chipped nail and at Sophie who nodded in agreement. She liked letting Georgey take control. She did not feel up to making any decisions today, even if it was something as simple as ordering food.

"Oh, and a bottle of red," she said in a melodramatic tone to the waiter.

"Sure thing," the waiter said with a smile, gathering up the unopened menus.

"Nice choice, but I can only have a small one," Tilly said. "Can't be picking up my girls sloshed now, can I?" she said with a giggle. "Now wouldn't that give the other mums something to gossip about!"

"Ugh, they can talk all they like! You never need take any notice of them!" Georgey said defiantly.

"You wait till you have kids, Sophie. You'll be fending off the judgement from all sides. I just don't understand why mums can't just stick together," Georgey said, rolling her eyes.

"Women," Tilly said, pursing her lips. "Can't trust a damned one of them."

"I'll drink to that," Georgey said as the waiter poured the wine into the extremely large glasses set on the table.

"Cheers to the only bearable women in Dover," Tilly said, as they clinked glasses.

Sophie drank deeply. She was enjoying the company, the easy banter, relaxed setting and delicious wine. She sat back in her chair and laughed along with their jokes and tucked into the food once it arrived. It probably was one of the best fish and chip meals she had ever had.

"Right, girlies, that's me off," Tilly said, as she drained her glass and threw some cash on the table. "Not sure how much it is but I'm sure that will cover it. Got to go get my lovies!"

"See you, give them big kisses from me," Georgey said, waving goodbye with the wine glass she was holding, nearly spilling half its contents on to the pearly white tablecloth.

"It was great meeting you," Sophie said, smiling.

"You too, darling! Hope to see more of you," Tilly said, as she sashayed off in her clinking heels.

"Well, let's get the bill then, shall we?" Georgey said, flagging down the waiter. "I bet she's short-changed us," Georgey added, gesturing to the door in feigned annoyance. "You know, me and Till go way back. We first met in primary school, can you believe it!"

"Wow, that's amazing! I wish I had friends I went that far back with. What's Tilly short for?" Sophie asked curiously.

Georgey let out a snort of laughter. "It's short for Mathilda, believe it or not! Swear you will never tell her I told you! She tells everyone it's Tilly on her birth certificate. Neither of us can stand our full names." She chortled. "You're lucky, your parents gave you a good one!"

"I never really thought about it, I guess," Sophie replied.

"You didn't have to," Georgey replied. They paid the bill and tumbled out into the high street. "What do you say we get our nails done? I know a great nail bar just down the road and it's not too pricey!"

Sophie had nothing else to do for the rest of the day and felt like being a little spontaneous. "Yes, why not?"

They linked arms and were giggling like little schoolgirls as they crossed the road and headed to the nail salon. Sophie had her nails painted a pale delicate shade of pink which had a gold reflection when caught in the light. Georgey went for fluorescent orange.

"I could stop traffic with these nails," Georgey said, pleased with the finished result. "Could come in handy when I'm running late!"

Sophie laughed and looked over her shoulder admiringly. "Absolutely gorgeous!"

She liked Georgey's big, bold character. It was so unlike her own. Perhaps that was the appeal.

As they walked together, Sophie remembered her first day exploring the high street. "Hey, isn't there a cute little café here somewhere? I saw it on my first day. It was called Tea and Biscuits, or something," Sophie said.

"Tea and Biscuits?" Georgey replied, brow furrowed. "Nope, don't think so, darling. I would remember such a name."

"Are you sure?" Sophie asked, slightly confused. "It was right around this corner. It has an old-fashioned theme, like you were entering a time capsule."

"I know this place like the back of my hand," Georgey replied. They turned the corner and sure enough, there was no Tea and Biscuits café in sight. Slightly down the road was an off licence, and on the other side was a post office, but no old-fashioned café.

"See, no Tea and Biscuits here, darling. You'll have to get your cuppa elsewhere," Georgey said, smiling.

Sophie nodded, feeling disconcerted. She could see the place in her mind's eye. It had been right there, opposite the post office. She could see the sign with the teacup and biscuit swaying gently in the breeze. She couldn't have imagined it, could she? How strange.

Georgey's voice cut through her thoughts. "You know, I've loved our girly day out, but I've just got to see my boys! I think I'm going to meet Jim at the ice cream store down the road. Apparently they're all in there, probably a sticky mess by now. They may drive me insane, but I can't go a day without them."

"Of course, like I said before, you have a gorgeous family!" Sophie replied, hugging her goodbye.

"Come along if you want. You can meet Jim," Georgey said warmly.

"No, it's ok. I've got to start heading home myself. But let's do this again sometime. I had so much fun with you guys!"

"For sure, doll! See you around. You take care of yourself!"

Sophie was slightly wobbly on her bike as she rode home. She checked her watch as she let her bike clatter to the ground in the front garden. It was 5:00 pm. She looked at the small, unassuming cottage for a moment before walking up the pathway to the main door. It looked as if a dark curtain had been draped over it, engulfing it in folds of shadow and pockets of dim, ghostly light. An odd feeling penetrated her skin and entered her very bones as she unlocked the door. She felt like the caretaker, not the owner.

Although she had cleaned every corner of the house, dotted her knick-knacks around it and hung up her pictures, it still, somehow, was unfamiliar to her. She thought back to the strange man with lilac eyes. Maybe this was all his fault. Perhaps this was just a self-fulfilling prophecy since he had sown seeds of doubt in her mind before she had even arrived at her new home. After all, this house was meant for her. She had been certain of it the second the picture popped up on her laptop. Home. It had called out to her. This is home.

As she entered, she dumped her bag and coat on the bannister. She was about to dash upstairs to do the laundry when she heard the floorboards creak slowly overhead, as if someone was stepping gently on them, trying not to be overheard. She froze. She heard one more creak, and then there was nothing but silence. She had heard creaking floorboards the very first night she had spent here but she hadn't heard it since. Sophie felt rooted to the floor. She tried to fight the wave of nausea churning in the pit of her stomach. She didn't want to go upstairs. A stray animal could have made its way into her house by accident, she told herself. She gently picked up a saucepan that was lying on the drying rack. The now familiar sense of fear was pulsating through her veins. She edged up the stairs slowly. Each creaking floorboard grated on her nerves. The wine swirling in her stomach made her feel vaguely sick. Her hands were shaking as she gripped the saucepan so tightly her knuckles turned white.

Once on the landing she stood facing her bedroom door which was closed. She was sure she had left it open when she made her mad dash to work earlier that day. Of course she could be mistaken. Her memory seemed to be playing tricks on her in this house. As she stared at the door she felt a current of energy radiating through the cracks, trying to burst free. As if in slow motion, she crept closer, sensing a presence on the other side. Barely able to breathe, she pushed it open, holding the saucepan up high. She let out a scream as a dark shadowy figure flew past her, nearly knocking her off her feet and causing her to drop the saucepan. Only when she heard the loud, angry caw of the bird did she realise it was a raven. She ran downstairs and flung the front door open. It flew out, huge wings flapping wildly. Sophie's breath came in ragged gulps. She was shaking all over.

"Dumb bird!" she yelled after it. "How the hell did you get in here?" she said more quietly to herself. She quickly went around checking all the windows and making sure the latches were secure. Not one of them had been opened. Bizarre, Sophie thought to herself. Either way, at least there was no intruder.

Sophie's attention was drawn to the china doll she had bought when she moved in. She had kept it perched on a chair in the corner of her room as a little decorative piece. She was certain she had never moved it, just left her sitting, staring blankly into space. The doll was not on the chair. Instead she was sitting bolt upright on the bed, one arm raised above her head, the other extended in front of her, as if someone had been playing with her and left her mid-game. Sophie stared. How did the doll get there? Sophie tried to imagine the different possibilities. Perhaps the bird had knocked it over with its massive wings. But even then, the doll would be on the floor, not propped up on the bed. Sophie shut the door slowly, the doll's glassy gaze sending chills down her spine.

When in doubt, make a cup of tea, Sophie thought to herself. She needed a soothing cup of milky tea for her poor frayed nerves and racing heart. None of this made any sense. Nothing in this house seemed to abide by the laws of nature, the dictates of reality. Sophie felt like Alice in Wonderland in this house. She felt as if she had been swallowed up by a gaping rabbit hole and was surrounded by elusive figments of her imagination. It was an endless tunnel of insanity, and Sophie couldn't make head or tail of it. The only difference between her and Alice was that she, Sophie, wasn't able to wake up.

She nestled into the couch and sipped her tea, taking deep breaths and exhaling slowly. Her grief counsellor would be happy to hear she was keeping up her breathing exercises, Sophie thought to herself. She switched on the TV and flicked through the channels. She settled on a documentary mysteriously called *The Curse on the Gypsies*. It looked like an old documentary. Her curiosity about the history of the town she now called home had been piqued ever since Luke had told her that short, enigmatic tale about the band of travelling gypsies and the coffee shop all those years ago. It looked like the documentary had only just started.

Black-and-white images of forlorn, dirty children dressed in rags flashed on the screen. The narrator began by introducing the gypsies as an ancient culture of unknown origin. They were a culture which evaded proper scrutiny. Their history was a web of secrecy and shadows. As gypsies didn't keep written records, everything that was known about them was through the eyes of outside observers.

Sophie was already gripped. The lilting, melancholy music that played in the background and the calm narrator's voice drew her in. She leaned forward, as if by moving closer to the screen she could somehow melt into a faraway, forgotten world. The narrator continued. Based on linguistic investigation, scholars had found many similarities between Romani, the gypsy language, and Sanskrit, indicating that gypsies were of Indian origin. One theory posited was that the gypsies were a lost band of travelling musicians. It is said that in an epic historical poem in *The Persian Book of Kings* that the Shah of Persia had been gifted thousands of entertainers and musicians, the gypsies, in the year 439 AD. Other theories claim they were warriors trying to push the Muslims out of India. A black-and-white battle scene flickered on the screen. Men precariously balanced on elephants threw sharp spears down at their enemies. The trumpeting of elephants and battle cries raged around Sophie, filling her ears. Men with sharp scythes and shields ran on foot or charged on horses across fields and became a confused muddle of violence. Atmospheric music with steady drums played in the background.

The gypsies were persecuted and enslaved in medieval times, an important scholar on the subject was saying. In order to escape this ill fate, in the 1300s they adopted false identities and pretended to be travelling religious pilgrims from Little Egypt. A plethora of supposed princes, dukes and counts led these pilgrims with signed imperial letters allowing them safe conduct. For a while, this scheme worked. They coexisted with their host countries and peoples, providing entertainment, fortune-telling and herbal medicines in exchange for food and alms. However, in the middle of the 16th century, in Europe the tide turned yet again against the gypsies.

Religion gripped society, and where light was associated with purity, the gypsies' dark looks and black eyes allied them with sin and the Devil. Once again they were persecuted. In 1547 King Edward VI of England had gypsies branded with a V sign and subsequently enslaved for two years. If they escaped and were caught, they faced a lifetime's enslavement.

And yet, with the Industrial Revolution, the tide of resentment ebbed, to be replaced by a new wave of curiosity. In Dickensian England, life was dark, gloomy and punishing. The gypsies offered an alternative life, a bright life, brimming with spontaneity, excitement and colour. They were not trapped by the same boundaries as everyone else. At the same time the idea of the noble savage rippled through literary and philosophical circles, its influence filtering down to the masses.

Sophie watched with fascination. Scenes of gypsy women wearing ruffled skirts and swirling around campfires drew her mind to the portraits in The Acorn Café. The music was enthralling. Imperceptibly her mind started to wander, and her eyelids fluttered heavily. The enchanting music softly lulled her to sleep.

Sophie woke with a start. She was shivering. It was dark outside and the programme about the gypsies had ended. Disoriented, Sophie reached for the remote and switched off the TV. To her shock, when she breathed out a cloud of mist swirled in front of her. Sophie stiffly got up and stumbled to the radiators.

"Nooo," she groaned inwardly. They were ice cold and she had no idea how to fix them. Sophie glanced at her watch. It was 2:06 am. She was surprised at how long she had slept. Well, it will just have to wait until tomorrow, Sophie thought to herself. She wrapped herself in the blanket that was lying on the couch and rubbed her hands together in an attempt to get warm. Sophie glanced out the window. The night was intimidating, a wall of darkness, pressing in on all sides of the house. She quickly drew the curtains shut. She was so cold her teeth chattered.

It was then that she heard it. It was so soft and gentle at first that she thought it was a figment of her whimsical imagination. The doleful notes of a flute floated in the air, encircling her. At first Sophie couldn't move. The song was so mournful she felt tears well up inexplicably in her eyes. She stared into nothingness, letting the music seep into her bones. It was a song of the silvery moon and gentle wind, of night and the smattering of stars tucked in their bed of the deep black velvet above. A soft carpet of stars. It was a song of secrets buried deep within the ancient earth, of the stirrings of life. Sophie felt lost in the melody. The sturdy walls of time seemed to crumble and disintegrate around her, leaving plumes of sparkling dust where they fell.

The past, present and future meshed together, bleeding into one eternity. It was a song of loss. Time's eternal theme. The one constant. Sophie opened her eyes with a start when she felt a cool tear trickle down her cheek. She sniffed, unsure of what she was crying over. For once, she knew she was not crying about Dan. This pain was greater than her and her memories. It suffused her soul, creeping into every molecule of her body. It was a collective pain, the pain of the earth's broken, accursed souls.

Sophie needed to find out who was playing this haunting music. It sounded as if it was coming from the garden. Barefoot, she padded to the front door and went outside. It was a still night with the merest hint of the wind whispering in the background. It was warmer outside than within the cold uninviting walls of the cottage. Moonlight flooded her front garden, yielding no mystery flute player. The music was waning but could still be heard through the trees, bushes and grass as if united with the patchwork quilt of air around her.

She stepped out onto the cold, wet grass. Icy dew drops clung to her feet as she trod lightly towards the willow tree. Its vines were swaying gently to and fro, almost hypnotic. They morphed between dark green, grey and silver hues, catching the moonlight before returning to the shadows once more. Sophie remained rooted to the earth as she stared up at the massive willow towering over her. She breathed in a sense of comfort and security from its timeless presence. Without knowing why, she parted the locks of the willow and reached her hand inside to touch the trunk. She felt its rough surface under her pale skin. She felt a surge of energy, life and vitality flow through her. Standing next to the tree, she felt connected to something bigger than she was. When she opened her eyes she realised the music was gone. There were no stirrings around her. Even the usually violent waves below were restrained and soundless. Sophie turned and walked slowly back to her cottage, a strange feeling of love and affection for the place blossoming within her. She walked upstairs to bed in a trance-like state, still feeling more than hearing the music drift through her mind. That night she slept well, dreaming of gypsies dancing slowly to the sorrowful flute music she was certain she had heard. They swayed to and fro like the vine leaves of the willow, their dark hair and long scarves glittering in the moonlight before being cast into the shadows once more.

When Sophie woke up it was 11:30 am. She had not set an alarm as she did not have work that day. She woke up feeling at peace with the world. She felt as if there were an aura of tranquillity bathing her, gently caressing her troubled soul. Sophie got up and started getting ready for the day. She didn't have any plans in particular. She could do anything she wanted, go wherever she pleased. As she brushed past the radiator in her room, she jumped back, surprised. It was no longer ice cold but its regular, warm working self. Sophie checked the downstairs radiators and to her relief found them all working like clockwork. Thank goodness I don't need to deal with any broken radiators and call in any repairs people, Sophie thought to herself, pleased.

She decided she would go to the beach. There would be no swimming this time though. She had checked the weather. It was supposed to be cold and sunny all day with an impending storm in the evening. She decided to make the most of the good weather and hopped on her bike to head to the beach. She tried not to think of potentially seeing her professor friend who apparently liked to go there every day to clear his mind. She hadn't seen him yesterday at the coffee shop. Would she miss him again today? Perhaps he never actually went to the beach to clear his head and had indeed been following her. On the other hand, Sophie was the one feeling kind of stalker-ish, trying to predict his whereabouts and movements based on her sparse knowledge of his schedule.

Sophie still had his number scrunched up in her bag. She could be a mature adult and just give him a call or send him a text rather than dwell on what he may or may not be doing. Sophie shook her head, as if by doing so she could shake off any thoughts of him and cast them into the open air around her. She wanted to expel any worries or stresses and send them out into the universe so that she could be free of them forever. She was sure, however, that like a boomerang they would just come flying back at full pelt and hit her with all maximum force. What was it her grief counsellor had told her, something about confronting her feelings rather than running away from them? She had said that geographical solutions were rarely the equivalent to psychological solutions, and that running off to Dover wouldn't help her escape the inner workings of her own mind, which was what she was really trying to run away from.

Sophie pondered this. She wasn't sure if she agreed. She knew she had to confront her feelings, but the change, the solitude had been good for Sophie. She wasn't just sitting at home crying herself to sleep every night. Being on her own had forced her into action, propelled her into momentum. It had forced her to engage in real life again and into making decisions that she would have let slide had her parents been there to fix everything for her.

Sophie parked her bike and chained it to a post. It was almost November and the cold stung her face. Nonetheless, she laid out her towel and took a seat on the rocky shore. She pulled out the banana and BLT she had packed. Sophie had not brought her swimsuit this time as she had no intention of semi-drowning herself again. She merely sat and watched the birds circulating above probably hoping they could snag some of her BLT. She dug one of her hands into the rocky shore feeling the smooth cold pebbles between her fingers.

When she finished her lunch, she got up and started to meander slowly along the coastline, breathing in the scent of the beach. Her feet made a satisfying crunching noise as she stepped on crushed shells and rocks below. She climbed up a set of rocks that formed a separation in the beach. She breathed heavily as she clutched onto the cool stones, trying not to lose her balance. Nestling her hands and feet into the little ridges, she made her way to the top. From this vantage point, if she looked straight ahead, the only thing she could see was miles and miles of ocean stretching out beneath her. A wave splashed the rock, spraying her face with foam. Sophie smiled, enjoying the sensation. The wind cut past her, sending ripples shivering through the little puddles between the rocks. Sophie watched as a tiny crab sidled out from the puddle and wedged itself into a crevice in the rocks. She watched this scene repeat itself with several different puddles and several different crabs. They didn't seem to mind her presence. They simply carried on their business for the day.

Her gaze shifted from the crabs to the expansive horizon stretching out in front of her. She didn't know how long she sat there, transfixed by the subtle movements and shifts in the water, wondering if all the answers she sought were somewhere wedged between the sea and sky in some unknowable land, just out of reach.

Sophie only realised how late it was when thunderous, dark clouds started rolling in, breaking up the bright blue haze. The storm must be coming early, Sophie thought to herself. The dark, swollen clouds were moving towards her fast. At first she was enthralled by the way they swept over the sky, casting foreboding black patches of shadow over the sea. They reminded her of illustrations out of a dark fairy tale, full of poison and rage. In a storybook these black clouds would have been sent by some wrathful God or evil sorcerer. It was only when she felt the first drops of rain that she knew she had to move. These rocks would get slippery in no time and she didn't want to be putting herself in danger again, especially since it looked as if her knight in shining armour had taken the day off. She had been peeping out of the corner of her eye at the few passers-by, but there was no tall, dark, handsome professor among them.

She managed to make it to the bottom of the rocks, slipping only once tearing her jeans and grazing her knee slightly. The rain was coming down harder now, thick droplets hitting her face. Sophie pulled her coat closer around her as she ran to her bike. By the time she had started cycling back, the rain was pouring down furiously, lashing her face and bare hands. Sophie's teeth were chattering as she tried to blink away the water dripping into her eyes. So much for an idyllic cycle home, she thought to herself. The roads were slippery, splattered with deep puddles. The rain continued to hammer Sophie while thunder rumbled menacingly in the background. Sophie was shocked to see a bolt of lightning flash what felt like right in front of her, a sharp, electric dagger cutting the sky into ribbons. The thunder continued to roll and more daggers of light unsheathed themselves, stabbing the earth below in a wild murderous rage.

Sophie pedalled harder, her muscles aching. Just then, a car whooshed past her, causing half the contents of a deep murky puddle to drench her from head to toe. Sophie wobbled on her bike trying to keep her balance. Everything around her felt surreal, as if she was pedalling deeper into a ghoulish nightmare. The landscape had turned into a blur. She felt she was in a watercolour painting where all the colours were melting off the canvas, dripping into a wishy-washy muddy swirl of confusion. She cycled past the familiar landmarks. She imagined the lettering for The Hope Inn sign sliding down, letters dripping onto the sodden ground. The cemetery was colourless. In her mind's eyes she saw lightening splitting each tombstone, sending sharp grey shards scattering in every direction. The pub was deserted and devoid of life, an empty shell. No more clinking glasses and laughter permeating the air. And the hills were empty expanses of spongy earth, soaking up heaven's tears. Nothing had ever looked lonelier or more desolate to Sophie.

She felt as if she had been pedalling for ages and yet time was warped, dragging her backwards. She pedalled furiously, feeling like she was getting nowhere, trapped in a torrential vortex, stuck in the eye of the storm. She couldn't focus on where she was. She let her thinking mind go and forced her stiff muscles to lead the way.

Somehow Sophie found herself in her garden. She threw her bike to one side and ran into the cottage. She was soaked. Sophie immediately peeled off her dripping clothes, leaving them in a sodden pile by the door. She dashed into the bathroom and grabbed one of her old, rough towels and dried herself off. She felt the warmth seep back into her skin. The rain continued to pound the roof and walls of her house. It sounded louder than Sophie would have expected, a continuing beat, like the drums of an impending war. It hammered so hard Sophie was scared the rain, like ricocheting bullets, would pierce the very roof. The windows rattled in their frames as the wind pushed violently against them, demanding to be let in. Sophie changed into dry clothes and towel-dried her hair. She made herself a very large mug of steaming tea and took out some digestives from the cupboard.

She then noticed movement. A string of ants were marching from an unknown crack, heading towards the gap under the back door. Sophie watched them, surprised.

Surely in a storm like this the ants would want to stay inside. Sophie shook her head. She was not an expert on ant behaviour. She did, however, have to call an exterminator. There weren't as many ants as last time but then, Sophie was not sure if she was even remembering "last time" correctly. It had been so strange, and the memory already had a blurry dreamlike quality to it. She had barely been sleeping back then and was prone to an overactive imagination.

She continued to watch the thin trail of ants as they continued on their journey. Sophie picked up the landline to dial the number for an exterminator in town. There was no dial tone. She jabbed randomly at numbers, but nothing happened. The storm must have messed something up, Sophie thought, irritated. She would just call them from her mobile. She rang their offices. The line crackled and hung up several times. Eventually, however, she got through and was able to make an appointment for the next day after her Acorn shift.

Somewhat relieved, Sophie sat back and wrapped herself in an old but favourite blanket of hers. Something about this storm didn't feel normal to her. It was too loud, the crashing felt almost intentional, as if nature was trying to batter her house to the ground. The wind was howling feverishly outside. A particularly strong gust rattled the upstairs windows. It sounded like thousands of chattering teeth, rattling with fear and cold. Sophie felt uneasy. She didn't want to be alone in this house on a stormy night. She went to the kitchen and glanced out the window facing Isabelle's house. She couldn't see much through the impenetrable wall of rain, but she could make out blurry lights in the house. Isabelle must be home enduring the same things she was.

Well, Sophie was going to be stuck inside for the entire evening by the looks of it. She decided she would try and make the most of it. She wandered over to her bookshelf crammed with books, hoping to find one to take her mind off things. She stroked their spines, reading the titles, taking her time deciding which one to read. One of the books caught her eye. It was the book she had bought from the Peacocks' Lair several weeks ago, *An All-Encompassing History of the Cliffs*. Sophie eyed it, flipping it over in her hands. Perhaps it was a good idea to read up on the history of the place she now lived in. It didn't promise to be a particularly exciting read. In fact, it looked like it was written in dull, factual prose, but she thought she would give it a go.

She flipped the pages, breathing in the scent of the old paper. Suddenly, a card slipped out. Intrigued, Sophie bent down and picked it up off the floor. When she had flipped through the book in the shop nothing had fallen out. Perhaps the card had been wedged in. It was lying on the floor face down. Sophie turned it so that it was facing her.

On the card was an old-fashioned-looking illustration of a young man carrying a white rose in one hand and a stick with a bag knotted to it in the other hand. His clothes were ragged and hung off his skeletal frame. He was standing on the precipice of a cliff, behind which were either aggressive-looking waves or spiky bluish mountains. He appeared oblivious to the little white dog barking at his feet. Sophie's eyes drifted down to the words written in spidery capitals underneath the illustration: **THE FOOL**. She rubbed the card. It felt dusty beneath her fingertips. What was this card and where did it come from? She sat down and examined it more closely. It looked and felt old. It had an other-worldly smell to it, Sophie thought, as she brought the card up to the tip of her nose. The smell reminded her of a collection of old classic novels she had once bought for a ridiculously cheap price at a charity shop. She had never been into card games but assumed it was part of a deck of cards. Maybe she would ask Isabelle or someone at work about it later.

She turned to the middle of the book where the glossy photographs were. She decided she would take a quick peek before reading the unpromising book. On the first page was a large black-and-white print of a ship sailing on smooth waters with the backdrop of the white cliffs soaring into the sky. Behind the ship was a little building dotted with black windows. Sophie flipped the page to a black-and-white sketch of a town in Dover. She looked at each of the townspeople in the picture. It was an entire world away from the one in which she existed. The caption claimed it was created in the 1820s. Women in long dresses and hats were going about their chores. A stooped man was pushing a wagon containing some sort of bundle. Another respectable-looking woman was holding her child's hand as they crossed the bustling street. It was a calm peaceful scene. Sophie's heart skipped a beat. She looked closer at the picture, scrutinising the details. The sketch drawing wasn't clear, but she was sure she could make out a sign with a scratchy drawing of a teacup and biscuit, Tea and Biscuits. Looking at the road with fresh eyes, it resembled the layout of the present-day road. She had never been able to find that teahouse again. She strained her eyes but couldn't be sure of what she was seeing.

Her heart fluttering like a caged bird, she quickly turned the page. She was confronted by a picture of a rather serious-looking man with a black bowler hat and stern expression. He had a thick beard and was wearing a dark suit. Sophie was surprised to read that this was a picture of a Henry Norton, a criminal who had been captured in Dover and jailed for embezzlement. His serious countenance had led Sophie to believe he was just another respectable, serious, Victorian man. How looks could deceive.

Sophie turned the page. She gasped. Her heart was no longer fluttering. The caged bird had been shot dead. Her heart was still. Her eyes focused on the black-and-white picture.

No, no, no, no, the word repeated itself over and over in her mind.

A cold sensation flooded through her body, as if her blood had turned to ice. She couldn't breathe. Sophie stared harder in disbelief and mounting horror. Her head was reeling, nausea rippling through her stomach in waves.

"No, how can this be?" Sophie said aloud, panic rising in her throat like bile. She slumped to the floor, feeling faint. She was clutching the book so tightly the pages were folding and crumpling under her grasp. Sophie felt the eyes staring at her, ripping into her soul, those lavender grey eyes which looked almost white in the monochrome picture. The man's silver hair was combed into a ponytail. He was standing next to a tree with a gnarled old stick in his hand. He wore ragged clothes with an assortment of patches and thick leather boots. Sophie had seen him before. She had seen those eyes, that stick, those patches, those boots.

Sophie felt she couldn't breathe. The eyes were following her. Her forehead gleamed with a sheen of sweat. She wanted to die. She wanted to be anywhere but here. Somewhere far away from this waking nightmare and this haunting man.

"There must be an explanation," Sophie whispered breathlessly. The words were swimming in front of her. She closed her eyes for a moment, trying to rein in her shallow breaths. Focus, focus, focus, she repeated to herself. As she opened her eyes, she tore them away from the old man's face and read the caption:

***Willowen Woodlock, 1814–1864, Leader of the
travelling gypsies who arrived in Dover in the winter of
1849. Disappeared shortly after arriving. Cause of
death: unknown.***

Sophie felt sick. "No, no, no," she muttered again
under her breath. Sweat trickled down her back. Her clothes
were damp. What was happening? Was she going mad? The
storm seemed to pick up outside. She felt it raging outside
the house but also inside her own head. The hammering
rain picked up in speed, smashing against the windows. The
house felt like it was rocking, being blown off its hinges,
uprooted from the earth. All she could hear was the
pounding storm. She could feel the thunderous vibrations in
her bones, white lightning lighting up the room in ghostly
flashes. Everything around her was spinning wildly.

His hoarse words floated back to her, the memory
burning in her mind causing her an almost physical pain:
"That house is not your own. I would rather be lost out
here in the open than in that godforsaken place."

She returned her gaze to the picture and stared at
the dates: 1814–1864. It was 2019 now. There must be
some mistake, she thought feverishly. She locked eyes with
those impenetrable milky-white orbs. She felt as if she was
being drawn into their gaze. The magnetic pull drew her
closer to the book until she realised her nose was nearly
touching the picture. Any closer and she felt she would be
dragged into its pages, into a black-and-white ghostly world
haunted by bygone years and ancient troubled souls.

Before allowing herself to get trapped in that book
forever, she slammed it shut. Sophie didn't know what to
do or think. This was beyond her. This was beyond all
reason and logic. Beyond time itself. Who was that man she
had seen on her first night in town? She could not bring
herself to acknowledge what she thought he might be. She

didn't dare believe it. He had been real. They had had a conversation. He had been so close she could have reached out and touched him. And then, in the blink of an eye, he had disappeared into the night, melting into the shadows as if he had never existed.

Sophie hugged her knees into her chest and rocked herself on the floor in the corner of the room by the bookcase. She felt the milky eyes watching her from somewhere. She shoved the book under the couch next to her, but to no avail. The sense of being watched heightened, as if the walls, or rather the house itself was a breathing, seeing, sentient being, with a life, or death, force that was stealing into her soul, melding itself with her. She was slowly becoming fused into its distorted architecture, imprisoned within its shifting shadows.

With shaky, clammy hands, Sophie pulled out her phone from her pocket. She couldn't stay here alone another night. Desperately she tried to control her trembling hands and type a message to Angie.

*Hey, Ang, can you come up earlier than Fri? Please. I'm in a bad way. I need someone here. Pls xxx*

She hit Send. She knew she would not be able to sleep tonight or any other night she was alone in this godforsaken place. She was afraid that if she let her mind drift into slumber she may never wake up again. She felt the house, like a disease, wanted to infect her soul, poison her with its malice. It wanted to eat her alive. She realised then how much she wanted to live. Instead of allowing herself to be stolen by sleep or her mind to conjure up those penetrating eyes again, she tried to focus on her breathing. She began counting it, trying to concentrate on something innocuous, something solid and real. She kept counting. She counted as the storm continued to batter the house from the outside, like an angry spirit hurling itself against the walls, trying to get in. She counted as night settled and the rain slowed. She continued counting as dawn broke through the sky with a gash of hazy pinks, crimsons, purples and oranges. She counted when her alarm rang indicating that she had to wake up and get to her shift. She was swaying, eyes half closed, mumbling, "Eight thousand nine hundred and forty-six, eight thousand nine hundred and forty-seven, eight thousand nine hundred and forty-eight." When the alarm went off she opened her eyes wide. They were itching with tiredness. She glanced blearily at the window. An innocent sun beamed back, winking at her through the glass, as if nothing had happened, as if it was just another day.

Had she imagined the horrors from the night before? Had it been a demonic nightmare springing to life, the storm and shadows playing tricks on her feeble mind? She did not dare check. Leaving the book wedged in its hiding spot she stood up shakily. Her muscles had cramped after being fused in the same position for so long. It was painful to walk. She hobbled over to the bathroom. The trail of ants had vanished. She splashed cold water on her face and looked in the mirror. The sight made her stumble back in shock. She looked deranged. Her hair had dried in tangled knots. Black shadows ringed her eyes. Her cheeks and lips were devoid of any colour, corpse-like. Her eyes were the worst. Bloodshot and open wide like saucers, filled with an expression she had never seen there before. What was it? At first she thought it was fear before she realised it was something much deeper than that. It was something beyond fear. It was the shadow of a faceless spectre, flitting behind her eyes, sowing a plague of doubt in her mind. It embodied the realisation that darkness haunts all corners of this world and that she was never going to feel safe again. Or perhaps she was just losing her mind. Perhaps this is what madness looked like.

She didn't have long to try and fix the mess she was before going to work. She felt completely drained, mentally and physically. With what little strength she had, she scraped her hair into a ponytail. She scrubbed her face and applied a thick layer of foundation before fluffing on some blusher, trying to bring life back into her face. Quickly she layered on the concealer around the eyes and went for a heavy black liner look with half a ton of mascara. To finish, she slapped on a dark purple lipstick. That should distract people from the strangely hollow look in her eyes, she hoped. She had tried to avoid looking at her eyes as she did her make-up. They looked like two dark cavernous wells, extending into nothingness, indistinct echoes of a nightmare floating to the top.

She saw a message pop up on her phone. It was Angie.

*Hey, are you ok? Can I call? You don't sound ok, I'm really worried! Of course I can figure it out and come by earlier!*

Sophie was in the middle of texting back when the phone rang. Sophie jumped about a mile in the air.

"Sophie, are you ok?" Angie's worried voice sounded through the phone.

"Yes, I'm fine. Look, I'm really sorry if I scared you or anything. I just wasn't having a good night last night. If you're busy with work I totally get it," Sophie said, her voice strained and unfamiliar.

"No need to apologise, Soph. I've already figured things out. I'll just work from your place for a bit. I'm going to head down today around 3ish if that's all right," Angie replied, her voice tinged with concern.

"That would be amazing, as long as it really is ok with you! I don't want to be getting you in trouble or anything!"

"Soph, you don't need to worry about that. I get myself in trouble all the time and none of my clients have fired me yet," Angie replied.

"Great, see you later then. Thanks so much for this. I'm just finding it hard being alone," Sophie said, swallowing a lump in her throat.

"Of course! I can't wait to see the place. You've been secretive about it. You haven't even sent any pictures," Angie said.

"Well, I'll give you the grand tour tonight," Sophie managed, hoping she sounded relatively normal. "It'll probably take the best part of a minute considering the size of the place."

"Sounds like an excuse to celebrate! I'll bring wine and maybe a bottle of gin. And some chocolate," Angie said excitedly.

"Can't wait! See you soon!"

"Bye, Soph. You take care of yourself until I get there," Angie said, before hanging up.

Sophie breathed in. She felt such a strong wave of relief soar through her that she could almost sprout wings and fly to work.

She managed to get to the café just in time. She had put some eye drops in her eyes to try to get rid of the redness. She had also brought the card with The Fool on it, wondering if anyone at The Acorn Café could tell her what it was for. It somehow felt like a clue, a puzzle piece of the mystery that was unwittingly becoming her life.

"Hey, Sophie," Chris called. "Ooh, like the new look. Very… gothic," he said, gesturing to her dark lipstick and heavy liner.

"Yeah, thought I'd try something different," she replied furtively. "Hope I don't scare the customers away."

Chris laughed. "No chance. It's cute gothic, not scary gothic!"

"Oh, I didn't know there were variations," she replied as she started clearing the tables and stacking the dishwasher.

It was a busy morning but by 11:00 am the flowing crowd of people had reduced to a mere trickle.

"Hey, Chris, I've got a question," she said, fishing out the card. "Do you play cards? Or know what this is? I just found it the other night and was wondering if it might be part of a set. Something about it and the illustration interests me, I guess."

Chris glanced at it. "Oh, I think I know what that is. It looks like a tarot card. You know, stuff fortune tellers use to see into your future. I don't know much about fortune-telling with tarot cards, but I had an ex who was really into this stuff. Let's see which card you have," he said, taking it from her.

"Wow, this looks really old," Chris said, turning it over, impressed. "Looks like you've got The Fool. Hmm, I can't really remember the meanings of the cards. There's so many, more than you might imagine. But if I remember correctly, The Fool was also known as The Beggar or The Madman. He has something to do with making big changes in your life and taking risks. I think it's one of the most powerful cards in the deck symbolising new beginnings and having faith in the future." He handed the card back to her. "Sorry I couldn't be of more help. If you can get your hands on more cards in the deck that are this old, you'd probably have a very valuable collection."

"That's really interesting. Thanks," Sophie said, glancing down at the card, wondering if it held any answers within its papery depths.

"You thinking of ditching us here at the café and going into the fortune-telling business? You would look the part with that hair and liner," Chris said, with a smile.

Sophie laughed. "You know, I somehow don't think that's my calling. But good to know if all else fails I have a viable backup plan." She slid the card into her back pocket.

# Chapter 12

## *Samuel*

It was getting worse. The waking visions, the hallucinations and the sensations had only gained acuity since he'd sold the house. It was worse than anything he had experienced when he lived there. How could that be? He had sold the house to be rid of all this madness, to free himself at last. And yet, like a cruel twist of fate, the tenuous boundary between the real and imagined was evermore distorted, threatening to snap at any moment. He no longer could tell when was day and when was night. It was all meshing together in some diabolical nightmare. He couldn't understand its incessant force. It had gained in urgency, strength and energy ever since Sophie had moved in. Since then, not a day had gone by when he wasn't affected in some way by these haunting visions. He hoped if he was absorbing the majority of the bizarre activity and energy of the house then maybe it was being deflected from Sophie. He hoped that by suffering the visions and apparitions he was at least protecting her from experiencing them. But he had no idea of knowing since Sophie had not replied to his letter.

Samuel was also having the same nightmare almost daily. He had been dozing in his armchair that afternoon and had tumbled straight into it. The faceless man was placing crate upon crate onto Samuel's chest. Samuel tried to call out, to tell him to stop but could barely muster more than a weak rasp. The man turned at the sound of the splutter coming from below. Samuel, expecting to see the swirling shadow that consisted of the man's face, was shocked. The hazy dark cloud had lifted to reveal none other than Samuel's own face. Those were his own hands burying him under the crates. The eyes that met his gaze were his own, except devoid of life or expression. The faceless Samuel continued to load the crates mechanically onto Samuel's chest, never once taking his hard, stony eyes off the suffocating man on the floor.

Samuel woke up in disbelief. At least, he thought he woke up, or perhaps he had exchanged one dream state for another. Perhaps he was on a train, disembarking at different stations with different realities until he made it back to his own. When he opened his eyes he was not greeted by the comforting sight of his cosy armchair or his knick-knacks dotted around the house. Instead he was in the earthen shack. The floor consisted of dirt, and the walls were mere planks of wood jammed together. Samuel was familiar with this room. He wasn't alone. He could sense it. He turned around slowly and saw the volatile gypsy, the one who could speak with the dead, the one with the sapphire eyes: Erosabel.

Samuel could hear children playing outside, their shrieks of delight drifted through the air as they threw pebbles over the cliff edge and danced around in the garden. Erosabel seemed oblivious to them, as if she were encased in an impermeable membrane where no outside smells or sounds could reach her. She was alone, shuffling and re-shuffling a deck of cards. Four massive ravens stood like sentinels around the room to keep her company. She was muttering to herself.

Slowly, she slid one card out of the deck and put it face up in front of her. The Fool was the first card she laid out. She continued shuffling the cards absent-mindedly. Carefully, she slid out the next one, The Hanged Man. Erosabel let out a derisive snort as she laid the next card out on the earth in front of her, a picture of a man lying face down, stabbed in the back. It was the Ten of Swords. Erosabel continued shuffling, letting her hands warm the deck, transferring her energy into the cards. The next card was The Devil, and her last card, Death.

Erosabel started laughing. It was a low, ominous laugh building up to hysterics. It was a hollow sound, devoid of any true joy. Instead it sounded as if it was being dredged up from the belly of an enormous beast awoken from a thousand-year slumber. The laugh rasped and crackled, grating on Samuel's nerves. The ravens shifted uneasily on their spindly legs. Willowen entered the hut.

"What's going on in here?" he asked sharply. "Roz, you're scaring the children. They can hear you out there."

Erosabel continued cackling, rocking slightly backwards and forwards.

"What are you doing?" Willowen asked sternly, looking at the ominous cards splayed out in front of her.

"Look," Erosabel said, still snorting with laughter. "Look at my future. It's a cauldron of death, failed decisions and disaster. It's brimming with upheaval and change, risk and sacrifice. It portends a great destroyer on the horizon and it's going to eat us all alive!" She stopped laughing abruptly, as if someone had suddenly pressed a mute button. The heavy silence was almost worse than the insane cackle.

"Erosabel, this is crazy! You're taking this too far," Willowen said, snatching up the disturbing cards and pocketing them.

"I have no control over the cards. They are destiny and this is mine. Wreck and ruin," Erosabel said, staring glassy-eyed at the empty space in front of her. Her face was expressionless, a blank canvas waiting to be painted on.

"Roz, you need to pull yourself together, for the children! You're scaring them with all this!" he repeated, gesturing to the ravens perched in the corners of the room.

"Leave my birds alone," Erosabel said, with no hint of emotion in her voice, a command landing on Willowen with the force of a blunt axe.

"You seem to care more for the birds than your own children," Willowen said flatly, watching her expressionless face. "You feed the birds. You spend ages in here petting them and flipping through cards. This isn't normal. I'm trying to help you."

"It's better here than out there where they're trying to kill us! They're already butchering and murdering everyone I care about!" Erosabel spat. "But the birds are safe. They'll never get the birds," she muttered.

"I know, I know," Willowen said in hushed tones ignoring the birds comment. "We'll leave as soon as it's safe. And there's still me and the children. Even if you don't care about me, please don't forsake the children. They need their mother."

Erosabel didn't seem to hear him. Her mouth was pressed into a tight, thin line. She stared vacantly ahead, not blinking. Samuel tried waving a hand in front of Erosabel's face, not that anyone could see or feel him in this world. She remained as she was, still as a wax statue. Willowen knelt down beside her, tears streaming down his face.

"Come back to me, Erosabel. Come back to me, my love," he cried into her soft hair.

She didn't move a muscle or give any sign that she was even aware of his presence. She continued to stare, a lifeless doll, her soul transcending to another world completely.

# Chapter 13

## *Sophie*

Once Sophie had finished her shift at the Acorn, she hurried back home to meet the exterminator. She arrived just as his van was pulling up.

He strode up to her. "Are you Sophie Parker? An ant infestation, you say?"

"Yes, that's me. Come on in," Sophie replied.

They entered the house together. There was no undercurrent of emotions today skulking unseeingly through the house. Sophie had realised this about the place she now called home. Whether it was her projecting her own emotions or something else at work, she felt the house was in a constant state of silent change. Its moods fluctuated wildly without the slightest provocation. It was as if the house was breathing and with each exhalation the atmosphere shifted. The walls, floors, ceilings, everything around her had a brooding feel to it. It made her hairs stand on end.

"So where's the problem, Miss?" the man said, cutting into her consciousness.

Sophie realised she was just standing in the doorway, staring into space. The exterminator was looking at her in a curious manner.

"Right, it's this way, in the kitchen," Sophie said quickly.

"Great. Well, let me take a look."

She led him into the kitchen, explaining, "There was a trail along this wall here and spread across the floor. I'm not sure where they're coming from."

The exterminator knelt down and felt along the cracks and crevices of the wall. "Ok, well, I'll see if I can find the nest. That's the best way to get rid of ants, find their queen and exterminate the root of the problem."

Sophie nodded. "Can I get you some tea, or a coffee?"

"A tea would be lovely. Milk and two sugars, please," he replied as he opened up the cabinets below, eyeing them with his expert gaze.

Sophie made tea for both of them. She sat sipping hers, watching him as he continued his inspection.

"Well, sorry to tell you, Sophie, but I can't find any sign of ants round here," the inspector said, getting up from all fours. "In order to eliminate the infestation, I've got to eliminate the nest otherwise they will just keep coming back. Do you know where the trail of ants started when you saw them?"

"Uh, no, not really," Sophie said, trying to remember. They had just seemed to appear out of nowhere. "They were heading outside through to the back garden."

"Hmm, do you keep the bins out there or something? Worker ants are on a mission to find food for the queen who does not leave the nest. Check if there are any sources of food around there. Also I've got some homework for you. Next time you see them, watch where they are coming from. Once they get food, they will always go back to the nest, which is what needs spraying. I don't want to just spray the cabinets with insecticide now because to me it's a waste of your money and I can't guarantee they won't come back."

"Ok, no problem. So I should just follow the trail?"

"Yup, and then give me a ring. You could also leave out some food as bait if you want to speed up the process. Some people leave out honey to trap and kill the ants but that's not a long-term solution as it doesn't destroy the core."

"Right, ok, well, thank you for coming over. Sorry, I feel you wasted your time. How much do I owe you?"

"Nothing at all," the exterminator said, raising his hand. "Just give me a ring next time you see them and remember, follow the trail."

She smiled and walked him to the door. Follow the trail, she thought to herself.

"The name's Bill by the way," he said just as he was about to leave.

"Thanks, Bill, I'll probably see you around," Sophie said as he walked back to his van.

Sophie collapsed on the couch, exhaustion pounding through her head. How annoying about the ants, she thought to herself. She would have liked to exterminate them before Angie's arrival. Where was that beastly queen hiding? Without realising, her eyelids drooped heavy with sleep. The waking nightmare from the night before melted away. Within seconds she was fast asleep.

The fire slithered and hissed into her dreams like a nest of angry snakes. She was outside by the willow tree. She could smell its singed vines. She looked up. Its trunk was mottled and black. The ashy vines drooped heavily, weighted like hung men in the gallows. As she went to touch one of them, the wispy vine instantly turned to dust and disintegrated into the air, another one of earth's forgotten memories. It was an empty, charred wasteland. The sky was a colourless block of grey. The only sound that echoed was the screech of a raven.

Something drew her gaze down to a pile of ash at the base of the tree. Sophie knelt down, slipping her hands into its soft powdery depths. At first she could only feel the feathery substance slide between her fingers, until she touched something solid. She pulled it out, exhuming dusty clouds, watching them float gently upwards spiralling towards the heavens. It was a deck of cards placed face down. She turned it over in her hand, wiping off the layer of grey ash that coated them.

Cold fear gripped her heart. Depicted on the card was a skeleton dressed in armour and holding a black flag. The grinning skeleton was riding a white horse. Lifeless bodies were strewn on the ground surrounding this grotesque sight. Standing in front of the horse was a man, his hands in a pleading gesture. He wore golden robes and his face was a mask of despair. Sophie's eyes slid down to the wording below the horror scene. In capitals, it read, **DEATH**.

The smell of fire grew stronger until she could feel a burning dryness in her throat. She tried to swallow but her mouth felt like a parched desert, her tongue rough as sandpaper. She continued to stare at the deck of cards. As she flipped through them she realised they were all the same, Death. There were thirteen cards in total, twelve of them depicting the malicious skeleton. When Sophie reached the last card, she saw that it was blank. She flipped it over and with horror saw her own face reflected, a ghostly image on the card. Sophie threw down the cards and turned to run. She was met by the sight of her house ablaze in dancing scarlet and crimson. Olympian clouds of smoke billowed around her obscuring her vision. Disoriented, she tried to run in any direction, but found she couldn't move her legs. They were rooted in the earth like little tree stumps. The blizzard of ash was engulfing her, burying her alive. She let out an ear-splitting scream only to be smothered with ash, dirt and smoke. The grave of ash reached her neck and Sophie knew she could fight no longer. Her limbs, suspended in the mound, were immobile. She let the ash pour over her and reach the crown of her head. And then, all was oblivion. It was over.

Sophie woke up with a start to the sound of rapping on her door. She was drenched in sweat. Wildly Sophie looked around her. There was no fire, no ash and no skeletons. She checked her watch. It was 4:30 pm. The rapping sound came again, more impatiently this time. Sophie gathered herself together and opened the door, feeling out of place and dishevelled.

"Sophie!" squealed Angie. "Oh my God, no offence, but you look a mess!" she said, looking her up and down.

"I was just sleeping. I was having some really weird dreams," Sophie replied groggily.

Angie reached out and pulled Sophie into a tight hug. "Are you sure you're doing ok out here?" Angie asked, looking Sophie directly in the eye, searching for clues. "I mean, you know you can always come back home whenever you like. And you don't have to go to your parents' house either. You can always come live with me. It would be our never-ending slumber party." Angie grinned.

Sophie smiled. "Thanks, Angie, but I only just bought this place. This is my home now. Let me just get changed quickly and then I'll show you around. I like the hair by the way," Sophie said, commenting on Angie's new angular bob cut as she led her through the entrance. "Very cool, graphic designery."

"Oh, why, thank you. You know, gotta look the part," Angie said, flicking a short stray hair for dramatic effect. "The salon next to Marty's bar was doing crazy discounts. I just had to make the most of it!"

Angie had curly black hair. Now it was short, the ringlets formed a little cloud around her strong features and permanently tired-looking eyes. "Who needs sleep when there's so much to do? You can sleep when you're dead," was her usual response when Sophie confronted her about it. Angie lived on coffee, bagels and cigarettes. She was average height and athletically built with wiry arms and legs, toned stomach and flat chest.

"Do you mind?" Angie asked, a cigarette perched between her lips. She was already lighting up before Sophie could answer. Instantly Sophie felt a cold fear ooze through her bloodstream as she watched the flame from Angie's lighter come to life. She stared at it as it flickered and burned the end of Angie's cigarette making a light sizzling sound. Angie breathed out a plume of smoke.

"Hey, I'll put it out if it bothers you," Angie said as soon as she saw Sophie's transfixed stare.

Sophie shook her head slightly. "No, no, smoke. It's fine. I'm just tired. Sorry if I'm being a little weird."

"I thought I was supposed to be the permanently sleep-deprived, moody, tired one in the relationship," Angie quipped. "We can't have two crabby gals now, can we? We'll tear each other to bits." She put her arms around Sophie. "Ok, so the place is small but..." Angie paused, scrunching up her nose as if trying to decide the best word to use, "cute." She raised her eyebrows as if it was more of a question than a statement. The tendrils of cigarette smoke curled wildly in the air, like a trapeze artist doing summersaults as Angie gesticulated. She talked as much with her hands as her actual mouth.

"Hey, it is cute! Here's the living room," Sophie said, remaining stationed by the staircase, pointing to where Angie should look. "There's the kitchen. And beyond the kitchen is the bathroom. Isn't this a great tour? You don't even have to move and you've pretty much seen the entire place," Sophie said, laughing.

"Well, as long as you're happy, Soph, I'm happy! Now how about we crack into this wine then, huh! I got your favourite, Oyster Bay," Angie said, shaking the rustling bags in her hand, creating a satisfying clinking sound.

"Let me get the glasses," Sophie said enthusiastically.

She quickly changed into comfy clothes in the bathroom and then rummaged in the cupboards for two wine glasses. With Angie's familiar presence, Sophie felt calm, the worry rolling off her like pebbles tumbling down a hill. She grabbed two glasses and snuggled herself next to Angie on the couch. Angie poured two very generous glasses of white wine.

"To my little Soph, all grown-up, a homeowner and a dishevelled wreck," Angie said, laughing.

"Ok, Miss Hipster, you can give me a make-over tomorrow," Sophie said, raising her glass in toast.

"Deal."

"Speaking of which, I've made a friend next door. Her name is Isabelle and she said she would really like to meet you when you came to town. What do you say we have tea with her tomorrow or sometime during your stay? She really is the absolute sweetest. You'd love her," Sophie said eagerly.

"Sounds like a plan," Angie replied. "So how have you been spending your time these days? What is there to do?"

"No need to sound so sceptical," Sophie said, smiling. She knew Angie loved the hustle and bustle of London. That city ran through her veins and throbbed in time with her heartbeat. "It may not be London but there are still things to do around here. I've got a job as a barista at The Acorn Café. You need to check it out. We do the best coffee in town! I've also been spending a lot of time by the beach. Obviously it's cold but I love just walking along the shore. It's really beautiful. I'll take you down there at some point. And I've met these two really great mums, Georgey and Tilly. They're hilarious, maybe you'll meet them too while you're here."

"Wow, I'm impressed, Sophie. You've really settled into this new life of yours. Good for you. If I'm totally honest, I thought your mum was right when she said you'd be back in a matter of weeks. But look at you. You're doing great. You've really got everything on track and running smoothly," Angie said, patting Sophie's leg.

Sophie rolled her eyes at the mum comment. She knew her mum did not trust her to operate a microwave let alone live by herself. She knew the worry was because she cared, but Sophie was glad to have proved them wrong.

"You know, it's strange, I've only been here a short while but this place, this town, already feels like home," Sophie said.

"Yeah, I can tell," Angie said, studying her friend's face. "Top-up?" she offered, as Sophie drained her glass.

"Of course!" Sophie said, offering her glass to Angie who also topped up her own glass to the brim.

"Well, things are going great with me, thanks for asking," she said in mock sarcasm.

"Oh, I'm sorry, Angie, you must think I'm so selfish!"

"Never, Soph. I was only joking. But really, I've met this guy. His name is Brad." She paused, looking at Sophie's disgruntled face. "Hey, what is it? How can you judge him already?"

Angie had a track record for choosing the wrong guys. Wrong meaning commitment phobes, mama's boys, serial cheaters and even a flamboyantly gay man who Angie found out later was starring in a reality drag show on TV. The only thing these guys had in common was Angie.

"Nothing good ever came from a guy named Brad," Sophie said, raising her glass in warning.

Angie hit her with the cushion wedged between them. "You listen, I'm sure even you will like him! We'll be just like Brad Pitt and Angelina Jolie! The ultimate power couple! Anyway, he owns his own music studio and he's working on a hit record. His voice is amazing and he plays the guitar. I'm not so keen on his nipple piercings but he's got such an interesting character. He's so well travelled. He's been all over Asia and the Far East. He's super spiritual and spent like six months in a monastery without talking even once. He has a tattoo of a giant squid on his leg which he got done on a scuba diving trip to Thailand. It was totally spontaneous. He said he came face to face with this massive squid in the middle of the sea. They were just floating there together, suspended in endless water. He said it was watching him intently, looking deep into his eyes. They stayed facing each other for ages. He said he could feel the creature's ancient wisdom pour out of it and into him. He said it was a turning point in his life. Gave him a new perspective."

Sophie raised her eyebrows. "Sounds like one heck of a squid. Maybe it was sizing him up preparing to eat him?"

"Haha, very funny, Sophie! The way he told the story, even you would understand!"

Sophie smiled. Angie did tend to get carried away with stories and words. She had a tough exterior but was secretly a soft romantic at heart.

Angie paused, uncomfortably. "What about you?" she said in an exaggerated light-hearted tone. "Any cute guys around here?"

Sophie knew this was coming. She had been waiting for it. She felt like she had when she was a child waiting in the dentist's office, praying they wouldn't call her name.

Angie had told her she needed to get out there and see other people. Sophie had not been ready at the time and Angie withdrew. Now she was back, full force, asking the question Sophie wanted to hide from for the rest of her life. She sighed, swirling the wine in her glass, watching it swish hypnotically.

"Sophie, I'm only asking because I care," Angie said softly. "I know no one can replace Dan. He was one of a kind and I miss him too, so much. But you're not looking for a replacement, just something different."

Sophie nodded. She cleared her throat and latched onto the first thing that came to her mind to fill the void of silence that was blossoming like a dark flower between them.

"There is this one guy from the coffee shop."

Angie perked up, nodding her head encouragingly. When Sophie remained silent, she said, "And…"

"And he's tall, good-looking. We spoke a little at the café and then I saw him again at the beach. He was really sweet and drove me home. He, erm, gave me his number," Sophie said, looking down sheepishly.

"Have you messaged him or anything?" Angie asked, literally perched on the edge of the couch.

"Not yet. That was all a few days ago now. I'm sure he's forgotten all about me. He has a kid," Sophie finished, glancing up at Angie.

"Ah, well, that throws a spanner in the works. How old is the kid?" Angie asked, leaning back into the couch.

"I don't know, he didn't say."

"Any mention of a wife?" Angie asked, trying to puzzle this mystery man together.

"Nope, no mention of a wife, but I'm sure guys like him are happily married with perfect children and perfect lives," Sophie said miserably.

"Sophie, he gave you his number. Maybe he's separated or divorced or something."

"I know, or maybe he just wants a fling!"

"Ok, what's so wrong with that? You could do with a fling." Angie winked.

"Angie, I'm not getting involved with a married man!"

"Easy, calm down, we haven't yet established he's married. And there's only one way to find out. Call him!" Angie ordered.

"What, are you insane? No way am I calling him!" Sophie said, taking a deep sip of wine, mock frowning at Angie.

"Ok, scaredy-cat, then message him. Come on, let's draft it together."

Sophie looked suspiciously at Angie before retrieving the two mementos from her mystery man.

"Hey, what's that one say?" Angie said, pointing to the other note.

Sophie opened up the crumpled paper: *Thought you might need this ;)*

"What does that mean?" Angie asked.

"I forgot my bike in his car when he drove me home. He obviously came back and left it by the door with this note in it."

"Sophie!" Angie said, shaking her best friend, sloshing some of her wine on the carpet. "Look at that winking face. He is clearly into you."

Sophie couldn't help but smile at Angie's bubbling excitement. "So, what do I write?" Sophie asked, armed with her phone and liquid courage.

"Write: '*Hey, handsome, been thinking about you. Winking face*'," Angie said, putting on a deep manly voice.

"That's no help at all!" Sophie said, trying to be serious but breaking out into a grin as Angie doubled over in laughter.

"Ok, ok, I got it. Write: '*Hey, man – are you married, now would be a good time to tell me. Winking face*'," Angie said again before bursting into peals of laughter. Sophie couldn't help but laugh too.

"How about: '*Hey, have you checked out a giant squid recently? Heard it's life-changing. Winking face*'," Sophie said, gasping for breath. Angie rocked back and forth in laughter.

"Write: '*Wuddup, dude, let's hang. Winking face*'," Angie said.

They couldn't stop laughing as they rolled about on the floor, coming up with ever more outrageous messages to send.

At last, Sophie cleared her throat, her stomach cramping and face muscles aching from the laughter. Her back was against the couch. "Ok, ok. I'm really going to send this one. We spoke about getting coffee or something, I think. I'm going to write: '*Hey, it's me Sophie, from The Acorn Café. Thank you for dropping my bike off the other day. How about grabbing that coffee we talked about? Let me know when suits you! S*'."

"Don't forget – winking face," Angie said, trying to rein in her giggles.

"I'll add a smiling face – forget the winking face!" Sophie replied, as she drafted the message.

"Ok, but it's a bit wordy. I know men, and I don't know if he'll make it to the end of that essay you've written there. Here, give me the phone!" Angie said, snatching the phone from Sophie's hand. Sophie, feeling weak from the laughter and slightly dizzy from the wine, let Angie get on with it.

"No need to explain who you are," Angie muttered. "I'm sure he remembers. And no need to be so thankful yet, you're not marrying him. Here you go, what do you think?" Angie said, handing the phone back.

It read: *Hey there, it's Sophie. That was really sweet of you to drop off my bike the other day! Are you free for a coffee this weekend?*

"There you go. It's direct, to the point and we've thrown in a compliment to stroke his ego. If you don't get a reply in a matter of milliseconds then I will eat my hat."

"You don't have a hat, Ang," Sophie replied in a quiet, serious undertone.

"Then I will find one and I will eat it!" Angie said determinedly.

"Ah, here we go! Send," Sophie said, closing her eyes for dramatic effect as she hit Send.

"CHEERS!" Angie bellowed to the room. "Here's to you and, wait, what's his name?"

Sophie laughed. "Small detail, huh! It's Matthew!"

They clinked glasses loudly and took deep swigs of the wine.

"Top-up!" Angie cried, holding the bottle at a precarious angle while attempting not to spill any.

"He's not going to reply, you know. I think you'll end up having to eat someone's hat," Sophie said seriously, slurring her words slightly. "You know, Isabelle over there had a very sweet-looking hat hanging on a peg by her front door. We may need to go hat hunting there."

"Well, we don't want to wake her up. It is nearly 9:00 pm. We'll just have to break in," Angie replied, mirroring the gravity of the situation.

"Yes, but quietly," Sophie said, her voice hushing to a whisper. "We can't actually break anything. We need to find a lock picker!"

"I know! Ask Matthew, guys are good at this stuff," Angie said, sipping her wine.

"Yes, but if Matthew replies we won't need the lock picker because you won't need to eat Isabelle's hat because the whole point of eating the hat was if Matthew didn't reply," Sophie explained as if she was teaching a very dense student basic addition.

"Ah, right," Angie said, nodding at the logical conundrum presented to her. "Good point there, Soph."

Just then Sophie's phone beeped. Angie and Sophie looked at each other and simultaneously let out a high-pitched squeal.

"I can't look," Sophie said, shoving the phone at Angie. Looking at her through the prison bars of her fingers she asked, "Is it him?"

Angie paused, expressionless before breaking out into a whooping cheer. "It's Winking Face! Here, read the message," Angie said, throwing the phone back, delirious with excitement.

*Sophie – I'm so glad you messaged. I'd love to get a coffee, how about tomorrow at 1:00 pm? I know a great place by the beach we could go. Pick u up at 1? ;)*

"Well, no hats are going to be devoured tonight," Sophie said, breathing in. "Ok, I'm going to reply with: 'Sounds good, see you then!'"

"Sure, but add an x. He's put the winking face. It's only fair you add a kiss," Angie said, nodding her head sagely, clearly an expert on matters of the heart and emoticons.

"Right. Here goes: '*Sounds good, see you then! Xx*'."

"Ooh, two kisses, how very French," Angie said, looking over her shoulder. "Perfect, now send it!"

As she sent the message, Angie raised her hand in a high five. Sophie slapped her hand hard, making both their hands tingle.

They continued chatting and giggling into the small hours. Angie then crashed on the sofa while Sophie crept upstairs to her room. Full of wine laughter and a text from Matthew, she collapsed onto her bed with a smile on her face and a warm glow nestled deep within. She was asleep in an instant.

Sophie woke the next day with a throbbing hangover. She rolled out of bed and tiptoed downstairs where Angie was snoring loudly, her face lost in a tangle of curls. She popped an aspirin before making a breakfast of plain omelette, toast and cheese. She had even bought some orange juice for the occasion. She wrapped a portion in aluminium foil and set it aside for Angie. As there was no dining table and Angie was taking up the entire couch, Sophie ate her breakfast standing up in the tiny kitchen.

Sophie stopped chewing mid-bite. She felt their presence. Instead of the hard, cold stare piercing the back of her skull, she felt a different sensation. It was as if she was being caressed gently by the softest, silkiest of feathers. She turned slowly. The ravens were perched on the windowsill. Their dark eyes, like mysterious bottomless wells, were drawing her in. She wondered how she could ever have thought of them as hideous. The one on the left twitched an elegant sleek wing as if in greeting. A small smile played across Sophie's lips. She felt there was a secret between them, an unspoken energy transferring from their souls to hers, merging them together.

Her phone beeped, snapping her out of her reverie. Sophie glanced down. It was Matthew confirming their date for the day. She suddenly felt butterflies awaken in the pit of her stomach, stretching their wings and doing pirouettes around her intestines, distracting her from her new friends. She was seeing Matthew today! How could she have listened to Angie and set up this date? She was not ready for this. Her breathing felt restricted as her palms grew sweaty. She got in the shower and covered her eyes with her hands as the cold water trickled down her body, making her shiver.

"I wish it was you I was seeing," she breathed, thinking of Dan. The water dripped down her face. She didn't realise she was crying until she heard a tap on the door.

"Hey, I really need the loo. I might puke. I've got a bucket in tow but just letting you know," came Angie's voice, thick with sleep and too much wine.

Sophie sniffed and wiped her face with her wet hand. "Sure, nearly done." She hoped her voice didn't sound too shaky. Then again, Angie was hungover and probably not listening to anything she said anyway. Sophie breathed in. Her thoughts drifted back to Dan. Here she was, going to meet a perfect stranger, sit through the agony of awkward conversation only to find out at the end that he was probably married and looking for a bit of fun. Dan had been her comfort and security. It was warm and easy with him. Now she would have to do it all again. Six years of dates, fights, tears, love culminating in a fairy-tale engagement had been ripped from her, leaving her an empty hollow shell trapped in the body of her previous self.

She heard violent retching sounds. She quickly turned off the water and wrapped herself in a towel.

"Oh no," she said, as she saw Angie bent over the bucket Sophie used to mop the floor with. "Guess it's too late to make it to the loo," she said, combing back Angie's hair and holding it out of the way of the stream of vomit.

Angie groaned. "Sorry about this. You know, I really thought I'd have figured out my limits by age twenty-nine," she said, before heaving again.

"I thought I'd have figured out life by age twenty-eight," Sophie half whispered to herself.

"I'll clean this mess up," Angie said. "You get ready for your date, with that winky face guy." She let out a weak smile before groaning again.

Sophie rubbed her back. "Well, when you're up for it your breakfast is under the foil. It's—"

"No, don't talk about breakfast," Angie interrupted. "Don't think I could handle talking about consuming anything except water right now! Even that's a stretch."

"Got it. I'll leave some water and aspirin on the counter," Sophie said. "You going to be all right? I'll just get dressed and my make-up sorted, and I'll be right down."

"Don't worry, I'm used to these shenanigans of mine. I can handle this," Angie slurred as she cradled her head in her hands.

Sophie dashed upstairs, contemplating what kind of look to go for. She settled on the natural look, applying nude eyeshadow and a thin black wing of liner. She layered on two coats of mascara and dabbed on a peachy pink lipstick and matching shade of blush. Time to tackle the wardrobe, she thought to herself. She opened the wardrobe and eyed her clothes. What could she wear that was appropriate for the winter weather and still relatively cute? Her favourite, go-to look was a pair of thin, faded jeans and oversized pullover; comfortable but decidedly not cute.

After a couple of outfit changes, ending up with a pile of clothes strewn across the floor, Sophie had decided on a thin, fitted, white V-neck jumper that clung to her figure nicely. She paired it with a miniskirt with a purple zigzag design. She chose a pair of tights and flat ankle-high black boots to go with it. It was cute but casual, she thought. She gave her hair a quick blow-dry and ran her brush through it. Her light brown hair cascaded several inches below her shoulders in smooth rippling waves. She was surprised at how long it was getting. She had always had her hair cut relatively short, but she liked this new look. It was soft and gentle. She turned to the side and ruffled her hair slightly. She liked the effect, not overly done up. She spritzed herself with her favourite Lancôme perfume and slid a pair of dangly silver earrings through her ears. She looked herself up and down, pleased with the overall effect. She hadn't properly looked at herself in months, she realised. Her skin had a healthy glow about it. The fitted jumper hugged her slim waist, showing off her slight curves. Her long legs looked sleek and shapely in the black tights.

Sophie grabbed her purse and went downstairs to see if the outfit got Angie's stamp of approval.

"Oh my God, you look like an angel," Angie said when she saw her. "I would hug you, but you smell so sweet and perfumed you don't want my vomit breath on you! But you are missing one thing. Wait right there," Angie said, scooping herself off the floor and moving slowly to her suitcase which lay untouched in the corner of the living room. She bent over it and pulled something out. "You know I went to Greece for a long weekend with that weirdo ex of mine, Fender, I mean, who is called Fender? Now that's a name to look out for! But I did get this for you. I kept forgetting to give it to you, but it's been in its box safe and sound waiting for my forgetful brain to function properly." Angie pulled out a small silver box. "For you," she said, handing it to Sophie.

"Angie! You didn't have to get me anything," Sophie said, surprised at the unexpected gift. She opened the lid and saw a twinkling blue and silver eye in the shape of a teardrop hanging on a delicate silver chain.

"It's supposed to ward off the evil eye and protect you when I can't," Angie said softly, her hand on Sophie's arm.

Sophie felt her chest swell with emotion. "It's beautiful," she stammered.

"Don't you dare cry and ruin that beautiful make-up you just put on for Winking Face!" Angie commanded.

Sophie nodded mutely, unable to talk. Angie took the necklace carefully out of the box and placed it around her friend's neck.

"There, you're perfect," she said, a tear sparkling in her eye.

Sophie pulled her friend into a tight embrace. An undercurrent of love and friendship flowed freely and deeply between them. The spell was broken by a sharp tap on the door. Sophie widened her eyes and breathed in deeply.

"Sophie, relax, stay calm. You got this!" Angie said, smiling. "Now if you don't mind, while you enjoy your date with your knight in shining armour, I'll enjoy mine with your beautiful loo and its shining basin!"

"Feel better," Sophie said, clapping her friend on the back. "I won't be long. We'll do something fun tonight, I promise!"

"Just go," Angie said, waving a hand at her as she disappeared into the bathroom.

Sophie walked up to the door, swallowed hard and opened it.

# Chapter 14

## *Sophie*

*Dear Daniel,*

*A dark curse hovers over me,*

*A curse cast by your own hand,*

*Its bitterness lingers with all the love I poured into you,*

*I loved a soul that belonged to the world of the damned.*


*Your curse has bent me into a weeping willow,*

*My tears of leaves mourn, kissing the ground below,*

*From my stiff branches they drip down,*

*Weeping my heart's eternal woe.*


*Your curse transcends time as this wretched tree will age,*

*I'll forever be arched in agony and sorrow,*

*My vines tying knots deep within me, twisted with rage,*

*Only a hollow emptiness inside me does grow.*

*You cursed my soul to be as black as night,*

*You cursed my heart to be a leaden grey,*

*You cursed me to love you with all my soul's strength and might,*

*Your undying curse descended upon me the day death stole you away.*

*Sophie*

"Hi," Matthew said, grinning, a bunch of white lilies in his hand.

Sophie blushed. So this was a date. Flowers clearly signalled a date. "Wow, thank you. These are beautiful. Let me put them in a vase," Sophie said, gathering the bouquet of gorgeous-smelling pearly white lilies. "He got me flowers and I don't have a vase," Sophie whispered to Angie who was picking at the breakfast Sophie had left for her.

"Just leave them in the sink and I'll create a makeshift vase. Maybe I'll use one of the empty wine bottles or something," Angie said. "Wow, you must really have made an impression on this guy. These are gorgeous." Angie took the flowers and stroked one of the velvet, delicate petals.

"Wish me luck," Sophie said in hushed tones as she headed back.

"Darling, you clearly don't need it," Angie replied, winking.

Sophie tucked an imaginary lock of hair behind her ear as Matthew escorted her to his car. He opened the door for her, and she slid in.

"I'm so glad you messaged. The only way I could contact you is if I showed up on your doorstep, which I think would have been a bit weird," he said, flashing her one of his wide smiles.

Sophie fidgeted nervously in her seat. She felt out of practice. She couldn't tell the difference between friendly banter, mischievous flirting and banal conversation any more. She did realise, however, that she couldn't just sit there weirdly mute.

"Yeah, I mean, I really just want to say thank you again for helping me out on the beach and dropping off my bike. That was really nice of you," she said, smiling. "I didn't see you at the Acorn the other day. Are you cheating on us with another café?" Or are you currently cheating on your wife, she thought savagely. Come on, out with it. She looked up at him innocently, examining his face to see if she had hit a nerve.

Clearly she hadn't as he chuckled in his low relaxed way. "Did you miss me?" he asked, glancing at her playfully before returning his eyes to the road. "Nah, I just couldn't make it that day. My daughter was sick, and I had to get a child-minder at the last minute. I was late enough to work as it was let alone adding another twenty minutes just to get a coffee. Although I would have done if I'd known you were working the morning shift that day."

Her cheeks flushed again, making her wish she had worn a looser-fitting jumper. Perhaps he had turned the heating up too high in the car. It wasn't that cold outside. It was a whopping four degrees today, who needed the heating on at all with such soaring temperature? She dragged her thoughts back to their conversation and his sick child and her next line of questioning: why couldn't your wife take care of your daughter? Is she above babysitting? Is she too good to look after her own children? What kind of woman is she? The interrogation was flashing through her mind, taking somewhat absurd twists and turns like an out-of-control rollercoaster.

Instead she said sweetly, "How old is your daughter?"

"She's five and a total drama queen already," he said, laughing. "Her name's Heather. Hopefully you'll meet her someday," he added casually.

Will I have the pleasure of meeting your wife as well? It wasn't so much word vomit as thought vomit with all the unwanted thoughts regurgitating and churning around in her mind.

"That would be nice," she replied. "So where is it we're going?" She had to turn the conversation away from his family life before she said something utterly deranged.

"Patience, we're nearly there," he said, smiling.

As they parked he jumped out of the car to open the door for her. An old-fashioned gentleman, Sophie thought. Lucky old wife, her sarcasm quipped back. Matthew took a basket out of the boot and heaved it over his shoulder. They walked down the beach, the crashing waves filling the silence for them.

"It's that building right over there," Matthew said, pointing to a tower.

"Isn't that a lighthouse?" Sophie said, squinting.

"Yup, it's no longer used. It was abandoned years ago."

"And that's where we're going?" Sophie said, raising a brow sceptically.

"Yeah. I saw you having what looked like a picnic on the beach last time you were here. I thought you were more a picnic type of girl than a fancy restaurant one."

Sophie could not fault his deduction there. She always preferred the great outdoors and didn't understand other people's desires to dine out in as many fancy restaurants as they possibly could, just ticking off their imaginary boxes.

"Strange place for a first date." Sophie smiled.

"Ah, so this is a date?" he asked, glancing down at her, his free hand brushing against hers.

Sophie bit her lip. Oops, now he will tell his wife I came onto him, she thought. She shook her head slightly. That nagging, sarcastic voice in her head needed to shut up. They walked on in silence until they reached the lighthouse.

"I love this place," Matthew said enthusiastically. He pushed open the door.

Sophie's rational mind told her it was a bad idea to go into an abandoned lighthouse with a total stranger carrying a basket full of what could potentially be torture devices, weapons of mass destruction, taxidermy animals, the list could go on. But her instinct told her to go inside.

"Wow," she said, as she glanced up at the spiralling staircase, feeling the smooth wood beneath her fingertips. In front of her was the entrance to the staircase and straight ahead was a door which opened up into a kitchen. The trapped air smelt of ageing wood and carpets of dust. A tangy metallic taste hovered on her lips. The atmosphere was heavy with time gone by. She felt the spirit of the lighthouse clinging onto its memories, keeping them alive through the undercurrent of energy that spiralled up the winding stairs and onwards to the heavens.

"It's beautiful," she whispered, feeling her voice did not belong amidst the layers of life that papered the walls and scented the very air she breathed. She felt like an intruder.

"I knew you would like it," Matthew said, beaming. "You're like me, just the type to appreciate the world's forgotten things."

Sophie turned to face him. "And what type is that?"

Matthew was silent for a moment, contemplating his answer. "I don't know," he said slowly. "You're the type of person who is nostalgic for a life that was never yours, nostalgic for the past and history. You belong to a bygone era, not quite slotting into the mayhem of the 21st century. Woah, that's deep," he said suddenly. "Maybe I was just describing myself there. I promise I don't always talk like that. Come on, let me show you the best bit!"

He took her hand gently in his. Sophie felt his light touch pulsate through her body. It felt strange holding someone's hand in such an intimate way. His hands were big and slightly rough to the touch. He was holding her hand as if it were a fragile feather and he was afraid of bending it the wrong way. The palm of his hand lightly caressed hers while his fingers wrapped themselves around her long, dainty ones.

Their footsteps coughed up clouds of dust as they left prints on the stairs' surface. They clambered upwards, their shoes leaving their fading signatures in the lighthouse. They passed a landing which opened up into two bedrooms. She glanced sideways at Matthew, hoping this was not "the best bit" he was talking about. He didn't stop there. With her hand still clasped in his, they reached the top of the stairs. Sophie blinked and had to do a double take. She felt breathless. It was the most beautiful sight she had seen.

They were surrounded by glass-panelled windows. From all angles the sea spread out beneath her, a royal blue carpet of mysteries. Olympian white clouds sailed by dreamily. It was the essence of peace and tranquillity up here. It was so beautiful it could hardly be real. She must have stumbled into the illustrations of a children's storybook or a painter's canvas. She stepped forward and put her hands gently on the cool glass panel, allowing her breath to fog up the window. It was a sheer drop beneath her if the glass were to suddenly vanish underneath her touch. She was aware of Matthew watching her intently. She swivelled around. "Matthew, this place is like a dream," she said breathlessly.

"I know. Glad you like it. I know we said we would have coffee, but I hope you brought your appetite along." He pulled out a red-and-white striped blanket and laid it on the dusty floor. He then began to take out the contents of the basket and arrange everything on the blanket.

Sophie eyed the basket, definitely no torture tools, weapons or stuffed animals in there, she concluded.

He took out a decanter of lemonade and a flask of what was presumably coffee. "I wasn't sure if you were a carnivore or herbivore so I came prepared with options," he said, as he took out several bacon, smoked salmon, and cheese and pickle sandwiches. He took out what looked like a potato salad, a packet of berries, chocolate Hobnobs, crackers and cheese and an assortment of muffins.

"I hope this will be enough," he said, eyeing the spread in concern.

Sophie smiled. "It's plenty. This is amazing. You didn't have to go to all this trouble."

"Well, it's a first date, need to make a good impression. Coffee?" he asked.

Sophie fiddled with the imaginary lock of hair by her ear. "Yes, please."

He took out a Styrofoam cup and poured the dark, heavily scented, rich coffee into her cup.

"That smells heavenly," Sophie said, inhaling deeply. Before she became too intoxicated with the romantic backdrop, delicious aromas and dizzying heights, she knew she had to get it off her chest and ask about Heather's mother. She glanced at his hands, no ring. She needed to bring it up in a subtle, tactful way. In a way where he didn't even notice she was asking. She had to be an artful detective and tread lightly around the subject. She resolved to embody the phrase "walking on eggshells" in her questioning techniques, to avoid any explosive or emotional outbursts.

"So, is Heather's mum in the picture?" she said, freezing after the words tumbled dreadfully out of her mouth, hitting the floor in between them with a solid thud.

Matthew choked on his coffee, coughing several times before looking up, a smile playing on the corner of his lips. "I'm divorced," he said simply, studying her expression. "I noticed you're wearing a ring though. Is that an engagement ring?" he asked, his brow slightly furrowed.

Sophie looked down at her hands. The ring was catching the light, shining brighter than usual. She felt its blinding glare was accusing her, reminding her that she was not being faithful to Dan's memory. But he was gone. He had left this world and her behind. How could she be faithful to the elusive memory of a man?

Finally she spoke. "I was engaged. He died." She stopped herself, not wanting to cry in front of Matthew.

He reached out and clasped her hand in his. She lifted her lashes and met his warm gaze. A sheen of sadness glistened over his eyes. "I'm so sorry. That's tragic."

She swallowed hard and nodded, determined to fight back the tears edging their way to the corners of her eyes.

"I knew I should have spiked the lemonade," he said.

Sophie let out a surprised snort of laughter. Rarely had anyone made a joke after she announced the death of her late fiancé, and yet, not in a cruel way; it seemed like just the right thing to say. It enabled her to swallow her tears and shake away the sadness, like shaking the rain out of her raincoat after a stormy day. She looked at him with glassy eyes, full of gratitude.

"Why did you and your ex-wife divorce, if you don't mind my asking?" Sophie said.

"Well, she had an affair. She went off on a world trip with this guy, Gustav, and then settled in France. Gustav doesn't like children so she doesn't have much to do with Heather. It broke poor Heather's heart at the time, but I've done my best to make up for her mother's absence." He sighed.

"That must be difficult," Sophie said sympathetically. "It's hard enough being one parent, let alone two."

"I know. But I do blame myself. Not for her affair, but for making the wrong choices. I chose to marry her when from the very beginning I had an inkling it was the wrong thing to do. I was pretty sure she had a thing for my best friend at the time. Maybe that's what spurned me on. I don't know. I was very young, twenty-five, but that's no excuse. You realise as you march on through life that everything really is all about the choices you make. Making good choices really does mean something," he said, looking at her. He picked up a bacon sandwich and took a big bite.

"I agree. But sometimes things happen outside of your control. Where does your choice theory fit in there?" Sophie asked, going for a smoked salmon sandwich.

"True, we can't control everything that happens to us. But then we can choose how to react to it. We can decide how to deal with the situation and how to cope," he said, looking at her softly.

Sophie nodded. "I can tell you're a professor by the way you speak. You're lecturing me, aren't you?"

Matthew laughed. "Sorry, it's hard sometimes to switch off from being a professor and just be normal!"

"No, I like the way you speak. You're so sure of yourself," she said. "What is it you teach?"

"Philosophy," he replied.

"Oh no, from my experience philosophers love to argue," Sophie said, laughing. She popped a raspberry in her mouth. "This really is delicious!" she remarked, taking a bite of a mini blueberry muffin.

"I'm glad you like it," he said, reaching over and brushing a stray crumb from her lip.

Her eyes locked with his. She caught her breath and glanced away, her breathing becoming more shallow.

"Has anyone told you how beautiful you are, especially when you blush?" he said, a half-smile playing on his lips.

She felt as if her skin was on fire under his intense stare. "Um, it's just warm in here," Sophie said, standing up quickly, walking to the glass. A wave of confusing emotions coursed through her. The butterflies were flapping their wings wildly in the pit of her stomach. An electric sensation spread downwards, a deep longing awakened. She avoided his gaze and cleared her throat, trying to distract herself. Her mind felt as if it was lost in a hazy cloud, drunk on food and an uninvited wave of desire.

"I think I need some air," she said more breathlessly than expected.

"Of course, there's plenty of that out by the beach," he replied.

She went down the stairs ahead of him, skipping several steps at a time. Her footsteps clattered loudly in the heavy, timeless silence. She deliberately looked away from the bedrooms, their doors left mischievously ajar.

She burst through the door where the cold air slapped her in the face. She breathed it in, savouring the sensations, feeling her frenzied inner state relax back into its equilibrium. She leant against the lighthouse and stared at the waves, recklessly hurling themselves at the rocks.

"You ok?" Matthew asked, joining her. "I hope I didn't do anything wrong in there." He shoved his hands deep inside his pockets, looking down.

Sophie smiled and shook her head. "I really just needed some air."

Matthew nodded, still looking down at his feet. "Hey, I wanted to ask you, are you a professional swimmer or something?" Matthew asked quietly.

"No, not really," Sophie said, taken aback by the question. "Why?"

"Well, the only people I know who go swimming in the sea when it's October are hardcore swimmers or drunk boys trying to impress the girls. You don't fit into either of those categories. What were you doing out there in the dark all by yourself?" he asked, his eyes fixed on the waves lapping the shore.

Sophie wished he hadn't asked. She felt he knew the answer already. She had literally been drowning in her sorrow, trying to find a way out. She looked away from him. "I don't really know what I was doing, if I'm honest. I just acted impulsively, I guess," she said, turning back with what she hoped was a convincing smile.

He nodded, pensive. "Please don't do it again," he said simply, his eyes still fixed on the sea.

Sophie looked up, slightly confused by the strength of emotion in his warm, deep voice. "I won't. Pinky promise," she said, sticking out her pinky finger, making light of the situation. "Come on, you have a five-year-old girl. You must know how pinky promises work. Don't leave me hanging."

He gave a reluctant laugh and hooked his much larger finger around hers. In an instant he drew her closer to him and kissed her. It was a slow, lingering kiss. Sophie froze. She couldn't move and barely knew how to react. He tugged gently at her top and bottom lip before stepping back. Dazed, Sophie blinked several times, trying to clear her head.

"It's getting dark. Let's get you home," Matthew said softly.

Sophie nodded, mutely, still unsure of what to do or say. Matthew didn't seem to mind her confused silence. He glanced down at her several times as if to check she was still there and hadn't vanished into thin air. He didn't reach for her hand this time as if he knew she needed some space to process what had just happened. As they walked, Sophie felt she had lost control over her limbs. She felt her arms swing wildly by her sides while her hands went limp, unsure of what to do. Her legs continued to extend and propel her forward, one after the other, yet she somehow felt awkward and uncoordinated in her movements.

Matthew didn't seem to notice her inner dilemmas. He switched on the heater as they got into the car. "I had a great time today with you, Sophie," he said, his eyes searching hers for some sort of reflection of those feelings.

Sophie honestly did not know what she felt. She felt guilt and anger towards Dan for putting her in this strange, almost surreal, situation. She felt a pull towards Matthew and enjoyed his company, conversation and, admittedly, kiss. It stirred feelings in her that she hadn't felt in a long time.

"Me too," she said at last. Disappointment flashed across Matthew's face. Sophie quickly added, "I really enjoyed it. I had a beautiful time. Just…" She paused, thinking of what she wanted to say.

"What is it? You can tell me what it is you're thinking," Matthew said, shifting to his side so that he could meet her gaze.

"I don't know, just be patient with me," Sophie said, shrugging her shoulders, as if it was a silly request.

"Of course," Matthew said quietly. "And you, just remember my request, no, command, that you take care of yourself."

Sophie nodded. She flicked through the radio stations as they drove off, settling on a station playing oldies from the eighties.

"Good choice," Matthew said, nodding in approval. "I just can't listen to that modern stuff they call music these days!"

Sophie laughed. "You can't be that old. Let me guess. Thirty-three?"

"Ooh, close," Matthew replied. "Thirty-five actually."

Sophie nodded. "Can you guess my age?" she asked.

"No, no, I'm not getting into that game. Whatever I say, I'll get crucified." He laughed.

"Really, just one guess! I promise I won't get mad!" Sophie said eagerly.

"Hmm, ok, I would guess twenty-nine?" he said, squinting in a mock pained expression.

"What! You just aged me by an entire year!" Sophie replied, tutting her tongue against the roof of her mouth.

"Twenty-eight! Dammit, of course I was going to say twenty-eight!" Matthew said hurriedly.

"It's ok, I'll forgive you this one time," Sophie said, raising her index finger as if in warning.

He parked outside her house. "Goodnight then. Let's do this again sometime," Matthew said.

"Sure, goodnight." She smiled at him and quickly slipped out the door so that there was no confusion as to whether or not there was going to be a goodnight kiss. She turned and gave a little wave, to which he raised his hand off the steering wheel briefly, waiting for her to get safely inside her house before driving off.

Angie was inside watching re-runs of *Doctor Who*.

"Ugh, I hate that show, Ang!" Sophie exclaimed as she walked in.

Angie quickly muted the TV. "Sophie! You've been gone for over five hours. I was beginning to get worried. What were you doing that whole time! You don't have to tell me the details, but I'd prefer it if you did," she said, with a giggle.

Sophie smiled. She had not even checked her watch once while she'd been out. They had been locked in their capsule of time within the walls of the lighthouse where nothing could reach them.

"Sophie, come on, you've got to give me something. Was it a good date? I mean, it must have been!"

Sophie plopped herself next to Angie on the couch. "It was great. He took me to an abandoned lighthouse where we had a picnic he had prepared, and we just chatted there for ages. He is divorced and the wife is in France, so there's a whole lot of sea separating us," Sophie said. "Um, what else? His daughter is five and her name is Heather. We walked along the beach and chatted some more," Sophie finished.

"An abandoned lighthouse? Well, he gets points for creativity in my book," Angie replied. "So I gather you did a lot of talking. Did you get around to doing anything else?" Angie asked mischievously.

Sophie looked down. "Well, we may have kissed."

"What! No way," Angie said, her eyes dancing. "How was it?"

"It was different. I kind of froze, Angie," Sophie said anxiously. "It was more like he kissed me, and I let him. I didn't really kiss him back. I don't know what stopped me. I mean, I like him and we had an amazing date, but I literally froze."

"Hmm, ok, well, it could be worse," Angie said, attempting to salvage the situation. "As long as he didn't run in the opposite direction after it happened, it can be fixed!"

Sophie laughed as she imagined him fleeing in horror. "That would be one hell of a rejection, wouldn't it?"

"Laugh all you like, that was pretty much the case with me and Hank," Angie said, rolling her eyes.

"Oh, you mean Henrietta," Sophie said, referring to Hank's new drag name.

"Hey, we're not changing the subject to my disastrous train wreck of a love life!" Angie cut in quickly. "But yes, my apologies, Henrietta. So it was just the one kiss?"

"Yep, just the one. We also held hands," Sophie added.

Angie smiled. "Well, aren't you adorable." She put her arm around Sophie. "I'm glad it was a good date. Did you guys plan the next one?"

"He said he'd like to see me again, so I'm guessing there will be a next one," Sophie said.

"Of course he would!" Angie replied. "Now, it was just getting to the really good part," she said, as she pressed the mute button again.

Sophie's eyes were glued to the flitting images on the TV screen, but her mind was wandering a million miles away. She had to admit, she really liked Matthew. It was as if there were two forces within her, one pulling her towards him and the other pushing her away. She couldn't help but feel that the one pulling her in his direction was the force that was propelling her into the future whereas the other was attempting to drag her back to the murky depths of her past.

The next day Sophie had an afternoon shift and was spending the morning with Angie. They had both risen early and were getting ready to spend an hour or two walking by the beach. Sophie tumbled down the steps and was met by a sweet smell wafting from the kitchen.

"Good morning, I'm making pancakes!" Angie said enthusiastically. "And coffee, lots of coffee!"

Sophie set the table in the living room and helped Angie bring the plates out. They sat in comfortable silence, eating their pancakes as the sun lazily woke up, its rays stretching through the feathery clouds.

"Looks like it's going to be a nice day," Angie observed.

"Yeah, but wrap up. It's cold by the beach. I'm kind of used to it now but you, with your mild London weather, might suffer," Sophie said, savouring her cup of steaming coffee.

"Ok, Mum," Angie said, laughing.

They finished their breakfast and Sophie gathered up the plates. It was a still, calm morning, a morning where time felt as if it were gliding through treacle. Sophie enjoyed the slow-paced, relaxed momentum as she did the dishes.

And then she felt it. Eyes watching her. Behind her. The presence felt so close she could almost feel its hot breath tickle the back of her neck. She spun around, splashing dishwater down her pyjamas. Angie was still in the living room. Her gaze was then pulled inevitably to the window where two large, black ravens stared, their dark soulless eyes cutting through her. She no longer saw the strange, fleeting beauty she had seen in them the other day. They remained motionless, like hideous charred statues. One of them slowly opened its beak. Sophie stared hard. She felt she could hear whispers infiltrating through the window, emanating from its sharp open mouth. Low whispers slithered through the cracks, muffled and indistinct. The breath of a curse fogged up the windowpane. These were not normal birds, Sophie thought to herself. She tore her gaze away from the sight and turned her back on them.

Angie walked into the kitchen. "Hey, let me finish this up. I'm pretty much ready. I'll get the dishes done and you get ready so we can head off early and make it back in time for your shift," she said brightly.

"Sure," Sophie mumbled. "I wish those ugly birds would just go away. They're there almost every day, just watching me. It's kind of freaking me out," Sophie said, gesturing behind her, without turning around.

Angie glanced over her shoulder. "What birds?" she asked vaguely.

"Those ones…" Sophie said, pointing at the window. To her surprise, she saw nothing except the overgrown grass in her back garden bending slightly in the breeze in a reverent bow to the cottage. The ravens had seemingly vanished into thin air without leaving a trace, not even the echo of their caw.

"I don't see any birds, Soph. You must have scared them away," Angie said, playfully flicking some soapy dishwater at Sophie. "Now go scrub up. We've got to get a move on."

Sophie nodded, distracted. Was that all she had to do? Say she wished they would leave and then like magic they disappeared? Sophie felt unsettled by their vanishing act. Why had they disappeared when Angie turned around? Angie had laughed it off but something about what had just happened, something ephemeral Sophie couldn't quite explain, had unnerved her to the core.

As they were leaving the house, Sophie ventured, "Angie, how was it being in the house alone? Was everything all right when I was out on my date?"

"Yeah, I had my programmes and coffee to keep me busy," Angie replied light-heartedly.

"So everything was normal? Nothing weird happened?" Sophie couldn't help but ask.

Angie turned to face her. "What do you mean, Soph? Are you ok living here alone?"

Sophie considered her answer. "I like living alone and I love this town. But there's something about this house that I just find strange. It puts me on edge. I just wanted to know if you got the same feeling, or if it's just my overactive imagination."

Angie took Sophie's arm and gave it a squeeze. "If you're not comfortable here you can always come home with me. I didn't feel anything strange in the house, but I haven't been here that long. What specifically has put you on edge, Soph?"

Sophie felt stuck. She didn't know how to answer without sounding crazy. She couldn't even pinpoint the specifics. It was just the overall atmosphere of the place and its constant shifting. She felt as if she was balancing on tectonic plates which were slowly moving in unpredictable directions. If she lost her balance for a moment, she would fall into a dark abyss and into a different world entirely.

"I don't know," Sophie replied finally. "Never mind, forget I said anything. I think I'm just getting used to living alone. I've been a little jumpy these days is all." An image of pale lavender eyes swam into focus in her mind's eye. She shook her head slightly, trying to rid herself of the image, trying to stash away that inexplicable encounter in sealed box in the far corners of her mind.

Angie looked concerned. "Sophie, come home if this place isn't for you. I mean it. You've made the place really cute and cosy and you've done great at setting up your life here. But if your heart's not in it, if there's something that feels amiss, that's probably because something is amiss."

Sophie nodded, letting Angie's words sink in. "I'll think about it," she replied, smiling at Angie. "Now let's go while we've still got the time!"

As much as she tried to shake off the creeping feeling, neither the sharp beach air nor the warm, inviting comfort of the Acorn could eradicate the crawling sensation. She felt it was outside of her, hovering around her, a black aura. Even more frighteningly, she felt there was something inside her, under her skin, that hadn't been there before, and like a poisonous snake it was slowly unfurling and uncoiling, slithering its way through her bloodstream, taking over her mind, body and soul.

# Chapter 15

## *Samuel*

Samuel was lying in bed awake. It was midday. Samuel rose early, around 5:00 am on most days. He could not remember the last time he had awoken past 7:00 am. It was unthinkable for Samuel to be in bed so late. But it had happened again. Last night he had been accosted by a particularly vivid hallucination, and he couldn't get it out of his mind.

When the apparitions and bizarre dreamlike experiences first started happening, Samuel had been terrified. He had lived with creepy, unexplainable phenomena for years when he lived in the house on Edgeware Lane, but nothing had ever been this intense. He had felt crawling sensations, temperature changes and the ghostly appearances and disappearances of Willowen, but he had never been transported to different times and places, witnessing a small section of history unfold before his very eyes.

Samuel was no longer terrified of the experiences he was now having. He actually looked forward to them and would try to figure out ways to induce them. They were like Hansel and Gretel's breadcrumbs, each one a little clue leading him to his house of answers, answers he had been seeking for years. Only now, since Sophie had moved in, was the trail revealing itself to him. It was as if the confused, decaying leaves of the past had been swept away to expose a golden pathway. What connection did Sophie have with the house? Was it a coincidence or was there an explanation? The hallucinations continued to leave Samuel breathless and his body battered, but at last, the truth was shining through the darkness that had shrouded his life for so long.

Last night had been different from the other hallucinations. It had been so clear, as if Samuel had been watching the scene from a high definition television. It didn't have the blurred-around-the-edges, surreal effect of the previous visions. The outlines were sharp and crisp. The voices had been penetrating and continued to echo in Samuel's mind like the memory of a pebble tumbling down a well. He had been inside the ramshackle hut again, the decrepit ancestor to the house Sophie currently lived in. There had been a group of eight people crammed inside, talking in hushed voices.

"They're coming to search the place again and this time they won't leave a stone unturned. They will search the house and the cliffs themselves," a middle-aged, well-dressed man was saying. "You have to take your family and leave tonight, Willowen. You don't have a choice."

Willowen nodded solemnly. Erosabel was standing by his side, her piercing blue eyes narrowed in concentration. The children were supposed to be playing on the earthy floor, but all of them had ears like satellite dishes, directed towards the adult conversation.

"You have been so kind, Mr. Davies, coming to warn us like this," Erosabel said, giving him and his wife a small smile. The middle-aged couple were holding hands, looking at the gypsy family and each other in concern.

"Of course, we've come to see you and your children as dear friends. Our William will be so sad to lose his playmate Danior. But it must be done. For your safety, you have to leave," Mrs. Davies said, sadness and resignation hanging in her eyes like a line of limp washing hung out to dry in a storm.

"I'm sorry it's had to end like this, and I can't explain the behaviour of our fellow townspeople. They seem to have been driven into hysteria by this most recent pox outbreak. I'm sorry the blame has fallen upon you and your fellow travellers. But the situation is dire, and you must leave," Mr. Davies said sternly. "There will be a storm tonight. Leave then. We can arrange a carriage to take you to the next town over. It will be a dark and dangerous road, but because of the storm you will probably slip through the police's fingers."

Willowen was looking sadly at the children. "Do you know anything of our fellow travellers? Are they still being held captive in prison or…" He let his voice trail off.

Mr. Davies merely looked sorrowfully back at Willowen and gently shook his head. "You need to look out for you and your family, that is it," he replied.

"Right," Erosabel said firmly. "We will pack a small bundle each, basic provisions, and we'll be off tonight."

Mrs. Davies gave her a quick embrace and ruffled the children's hair. Mr. Davies and Willowen shook hands.

"It's been a pleasure knowing you. Safe travels," Mr. Davies said as he and his wife turned to leave.

"Thank you for all you've done for us. We're forever indebted to you for your kindness," Willowen replied.

As they left, Erosabel propelled herself into motion. Dark clouds were creeping over the horizon, spreading like a purplish, painful bruise.

"Children, go get any of your toys or trinkets you have that are lying around in the garden. Edwina, if you've left any of your dolls up in the tree, I think you should bring them down if you want to take them with you," Erosabel said hurriedly.

"Mommy, do you think we'll be able to do it? To get away without them noticing?" Joni asked her mother, fear haunting her eyes.

"Yes, sweetheart, I think exactly that. We'll manage. You heard Mr. Davies, there will be a storm later. The police will be too scared to leave the warm safety of their homes to chase a little gypsy family."

"What about all our friends? We're just going to leave them?" Logan asked, bitterness and anger saturating his voice.

"We don't know what's happened to them and we can't find out. It's not fair but it is what it is. Life isn't fair, Logan. We're simply pawns in more powerful people's games," Erosabel said. "Now, hurry, get whatever you want to bring with you and leave the rest."

"Let's go." Logan sighed, slapping Danior playfully over the head.

"Hey, watch it!" Danior piped up, chasing his older brother out of the hut.

"What about you, mommy? Are you ok?" a high-pitched girlish voice asked. The question was thin and tenuous, taut like a string that was about to snap.

"My love, I'm fine," Erosabel said quietly, scooping Edwina up in her arms and planting a kiss on the little girl's forehead. "I'm feeling much better today."

Edwina nodded, smiling uncertainly. "Ok, I'll get my dolls from the tree house. They've been keeping guard for us and keeping us safe this whole time, you know!"

"I'm sure they have, Eddie." Erosabel smiled as she put Edwina down.

Once Edwina had left the hut, Willowen turned to Erosabel. "Is that true? You're feeling better today?"

Samuel watched Erosabel's expression crumble from being strong and determined to fearful and defeated.

"No, Willowen. It's not true. Of course it's not true. Things get worse by the day, by the hour and by the minute!" She was rubbing her temples aggressively, as if she was trying to erase her brain altogether. "It doesn't stop. They don't stop!" she whispered, collapsing on the floor.

Willowen knelt down beside her. "It's going to be ok. Once we get away from here we'll get you the help you need."

Erosabel snorted. "Help? The only help out there for people like me is a bed with chains. You know they'll lock me up and I'll never be able to see the children again. That's worse than death for me!"

"We'll think of something, Roz. We'll manage this," Willowen said softly, trying to convince himself as much as Erosabel.

Erosabel smiled weakly at him. "Of course we will. How about you gather up some food to take with us?"

"You'll be all right in here?" Willowen asked, brows furrowed.

Erosabel nodded, exhausted. "I just need to rest before the journey."

"Sure. I'll a pay a quick visit to the Turners. They've been so helpful with getting us supplies and food. I'm sure they will grant us this last favour."

"Say goodbye to them for me," Erosabel said, her voice barely above a whisper.

Just as Willowen was about to get up, Erosabel grabbed his ragged shirt. "Please be careful, Will. I love you," she said softly.

"I will. I love you too, Roz," he replied, kissing the top of her head.

When the door shut, Samuel turned to see Erosabel sitting, frozen like a statue on the floor. Suddenly, she let out a low grunt and her body contorted, her limbs twisting and sticking out at odd angles. He watched as the transformation took place, rooted to the spot in horror. He wanted to sprint after Willowen, beg him, plead with him not to leave Erosabel on her own in this state. In this world, however, he had no say, no control. He was merely a silent observer.

Erosabel continued twisting her body. Samuel heard several sickening cracks as she writhed like a snake on fire. A low growl rumbled through her body as she intertwined her fingers into her tangled hair.

"Go away," Erosabel hissed in a harsh voice, one completely different from the voice she was using moments ago with Willowen. At first Samuel thought she must be talking to him. No one else was in the room. But instead of turning to face him, she knelt on the floor and as quick as a flash, slammed her head with full force into the earth. A cloud of dust erupted around her.

"Just stop and leave me alone," she snarled again before slamming her head a second time into the earth. A faint imprint remained. Samuel wanted to reach out and stop her. He wanted to stop her from hurting herself but was powerless to do so.

"Shut up, shut up, shut up!" she said more ferociously, before hitting her head several times in a row.

When she rose from the haze of dust, Samuel saw a tear of blood trickle from her forehead and down the side of her face. What happened next made his blood run cold. All he wanted was to be transported back to the present day, away from this monstrous scene. In that moment he yearned for the comfort and security of his old armchair and a warm mug of tea. Erosabel grabbed fistfuls of her hair and yanked as hard as she could. Thick clumps of hair were torn from her scalp making an audible, nauseating sound. A low sinister laugh permeated the room, flooding every corner with stomach-churning terror. Samuel watched in horror as Erosabel slowly let her head loll back as she let out that inhuman, blood-curdling laugh. She continued laughing as she grabbed handfuls of dirt and smeared it across her face. The hideous laughter was a continuous string, an unending note stretching, expanding, contracting, and obliterating everything in its path. There was no pause for breath, no variation in tone. It was a flat constant, unchanging and unnatural.

As quickly as it started, it stopped, leaving the room empty. Erosabel stood up slowly, dropping the wiry black tufts of hair. Her eyes were glazed over, lost in a trance. Samuel peered outside through the gap in the wall. The storm was upon them. The heavy rainclouds began pelting down bullets of rain, hurling them at the earth below.

"Time to come inside, children," Erosabel said flatly. As she opened the door, two ravens swooped inside, cawing loudly. "There there, my lovies. It will all be over soon," Erosabel cooed in an unnaturally light, airy voice.

Samuel charged after her. She left the hut, walking slowly but deliberately. He felt an uncontrollable urge to grab her, to shake her awake. He reached out and tried to touch her arm. Instead of feeling flesh and bones, his hand swiped through the air. He looked up. Erosabel and the stormy scene were melting away before his very eyes. The last he saw was Joni, Logan and Danior gathering what looked like leaves and twigs by the cliff edge. Their silhouettes were moving busily as their mother drifted towards them, a liquid shadow creeping up silently from behind.

Samuel had woken up from the vision feeling disturbed and disoriented. It had been so real it made the world around him feel like an illusion. He had a bad feeling about what he had seen. He wanted to tell someone about it. But who would he tell? And who would care about a mother behaving bizarrely over a century ago? They were all long dead and buried. But their stories continued. Samuel felt the family story had been lying dormant for decades and was only now breathing life again. It had a secret it needed to tell.

Samuel heard a tapping on his windowpane, anchoring him back to the present day. The tapping grew louder and more relentless. Samuel heaved himself out of bed to investigate, imagining a tree branch swaying back and forth in the breeze. He parted the curtains and gasped. He stared in dismay at the figure perched on his windowsill. A massive solitary raven was staring back at him, transfixed and unmoving.

# Chapter 16

## *Sophie*

*Dear Daniel,*

*Darkness consumes my very soul,*

*It creeps like a shadow within me,*

*Slowly, malevolently, it whispers stories, truths untold,*

*It showers me in pain and misery.*

*My heart is a dusky wasteland,*

*Where the black angel of death spreads her charred wings,*

*She tells me to trust her, take her withered hand,*

*Hope is dead, she sings.*

*For the longest time I believed her,*

*For the longest time she ruled over me with a heart of stone,*

*Yet now I see dawn breaking on the horizon,*

*Now I feel I'm not alone.*

*A trickle of lights filters through the cracks,*

*My heart and soul yearn for its warmth,*

*I feel I'm returning, I'm coming back,*

*From the depths of hell, I've been reborn.*

*Truth stretches through the sky and breaks free,*

*Filling me with the hope the dark angel did steal,*

*I can see life beaming with my new-found clarity,*

*I can finally begin to heal.*

*Sophie*

The night before Angie was due to leave, Sophie felt nervous. Apart from the disappearance of the ravens, everything had been so normal during the week Angie had spent with her. She had even stopped having those bizarre dreams brimming with fire and ash. Sophie couldn't help but doubt herself, thinking stress and anxiety had overcharged her brain, causing her imagination to overreact to what were actually mundane occurrences. She was certain her grief counsellor would explain away the strangeness of the past month and put it down to Sophie's overexertion with the move, new job, new town and so on.

Whatever the explanation, Sophie continued to toss and turn in bed, wishing Angie could stay just another couple of days. She knew she couldn't ask that of her friend and that tomorrow morning she would be left alone in the house. Except, the strange thing was, Sophie never really felt alone.

They had planned to see Isabelle during the morning before Angie had to head back to London. Angie had baked some deformed, lumpy cookies which she had intended to bring over for tea with Isabelle.

"Do you think I should bother taking these over? I mean, maybe she would take it as an insult?" Angie said, eyeing the cookies sceptically.

"Here, let me taste one," Sophie said, peeling one off the pan. She took a bite of the strangely shaped mass. "It tastes great, all gooey sugar and chocolate, exactly how a cookie should taste!"

"Yeah, but they look like those little alien babies we used to beg our parents to buy us, right?" Angie replied.

"They don't look like alien babies!" Sophie laughed. "They taste great, and that's what counts. Let's put them in a Tupperware. Isabelle will love them. Anyway she keeps telling me her sight isn't what it used to be. I don't think she will even notice that they look slightly off."

Angie chuckled. "All right, you've convinced me," she said, helping Sophie peel the cookies off the pan and into the Tupperware.


"Oh, how lovely!" Isabelle exclaimed happily at the sight of the cookies. "Please come in, let me make us some tea and we'll have these with it! So you must be Angie," she continued, bustling around with dainty china cups and plates.

"Here, let me help you with this," Angie replied. "And yes, I'm Angie. I love this town and the seaside. It's such a lovely break from London!"

"Oh yes, it's all peace and tranquillity in these parts. We can't keep up with the fast-paced life of London," Isabelle said.

Once the tea and biscuits were served, they all settled comfortably into the plump, overstuffed couches, and easy, light conversation ensued. Isabelle asked Angie about her work, city life and her relationships. She hid her surprise as Angie delved into some of the details about her string of unsuccessful, harrowing relationships. They chatted for a couple of hours, nibbling on crust-less sandwiches, lumpy biscuits and a home-made sponge cake Isabelle had whipped up for the occasion.

"Well, it really is time for me to go now. It was so lovely meeting you, Isabelle," Angie said.

"Oh, the pleasure was all mine, dear," Isabelle replied. "Please visit again whenever you are in these parts."

"Of course," Angie said.

"See you, Isabelle," Sophie said, giving Isabelle a hug before heading back to the house to help Angie gather her things.

"You take care of yourself, Sophie," Angie said, hugging her friend once they had packed everything into her car. "And let me know if you ever need anything. I'm just a phone call away."

"For sure. Thank you so much for coming down. I had the best week with you," Sophie said. "We must do this again sometime. Maybe I'll come down to London for a bit."

"Please do, mi casa es su casa," Angie replied. "You sure you'll be ok?" she asked, the concerned glint in her eyes betraying the light-hearted tone of her voice.

"I'll be absolutely fine. Besides, I have Matthew to protect me," Sophie said, with a smile.

She and Matthew had been on two more dates since their first one at the lighthouse. They had gone for coffee at The Crown Cup in town and for a candlelit romantic dinner in Canterbury near the university where he worked. Both outings had been just as magical as the first. They found they had so much to talk about. Once dinner plates, coffee cups and desserts had been removed, they continued to sit and chat for hours. Conversation flowed between them like an invisible stream of words, thoughts and ideas. Whenever there was a lull in conversation, whenever the words ebbed, withdrawing from the shoreline of their conversation, an amicable silence settled between them, like snowflakes drifting serenely in the air before melting into the earth below. They had also shared two more kisses on these dates. Fortunately, Sophie did not freeze up like the first time, but relaxed into his embrace, enjoying the electric sensation rushing through her body.

"Oh, that one's a keeper, he is," Angie said, breaking into Sophie's dreamy reverie. "I'll miss you, Soph."

"I already miss you!" Sophie called after her. "Let me know when you reach London. And please drive safely!" Angie was a reckless driver and had bashed her car up more times than Sophie could remember.

"Don't worry about me, I'll be fine," Angie said as she waved.

Sophie waved back, staying outside until Angie's car was out of sight. She turned around and headed back to her house. It was Saturday and Sophie was meeting Matthew in a couple of hours. He was picking her up and taking her to Canterbury again. They were planning on visiting the cathedral together. He had visited it many times but said that he could visit it every day and never get bored. Every time he went he claimed to discover something new about the cathedral and that the experience was always different somehow. Sophie loved visiting museums, ancient architectural sites and forgotten dilapidated churches and was excited about this excursion.

Sophie got ready, pulling on a pair of faded blue jeans and a deep purple pullover. She spiced up the outfit a bit with a chunky pair of cameo earrings and statement necklace. She was about to head downstairs to make herself a cup of tea before Matthew arrived when the ring on her finger caught the light. Matthew had gently asked her about Dan on their last date and what had happened. He hadn't mentioned the ring, but Sophie could feel him glancing at it surreptitiously throughout the evening. Sophie felt her stomach tie itself into knots. She felt guilty wearing it and guilty taking it off. With the utmost care, she twisted the ring off her finger. It sparkled in the palm of her hand, reflecting memories and a dream of a different life, a life she never had. A tear splashed the shiny band, followed by another. Sophie sat down and curled herself into a ball, rocking silently on the floor.

"I miss you so much," she said to the empty room, her eyes transfixed on the ring, as if by removing it, she was amputating part of her soul. She felt a physical pain shoot through her body. An ache deep within her bones weighed her down. "I just want to talk to you, to see you one more time. I just want our life back," she said, before collapsing into a puddle of tears on the floor.

Minutes trickled by as she lay there, her face resting on the cool wooden floorboards. Eventually she managed to catch her breath between the sobs and drag herself up. Gravity felt as if it had doubled in strength, every movement she made required immense effort. Slowly but surely, she managed to stand.

She checked her watch and realised she had twenty minutes before Matthew arrived. She looked at her tear-stained, blotchy face in the mirror. Time for make-up to work its magic, she thought to herself. She quickly washed her face and layered on as much make-up as she could to conceal all the crying she had just done. Her eyes still looked a little red and puffy by the time she was finished but it was the best she could do. She placed her beautiful rose-gold engagement ring in one of her cushioned trinket boxes, whispering, "I love you," as she closed the lid softly. It felt like a symbolic moment, as if she was closing the door to the life that had passed her by, the life which had been swept away like the broken shells littering the beach, one moment there, the next gone. The vast love between her and Dan which once had been so real and had permeated her entire body was now trapped, captured like a fragile butterfly within the walls of the little trinket box beside Sophie's bed.

Punctual as ever, the sound of the doorbell chimed through the house. Sophie forced herself to smile as she opened the door.

"Hey," she said self-consciously, her fingers feeling stripped and her heart shattered.

Matthew took one look at her and the sadness etched deep within her eyes. Those large wounded brown eyes tugged at his heartstrings. Without saying anything, as he didn't believe there was anything he could say to make her feel better, he pulled her close, wrapping his big arms around her tightly. Sophie breathed in deeply, refusing to cry again. Matthew smelt different from Dan. Dan had smelt of fresh soap and his favourite cologne, like a clear spring morning. Matthew emanated a deep, warm, wood-like smell with a note of chocolaty sweetness. Sophie nestled her face into his jacket, seeking refuge, comfort, security, something, anything, to make the pain stop.

# Chapter 17

## *Matthew*

Matthew put his hand around her head and stroked her soft hair. She reminded him of a fragile, broken bird he had once seen on the grass having just tumbled out of its nest. He had scooped up the little bird and placed it back in its home after smoothing out its ruffled feathers. He wished he could help Sophie in the same way. He wished he could make the constant pain she felt stop. She was the first woman he had been drawn to since his messy divorce with Clare. Matthew had never been a believer in soul mates but there was something about Sophie that made him think differently. There was an aura surrounding her that, like a magnet, drew him in. He was drawn to the way her eyes would sometimes drift and cloud over, another world away. He loved the way she fiddled with an imaginary lock of hair behind her right ear. The blush that blossomed on her cheeks when she was nervous was beautiful, making her look like a china doll. He felt she was enveloped in layers of mystery, and even if he lived a thousand lives with her he would never quite know the secrets locked in the treasure trove of her mind. Her fluid movements and low dreamy voice sometimes made him feel like she was a mere illusion and if he blinked she would disappear.

"You ready to go? We could do this another time if you want," Matthew said, releasing her and holding her at arm's length so he could see her expression.

"No, I want to go today, with you," she replied, smiling weakly up at him.

"Right, then let's make a move," he said warmly.

They clambered in the car and sped off towards Canterbury and its towering cathedral.

They parked and bought their tickets. Matthew had tried to lighten the mood and chatted about work, how he was trying to prepare his students for their upcoming exams as well as get an article published in an important philosophy journal. Sophie sat next to him nodding serenely, offering the occasional comment or words of advice.

Once they arrived, Matthew insisted on buying their tickets. They entered into the nave of the cathedral. Matthew could tell by Sophie's expression that she was instantly captivated. He couldn't help but feel a glow of pride at having chosen the right place to take her. An overwhelming sense of quiet descended, like thick velvet curtains blocking out the loud bustle of the outside world, separating them from reality. Hushed voices rustled around them, the walls absorbing the endless stream of secrets and whispers. It felt still and cold. Matthew watched as Sophie's eyes followed the soaring pillars, craning her delicate neck to look at the high ceiling. Light was drifting in mystical swirls through the windows, bathing Sophie in an iridescent glow. Sophie's eyes darted from one corner to another, drinking in every detail around her. The beautiful stained-glass windows and the other-worldly air that had been captured in the cathedral spun stories of a lost time, a bygone age.

She and Matthew continued walking slowly together, Sophie's gaze enthralled by the cathedral while Matthew watched how her expression flitted from awe to a glimmer of sadness to furrowed concentration as she read the inscriptions in the walls and floor. They walked up a set of stone steps and veered to the left.

"This is the Altar of the Sword's Point where Thomas Beckett was murdered all those centuries ago, back in 1170. They say his ghost still haunts these parts," Matthew said quietly. Sophie's eyes fell on three black jagged swords pointing downwards, symbols of death. He noticed her shiver ever so slightly. He put an arm gently around her, wanting to protect her from the cold, the daggers, Thomas Beckett's ghost and most of all, the ghosts that haunted the architecture of her mind. Statues of saints and carved angles peered down at them through the centuries, their white sightless eyes following them as they walked.

They walked into the choir area where candles in glass tombs flickered along the walls. They passed rows of dark wooden benches which had been roped off. Quietly they stole into the trinity chapel. A chandelier dangled from the ceiling, spilling light onto the tombs surrounding them. The tombs were encased in black metal bars, death's eternal prison. Sophie walked up to one of the eerie tombs and read aloud what was written beneath it. "The Tomb of the Black Prince." The dates below read 1330–1376. Sophie peered into the Black Prince's final resting place. The figure of a man clad in armour lay there. His blank eyes staring into nothingness, his hands placed together, as if in silent, eternal prayer. She drifted to another tomb where King Henry IV was resting next to his second wife, Joan of Navarre. They wore regal bejewelled crowns on their heads, their expressions frozen in time. Sophie looked at the detail of their dress, the folds in the illustrious alabaster robes.

"It's beautiful, isn't it?" Matthew said, his voice echoing behind her.

"Yes," Sophie replied in hushed tones.

"Do you want to see the crypt? We can go from there," Matthew said, pointing.

Sophie nodded, following him. They passed a group of school kids who were jotting down notes in their journals and descended into the crypt. There were wooden chairs arranged in a circle, behind which more rows of chairs were set out, awaiting some sort of congregation.

Sophie stared at the chairs.

"What are you looking at?" Matthew asked.

"Nothing," Sophie said quickly. She paused before continuing, "Just imagining people sitting in those chairs, ghosts from another time watching and listening as we walk right past them. You know, sometimes I can envision something so perfectly in my imagination it's almost like I forget that it's not real. That nothing is actually there." She continued walking, the long shadows trailing after her as her soft footsteps echoed in the distance.

It was Matthew's turn to feel an involuntary shiver down his spine. Sophie fascinated him but there was something about her which he couldn't understand. And that frightened him. There was a darkness deep within her, probably something that was born out of the death of her fiancé. When she went to that place of darkness, Matthew felt an invisible veil separate them. When ensconced in that mysterious cocoon, she was unreachable.

He also didn't know how he felt about Dan, her ex-fiancé. This was a situation he had never been in before. How could he compete with such a man? Sophie had shown him several pictures of him. Dan was handsome, fit and had a big smile, which most of the time was directed at Sophie. Matthew felt a heavy sadness when looking at those happy pictures. Sophie could have had a completely different life, one where he, Matthew, did not exist at all. A sharp pang of jealousy tinged the sadness he felt when looking at those pictures. He knew if he were to fall in love with Sophie, he would have to accept Dan and the tragedy that would colour her life forever.

"Let's go back up," Sophie said quickly, linking arms with Matthew in a sense of urgency.

"Sure, everything ok?" Matthew asked.

"Yes, just feeling a little claustrophobic is all," she replied, slightly breathlessly.

Matthew took her hand and gave it a gentle squeeze. Together they emerged into the open air of the outdoors. For a moment neither of them spoke, both letting what they had felt and seen settle somewhere deep within them.

They had been in the cathedral for a couple of hours. Matthew heard his stomach rumble.

"Hey, you hungry by any chance?" he asked.

She smiled up at him. "Ravenous!"

"Great, I know this lovely little Italian place. Great food and even better wine!"

"Sounds like my kind of place," Sophie replied, grabbing his hand and swinging it childishly in hers. Just then, the clouds in the heavens above broke into a light, spitting rain.

"Quick, I don't have an umbrella. Let's go," Matthew said, breaking into a run.

Sophie ran, allowing the rain to kiss her face. She started laughing. It was a light, carefree sound. The sound was music to Matthew's ears.

"Guide me," Sophie said, closing her eyes.

Matthew glanced at her, watching the rain sprinkle her hair and face softly. "Ok," he replied.

She closed her eyes and he grabbed her hand tighter. They jogged slowly, Sophie giving herself up to the sensations around her. She could hear and taste the drizzling rain, the bustle of cars and people go by. She could feel Matthew's warm hand encasing hers. Matthew glanced back at her to make sure she was ok, running blindly through Canterbury with him. She was half smiling in an enigmatic way, reminding him of Leonardo da Vinci's famous *Mona Lisa*. A look of peaceful tranquillity had softened her face. In that moment, she looked utterly free, angelically beautiful. Matthew wished he could capture that moment and keep it forever.

They reached the restaurant.

"Open your eyes," Matthew said.

Sophie lifted her rain-studded lashes slowly, feeling dreamily disoriented. "Wow, I feel kind of dizzy," she said, smiling through the rain.

"I'm not surprised! Let's get you inside before you have any more of your crazy ideas," he said, putting his arm around her and escorting her into the warmth of the restaurant.

The waiter led them to a table next to the window so they could hear the soft patter of the rain.

"The cathedral is absolutely stunning," Sophie said enthusiastically. "I could go back a hundred times!"

Matthew laughed. "I've lost count of the number of times I've been there. I used to go there a lot when I was going through the divorce. Something about being in the company of such great men and women, lost in time, made my troubles feel almost insignificant."

Sophie nodded, seeming to understand this feeling.

"You know," he said slowly, "my daughter, Heather, has been asking a lot about you. She wants to know who I've been spending so much time with."

"Oh no, you mean, she wants to know who's been stealing her daddy away," Sophie said, an expression of guilt flitting across her face.

"No, don't be silly! It's not like that. But she really wants to meet you," he said, looking down, fiddling with his napkin. "I mean, I get it if you feel it's too soon but it would mean a lot to me if, maybe, you could come to my place, and have dinner or something with me and my daughter," he finished, glancing up anxiously.

Sophie paused, her expression unreadable. Matthew shifted uncomfortably in his seat. He knew it had been too soon to bring this up. He pretended to read the menu, waiting for her response.

"I'd love to meet her," Sophie said softly, reaching out and placing her palm gently on Matthew's hand.

A wave of relief eased the fine lines gathering in Matthew's face. "Thank you, that really means the world to me," he said, smiling. "Heather will be so excited when I tell her!"

They chatted some more about the cathedral, after which Sophie opened up about her love of writing and how she hoped to write something of significance one day.

"I mean, I write poetry and I was working on a short story before..." Sophie let her voice trail off.

Matthew glanced down, nodding. "Can I read your poems one day?" he asked.

Sophie blinked. "Yeah, maybe one day," she said hesitantly. "I've never actually shared my poems with anyone before."

"Well, it would be an honour for me to read them!" Matthew said enthusiastically. He wanted something that was just his and Sophie's. Something she hadn't shared with anyone, just him.

"If you ever finish your short story or decide to write something else, I know a guy who's a literary agent. He's always looking for fresh, young talent. I can pass your work to him anytime. Besides, he owes me a couple of favours so he'll have to read it," Matthew said, with a wink.

"That would be amazing," Sophie replied.

They continued to chat easily over lunch and polished off a large dessert before Matthew signalled for the cheque and it was time to head home.

Once in the car, Matthew said, "I can't tell you how much I've been enjoying your company. Since Clare, I haven't been interested in anyone or anything, except my Heather, of course, until I met you. You're like a bolt of lightning, shocked me into living again." He laughed.

"I could say the same about you," Sophie said quietly, glancing shyly up at him.

As her eyes met his, Matthew felt an undercurrent of energy ripple through his body. All he could think of was touching the softness of her skin as her breath caught in her throat. He leant forward, cupped her cheek with his hand and gently kissed her. His warm lips caressed hers as his other hand glided slowly down her neck. His light fingers trailed the contours of her collarbone and continued down to her breasts. Sophie drew a sharp intake of breath. He felt her chest swell as a rush of desire rippled through him. He squeezed her breasts lightly before touching the softness of her stomach as his hand travelled lower. Sophie's breathing intensified. As his hand stroked her inner thigh, a moan escaped the back of her throat. Matthew kissed her harder as he bit her lower lip.

Just then lightening streaked through the sky followed by a crack of thunder. Matthew withdrew for a moment, looking outside the car window at the rain lashing around them. Sophie inhaled sharply and quickly fixed her clothes which had become somewhat dishevelled.

She cleared her throat. "We should probably head home before the roads turn into waterfalls."

Matthew nodded, trying to recalibrate himself. "Good thinking." He smiled softly at her before starting the car and driving in the direction of the cliffs.

Once they arrived, before Sophie could hop out of the car and make the mad dash to her house to avoid getting drenched, Matthew grabbed her hand. He kissed it slowly and gently, rubbing her delicate fingers with his.

"I'm going to miss you," he said.

Sophie laughed. "We have our date with your daughter next weekend. It's not that far away."

Matthew nodded pensively. "I'll be thinking about you every second of every day until then."

Sophie smiled again and waved as she hopped out and sloshed through the rain to her house.

As Matthew drove away he couldn't stop thinking of Sophie, of how she felt, of how sugary sweet her lips tasted. He played the memory of them in the car over and over again. He didn't know how he would be able to survive an entire week without her.

# Chapter 18

## *Sophie*

*Dear Erosabel,*

*As my fragmented, fractured mind slips away,*

*I fear more and more for its decay,*

*As I stumble, as I wander,*

*From this world, my mind is torn asunder.*


*I fear I am falling deep,*

*Into a schizophrenic sleep,*

*Where gruesome dreams take control*

*Commandeering mind, body and soul.*


*Where death and uncertainty lie,*

*Piercing me with ghoulish, golden eyes,*

*I feel the heat of its gaze upon me land,*

*Innocently I stand and take it by its claw-like hand.*


*It leads me through tunnels awry,*

*Twisted and crooked as a broken spine,*

*Through the dreary underground depths of hell,*

*It wraps me softly in its hypnotising spell.*


*Deeper I go into the depths of madness,*

*Where I experience a sudden gladness,*

*Slipping through the tunnel of insanity,*

*Has broken my anchor to this world and I am finally free.*

*Sophie*


As she opened the front door, she swore she could hear a cat howl. She quickly glanced around, but everything was blurred in the heavy sheet of rain. She waited to hear the cat's cry again and see if she could discern where it was coming from. When no sound emerged, she quickly stomped her dripping shoes on the doormat and shut the door.

Sophie collapsed, weak-kneed, onto the sofa, still lost in a dreamy haze. Shaking off her wet clothes, she changed into her soft, cosy pyjamas. She sat cross-legged on the sofa, a romantic novel in one hand and a warm mug of steaming tea in the other. It was the perfect night to get lost in a novel, Sophie thought happily to herself. Thoughts of Matthew and their intense kiss lingered in her mind. She could still feel his strong hands as he touched the curves of her body.

Just as she was settling in, she heard a sharp rapping coming from the kitchen. Annoyed, she heaved herself up from her comfy seat to investigate. It was probably a broken branch knocking on the window.

Suddenly she felt as if she was swimming in slow motion while a cloud of fog infiltrated her mind. Everything around her seemed to shimmer and lose its distinctiveness, as if it were dissolving into the air around her. Once solid objects looked as if they were made of misty vapour. Sophie blinked several times in an attempt to restore her vision. When she reached the window, her eyes locked with the dark hallow eyes of the raven. The raven that had not been seen since Angie's arrival. It opened its beak slowly, letting out a gentle hiss. At first it sounded like the whistling of a boiling kettle. Sophie leant closer, her breath fogging up the glass pane separating her from the bird.

It wasn't a hiss. It was whispering to her. It was saying, "They're coming."

The bird opened its beak wide, so wide it looked like its jaws would snap at the unnatural movement. It let out a massive blood-curdling caw and spread its wings like a black angel of doom unfurling in front of her. Abruptly, the trance-like state was shattered. Everything came into sharp focus. The cloud dispersed, scattering to the far corners of her mind. Fear returned, pulsating hard through Sophie's veins. Her pulse quickened and the all-too-familiar sensation of dread settled heavily in her bones.

She felt it before she saw it. The floors and walls started to rattle. It was as if the house itself was trembling in fear. The rattling grew stronger. Books slipped off the bookcase, landing in a heap on the floor. The glasses left out on the table smashed, glass deflecting in every direction. And then the birds. All of a sudden all Sophie could see was a fast-moving swarm of black feathers engulf her house. It was a loud, black blur. Their wings flapped wildly, slapping the windows and doors. Sophie thought the house would collapse under the force of their blows. She stepped away from the window, the Kafkaesque nightmare unfolding around her.

In that moment, Sophie felt nothing. Not even fear could reach her. She was paralysed in shock as she watched thousands of ravens dance madly in circles around her house, their screeching echoing in her ears. She could see a scarlet slit of sky behind the solid mass, as the setting sun slipped away into oblivion, cowering out of sight. The crimson light reflected off the backs of the moving birds, making them look as if they were a shadow bathed in blood.

Sophie stood there motionless, continuing to stare transfixed at the swirling tornado of birds battering her house. Their continual churning made her sick with nausea. She then heard another screeching caw echo above the rest, and suddenly the birds turned in that direction. Their demonic wings flapped, moving away from her house. As quickly as they had come, they morphed into the black storm clouds above, an undulating bruise in the darkening sky behind.

Sophie remained rooted to the kitchen floor, unable to move or breathe. She had no idea how much time had elapsed before she regained control of her limbs. Not only did she have to move but she had to do something. She had to understand. She needed answers. She turned defiantly away from the kitchen and back into the living room. Her romantic novel lay discarded on the floor, while her stone-cold tea had been knocked over sideways, its contents dripping onto the carpet. She knelt down by the couch, closing her eyes and breathing heavily. She counted several breaths before shoving her hand underneath. She felt it immediately. It had been waiting patiently for her return. She pulled out Samuel J. Woodlock's book and wiped away the layer of dust from the cover. If she wanted answers, her instinct told her this was the place to start.

She did a quick clean-up of the destruction around her. Surveying the scene, it looked as if a monster had grabbed the room with giant fists and given it a violent shake, tipping the contents upside down. Sophie made herself a fresh cup of tea and settled down to read the book in trepidation. She sat on the couch and opened the first page.

*Welcome, reader. Let's embark on this history with an open mind and eagerness to learn about the history of these glorious cliffs of ours.*

Sophie breathed in deeply and began that journey. She continued to read through the night and into the early hours of the morning. It wasn't until she had read the book cover to cover that she put it down and closed her eyes, slipping into a sleep so deep not even the Devil himself could reach her.

Bizarre, dark dreams shifted and morphed in the corners of her mind. Their vividness blurred the boundaries between what was real and what was a dream. She was in her home, but it was completely different. Rough, splintered wood hammered together made up the walls, and the floor was hard earth, cracked and dry. She raised her hands, the same colour as the earth, to her face. Her cheeks were damp. She was crying. Sensing that she was not alone, she looked up.

Four ghastly ravens were facing her, staring directly at her. Although their beaks were shut, she could hear a low hissing emanating from their direction. It was as if they were whispering amongst themselves in a language beyond her comprehension. Their gaze, however, remained fixed on her.

Time was suspended in the dank hut. Sophie couldn't tell if it was getting lighter or darker outside, or if both were occurring at the same time. The weak light filtering through the cracks and crevices in between the planks of wood could have been projected from a silvery moon or a blinding sun. Time was trapped in the hut, warped and crooked.

Finally, one of the birds opened its beak, letting out a low hiss. This time Sophie could understand it. Its words hit her with their solid weight, crushing her insides and bruising her soul.

"Kill them and set us free. Relieve yourself of this cross you carry, this burden. Kill them and end the curse," it whispered malevolently.

Sophie looked down at her hands. They were no longer damp with tears. Sticky, red blood oozed between her fingertips as she pressed them together in horror. Heavy droplets splashed to the earthen floor, creating thick scarlet puddles. She couldn't tell where the blood was coming from. It seemed to be pouring from an unseen gash in her own hands.

Acrid smoke filled her nostrils. She looked up. The hut was a swirling mass of thick heavy smoke and flames.

She stared, rooted to the ground as the birds lifted their wings in unison, feathers alight. With their bodies and wings on fire they looked like monstrous, accursed angels, glowing in fiery wrath. The scream pierced her ears. She tried to block it out by covering her ears with her slippery bloody hands. She closed her eyes and fell to her knees. The scream rose higher and higher until she was sure her eardrums would split.

She opened her eyes. She was slumped on her couch with the book resting on her stomach. She quickly held her hands up to her face. No blood. She felt her heart rate slow. It was just another strange dream. She turned over Samuel J. Woodlock's book in her hands, flipping through the pages, considering what it all meant.

The book, as Sophie had first thought, had been written in dull, informative prose. There was only one section out of the entire book which had intrigued her and where the author's own emotion seemed to have spilled out onto the page through the evocative words used. It was only a few pages about an occurrence in 1849. According to the book, a band of gypsies had drifted into the town. Sophie's mind was brought back to the mysterious Acorn who had started The Acorn Café. The timelines seemed to match up. The gypsies had at first been welcomed by the townspeople who enjoyed the crafts and wares they sold. The men worked to make repairs to carriages and anything else that needed fixing. Some of the town's women were drawn to the mystical fortune tellers who sat in the moonlight wrapped in perfumed scarves, their cards splayed out in front of them.

They lived for several weeks in harmony until a strange sickness seeped into the town, stealing infants, children, young men, women and the elderly away. The author claimed the sickness was probably some sort of plague or pox a group of sailors had brought with them when they docked in the port. The townspeople, however, blamed the gypsies. Once the claim had been made, mass hysteria spread like the disease itself through the town.

They claimed the gypsies were a godless bunch of heathens sent by the Devil himself and should be hung without trial. Scores of gypsies were rounded up and executed. There was a particular gypsy family the author dedicated an entire page to. It claimed that there was a man, Willowen Woodlock, who was the leader of this band of gypsies and the milky-eyed man in the picture. He was married to a wild, erratic-sounding Erosabel and they had four children together, Logan and his twin sister, Joni, Danior and Edwina. Usually there were no records kept of gypsies. However, since the sickness broke out, the mayor of the town ordered all gypsies who were staying to work and see out the winter to register their names. After building a large, solid registry of the names of gypsies in the town, the mayor issued death warrants for fictitious crimes, checking off their names, one by one.

It was said that Willowen and his family fled with their lives to the outskirts of the town, to the wild, dangerous cliffs. There, whether by accident or calculated murder by the town's police, three of the children disappeared. Two bodies were found bashed against the ragged cliffs above the raging sea. They were believed to belong to the oldest brother Logan and his sister Joni. No remains were ever found of the missing boy, Danior. The youngest daughter Edwina survived the massacre but mysteriously disappeared later. It was believed that Willowen and Erosabel continued to live in the outskirts of that accursed town, unable to leave their dead children behind. Rumours spread that they later committed suicide.

Sophie's eyes had been transfixed to the page when she read about the tragedy of the Woodlock family. Sophie wondered if the author, Samuel J. Woodlock, was a descendant of this gypsy family. He must be, to carry the same name. Sophie's curiosity was piqued. She decided to pay Isabelle a visit. If anyone knew the recent history of the town and its people it would be her. She gave her a ring to check that she was home and able to receive company. Isabelle enthusiastically said she had just put a chicken pie in the oven and that Sophie was more than welcome to stay for tea. Despite having stolen only a few hours' sleep, Sophie was alert, hungry for answers. She tidied herself up before heading to her neighbour's house.

"Hello, dear, I'm so glad you rang," Isabelle said as she ushered Sophie in. "This weather we're having is absolutely awful," she said, slamming the door on an icy gust of wind. "It's making my arthritis worse than ever!"

"I'm sorry to hear that. Is there anything I can help with?" Sophie asked. "Here, let me make the tea," she said, stopping Isabelle before she could bustle off into the kitchen.

"Oh, that is sweet of you. Thank you, dear."

Sophie made the tea and brought in some biscuits Isabelle said they could nibble on before the chicken pie was ready.

"Were you home last night?" Sophie ventured, hoping her voice sounded casual.

"Well, of course I was. I don't get out much these days," Isabelle said, with a twinkle in her eye.

"Did you notice a large flock of birds around the house by any chance? I mean, there were a lot of them in my garden yesterday. It was a little strange," Sophie said, watching Isabelle closely.

"Birds? No, I'm afraid not. That storm was awful though, wasn't it?" Isabelle replied.

"Yeah, it was pretty bad," Sophie said, vaguely looking into her teacup. "Isabelle…" Sophie paused, trying to think how best to start her line of questioning. "You said there was a Sammy who owned the house I now live in. What was his full name? What else do you know about him?"

"Oh, he had a lovely name, a name that somehow sticks in your memory, Samuel J. Woodlock. I never knew what the J stood for but a lovely name. Oh, you don't look so well, dear," Isabelle said, noticing Sophie's face turn white. "I suppose you never really talked with him when you bought the place. You must have just dealt with the agent. Are you ok, dear?"

Sophie regained her composure. "Yes, sorry, I'm fine. I just read his book last night, about the history of this town. It was an interesting read."

"I'm sure it was. He was an interesting man. But what exactly is it you want to know?" Isabelle asked, leaning forward in her armchair.

"There was just this part in the book about a gypsy family and what happened to them. It was all very tragic and I'm guessing he's descended from them. I guess I just want more information about where they lived exactly, that gypsy family, and what happened to them. The book doesn't go into detail," Sophie explained.

Isabelle leaned back in her chair, eyeing Sophie. Time stretched silently between them, until Isabelle finally said, "They lived right there," she said, pointing out the window, to the house layered with secrets next door — Sophie's house. "Samuel moved there looking for answers about his family lineage. I think he unearthed something he didn't want to find, something he never told me about. Listen, Samuel never really opened up to me. There was only once, in the middle of a stormy night, he came here, wild-eyed. He had seen something that scared him and refused to go back to his house. I thought he was sick or delirious at first but when he spoke, he wasn't talking gibberish. He was as lucid as can be. He told me parts of his story.

"Samuel was a child of the Second World War. He was barely twenty-three when the war broke out. Like many youthful, idealistic boys of his time, he signed up to go to war and off he went. He saw awful horrors. Death stalked him at every turn. He was shot in the leg and arm, making half of his body stiff and nearly useless in old age. When he came back from the war he was a changed man, aged a thousand years so he said. He never married or had a family. When I asked him why, he told me it was because of the curse. He believed his family had been cursed a century ago, or so the story his father told him goes. His father, Jason, never spoke about their ancestry. When Jason's wife died one year into their marriage, Jason turned away from the light forever. He locked himself in his study most days and began seeing things, people who weren't there, things that weren't real. Young Samuel was too afraid to disturb his father in his study but through the walls he kept hearing Jason mutter about curses. Before Sammy went to war, he asked his father about it. His father told him that his great-grandmother had dabbled in black magic and placed a dark curse over the family and all its descendants. The Woodlock Curse.

"I asked whether he really believed in black magic and curses. Sammy only shook his head. He was in tears at this point. He must have been in his mid-nineties when we had this conversation. He was fragile and old, weathered down by life's cruelties. He slept on the couch and left before I woke up. He never opened up to me about his life or what happened that night ever again."

Sophie sat, listening motionlessly, as if any movement might cause a disruption in the tale.

"I think Sammy is the one you want to talk to, not me," Isabelle said, reclining in her chair, weary. "I don't know what it is about that house, but there's something strange lurking in its shadows, something not quite right," she said, staring out the window unseeingly.

"Do you know where I can find Samuel?" Sophie asked breathlessly. She needed to find him. She needed answers more than her lungs needed air.

Isabelle nodded. She got up slowly and fetched an old battered address book. "Samuel isn't one for company, but something tells me he will like you." She turned to the back of the address book, her fingers scanning under W. "Here we go, this is his new address."

Sophie took out her phone and snapped a picture. "Thank you so much, Isabelle. You've been so helpful."

Isabelle nodded again, silently. She leant back in her chair, sighing. "Well, let's have some of that pie then. A full stomach can solve most of life's problems," she said, the smile on her lips not quite meeting the corners of her eyes.

# Chapter 19

## *Samuel*

Samuel was reclining in his old stuffed armchair. His ragged breath tearing through his chest, exhausted after the two-minute walk to the shop and back. He felt his lungs, heart, bones and muscles all wasting away inside him, crumbling to dust. Eyes closed, he breathed deeply. A dull pain was shooting up his side, stabbing him in the gut. He didn't mind the pain though. He accepted it, part of his eternal punishment.

His head was swimming. As he had been walking back from the shop, the white light had been creeping in at the corners of his eyes, threatening to explode in a volcano of pain. He rested his head back and closed his eyes. He didn't feel ready for another vision. He was still recovering from the one he had a few days ago. It had left him drained and with a deep sense of foreboding which he had been unable to explain or shake off.

He heard a timid knock on the door. Too tired to even open his eyes, he continued to sit motionless, hoping whoever it was would go away. He then heard it again, more urgent this time. Who could possibly want to talk to me at this time, or at any time, to be frank, he was not in the habit of having guests over, he thought to himself. With immense effort he gripped the sides of the faded armchair and with all the strength he could muster, heaved himself up. Once on his feet he shuffled over to the door prepared to sternly reprimand any kids in case this was some sort of prank.

To his surprise he didn't see any young impish faces staring up at him partly in fear and partly in awe. Instead he was met with the solemn face of an elegantly dressed young woman. She was wearing an open parker jacket, revealing a soft camel sweater underneath and thick black leggings with short furry boots. A deep brown, red and orange scarf was slung loosely around her neck, reminding him of discarded autumn leaves. His first thought was she must have got the wrong address.

"Can I help you, Miss? Who is it you're looking for?" he said, his voice creaking with age.

"I'm looking for a Mr. Samuel J. Woodlock. Is that you?" she asked, peering up at him through her thick dark lashes.

Taken aback all he could reply was, "Yes, that's me. Is there something I can help you with?"

"I believe so. Would it be all right if I came in? It's just I want to talk to you. It's partly about the book you wrote concerning the history of Dover and partly about the old house you used to live in. You sold it to me," she said, studying his expression.

"Sophie Parker," he said, letting her name hang in the void between them. For a moment they stood there, each scrutinising the other, until Samuel finally said, "Well, you'd better come in then."

"Thank you," Sophie said as he opened the door wide enough for her to slip in. She noticed he walked with a limp, slightly dragging the right side of his body behind him, while the left side did all the hard work. The house smelt dusty and was in dire need of a clean. Cobwebs dangled from the lampshades in the living room. The surface of the coffee table gleamed with some sticky substance. Sophie perched on the couch which was rough with crumbs while he sank into his armchair.

"To tell you the truth, I've been expecting you to reach out in some way or other." Samuel sighed heavily. "I suppose you got my address from Isabelle?"

"Well, yes," Sophie replied apologetically. "I wouldn't barge in on you like this if it wasn't an emergency. And Isabelle just wanted to help…" Sophie said, her voice trailing off.

"Of course. I completely understand. I'm just surprised you never replied to my letter," Samuel stated in an inquiring tone.

"Your letter?" Sophie echoed in confusion. "You sent a letter to the house? I never got it."

Samuel closed his eyes and let out a soft chuckle. "Of course you didn't. That is no ordinary house you live in. I'm sure you know that already otherwise you wouldn't be here," he said, the corners of his colourless mouth lifting in what could almost be construed as a smile.

"Well, yes, it's about the house and your book and how it's all connected," Sophie said, spilling out everything she needed to say. She needed someone to validate her experiences and tell her she wasn't losing her mind.

"Strange things have been happening in that house. Things I don't know how to keep explaining away with reason or logic. I mean, when I first moved in I kept hearing creaking floorboards and whenever I checked there was no one there. There was a bizarre occurrence I wasn't sure I dreamt when all the candles in my house lit themselves and were burning manically. Two birds have been watching me since I moved in and then when my friend stayed they disappeared only to come back, an army of ravens, the night she left. I keep hearing a cat howling by my front door and haunting music playing in the middle of the night only to find no cat and no musician anywhere near the premises. Since the first night I've had hideous dreams about the willow tree blazing and the house being consumed by fire and ash. In some of my dreams, I'm not myself. I'm someone else and I have blood on my hands. A tarot card with The Fool on it fell out of the book of yours I bought, and only later that night I dreamt of finding twelve tarot cards, all with Death on them, buried in ash by the tree. The thirteenth tarot card had my face on it. Whatever I do, wherever I go, I feel I'm being watched. I feel the memories of the house stalking me. The temperature has risen to boiling point and then gone below freezing with no explanation. A ghostly trail of ants appears whenever these weird occurrences start up. They're running to get out of the house, and I feel I should be too. I'm afraid, Samuel, I'm afraid my house has a spirit of its own which will overpower and consume me if I can't figure all this out!" Sophie was panting as if she had run a mile, tears welling in her eyes. She had left out the bit about the ghostly encounter with Willowen, fearing this may be too much for the old man who sat rasping for breath in front of her. This was the point where Samuel was either going to tell her she was a crazy fool and had to leave immediately, or offer some pearls of wisdom, some answers at last.

Samuel's watery eyes were fixed on hers until he finally said, "Yes, I wanted to figure it out too, but some secrets are best left buried. Why don't you just sell the house and leave?"

Sophie was taken back by his straightforward solution. Perplexed, she heard herself answer before her mind had formulated what she wanted to say. "I can't. The house chose me. When I was looking at places, none of the houses appealed to me. I can't explain why or how, but I just feel I was destined to live here, like this is just a piece of a much larger puzzle which I belong to. I am exactly where I'm meant to be right now. The house needs me," she said emphatically, not quite knowing where this certainty was coming from.

"Well, if that's the case, I hope you have some time for I'm going to tell you a story. It is a story which starts over a century ago, a story which echoes through time and haunts me still. It's a tale of tragedy, black magic, murder, curses and tears. It's a story I hoped to take with me to the grave, allowing all those poor souls involved, all those dark memories, to disintegrate into dust with me and be laid deep within the cemetery of a forgotten world. A world that doesn't bear remembering. But I see it is my fate to pass this burden on to you. Are you sure you're ready to hear such a story?"

Sophie's throat felt dry and constricted. She nodded silently. She was ready.

"Well, we start in 1916 when I was born. I was born motherless into the world. I was only a few months old when my mother died. I had heard from neighbours that my father had been a light-hearted, carefree man, wildly in love with my mother, Marie. She had been a red-haired beauty with clear green eyes, but some strange disease stole her life away. Her death killed something within my father, Jason, for I only knew him as a gloomy, recluse of a man, preferring to drink in the shadows, talking to the demons that festered within his soul. Growing up, I stayed out of his way when I was not cooped up in my prison of a boarding school. It was only the night before going to war I had the feeling I was never going to see him again and that that was the last chance I would get to know the only family I had in the world.

"I asked him to tell me a story, any story. Usually he would brush off any conversation attempts I made saying he had more important things to do than talk to children and idiots. I think deep down he also knew these were the last hours we would ever spend together so he sat me down. I was twenty-two at the time, but I felt like I was a kid again, enraptured by the enigma that was my father. Sitting across from each other he told me the story his father, Danior, had told him many years ago. It's a story that originates with my great-grandparents, the tragic lives of Willowen and Erosabel.

"Willowen was a gypsy who roved along the coast of England. Willowen acted as leader of the camp, making decisions regarding where they would stop, how they would eat and what they would do to survive. He was tasked with looking out for everyone. He was calm, gentle and thoughtful, from what Danior told my father. He then met Erosabel. She was the opposite, volatile and tempestuous as the sea. It was said that she harboured a demon inside her that was slowly eating away at her brain. This demon was to be her undoing. During her manic episodes, it was said her rage could be felt through the wind and earth for miles around. She had a wild spirit and was travelling alone when she stumbled across Willowen's camp. Willowen insisted she stay with them for a while. She was beautiful with coffee-coloured skin and deep blue eyes that scintillated like the deceptively smooth surface of the water. Little did

Willowen know of the dark secrets swirling hidden within their depths. Her hair was thick and dark. She used to put jewels, mainly sapphires, in her hair. She said they were fallen stars, drowned in the sea, and that she had plucked them out, saving them, nestling them in her hair to create a carpet of stars. She had a vivid imagination and during her lucid moments, she apparently would tell the most fantastic tales of monsters, demons, witches and princesses to her children. She had a book of fairy tales with beautiful, handcrafted drawings in them. I wish I knew what happened to that book. It would be priceless, probably one of the first fairy-tale books, written before Hans Christian Anderson or the Grimm Brothers.

"Needless to say, Willowen fell helplessly in love with my great-grandmother Erosabel. He was older than her and promised to take care of her. He said he would give her anything her heart desired. She told him that what she wanted most in the world was children. She wanted a family and to be surrounded by a brood of babies. Her childhood had been a heartbreakingly desolate one with a rejecting mother who was troubled in the mind. She had no brothers, sisters, or father to make up for it. Willowen gave her what she most wanted and felt she had lacked. They had four children together, Logan, Joni, my grandfather Danior, and Edwina. They lived happily, travelling across England until that fateful night at the beginning of October in 1849."

At this point, Samuel started to cough. He coughed so violently Sophie ran to the tap to get him some water. When she got back, she patted him the back and handed him the glass. He took it with a shaky hand.

"I'm not used to doing so much talking. I'm sure Isabelle has told you about my habits," he said, his voice sounding thin and feeble, hanging on by a thread.

"Are you ok? Has this been too much?" Sophie asked, concerned. She didn't want to overtax this already emotionally overwhelmed old man.

"No, no, let's continue. Where was I?" he asked, rubbing his temples and setting the water down on the floor next to him.

"They just arrived in the town in October," Sophie said helpfully.

"Yes, at first the townspeople were intrigued by this mystical, glittering bunch of people carrying all their worldly possessions in heaps in small crooked caravans. The women did sewing for the local townspeople and the men helped on farms, building sites, metal works, any odd job they could find. I'm sure you read in my book a disease struck the town, coinciding with the arrival of both a group of sailors and the gypsies. Religious zealots claimed the gypsies were heathens, sent by the Devil himself to wreak havoc upon their town. They claimed God was punishing the town for opening its arms up to the Devil. With religion and spiked truncheons in their arsenal, the police scoured the town in search for the gypsies. They were persecuted mercilessly."

"Yes, Willowen and his family fled to the house where I now live. Is that correct?" Sophie said, mentally slotting a puzzle piece next to its neighbours.

"That's correct. It was a ramshackle hut at the time, not the house that is standing today. But they made the most of it. It is uncertain what happened at this point. The accounts are veiled in mystery, confusion and contradicting statements. It was said that Erosabel wanted to leave the town with her family as she was scared for their safety. Willowen, however, felt responsible for the other gypsies, the ones who had been captured. As first he harboured thoughts of freeing them but that soon became impossible. They had no choice but to leave. Each day they stayed, Erosabel got worse, her mental state deteriorating rapidly. Danior told his father that she started to ignore her family and adopted ravens as pets. She was seen spending hours talking to the ravens as if they were her children. She would sit with them, pet them, smooth out their feathers and cast spells on them. She doted on them while enslaving them with her magic. The ravens became her life."

The mention of the ravens sent a violent chill down Sophie's spine. As if reading her mind, Samuel said in a low voice, "Those ravens are no earthly creatures. They are figments of Erosabel's curses and spells breaking the boundaries of age and time."

Sophie swallowed hard, curious to learn more. "What happened to her actual children? In your book you said at least two of them died. Is that true?" Sophie said, feeling a sadness pull at her heart.

"Yes, no one knows for sure what happened that night. There was a violent storm brewing. It was a storm where the atmosphere itself felt electric. According to my father, Danior claimed his mother had been sitting on a smooth rock facing the ocean the day before the storm. She sat there staring and humming as if in a trance. There was nothing anyone could say or do that would stir her from the hypnotic state she was in. It was an eerie calm which sent shivers through anyone who saw her. Not once in her life had she ever been so still. It was an omen. It was almost as if she was brewing the storm in her mind. All the pent-up angst and madness within her found its release.

"The next day she had been lucid and rational. Police were rumoured to be conducting a final brutal purge of the town, purifying it from gypsy vermin. By the time the storm came, the night was blacker than black. There were no stars. Not even the moon dared show its face on such a bleak night where the stirrings of evil could be felt through the seething wind and sea. The heavens split, raining down hail, lightning and black tears.

"It is unknown why at least three of the children were out on the cliffs that night. Usually Willowen never left them alone but he had needed to get provisions for the long journey. Was it an accident that resulted in two of the children's mangled bodies being found the next day on the rocks below? Or were they pushed? It is conjectured that the police did a surprise raid, catching them off guard while Willowen was away. There could have been a nasty tussle where the children accidentally fell. Worse yet, perhaps the police deliberately pushed them, thinking it would be easier to eradicate the family over the cliff edge than take them to the already crammed prison cells where the rest of the gypsies were awaiting their doom. Danior told my father he remembered nothing from that night. All he remembered was flying through the air and crashing into a wall of murderous water."

"He survived? Well, he must have lived to pass on this tale to your father. How did he survive the storm and sea?" Sophie asked, on tenterhooks.

"He doesn't remember. All he remembers is being washed up against some other shore far away from his family. The people who found this semi-drowned young boy said it was a miracle. Danior lived on the streets for several years as a petty thief. He then joined a travelling circus where he did magic tricks. Desperate to have a better life and marry, he left the circus when he was probably in his late twenties and headed to the countryside where he did odd jobs on farms and masonry work. It was in one of the many pubs dotted along the rolling hills where he met Greta, a barmaid, and his future wife.

"After they married, Danior was determined to settle down and find stable work. His perseverance paid off. It was a summer's day and he was said to have collapsed from exhaustion underneath an old apple tree in one of the winding country lanes. He opened his eyes to see a kindly old man sitting next to him, handing him a flask of water. Danior always said this man had been sent as an angel from heaven for him and his family. Greta was pregnant at the time with my father-to-be, Jason. She was sitting, waiting for news from Danior, in the small rented room they had been living in for the past few weeks, constantly on the move.

"This man not only offered him water but a job, to help him out on the farms. He had only one son who had been killed by a runaway horse and carriage. Now it was just him and his wife on the farm and they were both getting older and couldn't manage it without young blood. Immediately Danior jumped at the prospect. That same day he brought Greta over to the farm where she took up work as their housekeeper.

"Just when Danior thought all the cards were in his favour, Greta died during childbirth. Not long after, the old couple who had been so kind to them also died, leaving the entire farm to Danior and his son Jason. Danior was determined that Jason would have a better life than his. Danior was in his forties at his point and not the young man he had once been. He couldn't maintain the farm and had to sell it. Danior went to the city with a young Jason and invested all of the farm money in a little store. Danior knew about herbal medicines and healing from what he had learned during his time with the gypsies. Before his mother, Erosabel, had descended into necromancy and black magic, she had been a healer, using her potions and spells to help people. She was well known for her remedies and had a reputation for being one of the most successful healers among the gypsy travellers. He opened an apothecary full of natural medicines and flowery ointments, appealing to rich young ladies. He taught Jason the tricks of the trade as soon as Jason could walk and talk. As Danior aged and became too feeble to run the business, Jason took over.

"Jason ran the business well and it was smooth sailing for several years. Chaos descended upon the little shop when a fiery-haired gentleman's daughter entered the apothecary. My father claimed he had been instantly captivated. Her looks, her voice, her clothes were spellbinding. He had had to struggle for everything his entire life and here was this beautiful, pampered creature with soft delicate skin, turning the phials over in her small dainty white gloved hands. Not long after she first entered his shop, they started an illicit affair. Her name was Marie. Marie was engaged to be married to some other respectable gentleman, George. George was said to have an unruly temper and held on to grudges with iron claws, biding his time, waiting like a tarantula in the shadows to strike.

"Jason and Marie eloped that summer. Her family was furious; however, they softened once they heard a baby was on the way. George, however, continued to lurk in the shadows, a permanent stain on Jason and Marie's happy life together. One day when Jason was out with me, a neighbour reported seeing George slip into their house where Marie had remained. He only stayed a few minutes. The neighbour said she heard yelling and saw Marie shoving George out of the house. When Jason returned a few hours later, he found his wife dead in her bed. It was thought to be poison; however, no evidence was ever uncovered. On the official reports, doctors claimed an unknown disease had spread through her body and stolen her last breath. George was rich and influential and probably had the doctors on his payroll."

Sophie's hand flew up to her mouth. "That's awful," she whispered. "How can people be so evil?"

"I don't know. But whether it was George or a disease or a curse, I never knew my mother, nor the person my father was before her death. I was sent away to a boarding school at five years old only to be collected in a begrudging manner on Christmases and summers. It was a lonely existence in those large, draughty school rooms with cruel headmasters and their harsh relentless punishments.

"My father slowly disintegrated into the shadows over the years. His drinking became more excessive and the apothecary fell apart. He drank himself to death the year I left for the war in 1939. I never saw him again after that night he told me his haunted story."

Sophie sat in silence. There was nothing she could say that could truly describe what she was feeling. A deep melancholy had settled in the very bones of her body, spreading a dull ache throughout. Samuel's breath had grown ragged. He wheezed and leaned forward.

"I think that's all I can manage for the day," he managed to say through laboured breaths.

"Of course, I'm so sorry," Sophie said, unsure of whether she was apologising for overtaxing this man or for the story of his life which brought tears to her eyes.

"Don't be sorry, dear," he said, his voice barely above a whisper. "I'm ninety-seven years old. This is what happens to the body after so many years roaming this accursed earth. Will you be all right showing yourself out? I don't think I have the strength in my bones to get up."

"Yes, of course I can. Will you be all right? Can I get you anything or call anyone before I leave?"

Eyes closed, Samuel's lips curled in an ironic smile. "All those who ever meant anything to me have left this world and remain alive only within my mind. I'm looking forward to the day I can join them in their eternal rest. I never wanted to live this long. Perhaps it is all part of the curse."

Sophie felt anxious leaving him like this. She dithered by her chair.

"Come back later, Sophie. Our story is unfinished. I'll be waiting for you," Samuel said, noticing her unwillingness to leave.

"Ok, please take care. Here is my number if you need anything at all," Sophie said, placing a piece of paper on the sticky coffee table.

Samuel nodded in acknowledgement without opening his eyes. He heard her footsteps drift away. His door creaked open and then shut. Silence descended upon the house once more. His papery cheeks suddenly felt damp. Samuel raised a hand to his face where he felt tears streaming down. He sat there, letting the heartbreak that he had inherited over the years wash over him and cleanse his soul.

# Chapter 20

## *Sophie*

*Dear Erosabel,*

*I remember nothing except rage crashing within me,*

*A thundering anger that was not my own,*

*Through me a channel of rushing energy,*

*Someone else made my heart their home.*

*Years of heartache and pain seeped through my skin,*

*Bleeding through my soul and body,*

*This secret I've kept, this unforgivable sin*

*Needs to find release as I scream into eternity.*

*Sophie*

Sophie remained sitting in her car for several minutes before driving back home. Her hands were shaking so badly she could barely clutch the steering wheel. She tried to focus on her breath, but Samuel's story kept intruding on her mind, stealing her focus. Instead she decided to sit and wait, allowing herself to feel the range of emotions coursing through her veins and creating a cloudy fog in her mind.

Although she had unearthed some discoveries through Samuel's tale she was also brimming with even more questions. How did the twins, Logan and Joni, actually die? Was it an accident or murder? How could the townspeople be so cruel as to murder children in such a brutal manner? And what happened to the youngest, Edwina? How did Erosabel and Willowen continue their lives after the violent deaths and disappearance of three children? And how was all this connected to the house? The flurry of questions gathered like a snowstorm in her mind. She just wanted to go back inside Samuel's gloomy home and make him tell her the rest of the story. She then felt a wave of pity for him. He was living this lonely existence, waiting for death's mercy, with only ghostly stories of the past and lingering inherited memories to accompany him.

She realised she didn't want to be alone that night in the house. Without thinking, she picked up the phone and dialled Matthew's number. He answered on the second ring.

She had not planned this conversation and quickly improvised when she heard his voice.

"Sophie, this is such a nice surprise. How're you? Ready for tomorrow's lunch with me and Heather?" Matthew asked. She could feel his warm smile emanating through the phone.

"I'm all right. There's actually something I want to talk to you about. Can we have dinner today at mine?"

Matthew, sounding slightly taken aback, said, "Well, sure, of course we can. Is everything all right? You sound a little worried?"

"No, I'm fine. I'll be waiting for you around seven," she said, trying her best to sound calm. She wondered if he would understand or think her crazy, but she had already decided she was going to tell him. She felt she couldn't keep all her discoveries to herself any more. She needed to shine a light on the truth, and talking to others might help her understand more of what was going on around her.

She quickly realised she had no food to prepare for the promised dinner. The innards of her fridge contained half a bottle of milk, a loaf of bread, a tub of butter, slices of cheese and some grapes which had shrivelled and needed throwing away. She couldn't make an immaculate dinner with those ingredients. The best she could rustle up was a cheese toastie.

With steady hands, she started the engine and drove to the supermarket. She bought chicken breasts, potatoes, vegetables, some spices and two bottles of red wine. She wasn't much of a cook but had made rosemary chicken a couple of times for her and Dan's anniversaries. She felt strange making it for a different man now, but it was one of the few things she knew how to cook.

She busied herself in the kitchen once she got home, cleaning vegetables, peeling potatoes and preparing the chicken. She felt her nerves were on edge, listening, feeling for anything unusual. She kept glancing behind her shoulder until she felt a stabbing pain in her neck from swivelling around too fast. She needed to calm down. She felt the ghosts of Samuel's story all around her. She could actually feel them. The air was saturated by their presence, breathing down her neck. She could almost hear ghostly childlike cries by the cliff edge, lost in the howling wind and crashing waves. Their souls lingered, just out of sight, separated by the veil of death. She reached for a wine glass and poured a generous amount of dark red wine in it. After taking a long sip, she felt her nerves settle slightly.

Just before seven, she heard a knock at the door. Sophie dusted her hands on the floral print dress she was wearing and went to answer the door. Matthew stood there smiling, white lilies in one hand and a bottle of white wine in the other.

Sophie grinned, pleased to see him. "Well, those certainly are two of my favourite things, thank you!" she said, taking the lilies and wine from him. "Come on in. Dinner should be ready in about twenty minutes."

"Is everything ok, Sophie? You didn't sound yourself on the phone earlier," Matthew said, trying to unravel the mysteries locked in her eyes.

"I'm fine," Sophie said shortly.

"You said you had something you wanted to talk about?" he enquired.

"Let me get you some wine first," she said, fetching a glass from the kitchen and pouring the wine to the top.

"That's good," Matthew said, gesturing for her to stop pouring. "You trying to get me inebriated?"

Sophie smiled weakly. "Sorry, didn't realise what I was doing. So how's Heather?" she asked, uncertain of how to bring up her ghost story. Now that he was there she was nervous about telling her weird, twisted tale. Everything in the house seemed calm and still. Would he believe her if she told him she believed a ghost from a century ago still haunted these parts?

"She's so excited about tomorrow! She's already got her dress picked out. She's having a slumber party with one of her friends tonight," Matthew said, glancing at his phone. "I hope they don't stay up too late."

Sophie smiled, only half listening.

"So tell me, what did you want to talk about? I have to admit, you're kind of scaring me," Matthew said, sensing her distraction. He fixed his gaze on her, concern flashing through his eyes.

Sophie looked down, swirling her wine glass. "I'm going to tell you, but you might think I'm crazy when I'm finished."

Matthew paused. "Honestly, I already think you're a little crazy," he said, smiling. "Just say what's on your mind and leave it to me to make my own judgements about your mental state," he said in an attempt to lighten the suddenly sombre mood.

With a heavy sigh, Sophie launched into her tale, leaving nothing out. She began with Dan's death and how she thought she would never be released from the miasma of grief that consumed her body and soul. She then told Matthew about the house and how she felt it belonged to her before she even bought it. She told him all about her first night, how the GPS went berserk and how a strange man appeared out of nowhere to help her, only to disappear into nothingness moments after. From there, her story was awash with the ghostly occurrences she couldn't explain no matter how hard she tried. She finished by telling him about Samuel's book and how she had gone to visit him earlier and the accursed story he had told her.

By the time she had finished they had drunk the entire bottle of wine. She had taken the chicken out of the oven and it was starting to get cold. Matthew stared at her, a quizzical expression on his face.

"So, bottom line is, you think this place is haunted by a gypsy family from the 1800s?" he said, trying to summarise the creepy tale he had just heard.

Sophie nodded slowly. "I didn't want to admit it at first. I don't actually believe in these things but there's just no other explanation. I feel it in my bones that there's something strange about this place," Sophie said, hearing the pleading note in her voice. She was desperate for him to understand and not walk out the door thinking she deserved to be admitted to an asylum for the clinically insane.

Matthew glanced around the room as if seeing it for the first time. He stood up and walked around. "Maybe," he said eventually, shrugging his shoulders. "I don't know much about these things, Sophie," he said, looking at her, a strange, unreadable expression on his face.

"Do you believe me?" she asked.

"I believe you've been through a lot. You've been through unimaginable tragedy. Perhaps this is just how your mind is coping with it all. Have you thought about seeing a psychologist or a counsellor?"

Sophie felt her heart drop. He didn't believe her. He thought she was crazy. Matthew must have seen the dismal expression on his face. He quickly joined her on the couch and put his arm around her.

"Hey, crazy or not, I still love you. I'm in this for the long haul," he said, whispering in her ear.

Sophie gulped, that was the first time he had said he loved her. Sophie bit her lip. She didn't feel ready to reciprocate such feelings. As if he sensed what she was thinking, he pulled her closer and kissed her on the forehead.

"I only suggested a psychologist because I want what's best for you. I just want you to be happy," he said simply. "As for this house and the strange occurrences, I don't want you sleeping here alone tonight. I don't know if it is haunted but clearly something about it is setting you on edge."

Sophie shook her head slightly. "This is my house, where else am I going to go?"

"If it's all right with you, I'd like to stay here. I can sleep on the couch. If anything happens I'll be right here to protect you. I'm not one to typically believe in ghost stories but if there is a ghost lurking in the shadows here, I promise you I don't get spooked easily," he said.

Sophie decided to ignore the teasing note in his voice. "Are you sure? I mean, if you're worried about me, don't be. I've been here all by myself for some time now," Sophie replied.

"You're not getting rid of me that easily. Now, let's have dinner before that chicken freezes over," he said, helping her set the table.

Sophie couldn't help but feel a sense of relief that she wasn't going to be alone in the house tonight.

After dinner and another bottle of wine and light conversation, Sophie made up the couch for Matthew to sleep on. She wasn't sure if she should offer to let him sleep with her but that somehow felt like they were moving too fast. But he had used the 'L' word with her. Then again, perhaps he had only said that because he had planned all along to stay over and this was his way of getting in to bed with her. Sophie shook her head, ridding herself of her spiralling thoughts as she finished plumping up the pillows.

"Well, goodnight," she said, feeling oddly out of place.

"Goodnight. You just rest easy tonight. I'm on ghost patrol, you have nothing to fear," Matthew said, breaking into a Superman pose. Sophie couldn't help but giggle. "Come here, gorgeous, I love it when you laugh," he said, pulling her by the hem of her dress. He kissed her full on the mouth, wrapping his hands around her small waist. He let his hands wander, feeling the softness of her body under the thin dress. A fire of emotions lit up somewhere deep within Sophie. She liked feeling his rough hands caressing her skin. Her skin tingled as goosebumps flared up along her arms.

She leaned into him, kissing him with a feverish desire. Her hands were perched on his chest, feeling the swell of his breath. Sophie felt her breath catching in the back of her throat. She pressed her body closer to his, feeling the hard contours of his hips and the strong muscles in his chest and arms flexing. She felt an electric energy pulsate between her thighs. Every inch of her skin felt charged, sensitive to the lightest touch.

She closed her eyes, letting a soft moan escape her lips, all thoughts and fears dissolving into a liquid puddle. Gently, Matthew picked her up and laid her on the couch. His hand drifted up her dress. Sophie bit her lip, breathing heavily. An explosion of pleasure rippled through her body as he touched her between her thighs, first gently and then with more force, pushing his fingers inside her. She groaned, clutching onto the sides of the couch. Matthew peeled off her dress and softy kissed her breasts. Sophie felt the wave of pleasure course through her chest. She was panting as she pulled off his trousers and felt his hardness press into the softness of her inner thigh.

"Are you sure you're ready?" Matthew whispered in her ear through heavy breaths.

Sophie nodded, pushing him inside her. She let out a small cry of pleasure as he moved rhythmically against her body. She bit her lip harder as the feeling intensified, electrifying her senses. Just as she thought she couldn't take any more, she felt her insides tremble and convulse with spasms of relief. She let out a deep sigh just as she felt Matthew shudder inside her. He kissed her neck, still breathing heavily.

"Sophie, you're the best thing that's happened to me," he said, biting her earlobe. He looked down at her flushed face and smudged make-up. "You're the most beautiful woman I've ever seen."

Sophie shifted from underneath him and pulled her dress closer to her body. "Well, you might as well sleep in the bed with me tonight rather than on the couch," she said, blushing.

Matthew laughed. "Yep, might as well."

They slipped under the sheets of her bed upstairs. Matthew leant over and wrapped his arms around her.

"Don't worry, you're safe with me tonight," he whispered before they both fell into a hazy love drunk slumber.

# Chapter 21

## *Matthew*

Matthew stroked Sophie's soft brown hair as she slept peacefully. Her face was relaxed, no hint of stress or worry. His finger traced the curves of her body gently as he watched her sleep. The house felt comfortable and calm. Sophie had a vivid imagination. He could tell by some of the things she said, not just the recent ghost stories she'd recounted, but in general. There was an ethereal aura about her that made Matthew feel that only half of her belonged to this world while the other half of her was lost in another, a world totally unknown to Matthew. He felt this when she daydreamed, her gaze miles away. This was something he loved about her. But the story she had told tonight was slightly worrying. She truly believed what she was saying despite how bizarre it sounded. Her certainty was contagious, stirring doubts in Matthew's mind as to whether there could actually be a grain of truth to it. With these thoughts, Matthew felt himself drift off into a deep sleep.

It was 2:06 am when Matthew woke. Something was wrong. He could feel it. He turned over to check on Sophie.

Moonlight was shining through the room, illuminating the hard edges of the furniture in an icy silvery blue haze. He was alone. Sophie was gone. The calm comfortable aura the room emanated had vanished with her, replaced by a creeping sense of foreboding. Malevolence hung like a dark curtain in the air.

Adrenaline and fear pulsated through Matthew's veins. Where had she gone? He jumped out of bed, his eyes blearily adjusting to the semi-dark room. He scanned it but quickly saw Sophie was not there. He dashed down the stairs, tripping on the last step. He burst into the living room where the remains of their dinner lay and two empty wine bottles stood like sentinels on either end of the table. He darted into the kitchen, but Sophie was nowhere to be seen.

"Sophie," he yelled, feeling the quiet stifle his lungs, panic tearing through them. Beads of sweat glistened on his forehead as he turned around, feeling a creeping sensation that he was being watched. His eyes locked with those of a giant black bird sitting ominously on the ledge outside the kitchen. Then something caught his eye. Behind the bird was a shadow of a person, gliding like liquid through the inky black garden outside.

Matthew ran out, the cold wind biting through his thin clothes, shocking his system. He stood frozen for a second before he saw the black figure kneel down and perch on a rock precariously balancing on the cliff edge. He broke into a sprint.

"Sophie," he called out again, but the figure remained motionless. Once he reached her, he put his hands on her shoulders. "Sophie, what are you doing?" But when she turned to look him in the face instead of Sophie's warm brown eyes gazing up at him, he was met with black whirlpools staring coldly back. She was humming tunelessly as her gaze drifted towards the sea. She started swaying gently, mumbling something under her breath.

"Sophie, please come inside! You're scaring me," he said, trying to lift her off the rock but she felt like a deadweight. She stiffened, not moving a muscle. She continued to mumble as the waves crashed with increasing fury against the rocks. Her face was splattered by the icy sea spray, but she didn't seem to notice. Pearls of droplets shone in her hair, sparkling in the cold moonlight like a carpet of stars. Matthew leaned in, trying to understand what she was saying.

"The ravens… the ravens… trust the ravens…" she said repeatedly through blue lips. Her skin was a waxy white mask, as pale as the moon.

"What ravens? Sophie, this isn't funny," Matthew yelled, shaking with fear. "Ignore the ravens. They're just dumb birds. You need to come back inside."

Suddenly, quicker than the blink of an eye, she snapped her head to face him. "What have you done?" she said in a voice that was not her own. It was deep and husky, almost like a man's voice. "What have you done?" she repeated with a hint of wild-eyed panic. Then, in a barely audible voice, which could have been mistaken for a whisper in the wind, she said, "My babies."

Nothing prepared Matthew for what he witnessed next and nothing could ever erase it from his memory. Sophie stood up on the smooth, slippery rock, her nightdress billowing around her, her hair, like wild snakes, lashing her face. A blood-curdling scream ripped through the sky. Sophie was standing, her mouth wide open, emitting an unearthly ear-splitting cry that would have made the Devil himself tremble with fear. Matthew stood motionless, staring in shock and horror as the never-ending scream permeated the night and soaked the atmosphere in electrifying terror. The piercing howl tore through space and time, reverberating into eternity. Matthew felt the leaves and debris scatter in opposite directions as if a volcano had just erupted.

Then, as if in slow motion, Matthew saw Sophie lift one foot off the rock on which she stood. She stood for a moment, balancing precariously on her tiptoes with one foot dangling over the cliff edge, arms outstretched like an angel about to take flight. Then, she tipped her weight forward, facing the jagged swords of doom awaiting her at the bottom of the cliff.

Without thinking, Matthew jumped on the rock and grabbed her arm. Sophie tried to shake him off, hypnotised by the violent seas below.

"I need to be with my babies," she snarled, gnashing her teeth like a feral animal. Her feet slipped on the wet rock.

Matthew yelled over the screeching wind, "There are no babies! You need to be with me!" With a firm yank, he pulled her off the rock.

They both tumbled into the damp grass below. Sophie's eyes were rolling in the back of her head so that all Matthew could see were the whites of her eyes, blank and unseeing. Matthew quickly scooped her up in his arms and ran as fast as he could back to the house.

He carefully placed her on the couch in the living room and made sure she was breathing. She was shivering violently while white foam bubbled at the corners of her mouth. He stripped her of her sodden nightgown, drenched in sweat and sea foam and changed her into an old shirt. He cleaned her face and then lifted her gently, carrying her upstairs where he covered her with the blanket.

At first she slept fitfully, tossing and turning. She was muttering something in her sleep, a frown buried deep within her forehead. Matthew stayed up stroking her hair, whispering soothing words. He stroked her arms and legs and told her it was going to be all right. He gently massaged her temples and hummed a song. Eventually, the creases between her brows softened and smoothed over. Her breathing became more regular and her limbs weakened and became limp. Sleep washed over her body while Matthew sat bolt upright all night, staring at her, fearing that everything she had told him might actually be true.

The sun shone brightly the next morning, bathing the world in liquid gold. Sophie woke up, stretching. She rolled to her side and saw Matthew. He was sitting cross-legged on the bed, bolt upright, staring at her with wide bloodshot eyes.

"What is it?" Sophie asked, rubbing the sleep from her eyes.

Matthew eyed her closely. "You mean, you don't remember last night?"

"Remember what?" Sophie asked, perplexed. Was he referring to the fact they had slept together last night, because of course she remembered that?

"You don't remember running out into the garden at two o'clock in the morning?" he said, his voice strained with anxiety and lack of sleep.

"Matthew," Sophie said, sitting up to face him. "What are you on about?"

Matthew swallowed back his fear and looked away.

"What happened last night?" Sophie said, a strange feeling of urgency sweeping over her. "Did you feel it too? Do you believe me now?"

"I don't know," Matthew replied. "You were acting so bizarrely. You ran out into the night and stood on the rock just on the cliff edge. You screamed, Sophie. It was terrifying. You were talking about ravens and babies. You almost threw yourself off the edge of the cliff. You probably would have done had I not stopped you," he finished weakly.

"What?" Sophie said, horrified. "I don't remember any of that. How's that possible I don't remember that?" Sophie felt the all-too-familiar sense of panic spread its wings like a sinister butterfly unfurling within her stomach. She could be dead right now if it weren't for Matthew. The thought made her feel like vomiting.

"I don't know," Matthew repeated quietly. "But I believe you, and we need answers."

They sat for a while, both lost in their silent contemplations. Sophie breathed in deeply and exhaled slowly before finally speaking. "I think I know where to get them from." Her mind drifted to Samuel and his unfinished story. "But first, we have a lunch date with your daughter that we need to get to," she said, suddenly remembering the excited little girl with her outfit all prepared, without a care in the world.

# Chapter 22

## *Sophie*

*Dear Daniel,*

*The morning dew hangs heavy,*

*On the petals of a heavy heart,*

*As the teardrops trickle down the stem,*

*Sparkling sadly in the grass, forgotten gems.*

*Bending in the icy breeze,*

*The wilting flowers bow their heads,*

*Staring solemnly down,*

*At the cracked, crispy ground.*

*As one soft petal falls,*

*Landing deftly on the earth,*

*The rest cluster together and stall,*

*Not wanting to meet their grave of dirt.*


*But as months swiftly pass,*

*As winter blends into spring,*

*There will bloom a vibrant mass,*

*Of blossoms raising their heads to sing.*


*Singing for the blurry sun,*

*That spreads her hazy rays,*

*Or singing for the pattering rain,*

*That pours down in the month of May.*


*For even though there are times of despair,*

*When the blossoms melt away,*

*The fragrant beauty of their memories remains,*

*With every single dawning day.*

*Sophie*


They drove to Heather's friend's house trying to make light, inane conversation in an attempt to normalise the terrifying events of the night before. Once they had parked, Matthew got out of the car and knocked on the door. Sophie suddenly felt slightly nervous meeting Matthew's five-year-old daughter for the first time. When she had first met Matthew he had just been another customer, then that had developed into a friendship which quickly blossomed into a relationship. Now she was meeting Matthew as the doting dad.

Matthew waved goodbye to the mother of the play date. A little girl with hair in two slightly lopsided pigtails bounded towards the car.

"Is she in there? Is she in there, Daddy?" the girl asked excitedly. Matthew nodded, smiling up at Sophie through the windscreen.

As the little girl jumped in the car, Sophie turned around in her seat. "Hello, there, I'm Sophie. You must be Heather!"

Heather stuck her hand out in a grown-up manner. "Pleased to meet you." She giggled. "Are you Daddy's special friend?"

Sophie smiled. "Yes, I guess you could say that."

"What's your favourite movie?" Heather asked. "Me and Olivia just watched *The Lion King*. I think that's my favourite movie."

"Hmm," Sophie said, in exaggerated contemplation. "That's a good choice but I think *Pocahontas* has got to be my favourite."

Heather's eyes lit up. "Oh no, no that's my favourite as well. Yes, I think I like that more than *The Lion King*," she said, nodding vehemently.

Sophie and Matthew laughed.

"I hope that's not all you did, just watch movies the entire time!" Matthew said, glancing back at his daughter in the rear-view mirror.

"No, we also had fish fingers for dinner and played games with her Barbies. I accidentally pulled one of the Barbie's heads off though and then Olivia got sad so I squished it back on but Olivia didn't want her any more because she said she was ugly," Heather said, visibly concerned over Olivia and the Barbie's welfare. "Can we get Olivia a new Barbie for Christmas?" she asked enthusiastically. "She would be so happy!"

"Of course we can, Heather," he said, rolling his eyes at Sophie. "See the daily dramas I have to deal with," he added, laughing. "My life is all Barbies, Disney and stuffed animals at home."

"That sounds absolutely lovely," Sophie said, smiling, putting her hand over his.

Once they reached Matthew's place, Heather grabbed Sophie's hand. "Can I show you my room? I want you to meet my toys!"

"Of course, I'd love to meet them," Sophie said, skipping up the steps with Heather.

"I'll let you two know when lunch is ready. It won't take long," Matthew called up after them.

Before she knew it, Sophie was surrounded by furry little toys with large eyes, all with similar names such as Mr. Snuffles, Mrs. Rabbit, Fuzzims and the like. Sophie played along, grabbing some of the toys and putting on high-pitched childish voices that delighted Heather. They played together, delving into Heather's imagination until Matthew called them both downstairs.

"We're still playing! Just five more minutes," Heather yelled.

"In five minutes it'll be cold. Come down now and we'll go up and play together when we've finished lunch," Matthew yelled back.

Heather's cross little face made Sophie smile. "Look, how about we take one of the bears to the table to eat with us? Which one is your favourite?"

Heather took her time deciding amongst the sea of squishy toys until she finally picked out a small, somewhat mottled-looking bear with rough brown fur and a pink nose. "This one! Mr. Cuddles is my favourite!" she said happily as all three of them went downstairs together.

"Oh, and who is this joining us today?" Matthew said, feigning surprise at the sight of the bear.

"I believe this is Mr. Cuddles," Sophie replied formally. "May I introduce you? Daddy, Mr. Cuddles, Mr. Cuddles, Daddy."

Heather squealed with delight as Matthew took the bear's tiny paw solemnly in his big hand. "Pleasure to meet you, Mr. Cuddles. Please have some lunch with us."

The four of them sat and chatted at the table over a lunch of chicken escalope, peas and French fries. After lunch Sophie helped clean up and they then all snuggled on the couch to watch Heather's new favourite movie, *The Aristocats*.

Just before it got dark, Sophie thought she should head home. Matthew insisted on driving her. They all piled into the car and drove off. When they arrived, Matthew left Heather playing with Mr. Cuddles in the backseat while he walked Sophie to the door.

Bathed in the pinks and oranges of the setting sun, the light reflected in the windows of her house and winked back innocently at them. Had the horrors of last night really happened? It all looked so serene now.

"She is absolutely adorable. You're doing such an amazing job," Sophie said.

Matthew smiled. "She is my little angel. Listen, I don't want you to be alone in the house." His face was etched with concern as he glanced up at the foreboding house.

"I'll be fine," Sophie said uncertainly. "Tomorrow I'm going to visit Samuel again and see if he can finish his story."

"Sophie, you could have died. Please stay with Isabelle or something just for tonight until I can figure something out, or just stay with me. I can drive you back right now. We can go to Samuel's together tomorrow. I'm begging you, Sophie," he pleaded.

Sophie sighed. She knew Isabelle wouldn't mind. Isabelle had already told Sophie that Samuel had done something similar when he just appeared at her doorstep at midnight too afraid to go home. Sophie nodded. "Ok, I'll stay with Isabelle. It'll be easier that way. I have my car and everything here and I'd rather go to see Samuel by myself, if that's ok. Don't worry about me."

"Of course I'm going to worry about you," Matthew said, clutching her hands in his. "Please message me when you get to Isabelle's. And message before you go to sleep and when you wake up."

Sophie laughed, trying to make light of the situation. "That's a lot of messages."

"Sophie, this isn't funny. I'm serious. I need to know you're all right."

Sophie looked down and nodded. To be honest, she didn't feel as brave as she was making out. "Ok, sure, I will message."

"Thank you. Please take care of yourself," Matthew said, his grip on her hands tightening.

"I will but you've got to let me go now," Sophie said, glancing down at his hands over hers.

"Sorry, but you know I could never do that," he said with a small smile, as he watched her head to the house that exuded mysteries and tales untold. As she shut the door, he felt his heart beating faster. He saw a light switch on in the living room giving the house a warm cosy appearance. To Matthew it looked like a thinly veiled veneer of normalcy. He was afraid that the darkness that permeated the house would cave in on itself and collapse, taking Sophie with it. He tore himself away from the spectacle when he heard a tapping on the car window. Heather was looking at him expectantly, clearly finished with her game and ready to go home. Matthew trudged back slowly to the car. He took one last look at the house as he drove away, the chilling scream still echoing in his ears.

Sophie did as she was told and rang Isabelle asking if she could sleep at hers. As expected, Isabelle obliged.

"Of course, dear, anytime," she had said.

When Sophie showed up at the front door, backpack in tow, Isabelle ushered her in.

"Listen, you don't need to tell me why you're staying here. That is your business and you are always welcome here, anytime, day or night. Just promise me one thing," Isabelle said.

"Of course, whatever you want," Sophie replied.

"Please just pass by to say goodbye before you leave. That house had a string of residents before Samuel stayed for eight years. Most of them didn't last more than a few weeks. They upped and left, usually in the middle of the night. If you're going to do the same, just let me know. You're a lovely girl and I don't have many friends these days. When you reach my age, they start dropping like flies. Just the odd phone call every now and then would be lovely," Isabelle said, her eyes glazing over.

"Isabelle, I'm not going anywhere," Sophie said resolutely. "And if I were to move, of course I would tell you."

"Thank you, dear," Isabelle said softly.

They sat in her cosy living room and sipped tea, chatting about the weather, Sophie's work and what TV shows were worth watching these days.

"Well, it's past my bedtime," Isabelle said wearily as the clock struck 11:00 pm. "What are your plans for tomorrow? Shall we have breakfast together?"

"That would be lovely," Sophie said, helping the old lady out of her armchair. "I'm actually going to pay Samuel another visit. He's going to finish telling me his story."

Isabelle looked up. "I'm glad you two are getting along. He doesn't like many people, you know. But I just knew, like a sixth sense, that he would like you. Please send him my regards."

"Will do," Sophie replied.

Just as Isabelle reached the foot of the stairs, she turned around and looked Sophie earnestly in the eyes. "I hope you find what you're looking for and can find some fragment of peace at last. It can be an unsettling place around here at times. They say that about places near the sea. Something about all that water and salty air, it can get to you." She turned and made her way slowly up the creaking stairs.

Sophie stared at the spot where Isabelle had just been standing. She couldn't quite get her head around Isabelle's words. Was she implying that it was Sophie's mind that was unsettled, or that the house itself was unsettling? The latter was certainly true. If it weren't for the absurdities in the house, Sophie would be coping and moving on with her life just fine. She was sure even her grief counsellor would be proud of the work she had done.

She took out her phone and messaged Matthew as promised. She instantly got a message back.

*Thanks for messaging. Goodnight, sweetheart, talk to you tomorrow. I miss you so much x*

Smiling inwardly, Sophie curled up on the plump, cushiony couch and drifted off, letting her imagination succumb to the world of dreams.

Sophie woke up early the next day. She helped Isabelle make an omelette with slabs of buttery toast on the side. Sophie did her best to eat her portion. She struggled to swallow as she felt like a swarm of butterflies were doing somersaults and backflips in her stomach. She just wanted to be in her car, driving to Samuel's. Finally the affair of pushing her food around her plate was over and she excused herself.

"Thank you so much for letting me stay the night and for the lovely breakfast," Sophie said, hugging her fragile, old friend.

"Tell me how it goes with Samuel. How is the old crone anyway?"

Sophie laughed. "He's doing well. I'll tell him you said hello."

"Oh, just a minute," Isabelle said, bustling off to the kitchen. "He always loved lemon meringues. Terrible for the teeth but most of his have fallen out anyway," she said, chortling to herself. "Here we go. I made these the other day. Could you give them to him?" she asked.

"Of course, I'm sure he'll love them!" Sophie said, taking the box of treats.

Armed with the meringues, Sophie sped off down the road. Once she arrived at his house she knocked several times on the door. There was no answer. She knocked again. She peered into the windows, but all the lights were turned off and she couldn't see much. She was standing there thinking about what she should do when a young woman from next door appeared on her doorstep.

"Hey, you there," she called over. "Are you Sophie?"

Sophie walked over to the woman's house. "Yes, I'm Sophie. Where is Samuel?"

"I'm afraid he collapsed the other day," the woman said. "He was walking back from doing his shopping and fell down just over there," she said, pointing to the pavement. "Luckily my husband was around at the time and saw it happen. He called the ambulance immediately."

"Oh, is he ok? Where is he?" Sophie asked, her heart in her mouth.

"Yes, I think he's ok. He's at St. Margaret's Underground Hospital. When they were taking him away, he kept repeating one thing, your name, over and over as if he was trying to pass on a message to my husband. I'm so glad you're Sophie and I can tell you all this. I would have felt so guilty at not being able to pass on a dying man's last request."

Sophie nodded, taking all of this in. "I hope he can see visitors. I'm going to go there now. Thank you so much." Sophie paused. "Sorry, what's your name?"

"It's Lucy," she replied. "I hope he's all right," she said, wrapping her dressing gown more tightly around her. "Give him my regards," she called out as Sophie made to leave.

Sophie waved goodbye and immediately entered the hospital name into her GPS. She put her foot on the gas and sped off, hoping that she was not too late. Guilt trickled through her body, its icy fingers clutching her heart. Had her visit overwhelmed him? Had she put too much stress on him? Sophie shook these thoughts from her mind and concentrated on getting to the hospital.

Once she found the visitors' parking, she slotted her car in one of the spaces at a horrendously crooked angle and dashed out.

"Mr. Samuel J. Woodlock. He was admitted here. I need to see him," she said desperately when she got to the reception desk.

The young receptionist glanced at the manic look in her eye and sighed. "Just a sec," she said, lazily tapping on the keyboard. "Let's see," she drawled, taking her time. "Yes, we have a Mr. Woodlock here."

"Can he see visitors? I'm family. I'm his niece," Sophie invented wildly.

"He can see visitors. It's upstairs, second floor. He's the first door on your right," the receptionist replied listlessly.

Without thanking her, Sophie sprinted to the lifts and slammed the button. "Come on," she muttered to herself. Finally the lift arrived. Following the receptionist's vague directions, she managed to find Samuel's room where a nurse was fiddling with one of the wires implanted in his skin.

The nurse turned to greet her with a careful smile. "Are you family? We can only have family visitors at the moment and not for too long. He's very tired, you see."

Samuel lifted his head slightly off the pillow. "She's family, please let her come in," he croaked to the nurse.

"Very well, but like I said, please make this a quick visit. He needs his rest. You just press this button if you need anything, love," the nurse said to Samuel. He nodded compliantly.

"What happened? Are you ok?" Sophie said, feeling weak with relief at finding him.

"I'm fine. I just had a nasty headache and before I knew it I'd fallen onto the ground and hit my head. I've been waiting a long time for death. I'd prefer it happen sooner rather than later. It constantly seems to be playing tricks with me, prolonging my existence," he said, letting out a raspy laugh.

"Don't say that," Sophie said, gently taking his translucent, veiny hand in hers.

"I'm glad you're here," Samuel replied, trying to sit up. Sophie plumped up the cushions behind him and lifted him slightly. "We've got a story to finish."

"The story can wait, Samuel," Sophie said. "I just want to make sure you're all right. If talking is too strenuous we can just sit here for a while. Isabelle sent over some meringues. I forgot them in my car, but I can go get them."

"She is lovely, that Isabelle. But I don't think they'll allow me those delights in here," he said, rolling his eyes. "Now, we're going to finish my story whether you like it or not. We have started something we must see through to the end. If there is any reason for wanting to keep death at bay, it's to finish our story."

A steely glint reflected in his eye and Sophie decided it was best not to argue. Instead she settled down as comfortably as she could in the hard, plastic chair by his bed and listened as time seemed to fade into the background when Samuel started talking.

"So I think I told you most of my father and grandfather's stories. Let's continue where we left off."

Sophie nodded eagerly, curiosity flooding every inch of her body. "What happened to the youngest child Edwina?"

"Well, I know much less about her as Danior never saw his family again after that fateful incident on the cliffs. Willowen is said to have planted that willow tree as a symbol of his heartache for his missing children. For as long as the tree shall live, it shall be bent in sorrow, mourning those dead children. But now our story fast-forwards through time to 1949.

"It is said that Erosabel and Willowen died in mysterious circumstances. It was rumoured to be a double suicide or pact of some sort. No one ever stayed in that area by the cliffs since. No tramps or vagabonds took advantage of the shelter that hut offered. No matter how harsh the weather outside, the hut remained devoid of life with only ghostly memories drifting through it.

"One day in 1944, when the Second World War was coming to an end, an entrepreneurial woman called Sylvia Whisk is said to have bought the land that the hut stood on. She rebuilt it into a warm, cosy home open to the poor, derelict and destitute. Her family had been obliterated during the war and she made it her purpose in life to help those seeking refuge. She called the place Healing House. There's a small cupboard, hidden in the wall of the kitchen. If you don't know to look for it, you would never realise it's there. I constantly had a problem with insects and ants crawling all around the floor and countertops, so one day I tore the place apart. I found a logbook and diary stashed away in their secret hideout. The logbook was where she kept records of those who stayed at Healing House, and the diary, which is a far more fascinating read, included her notes and perceptions of those same people."

Sophie gaped in awe. "And you still have those books?"

"Yes, they are kept under my bed. If anything were to happen to me here, please take care of them. I have no family and do not care what happens to any of my possessions. I just want to know her books are in safe hands," he replied.

Sophie nodded. "Of course, I will take care of them."

Samuel smiled and continued. "It seems there were six long-term residents at the house. There was a mother, Joan, and her daughter, Lily. Joan's husband had died tragically in the last few months of the war. Joan couldn't keep up with the rent and had been evicted. She had gathered Lily up in her arms and searched desperately for somewhere to sleep for the night. She stumbled across Healing House. Her and Lily were the first residents and slept upstairs. The bedroom upstairs was soon partitioned off into two very small rooms when a crippled ex-soldier came seeking shelter. His name was Thomas and one of his legs had been completed shattered from a ricocheting bullet. He had a wooden leg from the knee down. Apparently, he was in agony most of the time and was constantly pacing. It was said in Sylvia's writing that the relentlessly creaking floorboards were of some annoyance to the other residents." Samuel stopped, pausing for breath, watching Sophie.

Sophie felt a strange feeling of realisation seep into her soul. Was that what she had heard? Had she heard remnants of the poor man's pacing in torment as the floorboards creaked above, seemingly by themselves?

"You hear them too, I take it?" Samuel said, watching her expression change. Before she could answer, he continued, "There was an old woman, Esther, and her cat, Evie. Esther had two sons who survived the war. Unfortunately, they were changed men. She didn't say much but she said she couldn't live with them and had to leave. I think they were violent drunks. On the brink of destitution with nothing but her cat she found Sylvia's Healing House. Sylvia of course welcomed both cat and Esther with open arms. Esther slept in the living room on a mattress on the floor. According to Sylvia she wanted to be as close to the door as possible so she could hear when her beloved cat was exiting and entering the house."

Sophie's heart skipped a beat. Samuel didn't notice and kept talking as the colour slowly drained from Sophie's face. The last resident to join was a young boy going by the name of Damien. He was orphaned at around the age of twelve, although no one knew for sure. He was a very peculiar boy and seemed to be obsessed with fire. The other residents complained when he set their clothing line alight once. Sylvia also wrote in her diary several entries about Damien supposedly talking to thin air. He would play games by the cliff edge as if he was playing with other children but there wasn't anyone there.

"Sylvia was concerned for his mental state and worried about him being lonely and creating imaginary friends. She confronted him about it one summer's day. Damien is reported to have just laughed childishly saying, 'They're not imaginary. They're children, just very old children'. Apparently he seemed confused by what he had just said, and Sylvia didn't want to press the matter, but she kept a close eye on him."

Sophie's mind was immediately drawn to the two children who had died on the cliff, stuck in children's bodies forever. Had it been their ghosts this boy had seen? They would be very old children indeed, over a century old, drifting unknowingly through time.

"This is where things get a little peculiar," Samuel said. "In one of Sylvia's last entries, she writes about a very old woman called Elodie coming to visit. The date of the entry is the day before the terrible fire, 31$^{st}$ October 1949. The very next day, Healing House was set ablaze. The fire was so great that sparks flew from the house and set the giant willow tree alight. It was a terrible tragedy. Everyone in the house died, their poor souls trapped in that infernal blaze. Sylvia wrote that she kept her most prized possessions, including the logbook and diary in a locked safe, which clearly survived the fire.

"The strange thing is the page after the entry announcing Elodie's arrival has been torn out. I searched all over the house for the missing page but couldn't find it anywhere. I was hoping it would shed more light on who this mysterious Elodie character was and why she came to visit Healing House."

Sophie sat speechless at the strange turn of events. "Do you think Elodie started the fire? Or could it have been Damien by accident?"

"That is just one of life's mysteries." Samuel sighed. "I'm afraid I don't have the answers. The answers must be on the torn-out page which has vanished into the folds of history. But I can tell you this, violence leaves its mark on the world's soul, whether you can see it or not."

It looked like Samuel was going to say something else but just then the nurse walked in, a disapproving look on her face.

"You're still here?" she said pointedly at Sophie. "I must ask you to leave now. He really needs to rest if he's going to get better!"

Sophie nodded. "Of course." She leant over Samuel and kissed his forehead. "Thank you for this and please get better soon! We will solve this mystery together," Sophie said firmly.

Samuel smiled wanly, nodding.

"Time for your medication," the nurse said, rattling a bottle of pills.

"Bye, Sophie. Take care," Samuel said, raising a feeble hand in farewell.

"Goodbye, Samuel," she replied, leaving him in the nurse's capable hands.

She drove home, thoughts flitting around in her head like a flock of frenzied birds. She felt a wave of sadness wash over her as she thought of all those poor people who had gone to Healing House to seek a better life only to perish in a hellish fire.

When she reached her house, she didn't feel the usual anxiety flow through her veins. Instead she just felt a melancholy air float through her like a cloud. Light was finally being shed on this house and the sad truth that lay nestled deep within its broken heart. Sophie entered the house, stroking the walls, furniture and tabletops. She was walking through the house with purpose, from room to room, feeling the texture of the walls, the creaking floorboards underfoot. Scents of old wood, lingering dust and a faint flowery smell filled her nostrils. Suddenly she felt a sense of déjà vu as if she had experienced this exact scenario before. She stopped in her tracks trying to dredge up the faint, blurry memory from the recesses of her mind. She then realised it wasn't a memory she was recalling at all but a dream. She had done this before, smelt these smells, felt these sensations in a dream she had had during the first few days of her stay in Healing House. In the dream she had heard voices echoing from another world away. She had assumed it was the TV in the background wittering on but now realised it wasn't. The voices had strange, lilting accents. She closed her eyes and concentrated.

She tried to listen to what the house had to tell her. She strained to hear the whispers that had permeated her dream. She kept her eyes shut, squeezing them hard yet she couldn't hear anything except the faint sighs of wind outdoors. She finally gave up and batted her eyelids open. She saw it immediately on the floor by her feet. Like a magnet it dragged her eyes down. The Death tarot card stared up at her. She realised this was what she had been waiting for all along. Death had been stalking her since she moved into the house, but now she was no longer afraid. She was going to take Death by the hand and walk alongside it, letting it guide her to the gates of another world. Her legs moved mechanically, as if driven by a force outside of her control.

She walked outside and knelt by the weeping willow. In her dream there had been a pile of ash with Death inside it. Sophie felt the earth around the tree. It was soft. She plunged her hands into the dirt, feeling the grit stick under her nails. She kept digging. Time crept by, her hands became sore and the hole got deeper yet she continued to dig. She knew it was here. The sun was starting to dip into the sea when her hands met something hard. Sophie quickly shovelled the dirt aside and fished out a small box. She opened the box and inside it was a yellowing old envelope.

The fragile paper felt as if it might disintegrate in her hands. With the utmost care she peeled it open and slid her hand inside. She withdrew what she had known would be there. It was the torn-out page from Sylvia's diary, buried deep within the earth, waiting in its hidden grave for the right person to find it. The paper was damp and stained. Sophie had to squint to make out the sloping, cursive handwriting of the long-deceased Sylvia Whisk. From what she could make of it, it read:

*31$^{st}$ October 1949 (11:05 pm) – I have been paid a visit by a most peculiar old woman. The story she has told me is quite bizarre and disturbing, yet I shall try do it justice and detail it in these pages. She says her name is Elodie, daughter of a gypsy, Edwina.*

*Our conversation is as follows (I had to record it as it was so unusual):*

*S: You are most welcome to stay here at Healing House, Ms. Elodie. It is a humble abode, but you will have everything that you need. If you stay a while, I can make you a good meal before you need to continue your journey.*

*E: I cannot stay. I can only warn you that you and everyone here must leave tonight. This place is cursed and only brings misery and tragedy to those who live within its walls.*

*S (I was much taken aback at her strange utterances): I'm sorry but we cannot leave. This is our home. What brings you to say such things?*

*E: I will tell you a story. I know this place. It haunts me as it has haunted my family throughout time. I was born to a gypsy, Edwina. She told me the story her mother told her. Her mother was Erosabel. Erosabel lived here by the cliffs as an outcast, a pest upon society. Edwina remembers her mother's vivacious spirit slowly dying by these cliffs. She said her mother's mind gradually slipped away from her. The warm, doting mother she used to know sank into the shadows to be replaced by a cold, unfeeling stranger. Mt grandmother sank into madness and preferred the company of ravens to that of her children.*

*She started calling the ravens by her children's names. She was confused, thinking that someone had performed black magic and had switched the souls of her children into the bodies of the ravens. She did not believe the actual children were hers. She heard voices that told her that if she killed the imposter children then the ravens would turn into her rightful children and the spell would be broken.*

*Edwina, my mother, overheard her mother's ramblings. She was playing with her dolls in the safety of her favourite tree when it happened. She watched as Erosabel approached her brothers and sister who had been gathering dry twigs for kindling outside before the storm collapsed upon the town. Edwina watched as her mother gently pushed them off the cliff edge, gazing at their helpless bodies as they crashed into the rocks and waves below. It is said that when lucidity returned to Erosabel and she realised what she had done, her scream tore through the rocks and seas and straight into hell itself. Edwina's father, my grandfather, Willowen, back from his journey, rushed out. All he could say was, "What have you done?"*

*When the ravens did not turn into her lost children, Erosabel saw her error. All she had left was Edwina who went mute for many years after the atrocity she had witnessed. She told Edwina that the land was cursed and had spread its black enchantments into her mind and that was what had killed her brothers and sister. Erosabel said that she and the children would never rest in peace until the land had been cleansed. The only way to cleanse it was to burn the place down so that no trace of it was left behind, so that the memories within the land's earth would turn to dust and ash. Soon after, Erosabel and Willowen committed suicide. It's believed they threw themselves over the cliff edge in search of their missing children. Edwina, my mother, took it upon herself to fulfil her mother's curse.*

*Edwina travelled with the group of gypsies. Soon she fell in love, married and became pregnant with me. Her husband fell into gambling, and when I was barely an infant he was murdered by people he owed money to. It was said to be a vicious murder involving multiple stabbings. Apparently I was in the room, splattered in my father's blood. Since then Edwina became obsessed with the ramshackle hut, perched on the edge of eternity. She would talk about its curses for hours, talk about how it had stolen her brothers, sister, mother, father and her own voice when she went mute for years. She warned me that the curse was hungry for more souls to devour and would never rest until all the Woodlocks were dead.*

*She made it her life's mission to burn the place down where she believed the curse originated and hovered over her still. When I was fourteen, she died, her mission left unfinished. She had been desperate to make money and had taken to selling wax dolls to little girls as well as other things to men. A jealous lover stole into the bedroom one night and strangled her.*

*I was orphaned and took it upon myself to right a thousand wrongs of the past. I am telling you this so that you leave now and never return to this godforsaken place. Death and danger lurk in every corner and shadow within these walls. This house and all its residents are living within the claws of a curse.*

*S: Needless to say I was shocked at this tale of murder, intrigue and madness. I told her I would think about what she had said. However, I couldn't just wake all the tired, weary souls from their peaceful slumber and turn them out of their beds in the middle of the night.*

*I think I will speak to Elodie about this tomorrow morning. Daylight tends to bring with it a certain clarity. I will see if we can come up with some peaceful solution. All the while I can't help but wonder if she has a disease of the mind, a touch of madness her grandmother seemed to have. There is something not quite right about her. There were moments in her speech where she would digress and mumble incoherently to herself, almost as if she was talking to someone else. She is a troubled soul in need of help. I fear I shall sleep very ill tonight. Hopefully with daylight all shall become clearer.*

*Until my next entry,*

*S.W.*

Sophie read and re-read Sylvia's last entry in tears. She wept for the persecution of the gypsies. She wept for the murdered children, killed by their mother's insanity. She wept for the tragic lives Edwina, Danior and Jason had suffered. She wept for the poor, desolate residents of Healing House and the fire that consumed them. Then she wept for Samuel, who after all these years carried the curse like a cross on his back. So many people had suffered because of the insanity of this Erosabel and her curses, so many lives torn apart.

She wanted to help all those tormented souls stuck in limbo within the memories of the house. She wanted to heal their sadness and take their pain away. She felt her own sadness and grief intertwine with that of the lost souls, until she could no longer distinguish the different stories, the various tragedies and the multitude of hurts that seemed to settle like dust in her soul. It was all one. All the pain of the past, present and future had come to collect and reside in her heart and it was up to her to heal it. But she was not meant to heal alone. She was meant to heal in there, in Healing House, with the ghosts of the past. After what felt like a lifetime, Sophie stood up and returned to the house, her heart finally open to its pain.

She had a dream that night she would never forget. She was in the house. All those lost souls who had come and gone, lived and died within the house, were there, suspended in time. There was Erosabel and Willowen, their four children, Logan, Joni, Danior and Edwina. Next to them was Sylvia, the landlady of Healing House, Joan and her emerald-eyed daughter Lily, Thomas, Damien, and Esther. Then there was her, Sophie, the thirteenth to join the spectral scene. In her dream she was looking down at the scene, as if she were floating from the ceiling above watching herself and the others. They were sitting in a circle, linking hands. No one was speaking. They were all just looking at her. She could feel their energy, their pain, their joy and their life force mingling with her own. Their collective spirits had become a part of her. Time and space collapsed around her, creating one shared moment of truth.

It was deathly silent until Willowen broke the chain and started playing his flute. They all listened, enraptured by the slow, poignant notes of Willowen's sad song. It soothed Sophie's heart. Like a healing balm, it stroked and calmed the throbbing wound she had been carrying since Dan's death. It was a song that, whenever she felt sad, nervous or anxious, she could always hear in the background of her mind and it would never fail to instil a sense of peace within her. It was a song that would stay with Sophie until she was an old woman, awaiting the angel of death to scoop her up in his wings and transport her to the other side, where they waited for her arrival.

# Epilogue

*Dear Samuel,*

*Truth and light emanated through your eyes,*

*Your heart shone with iridescent beauty,*

*Forever your memories will remain in this soul of mine,*

*You, my wise willow tree.*

*As your leaves would rustle and sway,*

*Whispering their stories of time lost to me,*

*I would delve into another world where you would lead the way,*

*It was your stories that set me free.*

*And yet your branches are now crumbled and broken,*

*Your leaves mere teardrops on the ground,*

*Your stooped trunk arched over and bent,*

*The toll of death sounds.*

*Sometimes death is cruel foe,*

*Stealing souls for its own mirth and glee,*

*But for the special few, it is a kiss withholding woe*

*For you, the angel of death embraced you with warmth and mercy.*

*Sophie*

The day after her ethereal dream, Sophie went to the hospital only to discover that Samuel had died peacefully in his sleep. She returned to his house to collect Sylvia's diary and logbook as Samuel had requested. While she was there, she stroked the old armchair that still carried Samuel's scent.

"I solved it for the both of us," she whispered into the air, sure that somewhere beyond the veil of their world he could hear her and was at peace.

Matthew picked her up from Samuel's and let her cry softly into his jacket.

It was one year later. Sophie and Matthew had decided to get married a few months earlier and were living together with Heather. Sophie had convinced Matthew to move in with her. Understandably he had been sceptical based on his earlier experiences, but she told him the place was different now. It was a calm, serene place. The terrifying undercurrent of energy that used to ripple through the body of the house was gone, released. Sophie didn't say it out loud, but she knew that if a curse had hovered over Healing House for all these years, it had now been exhumed, disintegrating into dust in the light of day.

They remodelled it together and added an extension to the kitchen, creating more space for their growing family.

Sophie still heard the creaks in the floorboards when no one was upstairs and still felt an other-worldly presence engulf her at times, but the ominous birds and the wrathful anger had disappeared. Whenever she felt the strange sensations and spiritual energies, she no longer felt the pulsating, frantic fear grip her. All she felt was love, love for the previous residents of the house, love for the house itself and even love for the murderess, Erosabel, who clearly had been grappling with inner demons of her own. Sophie sometimes heard Heather playing in the garden as if with a friend, even though she was alone. Sophie never told Matthew and nor did Heather confide in him. Once Heather came up to Sophie, holding the china doll Sophie had bought when she first moved in.

"She likes the doll," Heather said. "It's her favourite."

"Who likes the doll, sweetheart?" Sophie had asked.

Heather merely let her gaze fall to the garden, at the patch just before the cliff edge, where Sophie felt the children's presence the strongest.

Sophie nodded and said quietly, "I'm glad." She squeezed Heather's hand before Heather ran off to continue playing.


Sophie woke up one morning, excitement fluttering in her belly. She heaved herself up. It was not easy moving around when she was seven months pregnant. She patted her round belly making soothing noises as she felt the baby squirm and wriggle inside her. She waddled slowly down the stairs.

"Morning, sunshine," Matthew called out from the kitchen before returning to question Heather as to whether she had finished the homework assignment that was due that very morning.

Sophie opened the front door and saw it, a little package sitting patiently by her doormat. Feeling slightly faint, Sophie picked it up, measuring its weight in her hands. With the excitement of a child on Christmas, she tore through the packaging. A book slipped out. Sophie caught it. She caressed its spine with love and flipped through the pages, inhaling her favourite papery scent.

"It's arrived," she yelled as she slammed the front door and headed for the kitchen where a fight about homework was ensuing.

"The book?" Matthew said, wide-eyed. "Let's see it!"

Sophie held it up carefully as if it was made of glass. "The proof is finally here. This isn't the final copy. As long as I approve of everything, the cover, the design and all that then it'll be in stores by this autumn."

"*Healing House* by Sophie Blake," Heather read slowly. "Wow, you actually wrote all that?" she said, her eyes as wide as saucers.

Matthew wrapped her in his arms and kissed her. "I'm so proud of you! You've done it, Sophie. You've published your first book."

Sophie smiled, feeling a tear wind its way down her cheek. Matthew swept it away with his finger.

"Let's give Mummy a moment, shall we?" Matthew said quietly, steering Heather into the living room.

Grateful, Sophie dabbed her eyes with a tissue. She sat alone with her book. She had tried to capture the magic, heartbreak and unspeakable sadness that had saturated the very air trapped within the walls of the house when she had first moved there. She hoped that through writing about their lives, she could somehow heal the tormented souls of the past. She wanted to write about what Healing House really meant to her. It wasn't the scary place she had first believed it to be. It was one of those rare places where the past and present had somehow evaded the boundaries of time and blurred into one. It was a home, a refuge, a healing house to many before her. Sophie hoped that she had done Samuel's story justice and that what she had created could also transcend time and forever be considered something beautiful, timeless and true.

She flipped to the first page, back to where her journey with Healing House all began, thinking about how she had found the house through grief, had her curiosity piqued through fear, bonded with it through healing and finally remained out of love. She sipped her warm coffee, letting the tranquillity of the house settle around her, the sunlight warming her face. Although the book was finished, she knew the tales of the departed souls as well as her own were not yet complete. In this house, their memories and stories would continue to intertwine and unravel together.

# About the Author

Nicole was born in England in 1992 and has lived a peripatetic life from a young age. She moved with her family to various countries, such as England, Saudi Arabia, Lebanon, and the United States. She currently lives with her husband in the United Arab Emirates.

Nicole has a Bachelor's and Master's degree in Psychology and is a Board Certified Behaviour Analyst (BCBA®). She has been passionate about reading and writing for as long as she can remember and has written a multitude of short stories, poems and articles. Healing House is her debut novel.

You can find more information about Nicole and her writing projects on her various platforms:

## Author Platforms:

Website: www.nicoleplumridge.com

Instagram: @authornicoleplumridge

## Psychminds Platforms:

Website: www.psychminds.com

Instagram: @psychmindspodcast

Podcast: Psychminds Podcast

# Excerpt from Erosabel

# Chapter 1

CHILDHOOD FELT LIKE a dream, or should I say nightmare, away. A distant memory swirling in a mirky pool I dared not peer into. It felt like millennia had passed since I was that frail, feeble child whose mother used to knock about. I was rarely comfortable discussing my past, but it felt different with Willowen, a cup of broth clasped in my hands, its warmth embracing me.

I had travelled a great deal to reach this gypsy campsite, both in terms of physical distance and psychic. I had journeyed to the edge of my own sanity, looking into an abys that was threatening to consume me whole. At the very last moment, I had been pulled back, saved by the steady hands of Willowen.

Willowen was head of the camp. He had taken me in, a lonely, stray orphan with nowhere to go. When I had first arrived, brittle and broken, he had asked no questions, only focused on my health and healing. Now, however, he wanted to know. He wanted to know about my past, who I was, where I came from. Dread tied itself in knots in the pit of my stomach.

As if in deliberate contrast to my inner world, the caravan in which I had been convalescing had a sleepy, calm aroma to it. A stillness hung in the air. Willowen was perched on a three-legged stool opposite me in the bed, wrapped in thick fur blankets.

"You don't have to tell me your story tonight," he said kindly, noting my pregnant pause after he had asked where I was from. "You must still be exhausted."

Mother's face floated into my mind from the ether. I had tried to bury the image; pretend she had only been a figment of my macabre imagination. Suddenly, I felt words, rising like bile, creep up my throat. I needed to talk. I had to tell someone my story. I desperately wanted someone to understand. Someone to tell me that I wasn't going crazy. Someone to forgive the evil I had done. The smudged windows and thin walls of the caravan melted away, replaced by the dank, rotting walls of Mother's flat in East London. With the familiar taste of fear metallic in my mouth, I began to tell my story.

*The slap stung the side of my face. A blood-red tear trickled from the gash, burning my cheekbone. I tried to stifle the sobs heaving through my chest.*

*"You ungrateful little beast!" Mother shrieked, brandishing her broken, dagger-like nails, threatening to strike again.*

*I recoiled into a corner like a wounded animal, trembling in fear. My eyes were glued shut as I waited for the final blow, waited for her to cut through my skin and pierce my very heart with her claws. It was only when I heard the sound of muted crying that I squinted through one eye. In that instant I wished Mother would continue beating me until she cracked my bones and scratched me to shreds. It would have been infinitely better than what I saw.*

*Mother was curled up in a ball, rocking backwards and forwards, mumbling through her streaming tears, "I'm sorry, Erosabel. I'm sorry. It's the Devil, you know. The Devil whispers in my ear. You know how I suffer. I'm sorry." Mother repeated this over and over again, her eyes unseeing and glassy.*

*Barely able to stand on my shaking, scrawny legs, I stumbled over to the rocking lump that was my mother. I sat down cautiously next to her, never sure of what to expect. Slowly, I put my arm around her shoulders. Her once luscious fiery red locks hung in limp strands around her waxy, pale face. A shiny film of perspiration coated her skin, giving her the appearance of a distraught wax doll.*

*"It's ok, Mother," I said, my voice high-pitched and trembling with uncertainty.*

*"No, Erosabel, you deserve better than this," Mother said, her eyes puffy and swollen with tears. "I can't protect you. The demons will have their way."*

*Her eyes had a faraway gleam in them, as if she were half in this world and half in another, a world invisible to me. Although I couldn't peer into that strange world of hers, I knew it to be one haunted by dark corners, winding mazes that led nowhere, shadows and eerie echoing voices. I was terrified when Mother was drawn into that world.*

"What did she mean when she said the Devil talks to her? Could your mother actually hear voices?" Willowen asked, his brow furrowed.

I am no gypsy, but I have heard they can be superstitious about these sorts of things. I wanted to put his mind at ease but didn't know how. I decided to go with the honest truth.

"I believe she thought she heard the Devil talk to her. She was tormented by it and then she transferred that torment onto me," I said as plainly as I could.

Willowen nodded thoughtfully. I took his silence as a sign to press on.

*It wasn't the first time Mother had spoken to me like this. The previous week I had come home after delivering linens and fabrics to a nearby shop. I had hesitated before entering the room as I thought someone was there with her. She had been shouting at someone or something to leave her alone. My first thought was that the rent collector had been pestering her again.*

*I pushed open the splintered wooden door to find Mother standing by the fire. At the sound of the creaking, Mother spun around wild-eyed. A blank film coated her eyes and there was no hint of recognition when she saw me. She was alone.*

*"Who were you talking to?" I asked timidly, my voice barely above a whisper.*

*Mother stared at me before tipping what would have been our dinner, a broth she was heating in a pot, into the flames. It hissed like angry snakes just as my stomach growled in hunger.*

*"That's what you get for not holding your tongue. Only troublesome devils ask questions!" Mother spat at me.*

*I nodded, wishing I had never said anything, wishing the broth would wind its way back into the pot and from there into my hollow, aching stomach.*

*"The devils will get you too, you know," she said, pushing past me into the only other room in the hovel we called home.*

*We lived in a tiny flat above what used to be Mother's apothecary. My grandparents had run the shop, selling herbal medicines and ointments for refined ladies with white, delicate hands ensconced in fine silk gloves. When they had died Mother took to running the shop. From the few stories Uncle Benjamin told me about Mother, she had been a different person back then.*

"Where's your Uncle Benjamin now? Are you still in touch?" Willowen cut in.

I shook my head slowly, a hint of bitterness in my voice as I continued.

*Uncle Ben had made promises to us, promises he swore he would keep. He had escaped the squalor of London and sailed off to the new lands and with them, a new life, in America. I remember him letting me sit on his knee with a sad, wistful expression clouding his eyes the day he was set to travel.*

*Uncle Benjamin said, as if to himself, "I wish you knew your mother before. Before... things changed. The strength of her spirit could rival the sea itself. I always thought she would marry well and get out of this dump. She didn't lack suitors, that's for sure."*

*"I thought she married Daddy," I said, wide-eyed, staring up at Uncle Ben.*

*Uncle Ben looked down startled, as if surprised by my presence. "Of course. I meant after your father died. I thought she would marry again," he said, clearing his throat and shifting me off his knee. "You take care of your mother now. She's not well, so you have to do everything you can to help her get better," he added, his eyes misting over with tears.*

*I didn't understand what he meant. Usually when people weren't well they were in bed, coughing and sneezing. Mother wasn't like that. She never got sick. I simply nodded as Uncle Ben patted me on the head.*

*"You be a good girl. I'll send you treats, lace and dolls every month. It's a new world out there, a better one. And who knows, maybe once I'm settled you and your mother can join me!"*

*He planted a long kiss on my forehead before leaving the room to find Mother and say his farewells. I heard a pot smashing and peeped around the door to see what had happened. Mother was standing in the middle of the bare room as Uncle Ben hurried out. I remember his shoulders were hunched over, as if he were carrying the weight of a thousand worlds on his back. A delicate painted clay pot lay shattered on the floor.*

*"Good riddance. We don't need your charity anyway, you good-for-nothing layabout," Mother shrieked after him.*

*As she slammed the door behind Uncle Ben, I felt my small world close in on me. Curtains of darkness descended, and I knew then in that bleak winter of 1818 that my childhood had ended.*

Willowen and I slipped into silence. I could feel his brain working, whirring away, processing all I had told him. Usually I would feel panicked; wonder what he was thinking about me, but today I was feeling too mentally exhausted for that. I was being honest, perhaps, for the first time in my life. I was stripping layer after layer of my soul, leaving it bare. Somehow, it felt good, a welcome reprieve.

"Where was your father during your childhood?" Willowen asked, softly peeling back the fabric of silence that enveloped us.

"Father?" The word was unfamiliar in my mouth. All I knew was Mother. The word had encapsulated hope and wonder in my childhood, only to turn to bitterness, disappointment and then apathy as I grew older.

*The story was my father had died before I was born. I wasn't sure if I believed the story as it frequently changed, depending on Mother's mercurial moods. She sometimes told me he had been trampled by a horse and carriage one day on his way to work at the factory. Other times, he had drowned in the murky waters of the River Thames as he was scouring the banks for valuable fragments. When Mother was in a good mood, he had heroically died from smoke inhalation after rescuing a family trapped in a burning building. Occasionally, she would curse him, brandishing her fists in the air, muttering furious words as if he were still alive. When I confronted Mother about these discrepancies, she would slap me so hard I felt my teeth rattle.*

*"You hold your tongue, girl, before I cut it out of your mouth," she would hiss.*

*I learnt never to question her. She would glower at me, saying that I was the ruin of her life. If it hadn't been for me she would have escaped the doom of the slum we lived in. Sometimes I would catch her staring at me, a look of disgust contorting her once fine and beautiful features.*

*"You have his dark looks," she would say, shaking her head. "Anyone would mistake you for a heathen."*

*It was true. I had dark skin and hair blacker than the night itself. Before, when we used to leave the flat, people would stare at us. Mother, a tall, willowy, red-haired beauty, with skin so pale it was almost translucent alongside this small, scrawny, tanned urchin. The only reason Mother wasn't called a baby-snatcher was our eyes: they were unmistakeably the same, passed down the generations like precious sapphires. Our eyes were a deep swirling ocean blue with large inky black pupils dotted in the centre. A peddler of feathers and trinkets had once grabbed me by the arm and stared at me, frowning. "You have the eyes of a witch," he spat. "Cursed." He then flung me with all his force away from his wares, sending me flying into a puddle of muck and filth.*

*I remember avoiding my reflection for years growing up. When I looked into Mother's eyes, I saw nothing except a hallow emptiness, as if her soul had already transcended to the world beyond. I was scared that if I saw my own reflection, I would see the same lifeless gaze staring back, like the glass eyes of an empty china doll.*

*Mother's rage, and later what I understood to be madness, ruled our lives whilst we lived in the two dingy rooms above the shop which had fallen into disrepair. All I remember feeling was an incessant guilt, gnawing at my soul. Because of me, her life was in tatters. Because of me, we lived in a ramshackle hovel. Because of me, she lost her mind.*

"You can't blame yourself for your mother's unravelling," Willowen said gently. "You never did anything wrong. Whatever was troubling her had nothing to do with you."

I was about to agree when I felt a lump in my throat. To my surprise, tears had gathered in my eyes and were threatening to spill over. Although I had rationally told myself that I was not responsible for her downfall, I couldn't help but feel the weight of ephemeral guilt press down on me. Somewhere, deep down within me, I blamed myself for everything that had gone wrong in our lives. To hear a perfect stranger say otherwise and have it ring true made every fibre in my being quiver with this new realisation.

Willowen handed me a plain white shred of cloth. I hadn't realised I was crying. The gentle tears turned into heaving sobs, and before I knew it, I had lost control and my entire body was shaking. But it wasn't with sadness. Willowen put his arms around me and drew me close. He didn't say anything, just let me cry it out. As the tears were tumbling down, I searched within myself to understand what emotion was bubbling to the surface. It wasn't sadness or fear. Nor was it worry or heartache. I then realised what it was: relief. It was washing over me and within me, cleansing me from the inside out. I was relieved to know that it was not my fault. Someone outside of myself had validated me for the first time. As the tears ebbed, I felt more alive than I had ever felt in my entire life. Just as this new vitality surged through me, a heavy physical exhaustion settled within my limbs, making it difficult for me to move.

As if reading my mind through my movements, Willowen said, "I think we ought to call it a night. You must be tired."

I nodded. The very act of speaking felt like too much of an effort.

"Goodnight, Erosabel. Rest well," Willowen said, as he opened the door of the caravan. "You'll be all right?"

"Yes," I managed to say. "Thank you for listening to all that."

"Of course. I can't believe everything you've been through. But don't worry. I'm glad you found us. It's all about to get a whole lot easier," he said with a warm smile.

I managed a weak smile in return as I waved him goodnight. I hadn't realised how much I needed that release, how much I needed to tell my story aloud. But I wasn't done. Now I had a taste for it, I needed to continue. I needed to tell my story and for it to be heard.

# ENTER THE WORLD OF

# THE WOODLOCK CURSE...

 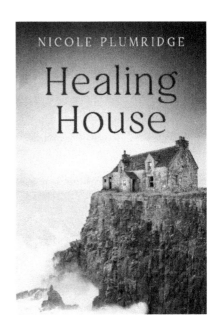

Printed in Great Britain
by Amazon

79542511R00192